THE TRAIL

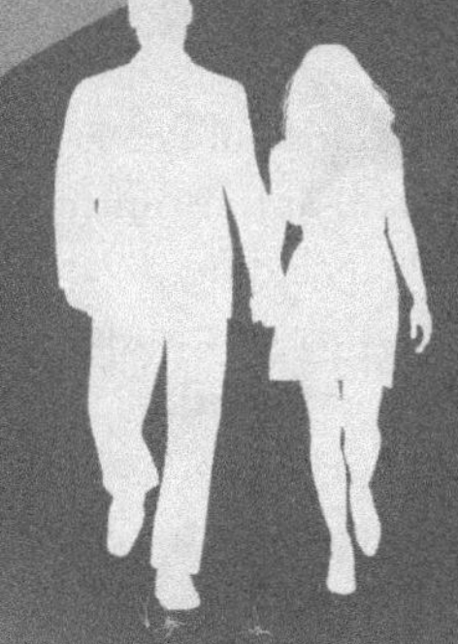

JAMES KENT

20 Twenty
Literary Group

The Trail
Copyright © 2024 by James Kent

All rights reserved. No part of this publication
may be reproduced, distributed, or transmitted
in any form or by any means, including
photocopying, recording, or other electronic
or mechanical methods, without the prior
written permission of the author, except
in the case of brief quotations embodied
in critical reviews and certain other non-
commercial uses permitted by copyright law.

ISBN
978-1-961250-80-2 (Paperback)
978-1-961250-81-9 (eBook)
978-1-961250-79-6 (Hardcover)

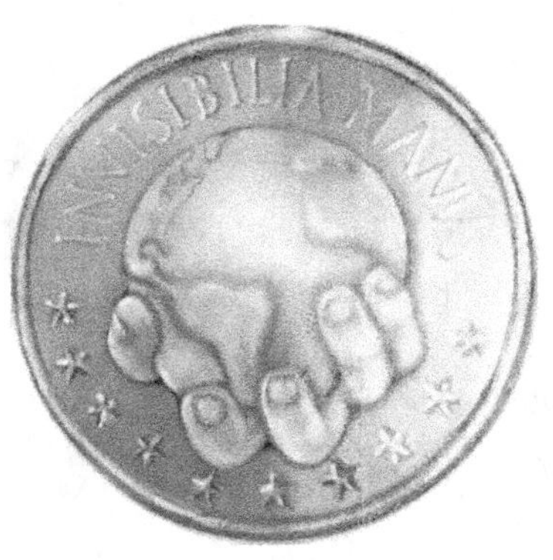

INVISIBILIA MANV

TABLE OF CONTENTS

IN THE DARK RECESSES

"Beneath the broad tides of human history there flow the stealthy undercurrents of the secret societies, which frequently determine in the depth the changes that take place upon the surface."— A. E. Waite

December 31, 1963
The Martel Family Chateau
Carcassonne, France

The Martel twins clutched their father's hands as they descended the staircase into the subterranean chambers of the sprawling country chateau. The cold, echoing corridor whispered with the weight of centuries-old secrets, and a sense of foreboding gripped them both. Glancing at each other behind his back with a mixture of fear and uncertainty, they remained silent, knowing better than to provoke him. With thick brows and a commanding presence, he led them to a heavy wooden door, a portal to their family's ancient traditions. Unlocking it with a turn of the key, he then ushered them into a room steeped in darkness, illuminated only by flickering torches. The air was thick with anticipation as they approached a stone altar, its surface gleaming with the ominous glow of a red-hot cauldron.

"This is your big day, my dear children," their father announced proudly, his voice echoing off the damp walls. "Today, you will receive your birthright, just as generations of Martels before you."

"*Père, où est la mère?*" his daughter cried out.

Annoyed, he looked down at her and scolded, "Your mother does not need to be here. This is not her business. You will do as you are told."

Kneeling before it, the twins watched in terror as their father took a glowing iron from the embers. Then, lifting both hands above his head and raising his eyes to the ceiling, he chanted the ancient incantation in a language they had never heard before. After what seemed like an eternity to the terrified children, he lowered it, looked down at his son, gripped the boy's left wrist, and thrust the glowing iron into his open palm. He repeated the age-old act on his daughter, while it seared an ancient and foreboding symbol into their flesh.

"*Invisibilia Manus in aeternum.*"

With those words, the transition was complete, and the Martel twins were forever bound to their family's legacy, their destinies irrevocably intertwined with the dark secrets of their bloodline.

Fifteen Years Later

August 12, 1978

Boldt Castle

The Thousand Islands

Alexandria Bay, New York

The blue and white tour boat drifted toward the mysterious structure in the middle of the St. Lawrence River. The intercom crackled with the sound of the tour guide's voice while she narrated the script that had been delivered a hundred times before.

"Welcome aboard Thousand Island Tours on this beautiful summer morning. You are on an expanse of the Saint Lawrence River known as the Thousand Islands. This archipelago of 1,864 islands begins at the northeast end of Lake Ontario, near Kingston. From there, they extend about fifty miles downstream to Alexandria Bay, New York. The largest island is more than forty square miles, while the smaller ones are occupied by a single cottage.

"But today, you are here to see one island in particular—the five-acre Heart Island with its majestic Boldt Castle. It was built by George Boldt, a wealthy turn-of-the-century hotel proprietor who operated both the Waldorf-Astoria in New York City and the Bellevue-Stratford in Philadelphia. Begun in 1900, Boldt Castle was the largest private home in America. George had it built for his beloved wife, Louise. Sadly, after her unfortunate death in 1904, Mr. Boldt ordered the hundreds of skilled tradesmen to abandon its construction. He never returned, and left the castle as an enduring monument of his love for her.

"I'm sure you will find Mr. Boldt's castle to be an unforgettable experience. So, feel free to ask questions of the guides as you stroll the grounds and roam through the 120 rooms. You will notice the buildings to be in a state of disrepair. Unfortunately, for the last seventy years, the castle and the other stone structures on the island have been deserted, exposed to the harsh weather and vandalism. Ladies and gentlemen, I see we are ready to disembark. In one hour, the captain will sound the ten-minute warning horn for our departure. Please don't be late."

Later that night

As the sun dipped below the horizon, casting shadows over the tranquil waters of the St. Lawrence River, Heart Island lay silent and still. The echoes of the day's tourists had long faded, leaving the majestic Boldt Castle shrouded in darkness. Under the cloak of night, two deHavilland DHC-2 Beavers descended upon the river, their engines humming softly as they touched down near the island's rocky shore. From the planes' cabins emerged a group of nine passengers, their origins spanning continents, united by a common purpose and a shared mark upon their left palms—a symbol of ancient lineage passed down through generations. These secret visitors, hailing from Europe, Iran, Turkey, India, Russia, and the United States, had come to Heart Island for an annual assembly steeped in secrecy, a tradition dating back centuries. Among them was a young woman from Carcassonne, France, her first journey abroad and away from the familiar embrace of her family and twin brother.

Led by their pilots turned security guards, the group navigated through the island's dense foliage, guided by the dim glow of flashlights. Hidden amidst the evergreens stood a seemingly innocuous garden shed, its exterior weathered by time and neglect. But within its confines lay a portal to the hidden depths below Boldt Castle—a labyrinth of tunnels carved into the bedrock by George

Boldt's hand-picked construction crew, now repurposed for clandestine activities.

Unlocking the gate and shed entry, the guards revealed a solitary elevator door, its entrance a gateway to the secrets concealed beneath the castle's grand facade. With hushed murmurs and a sense of anticipation, the group descended into the depths as they rode deeper into the subterranean labyrinth. Meanwhile, a technician from the Area C Technology Division in Detroit was visiting the island to install a new security system—a system designed to safeguard the terrifying secrets hidden within the walls. Two days later, local headlines would report a grim discovery—a body found floating in the waters of the St. Lawrence, a silent testament to the mysteries that lay concealed within Heart Island's shadowed embrace.

UNIDENTIFIED BODY FOUND NEAR HEART ISLAND

Kingston, Ontario, August 15, 1978
(The Daily Sentinel)

Police are seeking the identity of a man whose body was retrieved from the Saint Lawrence River near Heart Island last night.

The dead man is white, 5'10", and appears to be in his late 30s or early 40s, with a dark brown birthmark on his left temple. He was wearing khaki trousers with a pair of eyeglasses in a pocket. His hands were bound with a blood-stained, light blue shirt to which was attached an ID tag that read "McShane- Area C."

Police declined to give a cause of death, pending an autopsy, but evidence of blunt force trauma to the head was visible.

Anyone with information leading to the identity of the dead man or his attacker is asked to come forward.

CHAPTER 1

LE FEMME CAMILLE

THE THIRTEENTH STEP

June 22, 1981
Marseille, France

Hovering over me as I stirred from my slumber, the most stunningly beautiful woman I had ever seen coaxed me awake. Even after weeks together, her beauty still captivated me, ensnaring me in her spell.

"*Bonjour, mon* Sean, please get up," she whispered, her voice like a melody. "You must rise and greet the morning. I've prepared breakfast, with a special touch just for you."

But I was reluctant to leave the warmth of our bed, intoxicated by her allure. "Come back to me, sweetheart," I urged, my desire for her outweighing any hunger for food.

"Ah, but I've made crepes, fresh orange juice, and espresso just for you," she tempted, her eyes dancing with mischief.

As she tantalized me with promises of culinary delights, she reminded me of our pact. "You promised to tell me more about yourself today," she gently prodded.

Reluctantly, I relented, knowing her persistence would not wane. "Fine, but give me a moment to put on something."

As I came to the table, her impatience was evident in every word. "*Sean, dépêche-toi s'il te plaît,*" she urged. Her desire to please me thinly veiled beneath her insistence.

"Okay, okay, I'm coming—but how do you expect me to tell you anything with that pink camisole clinging to you? You do realize it really leaves very little to the imagination, and you know I can't resist you."

But even in her haste, she couldn't resist tempting me. "Hmmm, perhaps you would prefer it was a different color?"

"Are you kidding me?" I chuckled, unable to resist her charms. "You look fantastic in pink. But you would look great in red or maybe even black."

Her eyes lit up with mischief. "*Eh bien, mon amour,* maybe you can give me a red one for my birthday."

"Sure, and when would that be?"

"It's on New Year's Eve," she giggled. "Don't you think that's fun? Everybody celebrates my birthday."

"Oh my God, Camille, that's my birthday too. Out of curiosity, what year were you born?"

With a bashful grin, she bowed her head and pouted, "It's not polite to ask a lady her age. But if you must know, I was born in 1950."

"What? You've got to be kidding me, that's not possible. That's the exact same day I was born!"

"Oh, I see, now you're trying to tease me, but it won't work."

"No, no, I'm not kidding you. That's my birthday too. I was born on December 31, 1950."

"Okay, Sean, whatever you say. I'm going to put on my robe, too."

"Wait a minute. Camille, please listen to me. We were strangers when we met, but we have the exact same birthday. I think that's a remarkable coincidence, and yet you dismiss it as if it were nothing."

"Will you stop about our birthdays, Sean? Enough is enough. Like you said, we met by chance, so the odds of us both being born on the exact same day are not likely."

"I'm telling you, I could prove it if I had my passport with me, but it's back in my hotel room. Anyway, you're right about these crepes—they are amazing. What in the world is your secret ingredient?"

"Well, I can't tell you that, or it wouldn't be a secret anymore, would it?"

"Come on, Camille, sit on my lap. I want you close to me. And I'm really in no mood to talk about myself today."

"My goodness, when we first met, I had never seen anybody as uptight as you were. How wonderful it is that you can finally relax when you're with me."

"Yeah, with everything I know and what I've seen, that's what my job has done to me. It's turned me into a nervous wreck. Look, I just want to forget about work, and be with you. My God, you smell good!"

"Okay, you're just trying to distract me again, but it won't work. Sean, stop that! Don't touch me there. Your attention is not where it should be."

"For God's sake, why is my history so damn important to you?"

"*Mon amour*, you must realize, I've had few serious relationships, and none of them were lasting. But with you, it's different. We've only been together for a couple of weeks, but unlike the other men in my life, I have never felt so close to anyone like I do with you. It's wonderful to be with a man I have so much in common with. It's like I've known you forever. I feel like I'm finally at home when I am with you. Most of all, you seem to understand me more than anyone ever has. So, it's only natural I want to know more about you. For instance, you said you came here to Marseilles on business last month, but you never told me what it is you do. So, what's your job, and why does it upset you so much?"

"I'm an electronics technician for a company that sends me all over the world."

Pouting her lip, she whimpered, "Okay, now I see where this is going. You'll be here for a little while, and then go off on your next conquest with some other unfortunate, vulnerable woman."

"No, no, it's not like that at all. You know I'm crazy about you. I was speechless when you said it feels like you've known me forever. That's exactly how I feel about you. I dread the day when I have to leave France. I can't sleep at night trying to figure out how I can make this work for us."

"Sean, I want to believe what you say, but if we're going to spend our lives together, I need to trust you. So, please be patient with me."

"Well, come to think of it, I don't know much about you either."

"*Oui*, but unlike you, I have no problem telling you *everything* about myself. If you must know, I work for my family. They run a recruiting business, and I work in the employment office, where we screen prospective employees to make sure they are qualified for the jobs we send them out on. I haven't gone anywhere for the past year, so last month I asked for some time off. I came here to Marseilles to relax and do some shopping. Instead, I met you, and how wonderful it has been. So, there you have it; compared to you, I must sound very boring."

"I can assure you, nothing about you is boring. Okay, I'll tell you some things about myself. But first, I need another crepe and more espresso."

"*Bien sûr, mon chérie*, I knew you would love them. It will only take a minute."

"Okay, to begin, my home is in Michigan. I was married at twenty-two; we were both far too young. My ex-wife, Marlene, and I rented a flat next door to the guy who referred me to my employer. When I found out about the new technologies they were working on, I was so excited that I neglected her way too much. Unfortunately, our relationship suffered for it, and so she left me. Then I worked my way up the ladder until they promoted me to technical liaison. Since then, I've traveled all over the world and have experienced some pretty amazing things. And now I'm here with you. So, there you have it."

"No, no, Sean, I don't have it. Tell me about your job, and what brought you here to Marseilles. Where have you been and what have you seen? I'm sure it is incredibly exciting."

∗　∗　∗

Talking to Camille about my work or my employer was a serious violation of my employment contract, and I shuddered to think what would happen if they somehow found out. However, I was absolutely intoxicated being anywhere near her. My desire to be with someone I really cared about overrode the risk. So, I threw caution to the wind, sat down with her at the kitchen table, and told her things I had never uttered to another soul.

"I really don't like talking about my work. The projects I work on are highly classified. If they ever find out I'm talking to you about this stuff, I won't be around very long to say anything more to you, or anybody else for that matter."

"*Oh, mon Dieu*, how terrible. What kind of employer do you work for? That sure seems like a serious accusation. Perhaps you exaggerate?"

"I'm telling you, Camille, the less you know, the better. Anyway, I want you to trust me, so here goes. At first, I was dazzled by all the locations they sent me to, along with the intriguing job assignments. Then, in the evenings, there was the nightlife. Ah yes, the nightlife. But I can tell you, after a few years, the novelty of it wore off. You must understand, with the kind of job I have, my desire to settle down with one woman did not seem to be in the cards for me. What makes it acceptable is the amount of money my employer pays me to keep them happy. I'm building my nest egg so I can retire by forty-five, while I'm still young enough to enjoy my freedom with that one special woman. And now I know who she is."

"Oooh, Sean, do you think that woman could be me?"

"Look, I'm trying to be serious here, and you're teasing me again. Of course, you know you're the one for me. But there's something else you need to know before we go on. I have a passion. I'm telling you this now because I don't want it to come between us like it did with my ex."

"A passion, I like that."

"Please don't think I'm crazy, but ever since grade school, I've been pursuing my fascination with the Genesis Story of Creation. I have a theory that hidden in its thirty-one verses is a secret so amazing, that if I'm right, it will change everything. Nothing will ever be the same again."

"Oh, my goodness, that seems like a peculiar passion. I can certainly think of far more romantic passions."

"Yeah, I'm sure you can."

"So, Sean, does this theory of yours have anything to do with your employer?"

"No, not really. Why would you ask me that?"

"Oh, I don't know—just curious, I guess. So yes go on, and tell me more about your employer and your job."

"Okay, here goes. They send me to locations scattered around the world to install computer systems and other electronic components that we design and build in Detroit. Much of the technology is so advanced that it will take years for everyone else to catch up. However, what really puzzled me was where they get their seemingly unlimited source of money to fund these projects. But then, I found out."

"They have unlimited money?"

"Oh yeah, they sure do. My boss told me they are a humanitarian group who wants to make the world a better place. But I have seen and heard things that I was not meant to know. Interestingly, I have never met or even seen any the owners. So my imagination runs wild with other possibilities. Are they a covert government agency, or perhaps a Russian spy organization? Maybe they're a group of evil billionaires who want to take over the world, you know, like in a James Bond movie. I don't dare ask why they need all this technology. Anyway, each time I travel to one of their facilities, I feel the same sense of dread, like I might step on a land mine at any moment. So, every day I add more notes to my journal: what I see, what I overhear, who I talk to, and what they say to me."

"A journal! Oh my God, Sean! You keep a journal?"

"Yeah, I've kept a detailed journal ever since I started working for them. It's my insurance policy in case I needed it."

"An insurance policy? I don't understand. How awful it is to feel you must protect yourself from your employer. Sean, has anyone seen this journal?"

"Hell no! If they did, I'm sure I wouldn't be here with you right now. Anyway, over the last couple of years, I visited their other divisions, and just like where I work at—the Area C Detroit Division—each one is just as concealed. My first assignment was at the most incredible place I had ever seen. It's in Austria, a place they call Area A. They flew me on a private jet from New York to Vienna where a chauffeur driving a black van was waiting for me. He seemed nervous and didn't say anything during the entire drive. After about an hour through the Austrian countryside, we arrived at a desolate, foreboding area on the Danube. I couldn't believe it. He brought me to the ruins of an ancient crumbling fortress that merged into the rocky landscape. It turned out to be the Burgruine Dürnstein, a deserted medieval castle that was vacated in the 1600s.

"He then proceeded to escort me to a rocky outcrop, where an old, rusty iron gate was hidden in a tangle of thorny bushes. But before I could say anything, he ran back to the van and drove off, leaving me standing there alone. Well, you can imagine how I felt, with no idea of where I was or how I would get back. I just stood there feeling like a damn fool. Finally, after a few minutes, the gate creaked open to the entrance of a tunnel. Not knowing what to expect, I stepped into the darkness. Then, out of nowhere, a woman wearing a black uniform appeared. She instructed me to reveal the medallion that identifies me when I'm on assignment. After about a hundred feet into the cavern, we walked through a doorway into another dimly lit tunnel. It was guarded by a massive steel door that slowly shut after we passed through it. The walls were lined with laser detectors and guarded by sentries who held what appeared to be military-grade automatic weapons. We kept walking until we entered a complex of fluorescent-lit rooms."

"My goodness, Sean, you must have been terrified, but you were very brave to even consider going inside."

"Brave? I don't know about that, but crazy, yes. I'm sure at one time those rooms were dungeons hewn into the rock. I imagined they held enemies of the crown who were subjected to unspeakable tortures doled out by barbaric prison guards. However, now they are filled with people at work on computers, surrounded by monitors and file cabinets, next to other rooms with closed doors. Most imposing of all was the row of vault rooms I saw, protected by huge, gleaming, round steel vault doors. Of course, I never saw anything like that before. That's when I realized where my employer gets all their money.

"As I walked down the main passageway, one of the vault doors was left open, and I could not believe what I saw. The room was filled with row after row of gleaming gold bars. They were stacked about eight rows wide and five feet high, and next to them were hundreds of large metal drums and crates filled with heaven only knows what. We eventually reached our destination—a large, well-appointed office at the far end of the maze."

"Oh my God, Sean, you saw inside the-the—I-I-I mean, a vault room?"

"Camille, are you okay?"

"*Oui*, I'm fine. This is all very intriguing, that's all. So, then what happened?"

"Well, that's when I met Wagner."

* * *

"Mr. Phillips, I hope your journey here today was uneventful, and you are well-rested before you begin your assignment. Allow me to introduce myself, I'm Bruno Wagner. You may call me Mr. Wagner."

"Yes, sir, thank you. I must say, I have never seen anything like this place—I'm overwhelmed."

"Julian Marsh speaks highly of you. He has assured me you can be trusted with confidential information and with everything you observe while you are here."

"Yes, sir. That is true."

But then, Wagner's tone changed as he looked me straight in the eye. "Mr. Phillips, let me assure you, I do not trust you. Here in Area A, you are a stranger. I have no idea who you are or what your intentions are. As far as I'm concerned, you have already seen too much. I'm going to keep a close eye on you. One mishap, one wrong glance, one word spoken out of order, and your glory days will be over—forever. I promise you, I will personally make sure you are dealt with according to my rules. So, now that we understand each other, I have neither the time nor the inclination for further discussion. I will walk you over to meet Martin, the head of our technical team. You will talk with him and no one else. You are here only to lend your technical expertise and to assure me this intranet I've heard so much about gets properly installed as soon as possible. Marsh told me it should take no more than two weeks. When you're done, I will arrange your ride back to Vienna. Mr. Phillips, you better hope and pray we see no more of each other."

* * *

"*Oh mon Dieu,* Sean, now I understand what you are talking about. And, after meeting that awful Wagner person, I'm sure I would also want to keep a journal."

"Yes, yes, thank you for understanding; it means a lot to me. After Martin and I completed the installation, a van arrived and drove me back to Vienna. I decided to stay there for a while and get some much-needed R&R. A week later, they flew me to my next assignment, the Area B Media Division in Cyprus. Well, my beautiful Camille, are you bored out of your mind yet?"

"*Non, non,* please, go on, I have never heard anything like this before. It's thrilling."

"Okay then, you asked for it."

"When I arrived in Cyprus, I met Ahmet Kaya, the head honcho. He was far more hospitable than Wagner, and we shared many interesting conversations. He informed me that at one time Varosha was a modern tourist center, but then it was abandoned in 1974. The citizens fled when it came under Turk control, and they left the buildings to decay. The locals describe it as a ghost town, and entry into the area is forbidden to the public. I'm sure my employer was behind the public barring. The area reminded me where I work, hidden away in the old, abandoned Packard plant in Detroit.

"From Varosha, I flew to Belgium where an armed driver drove me to Liège, their Area D Information Division. Anxious to impress me with his knowledge of Belgian history, he told me the Dutch built the fort in 1817. Years later, it was turned into a Carthusian monastery, and then abandoned it in 1891. However, the monks who lived there at the time, carved out an elaborate tunnel system where they produced and stored the beers, liqueurs, and wines they were famous for. Ironically, those tunnels were so well concealed, the occupying forces during both World Wars never discovered them.

"When we got there, I was greeted by one of their armed guards who led me through a maze of dusty, dilapidated corridors. He then reached up behind a beam, where he pushed a button that opened a sliding section of the floor, into the hidden tunnel system below. That's when I met Marie DuPont, the supervisor-in-charge. During my two-week stay, most of our conversations centered on her political views, and quite frankly, I was astounded by her vast knowledge of international politics. Once my work there was completed, they sent me to France, and I arrived here in Marseilles last month, waiting to go on my next assignment. And that's when I was lucky enough to meet you."

"Sean, Sean, Sean, *ma chérie*, I don't know what to say. You must give me some time to think about all of this."

"Think about what? There's nothing to think about. Look Camille, you really don't need to trouble yourself about any of this. I already know what I'll do. I'm going to retire. I have a small fortune stashed away that will carry us through for many years until we can decide where we want to live."

Camille's eyes flashed with a mix of concern and determination as she reached out to cradle my head in her hands, her voice pleading. "Sean, you can't just brush this aside. Retirement isn't the answer to everything. We need to face this together, as a team."

But as her hands fell, I noticed it—a faded brand on her left palm, something she quickly tried to conceal. "W-w-wait a m-minute, Ca-Camille, I've been meaning to ask you. What is that?"

She hesitated, her facade crumbling for a moment before she regained her composure. "What do you mean?"

"On your palm, your left palm. It looks like a brand of some kind."

Quickly pulling her hands back, she mumbled, "Oh, that's nothing. Just a silly thing I did with some friends at a circus when I was very young."

But her attempt to divert my attention only fueled my curiosity further. "No, it's not nothing. Tell me the truth, Camille."

Sighing, she relented. "It's a reminder of a darker time, a past I thought I left behind. But enough about me, Sean. I'm worried about you, about what you're involved in. Please, let me help you."

Camille's voice lowered, her words dripping with urgency and secrecy. "Sean, now that you've peeled back the layers, I'm more worried than ever. Your safety is important to me. Can you trust me with your journals? I need to understand your world, your employer. We can't afford to keep secrets from each other anymore. We're partners now, with our future on the line."

An unconscious reflex stirred me as I glanced around cautiously, and in somber voice, I pleaded, "Camille, you're asking for a piece of a world I've kept hidden for so long. It's not just about my safety; it's about yours too. Once you've read them, there's no going back. My boss was emphatic that I was not to talk to anyone about my work. I've already told you way too much. I never even spoke to my ex-wife about any of this, but I do thank you for listening. It's been pure hell keeping this all bottled up inside of me for so long."

Reassuringly, she said, *"Eh bien mon* Sean, you will not put me in danger. You are very brave and I have you to protect me. And I can certainly keep a secret."

The air between us crackled with tension, heavy with unspoken truths and hidden agendas. But Camille's reassurances were like a lifeline to me, a beacon of hope in the darkness of my secret life.

"Yeah, but when I'm gone, I won't be here to protect you. Anyway, they're locked up in my hotel room, along with my passport. Camille, my life is in those journals. If they were to get into the wrong hands, well, I don't need to say more."

"Sean, we can't have any secrets between us, especially about your job, and why it troubles you so much. Besides, you promised me you would tell me everything. Come on, *mon amour*, I want to read your journals. I promise you, I will protect them with my life. I'll tell you what—I will read them while you're on assignment in Carcassonne."

Her mention of Carcassonne sent a jolt of alarm through me. "Carcassonne? Wait a minute! I never told you I was going to Carcassonne."

"Ahh, um, yeah." Suddenly flustered, she whispered, "Sean, I don't want to argue with you anymore about this stuff. You have made your point." She opened her robe, slipped her arms around me, drew me close to her and kissed me softly on the neck. "Can we pick up where we left off last night, Mr. James Bond 007? I want to play secret agent."

The Trail had put me on a series of steps I could have never predicted, and yet those steps led me to Camille. I thought I had my life mapped out, each step carefully calculated. Then I met her, and suddenly, everything I thought I knew was upended. It was like stepping into a parallel dimension where the rules were different, and danger lurked behind every corner. But despite the warning signs, I couldn't tear myself away from her magnetic pull. Even when she slipped up, dropping hints like breadcrumbs leading to a truth I didn't want to face, I chose to ignore them. The allure of her presence was too strong, blinding me to the stark reality staring me in the face.

CHAPTER 2

AND SO IT BEGINS

"Every man has his own destiny; the only imperative is to follow it, to accept it, no matter where it leads him."— Henry Miller

Destiny is just a comforting lie we tell ourselves. What I faced wasn't destiny—it was the Trail, a twisted path that dragged me through the darkest recesses of existence. I stumbled blindly, unaware that each action I took was leading me closer to the heart of chaos. It wasn't until I looked back, tracing a series of seemingly irrelevant and unrelated steps, that I saw the pattern emerge. The Trail wasn't a gentle guide—it was a merciless tormentor, forcing me to confront nightmares that lurked in the deepest shadows of my mind. And as I unraveled its sinister design, I found myself staring into the abyss of two cataclysmic events, converging like vengeful gods hell-bent on destruction. No one could have foreseen the horror that awaited, the final, brutal showdowns that

would shake the foundations of reality itself. But fate—
or perhaps some cruel twist of cosmic irony—chose me,
Sean Patrick Phillips, as the reluctant champion in this
battle against oblivion.

It all began in 1970, which marked the start of this
descent into madness, the innocent beginning of a journey
that would lead to the edge of sanity and beyond. And as
I stood on the precipice, I could only pray that I had the
strength to uncover the truth before the world succumbs
to its darkest hour.

THE FIRST STEP ON THE TRAIL

April 15, 1970

Back then, Danny Kirchner, my best friend and
roommate, and I lived in Ann Arbor where we attended
the University of Michigan. Our apartment was within
walking distance of the U-M, School of Engineering,
where I majored in both engineering physics and electrical
engineering, while maintaining a 4.0 GPA. At the same
time, I interned at several engineering firms where I got
the hands-on training and work skills I needed to land a
successful career.

This era was a turbulent time in American society.
Women's rights, civil rights, and the environmental
movements competed with the counterculture movement,
the energy crisis, and the Vietnam War. For me however, it
was this war that loomed in my consciousness. My student
deferment, which had sheltered me from being drafted
into this bloody conflict, was about to expire, and I was
terrified Uncle Sam would grab me for the draft.

One afternoon after classes, Danny started a conversation that I really did not want to have. We had been best friends since high school, and as far as he was concerned, he could say anything he wanted to me. He had absolutely no boundaries.

"Come on, Sean. All you do is study, work, sleep, worry, and mope around. What the hell is wrong with you? We never have fun anymore, and to be honest, I'm losing my patience with you. You definitely need something outside of school and work, my friend. I'm going to tell you one last time—you need to get a life. Maybe it's time you find a girlfriend."

"For Christ's sake, will you please stop hassling me about girls? You know damn well I haven't wanted to date anyone ever since Sheri dumped me. If I've told you once, I've told you a million times. I'm—not—interested!"

"My God, Sean, that was years ago. You need to quit feeling so damn sorry for yourself. Your incessant wallowing is driving me crazy. Okay, I'll tell you what. The only reason I even brought it up again is because Cindy's best friend broke up with her boyfriend a couple of months ago, and she's had it with the dating scene. She asked me if I would help her find someone. So, why don't you step up to the plate here, and help me out. The two of you can double with us this weekend."

"Je-Je-Je-Jesus, Danny, I d-d-d-don't know."

"Damn it, Sean, there you go with that stammer of yours again. You mean to tell me that asking a girl out makes you that nervous? You know what your problem is? You overthink everything. You really need to chill out. Look, I met her yesterday. Her name is Marlene West, and she seems really nice. She already graduated, and has a great job in home furnishings at downtown Hudson's. And, trust me when I tell you, she's an incredibly hot redhead. Quite honestly, if I wasn't already engaged to Cindy, I'd ask her out in a heartbeat. Ha, ha, you know what, maybe I'll do it anyway. Oh, oh, wait a minute—I forgot. I'm not supposed to joke around with you. Look, Sean, you're a good-looking guy; she's not going to shut you down."

"Okay, Danny, I'll do it. But she better not be like that weird girl you set me up with last time."

So, I bit the bullet, and as my stomach churned, I went on my first date in over a year. Danny was right though. Marlene was very attractive and full of self-confidence. Unlike me, she had no problem telling me exactly what was on her mind. A bright, ambitious, hard-working interior decorator, she was the first woman they hired as head of the creative design department at the iconic J.L. Hudson Department Store in downtown Detroit. It didn't take much for me to see that she was definitely out of my league. But at least, I wouldn't have to listen to Danny's constant nagging for a while.

Between her schedule and mine, it was not easy to get together during the work week. The drive from Ann Arbor to her place in Detroit was over an hour. But on the weekends, we doubled with Danny and Cindy going to U-M football games, rock concerts, and trying out the new ethnic cafes and bistros that were popping up everywhere. Over time, we became more comfortable and intimate with each other and ventured out on overnight road trips. That winter, we went up north on ski weekends and the following summer we relaxed at our favorite Michigan beach resorts. Most fun of all were the nature hikes up north, especially in Michigan's upper peninsula. Michigan is a water wonderland, with all the lakes, rivers, waterfalls, and fishing streams. We both loved hiking in the pristine national forests and meadowlands, where at one time there had once been an abundance of wildlife. But we could see that civilization was beginning to encroach on nature's beauty and the natural habitats. We had been reading reports that many of the once abundant species not only in Michigan but all over the world, were rapidly disappearing, and it would only get worse if things didn't somehow turn around.

We discovered we had a lot of things in common, and as we got to know each other, I became more comfortable with her. My doubts about us as a couple lessened, and I wanted to see her whenever we had the time. I finally became serious about making a commitment. It took about a year, but on October 21, 1971, on bended knee, and with beads of perspiration running down my face, I asked her for her hand. She looked me straight in the eye, and without hesitation, she said, "Yes."

I couldn't believe it. She actually chose me. At last, I found a girl who accepted me with all my weird quirks.

Marlene was a devout Catholic. As for me, my parents tried to raise me Lutheran, but since religion never made any sense to me, I vowed I would never step foot into a church again. She was a strong, confident, driving personality who always got her way, and she was determined to have a church wedding. But I was not about to reject my personal core principles, much less join a religion I knew nothing about and cared less about. So, we had a problem—a big problem. Even so, if Danny hadn't introduced us, I wouldn't have had the opportunity to take the second step, and my journey on the Trail would have ended before it really started.

CHAPTER 3

THE PROTECTIVE SHEPHERD

THE SECOND STEP

October 23, 1971

"Sean, we need to talk. I know how you feel about religion, but I've always wanted a traditional church wedding. I already know who I want for my bridesmaids, the photographer, the caterer, the florist and where I want the reception to be held. Please understand, this is a big deal to me, something I have dreamed about ever since I was a little girl."

"For God's sake, Marlene, you've known from the very beginning how I feel about church and religion. Why can't we just keep it simple and elope? Or better yet, we can say our vows in front of a justice of the peace, and then have a full-blown reception and invite everyone we know."

"Yes, Sean, I agree we'll have a full-blown reception. And, no, Sean, our wedding ceremony will be held in a church. And another thing: once we're married, you and I are going to church every Sunday. If you can't do that for me, well, then maybe we should just call this whole thing off."

"Wow, you're sure not giving me much of a choice here."

"Okay, I'll tell you what. I've been doing a lot of thinking. I'll make this easier for you. I decided I'd switch from Catholic to Lutheran. At least that way, the wedding will be held in a church and a religion you're familiar with."

After many emotional discussions and a great deal of soul-searching, she left the Catholic Church to accommodate me. That's when we joined the neighborhood church near our rented flat in Royal Oak, a suburb about twelve miles north of downtown Detroit. Exactly a year later, on October 21, 1972, we were married at Church of the Redeemer. I was twenty-two and she was twenty-four. Between my school and her work schedule, our time was filled, and so we postponed the honeymoon. Instead, we took the opportunity to move our meager belongings into our first home together.

Everything seemed great, except for the draft. The risk of being selected by the lottery was a constant threat. My student deferment was about to run out, which made me a ripe target for a call from Uncle Sam. Getting drafted into the military was the last thing I wanted. The risks of dying on the battlefield, coming home with missing limbs, or being captured and sent to the Hanoi Hilton to be tortured to death were high. After talking it over with some of my friends, I decided to try and enlist in the Army Reserve. Committing to six years of military service, along with the possibility of being called up for active duty at any time, was a real concern. But for me, the *possibility* of active duty in the Reserves was a far better option than the *certainty* of two years of active duty as a draftee in Vietnam. However, I soon found out the odds of enlisting in any of the Reserve units were slim, simply because thousands of other men also wanted to avoid the draft, and so available slots were limited. I had absolutely no idea what I could do. But it was Marlene's decision to join the Lutheran Church that led me to the next step.

THE THIRD STEP

November 5, 1972
Church of the Redeemer
Royal Oak, Michigan

One Sunday morning, our minister, Pastor Richard Jesse, delivered a sermon on the evils of war. He understood how hard it was for families when the draft forced their loved ones to fight in a war many Americans did not believe in. At one point, he mentioned his volunteer job on the selection committee at the local draft board. He said it was one of the most difficult positions he ever held. His words immediately got my attention. Even though he was not on the same draft board where I registered, I figured it was worth a try to find out if he knew of any options. After the church service, we cornered him in the hallway.

"Marlene and Sean, I'm really pleased to see the two of you. I don't think we've talked since your wedding. So, what can I do for you today?"

"Well Pastor, I have a problem. My student deferment has run out, and as you know, I could get my draft notice at any time. We heard you mention this morning that you serve on the draft board. I know it's a long shot, but do you think you can help us?"

"You're not the first one to ask me that. To be honest, Sean, I don't know if I can help or not, and I certainly don't want to get your hopes up. But I'll see what I can do."

"Thank you, Pastor. We would really appreciate anything you think might help."

Being the protective shepherd of his flock, Pastor Jesse went to bat for me. About a week later, I received a phone call from him. My face immediately broke out in a cold sweat and my stomach tightened into a tight knot. There was no way he could have done much to help me in such a short time. So, I prepared myself for the bad news.

"Good afternoon, Sean, it's Pastor Jesse. How are the two of you doing?"

"We're both okay. I'm still looking for a job, but it's probably a waste of time since I'm sure I'll be getting my greetings letter from Uncle Sam any day now."

"Actually, I'm calling you with some good news. There's an army reserve unit on the east side that will be enlisting half a dozen recruits. But you'll need to get there early next Thursday morning, no later than 6 a.m. The center doesn't open until 8, so you're going to be waiting out in the cold for a couple of hours. You'll want to be at the front of the line. And—very important—make sure you fill out the form on the clipboard they hand to you."

With words of deep gratitude, I thanked him for his help. That Thursday morning, I arrived at 6 a.m., but to my dismay, at least fifty other men were already waiting in the bitter November cold. My heart sank.

THE FOURTH STEP

November 27, 1972

Three weeks later, the unexpected happened. An officer from the enlistment center at Fort Wayne in Detroit called to schedule a time for me to swear into the United States Army Reserve. More than eager, I showed up at the appointed time. Standing in front of a sharply uniformed lieutenant, I raised my right hand and repeated the military oath, ending with, "So help me God." That oath would change my destiny forever. Ironically, the very next day, my "Greetings Fellow American" letter arrived in the mail. Uncle Sam had selected me for the draft. But timing was everything. Because I was already a reservist, regular army couldn't touch me.

I often thought about how damn close I was to getting drafted. If I had never met Pastor Jesse, that letter would have changed my destiny forever. The odds were high. I would have ended up in Vietnam, and only God knows what would have happened to me over there.

Several months later, my orders arrived in the mail for sixteen weeks of basic training at Fort Benning, Georgia. Eager to get this period of my life behind me was an understatement. I figured that after I put in my time playing soldier, I could come home to Marlene, begin my career as an engineer, buy a home, and start a family. The only thing was I would have to play weekend warrior and go to summer camps for the next six years. Even so, my life finally seemed to be predictable and back on track again, or so I thought.

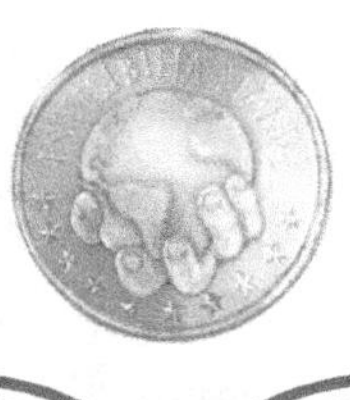

CHAPTER 4

BATTLE BUDDIES

THE FIFTH STEP

July 1, 1973

Several months after receiving my orders, I flew down to Fort Benning. As I walked down the boarding ramp, I figured the intense heat I felt came from the jet engines. Not so. It was the absolute hottest time of the year. The large thermometer on the Columbus, Georgia terminal read 102°, and that was in the shade. That's when reality hit me square in the face. I was alone in the Deep South, far from my wife, my family, and my friends.

Wandering around outside the terminal lost and confused, I eventually ran into a ragtag group of other recruits waiting for a bus ride to the reception station. When we arrived, a team of screaming drill sergeants greeted us and wasted no time transitioning us from civilians to soldiers. The routine was "hurry up and wait" while we stood in line after line to be processed for dental and medical exams, vaccinations, haircuts, uniforms, boot fittings, and paperwork.

That evening, they assigned us temporary bunks in one of the old World War II barracks. For the next three days, in the summer Georgia heat, we endured countless hours of briefings and humiliations from screaming, battle-hardened career men. That was when I met Eddie. He came from Cleveland, Ohio, and, like me, a college grad. With lots in common, we hit it off right away. Talking with him distracted me from my longing to be back home with Marlene.

During one of the morning briefings, aides taught us the buddy system. They had us select a battle buddy, someone we could trust to have our backs for the entire eight weeks of basic training. After we completed the three days at reception, we rode on olive-drab army buses to the Sand Hill Training Facility. I soon discovered that Eddie and I ended up in the same platoon. We would be battle buddies for the next eight weeks.

In the rare quiet times, we argued about the classic rivalry between our college teams, Michigan and Ohio. We talked about our careers and our families. Eddie liked to talk about his girlfriend, and, like me, he was already homesick for her. But we also talked about politics. At that time, America was in the midst of major social changes, transforming the way many Americans thought and behaved. We could not comprehend the 1960s anti-establishment, hippie, counterculture Woodstock generation. What we saw were nothing but over-indulged, lazy brats who lived for today with no accountability for their actions. We saw losers who obsessed over free sex and binge drinking, all the while spaced out on drugs and listening to hardcore rock and roll that idolized their lifestyle. To top it off, they used anti-war rhetoric as an excuse for their brazen behavior. They pissed us off because we could never figure out how in hell they avoided the draft without moving to Canada. In particular, we despised their disdain for traditional American values. We couldn't understand how they could disrespect the enormous sacrifices their parents' generation made fighting not one but two enemies who were hell-bent on destroying us. If it weren't for their parents who served in the military during World War II, we would likely all be speaking German or Japanese, or worse yet, locked up in internment camps. It was their bravery and patriotism that gave these spoiled baby boomer flower children the freedom to be complete assholes.

Eddie had already received his law degree and was excited about a career as a lawyer. Unfortunately, he was in the Regular Army and would not see an attorney's office for at least another two years. As a pastime, we spent hours reading and re-reading our letters from home. Constant complaining about his girlfriend became an obsession for him, and for good reason. Her letters had fallen off to one or two a week. And the tone of the few he did get was vague about almost everything, not at all warm and loving. The lyrics we chanted when we marched from one training site to another didn't help his morale either.

'Hut, two, three, four—I don't know, but I've been told; Jody's got your car and gone. Ain't no use in feelin' blue, Jody's got your girlfriend too—hut, two, three, four.'

To distract him from his woes, I would talk about my love of science and, in particular, my theory about Genesis. I explained that what really hit home for me happened in sixth grade when I read Mark Twain's book, *The Adventures of Huckleberry Finn*. I was especially intrigued by one of Huck's reflections on life on the river. Like Huck, I also questioned our origins.

'It's lovely to live on a raft. We had the sky up there, all speckled with stars, and we used to lay on our backs and look up at them, and discuss about whether they was made or only just happened.'

One Saturday afternoon, after the morning routines, Eddie asked me a direct question—one that was entirely out of character for him.

"Sean, I need to ask you something that I've thought about for a long time now. I'm sure nobody else has ever asked you, so I'll just be blunt. Do you believe in God?"

Annoyed by an unexpected question I struggled with, I replied without giving him a direct answer, "Well, I went to a religious school for eight years. Our teachers pushed Bible verses and other religious stuff down our throats every morning. I didn't understand much of what they taught us and cared less. If I questioned anything, they always gave me the same answer. The Bible is the word of God, and true believers do not question what the Bible says."

Not satisfied with my response, he repeated the question, "But you didn't answer me. Do you believe in God?"

Irritated by his persistence, I turned the question back on him. "Why do you want to know if I believe in God? Do you?"

"Hey look, Sean, you're the one who brought up Genesis. The reason I ask is, I've been thinking about God quite a bit lately. You're a science major, so let me pose another question. This one has puzzled me for a while now. I was taught that the universe began with a single particle during the Big Bang. Then, over billions of years, that particle expanded into everything that now exists. Science can't describe it, where it came from, what caused it to happen, or what existed before it. The physical laws don't seem to explain how it originated from absolutely nothing. So, is there a God who created that particle? Or, do you know something else I don't?"

"Not really, Eddie."

He finally realized that religion was not something I wanted to talk about. "Hey, never mind me. I guess I'm trying to distract myself from all my problems."

"No, no, don't worry about it. It's a question I also struggle with."

"Sean, let me be honest with you. I'm frightened—no, actually it's more than that. I'm scared to death. I never volunteered for this. I was drafted into this shit hole without a choice. Two of my friends from high school were also drafted. I just found out one of them is missing in action, and the other one was killed in a raid. I have confided things to you I would never tell another guy. We've been here for each other during basic. We're battle buddies. We're blood brothers. We've got each other's back, isn't that right?"

"Of course, Eddie, we made a pact. We're lifelong friends, you know that."

Then, out of the clear blue sky, he yelled, "Bullshit! I don't know why in hell I ever buddied up with you. We're not going to Nam together. You're going home and live the life of Riley with Marlene, while I get my ass blown up over there."

"Whoa, wait a minute, dude. You have no idea where they'll station you. They could send you anywhere, maybe even Europe. For God's sake, for all you know you could end up working in the motor pool or some office job with a typewriter. Eddie, I know you're scared, but dwelling on Nam is not helping. And yes, I'm going home, but I'm vulnerable for the next six years. I could get my orders to go there at any time."

Eddie should have never been accepted into the military. Like many other men, he was not cut out to be a soldier. He had deep-seated problems that not only prevented him from executing his role in combat, but could also easily put others in jeopardy while they constantly tried to help him. He simply could not carry his weight and was not a good battle buddy for me when I needed him to be.

During one of our training exercises, we practiced hand grenade drills. It was at night, and Eddie and I teamed up looking for a bunker where we were instructed to toss dummy grenades into. The rest of our squad was also divided into pairs, but they were out in the perimeter areas, so we were alone. Then, without warning me or saying anything, he suddenly pulled the pin on a grenade, dropped it at our feet, and began running. Even though it was a dummy, I instinctively dove to the ground and covered my head. My battle buddy was gone. I was so pissed off, I immediately got up and tore after him. When

I finally caught up with him, I threw him to the ground and beat the crap out of him. After he recovered, Eddie begged me to report the incident to the MPs. He was hoping to get discharged to avoid being sent to Nam. But I refused to rat him out. That was the last time we ever spoke to each other. I tried to understand his sudden change of attitude. Losing his girlfriend, the loss of his friends in Vietnam, and knowing he would part ways with me all took a toll on him. Nevertheless, his resentment toward me was extreme, leaving me feeling guilty for my good fortune.

Once we completed basic, I was ordered to Fort Rucker, Alabama, for my eight weeks of advanced infantry training. After I finished my stint there, I could fly back home to Michigan and Marlene. However, just before my discharge date, she sent a letter to prepare me. Our landlady had sold the Royal Oak flat we were living in, forcing us to move out. Once again, I lost control over my life, and I freaked out. I had no idea what we would do or where we would live. However, although I didn't know it at the time, the timing of my discharge was perfect and led me to the next step.

CHAPTER 5

BACK HOME

THE SIXTH STEP

November 3, 1973

I had always been capable and independent, and I always marched to the beat of my own drum. But now, I didn't even have a job and felt responsible for finding a place for me and Marlene to live. So, before coming back home, I called her.

"I have to tell you, sweetheart, after going through sixteen weeks of military life, I'm in no mood to have another obstacle stand in my way of us leading a normal life. Eddie is more than resentful of me for coming home, while they will undoubtedly ship him off to Nam. He's not fit to be a soldier, so I'm afraid I may never see him again. I don't have a job and will have to depend on you for the money. And now you tell me we don't have a place to live."

"Sean, will you please calm down and relax? Regardless of what you think, I'm quite capable of taking care of things. It so happens that my mother has a friend who owns a duplex in Birmingham, and fortunately for us, one unit just became available. The timing of your discharge is perfect before somebody else grabs it."

"Birmingham! You've got to be kidding. We can't afford Birmingham."

"For Chrissake, Sean, yes, we can, at least for the next couple of months until you find a job. Right now, the only thing you need to worry about is getting home; I'll take care of the rest. We don't have a lot of things to move, and my father said he would help me, so I'll be fine."

"Okay, if you say so. But there's one other thing. I have to tell you, I'm very grateful that I did not end up like Eddie, and I owe it all to Pastor Jesse for helping me when we needed it. The first thing I want to do is personally thank him as soon as I get back."

November 11, 1973
Church of the Redeemer
Royal Oak, Michigan

"Pastor, thank you for seeing us this morning. I know how valuable your time is, especially on Sunday. You have no idea how much your help has meant to us. It became clear to me after I left my army buddy behind. I'm afraid they will most likely send him to Nam."

"Of course, Sean, and welcome home. I'm happy it turned out so well for you and I was able to help. I'm truly sorry to hear about your buddy. He will more than likely have to face quite an ordeal over there. But really, there's no need to feel guilty about it. Sometimes that's just the way life is. So, is there anything else I can help you with today?"

"No, no, you've done more than enough. I just wanted to tell you how grateful we are."

"It must be a coincidence the two of you came to see me today or you read my mind. Please sit down for a moment—I have a favor to ask you."

"Absolutely, Pastor, anything we can do to help."

"I went to Jerusalem several years ago on sabbatical to study some ancient manuscripts that I thought might help me better understand scripture. When I was there, a couple of objects I found in a back alley shop caught my attention. After haggling with the merchant, I purchased them. Although they intrigue me, I never took the time to find out what they are. You're both intelligent college grads, and Sean, you're an engineer with an inquisitive mind. I want to give them to you. You're both young and have a whole life ahead of you. Perhaps, on one of your journeys, the two of you may have some time to find out more about them. I only ask one thing. Let me know what you find out. They have always excited my imagination."

"Sure, no problem. We'll be happy to find out whatever we can."

"The merchant put them in this box for me. Here, let me show you. I've never seen anything like them before. Anyway, I think they are made of some type of hardstone. To me, they resemble a roll of quarters. For something that small, I am intrigued. The figures etched on them are quite exquisite, and look like they must have come from some ancient culture. I have no idea what they were used for, who made them, or how old they are."

"You're right, Pastor, they're quite remarkable. I've never seen anything like them either. We would be happy to check them out for you. I'm not sure when we'll have the opportunity, but I promise we will keep them safe and always treasure them."

"That would be great, and that's all I ask. I'm in no rush."

Then he turned his attention to Marlene and asked, "And you, young lady, how are you doing?"

"I'm fine, Pastor. We're ready to start a family, and, pray, I will soon get pregnant. I'm not complaining though; I feel very blessed."

"Yes, I know how important a family is to you, and I will pray for you, too. For now, though, I hate to cut this short. The church treasurer holds a meeting once a month that I must attend." Extending his hand, he said, "Have a blessed week, and I will see the both of you next Sunday."

We took the box with the strange objects inside with us and put it in my dresser drawer. Initially, we were excited to find out more about them, but as it is with life, we had more important things to worry about. I needed a job. Marlene and I spent countless hours combing through the want ads. Going on dozens of employment interviews and armed with an engineering degree, I thought my search would be easy. However, such was not the case. Countless other college grads from all over the country competed for the same coveted positions in the auto capital of the world. Over the next several months, my pursuit of a well-paying job proved fruitless. That was when I met our new next-door neighbor, Don Campbell, who unknowingly led me to the next step.

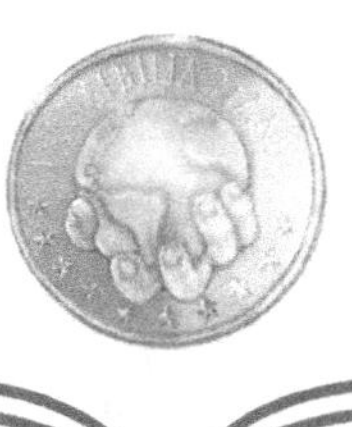

CHAPTER 6

AREA C

THE SEVENTH STEP

May 18, 1974

Several months after we settled into our new Birmingham duplex, I met Don Campbell. Don, a successful thirty-something real estate executive who serviced the metro area business community. Over time, we got to know him and his wife, Patti, and they became very good friends of ours. One Saturday morning, while cutting the lawn, he invited us over to their house for dinner that same evening to celebrate the birth of their baby. Our schedule was empty, so I accepted.

That evening

Ready to start a family and wanting a baby of her own, Marlene was envious of the Campbells' good fortune. "Patti, your baby is beautiful! What's her name?"

"We decided to name her Katherine after Don's grandmother, but we shortened it to Katie. Marlene, come over here for a minute, I want to show you the nursery. I'm really excited about it. I've been planning it for months, and now it's almost done, except Don still needs to finish painting the walls. He promised he would get them done by tomorrow afternoon. I certainly hope so." Then, suddenly distracted, she said, "Oh, oh, wait a minute, I see him waving at me. He's just about ready to serve his steaks, and he hates cold steaks. I'll show you Katie's new things after dinner, especially the cute little sweater my mother knit for her."

After we sat down, Don held up a bottle of wine. "Can I interest you in a new cabernet? We've waited over nine months to try it. With booze off limits, Patti can finally imbibe in one of her favorite reds. I guarantee it'll be the perfect pairing with these ribeyes."

"Hey, no problem, Don. I'm sure we'll love it."

"Sean, before we eat, I have some good news for you," Don said with a big smile. "I know finding a job has been difficult, but I may have a great prospect for you. One of my contacts heads up a company that is working on some exciting, new, cutting-edge technology. He claims it'll have countless applications, not only in the private sector but also in government and the military."

"Really, what is it?"

"I'm not familiar with any of it. He mentioned integrated circuits, computers, and other technical stuff. He said it would be revolutionary. He called it the 'internet.' I'm sure you know a lot more about these things than I do."

"Unfortunately, I don't, Don. These technologies haven't been around for long. Right now, I believe they're still in the R&D stages, and I have no idea at all about any of their commercial applications."

Ready to serve his steaks, he kept the conversation short. "I can't tell you anything more. Whenever I show some interest in his company, he immediately changes the subject. In fact, I've never been to his office, and the more I think about it, I actually don't even know their name or where it's located. I don't know, maybe they may work on some high-level government or military project. Anyway, I met with him for lunch the other day to discuss some personal real estate matters. That's when he mentioned their need for qualified engineers. He thought it would be easy to fill the slots, but evidently, that is not the case. Most graduates looking for jobs don't have the science background his company wants. Wanting to be of help, you came to mind. To cut to the chase, he would like to meet you. If you're interested, here's his number. Mention my name, and good luck."

"Interested, are you kidding? We are thrilled! You have no idea how much we appreciate your help, Don."

THE EIGHTH STEP

May 20, 1974

That Monday morning, I called the number Don gave me. A young woman answered the phone and identified herself as Rachel. She was very friendly, and after some brief small talk, we settled on a time for my first job interview. On the morning of my scheduled appointment,

I left the house at precisely 9. Four hours later, I returned home and yelled out, "Marlene, I'm home, and boy, do I have a story for you!"

More than excited, she ran to the door to greet me. "Come on, let's sit down. What happened? Tell me everything."

"Well, for starters, the place I went to was near East Grand Boulevard, about eight blocks from where my family used to visit our relatives when I was a kid. When I finally found it, shock doesn't even come close to what I saw. Turns out, it's located at the site of the old Packard assembly plant. I couldn't believe it. The complex was so large that it felt like I entered an endless maze. I found out it was once a state-of-the-art auto plant where Packard built American luxury cars. Back in the day it must have been quite the show place. Unfortunately, they decommissioned it and shut it down in 1958. Now, there's nothing there but weed-covered streets and abandoned buildings, with homeless people lying around."

Appearances were everything to Marlene. Compared to the posh offices where she worked, what I described was shocking. She could not contain herself. "You have got to be kidding. Please tell me you turned around and got the hell out of there as fast as you could."

"No, I didn't, and maybe it was a mistake, but I went anyway. Rachel told me to drive to Area C, but all I saw were old, run-down buildings and factories, nothing that remotely looked like a place where I could work. But you know how stubborn I can be, so I kept driving and finally ran across a group of five gray buildings. Eventually, I saw the small Area C sign wired to a chain-link fence, topped with razor wire that surrounded the buildings. That was enough to send chills down my back, until I remembered Don said he thought they might do government work."

"Don *thought* they might do government work. Are you kidding me? Sean, that's ridiculous. I really don't think the government would have one of their facilities located at a place like that."

"I know. You're probably right, but let me finish. I drove around until I spotted a guard shack. The guard asked to see my driver's license and directed me where to park. No sooner did I step out of the car when a second guard approached me. He patted me down, escorted me into the first building we came to, and handed me over to Rachel. She led me up three flights of stairs to a corner office. When I walked in, I certainly didn't expect what I saw. It was surprisingly attractive and ultra-modern inside, although I did think it was odd that there were no windows. You would think that an executive with a corner office would want windows. Instead, across from his desk was a summer beach scene mural, obviously there to create an outdoor illusion."

"Yeah, Sean, this whole thing sounds like an illusion to me."

"Ha, ha, very funny. Anyway, his office was impressive. In the middle of the room was a large conference table, and behind his desk were half a dozen computer monitors with flickering green screens. I had never seen anything like them before. They displayed charts, graphs, mathematical computations, and neatly arranged paragraphs of technical writing. On the desk was what appeared to be one of the most advanced computers

I have ever seen. It's certainly far superior to anything I used in school or at my internships."

"Okay, Sean, please just stop. Are you crazy? This does not sound right at all. I really don't understand why you didn't turn around and leave. We live in the car capital of the world, with three of the largest auto companies and hundreds of engineering firms. Why—in heaven's sake—would you ever settle for a place like that? I really don't get it."

"Yeah, you may be right, and I won't make any decisions until you and I talk it through."

"Alright, but I don't know what you can possibly say to change my mind."

"Well, we'll see. Anyway, Rachel brought coffee and donuts. That's when I met Julian Marsh. Surprisingly, he was dressed casually, with a Tiparillo dangling from the corner of his mouth. I really felt overdressed with my new Brooks Brothers three-piece suit. I found out he was definitely not impressed by attire. He looked at me, and then at the dossier Rachel put on his desk."

*   *   *

"Let me see here. Your name is Sean Patrick Phillips," he said, brushing away a stray cigar ash off his shirt. Then, he remembered. "Oh yeah, you're the one Don Campbell told me about." Standing up, he extended his hand. "Sean Phillips, of course, have a seat. I'm Julian Marsh. I hope you didn't mind our security measures. You'll soon understand why we take the precautions we do. I know you have a lot of questions, so why don't you go ahead and ask away?"

His offer to let me begin the interview threw me, but I asked anyway. "Yes, sir. First of all, what is this company? I don't see any signs. Who will I be working for?"

"My boy, you talk as if I already hired you. I like your positive attitude but keep in mind this is a job interview. We have not signed a contract yet. If we can come to an agreement, you'll work for Blackguard. Sean, let me save you some time. I understand you're Don Campbell's next-door neighbor. I've known Don for a long time and I trust his instincts. So, we took the liberty of completing an extensive background check on you before you got here. And, I must say, you seem to have all the requirements we're looking for. Correct me if I'm wrong. You have an engineering degree from the University of Michigan, along with a science major. You're a member of the U.S. Army Reserve. You're married to Marlene, so I'm sure you'll eventually start a family. Based on your religious background, I believe you're a man of your word and can be trusted with sensitive information. You have no negatives: no criminal record, no addictions we know of. You never participated in campus sit-ins, protests, or had any encounters with the police. Oh, and one other thing. Before I forget, for some reason that I'm unaware of, our employment office wants to confirm that your birthday is on December 31, 1950. We'll need to take a photo of your driver's license."

"Okay, but how in the world do you know all of this about me? Who are you, the CIA?"

"We are not CIA. Blackguard is a think tank. This complex is the Area C Detroit Technology Division. We are one of four divisions. The other three are located in other countries, and each one provides Blackguard with a specific service. The work we do here is highly classified. For now, that is all you need to know. If we agree on a suitable position, you will be sworn to absolute confidentiality on everything you know, see, observe, or hear. That means you may not discuss anything with anyone, not even Marlene. I don't mean to discourage you, but you must consider this position carefully. You'll face consequences from the higher-ups if you were to break our confidentiality agreement, and unfortunately, I won't be able to help you."

"C-C-C-Consequences? How much will you pay me to sign my life away?"

"Sean, my boy, don't worry about it. You will not be signing your life away. We want to hire you as a brilliant engineer with an impeccable background, and that's it. Keep in mind that initially, this is a trial period for both of us. If you're not happy, you can, of course, leave at any time. But the confidentiality agreement will remain in force for the rest of your life. Your pay will start at $50,000 plus medical benefits. And we'll enroll you in our retirement plan immediately. I'm sure any other company you might consider will only offer you $20,000 at the most and you'll have to wait a year for your benefits to begin."

Shocked by the offer, I stammered, "My G-G-G-God Mr. M-M-Marsh—$50,000! So, what does this position involve?"

"I'm sorry, I didn't realize you had a stutter. If you decide to accept the offer, you'll meet your team leader, Travis McShane. You'll work with him, and the other team members, on an exciting new project that will soon get underway. It's called an 'intranet.'"

"I've heard of the internet, but not the intranet. What is that?"

"Travis will fill you in on the details when you're officially onboard."

"Mr. Marsh, this all sounds too p-p-perfect. There must be a c-c-catch."

"Sean, will you please relax? I'm confident you'll have no problem adapting. With your background, I'm sure you will find our work here not only highly creative but inspiring as well. I can tell you, what we're doing will ultimately benefit all mankind. There's another benefit of your job—you'll travel to some pretty exotic locations, but there's a catch. We may have to relocate you to another city or country, depending on the assignment. Don't worry though, that won't happen for at least another couple of years."

"Wow, I don't know what to say. You've given me a lot to think about. I need to talk this over with my wife. She's very close to her family, so I'm not sure she'll go for the idea of moving."

"I understand and I don't mean to rush you, but I'll need an answer within three days. This project is getting off the ground on Monday morning. For your benefit, as well as ours, I want to get you started on the ground floor. So, yes, by all means, think it over and call me after you've made your decision."

* * *

"So, there you have it, sweetheart. Mr. Marsh went back to his desk and the interview ended as abruptly as it started. I don't know what to do. What do you think?"

Marlene's mouth began to curve into a broad smile. "Good Lord, Sean, now I'm not sure what to think either. I've been the breadwinner for a long time, and I sure could use some help, especially with the cost of living here in Birmingham. The benefits part sounds great, but a $50,000 starting pay—that sounds too good to be true."

"Okay, aside from the money, we need to talk about the negatives. What about the possible relocation?"

"To be honest, I don't like the idea of leaving Michigan. What about our families and friends? If we move, we will hardly ever see them."

"I know, but he did say moving is just a possibility. And if it were to happen, he told me I could leave at any time. We have three days to make up our minds. Let's take this time to weigh the pros and cons."

It did not take much time for us to decide. The generous income would offer Marlene some well-deserved relief, so the concern we felt gave way to the desire to finally have children and start a family. I called Mr. Marsh the next day. Delighted with our decision, he instructed me to arrive at Area C the following Monday morning.

CHAPTER 7

BLACKGUARD

THE NINTH STEP

May 27, 1974

On Monday morning, I arrived at Area C eager to begin my exciting new career. Rachel accompanied me to my work area and introduced me to my team leader, Travis McShane. Travis was a thirtysomething tech nerd. With his dark-rimmed glasses, light blue shirt, and khaki slacks, he looked like every other geek in America's corporate offices. He had a large, brown birthmark on his left temple, and I was sure he was a frequent target of unwanted stares. Even so, I found him warm, outgoing, and welcoming. He was someone with whom I immediately felt comfortable.

"Welcome to Team Internet, Sean. By the way, no formality here—call me Travis. Just relax, and I'll go over your new position. But first things first, I need some coffee. How about you? All we have is vending machine coffee, but it's pretty good."

"Sure, that sounds great."

"Let's grab a cup before I introduce you to our team."

"Travis, this is my first real job, so I have a lot of questions. I used to drive my professors crazy, but I take pride in my precision for detail. Getting answers as they come up simply minimizes problems for me. Don't laugh, but one of them had a nickname for me. I became known as the 'Curiosity Kid.'"

"Ha, ha, that's great. I can already see why Mr. Marsh wanted you on our team. So yes, go ahead and ask as many questions as you like."

"What's the deal with this company, or whatever it's called? I didn't see any signs anywhere."

"Blackguard is not a company in the traditional sense. It's is a high-level, classified, and interconnected global think tank. It has no official or legal name. You won't find it on any stock exchange, and you won't find any information about it in The Wall Street Journal or from your broker. Your paycheck will come from a shell company under a separate bank name, and your benefit package is entirely self-funded. Blackguard doesn't use insurance companies or outside investment firms."

"Where in the heck do they get the money from to run an operation like this?"

"Sean, let me assure you, you don't need to worry about the money. And I'll forewarn you now, don't ask too many questions about Blackguard. Mr. Marsh will tell you everything you need to know. Think of Area C as your employer and forget about everything else."

"Okay, so what does Area C do?"

"You must have heard about the internet when you were in school."

"Yeah, I heard about it, but other than that, not much else. A few of my professors touched on internet potential, but no technical details."

"Well, the internet is a global computer network that will provide a variety of information and communication services, made possible by interconnected networks and standardized communication protocols. In other words, every computer in the world will have the potential to communicate with each other. Our project here at Team Internet will be like the global internet, except our directive is to set up a dedicated network, what they call an 'intranet.'"

"What in the world is an intranet?"

"Only Blackguard and no one else will have access to it. In essence, they'll have a private intranet that is separate and impenetrable from the worldwide internet. Sean, I can tell you we are eons ahead of everybody else when it comes to this new technology. That's because Blackguard doesn't deal with regulators, corporate board of directors, red tape, or Congressional approval to fund these projects. Only the most talented people on the planet work for them."

"Okay, I don't know what else to ask right now, other than why all the secrecy?"

"Blackguard has four divisions completely separated from one another, and they maintain a zero-contact tolerance with each other. Think of it as a code of silence."

"Yikes, I've never heard of anything like this before. So, who knows the big picture?"

"I have no idea, but I can tell you they are people you have never heard of."

"Will I ever get an opportunity to meet any of them?"

"Again, Sean, your questions are reasonable, but I have no idea and I don't care. I've been with Blackguard for over twelve years now, and I have never met any of them. We have completed a lot of exciting projects here in Area C, I have loved every minute of it, and I always get paid on time."

"Okay. When can I meet the other team members?"

"Yep, that's next, so let's get acquainted."

My team members were both men and women. The youngest appeared to be around my age, and the oldest, maybe, early sixties. What struck me most was their diversity. I could see these people were selected strictly for their talents and skills, all seated for the imminent meeting and all their eyes on me. On one hand, I couldn't get over the nagging feeling that I was going to work for the most covert organization I could ever imagine—like something out of a Hollywood movie. But on the other hand, with all the new technology Travis told me about, I decided to settle into my new career working for Blackguard.

Over time, Travis and I became close friends, so there were many moments when he hung out with me and Marlene. The three of us would go out to dinner, play cards, or watch movies. On occasion, we went to some of the sporting events in Detroit and frequented a favorite downtown bar afterward. Once again, everything in my life seemed great.

After a year and earning a generous income, Marlene and I decided to move from our Birmingham flat and buy a house on one of the 350 inland lakes that dot Oakland County, Michigan. We bought a beautiful contemporary ranch on Orchard Lake, the perfect location to raise a family. Even though I made enough money to easily afford our new upscale lifestyle, all the secrecy left me feeling detached from my personal life. I couldn't discuss anything about my work with anyone, not even Marlene. When people asked what I did for a living, I made excuses like classified government works or boring technology.

To make matters worse, I would overhear water cooler talk and whispers from my other team members. During the few times I was included in their conversations, they would probe to find out what information I had about Blackguard. Like me, they did not understand how all this new technology would be used. Several of them had worked for other companies where their product lines were completely transparent to everybody. The higher-ups in these companies were also well known to everyone. But, other than Marsh, Team Internet had never met anyone even associated with Blackguard. These were smart people who felt the same way I did. Things just didn't feel right. That's when I decided to keep a daily journal. I documented my routines and conversations in case things turned against me, a suspicion I harbored ever since I first met Julian Marsh. It was of something he said: *'You must consider this position very carefully, because if you break the confidentiality agreement, I can't help you.'*

CHAPTER 8

WATER AND OIL

THE TENTH STEP

July 16, 1977

After three years of working for Blackguard, the once carefree and fun-loving relationship I shared with Marlene slowly went downhill. My workload evolved into ten-hour workdays plus five hours every Saturday. When I got home exhausted, I plopped into my chair and turned on the TV while she fixed dinner. Then, when we finally sat down to eat, we barely talked to each other. To make matters worse, after five years of marriage, she was still not pregnant.

Since I never took any time off for golf or sports, I lost contact with my friends. So, in my spare time, I worked on my Genesis Correlation project, which left her feeling even more detached than ever from me. Just like in college when I lived with Danny, I turned inward again and shut everybody out.

"Sean, I've been quiet long enough. I want you to tell me what's wrong."

"What do you mean?"

"You're always so distant when we're together, which by the way isn't that much anymore. I realize you can't talk about your job, but is everything over there okay?"

"Ah, yeah, I g-g-guess s-s-so. Sure, everything is fine. Don't worry about it—I'm okay. Look Marlene, I know things haven't turned out the way you expected, but I promise it will get better. This project we're working on is high-priority, but it's only a month away from being completed. I've built up a lot of vacation time, so I was thinking, why don't we go on that trip to the Caribbean for the honeymoon we never went on?"

"Sean, what a great idea, that sounds wonderful! I'll call my friend Laura. Her husband owns a travel agency and she told me the other day about some new promotions his company was offering. I'll call her tomorrow. But there's something else we need to talk about. When you're home, you're constantly distracted with this Genesis thing of yours. Not that I'm complaining, I know you need to do something to divert your mind from work. I guess it could be worse. At least I'm not a football or golf widow like what my girlfriends deal with. Maybe I've been too self-absorbed for not showing some interest in it, so tell me more."

"Sure, that would be great. I've been reluctant to bring it up with you because I thought you might think I'm crazy, or at least, it may bore the hell out of you."

"Don't worry, Sean, you know me. I'll tell you exactly what I think."

"Okay, you asked for it. I have come to the conclusion that the Genesis Creation Story may be scientifically accurate. I've put together enough evidence to begin my theory. I still have a long way to go, but the puzzle pieces are beginning to fall into place."

"Sean, I know you're not much into religion, but honestly, that sounds ridiculous."

"I knew that was what you would say, but hear me out. I'm sure you remember when they discovered the smoking gun that proved the universe had a beginning with the Big Bang."

"Of course, I remember, but what does that have to do with Genesis?"

"Well, if you recall, before that discovery, they theorized the universe was eternal, that it had always existed. They called it the steady-state theory. Ironically, the big bang theory proved the first three words in the Bible—*'In the Beginning.'* The universe is not eternal; it does have a beginning. So, naturally I was intrigued, and found more scientific correlations in other Genesis verses."

"You might as well stop right now. I believe God created everything in six days. On the seventh day, He rested. Then, He created Adam and Eve in the Garden of Eden, just like it says in the Bible. So, no matter what you say, I'm not going to change what I believe."

"Okay, Marlene, then how do you explain this? The Book of Genesis actually opens with two different creation stories, Genesis 1 and Genesis 2."

"What in the world are you talking about?"

"Well, Genesis 1 is about the creation of plants, animals, and then, verse 27 ends with the creation of man: *'And God created man in His own image, in the image of God created He him; male and female created He them.'"*

"Yes, Sean, I know that. So, what?"

"Genesis 2:7 contradicts that account. It restates the creation of plants and animals, although not in as much detail, but the creation of humans is an entirely different story.

"'*Then the LORD God formed man of the dust of the ground, and breathed into his nostrils the breath of life; and man became a living soul.'*

"Fourteen verses later, the Genesis 2 author states that God created woman: *'And the LORD God caused a deep sleep to fall upon the man, and he slept; and He took one of his ribs, and closed up the place with flesh instead thereof. And the rib, which the LORD God had taken from the man, made He a woman, and brought her unto the man.'*

"So, there you have it, you can't have it both ways. Genesis 1 states a biological fact that male and female were created together. Genesis 2 is obviously a myth, nothing more than an entertaining story. It's as if two different authors each wrote a different account of the Creation. In fact, they even refer to God differently. The Genesis 1 author refers to the Creator as *God*, while the Genesis 2 author calls Him *'Lord God.'"*

"Sean, no more! You and I are obviously worlds apart on religion. In fact, we don't have much of anything in common any more. You're still a workaholic, like when I first met you. It's like we're living two separate lives. We're like oil and water. So, let's get to the real issue here. I want to start a family, spend more time, and have fun with my husband, like we used to before you started working for

Blackguard. I want to lead a normal life like everybody else we know."

"Okay, okay. I understand, and so do I. Call Laura's husband and have him set up our trip. Please believe me, I really do want what those same things, too. So this will be a great opportunity for us to reconnect and plan our future, without any of the distractions of work."

CHAPTER 9

THE NOTICE

"If you find a path with no obstacles, it probably doesn't lead anywhere."— Frank A. Clark

THE ELEVENTH STEP

A year and half later
March 3, 1978

"Sean, I love you from the bottom of my heart, and I know you love me too. I give you a lot of credit; you've done remarkably well working at Blackguard. I really do appreciate how hard you work to make the money you make, and I certainly never expected to live in this beautiful house. But money isn't everything. I've given this a lot of thought. We've been married for over six years now. I hardly ever see you and we never talk about us. It's always the same thing. You bring your work home with you and sit behind your computer or turn on the

TV. And when you're not doing that, you're working on that ridiculous Genesis thing of yours. Sean, I need to bring this charade of a marriage to an end before I lose my mind. I hate to be so blunt, but I want a divorce!"

"Y-Y-You want a d-d-divorce? I don't understand. What about our wedding vows—until death us do part?"

"Come on, Sean, you know darn well what's wrong. I'm not happy, and I don't think you're happy being married to me. When you're home, we don't talk, at least not about things that actually matter and concern us. You won't talk to me about Blackguard. You're certainly not here for me emotionally. I haven't felt connected to you for a very long time now. And there's another thing: it breaks my heart that we still don't have children. I've been to three fertility clinics, and they all say the same thing: There is nothing wrong with me. They tell me it's stress. Our friends think we're weird. And by the way, you're so out of touch. I know you haven't talked to Danny for over a year. I bet you don't even know he and Cindy got divorced over six months ago. My parents, especially my mother, know how unhappy I am. You really have no idea how miserable it has been for me. I can't live like this anymore, or I'll get sick. Sean, I'm pulling the plug."

After six years of marriage, Marlene presented me with the notice of divorce. I really couldn't blame her. Looking back at it, I'm surprised she hung in for as long as she did. It was only because she was raised Catholic and no one in her family had ever resorted to divorce before. We did love each other, but we were far too young when we married, and the stress I brought to the marriage was too much for her. She ended up with the Orchard Lake house, and I rented an apartment in nearby Bloomfield Hills. If she needed this break from me, I wanted to give it to her. Occasionally, we would meet for dinner and catch up on what was going on in our lives. It seemed as if we had a better relationship separated than when we were married. As the years passed, life matured both of us and I was confident that, given enough time, we would get back together again.

Eddie was on my mind a lot, too. I should have felt grateful for not ending up like he did, but instead, I felt guilty. I guess I knew right from the beginning when I first met him that I would not be his battle buddy in actual combat. I should have probably buddied up with another reservist, but I didn't. Eddie simply reminded me of another loss in my life.

Shortly after our divorce was final, I suffered another loss. I came into work one morning and Travis informed me that Blackguard was sending him on a highly confidential assignment. He was ordered not to mention anything to anybody. When I came in to work the next day, he was gone. A memo on my desk from Mr. Marsh notified me that I would be filling in for him as temporary team leader. After that, I never saw Travis McShane again.

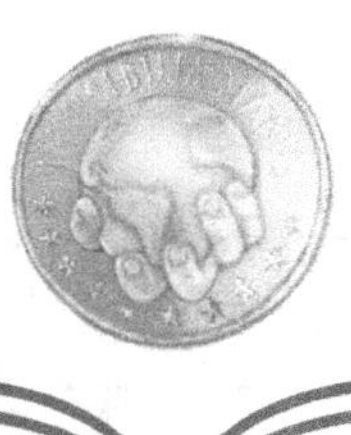

CHAPTER 10

THE PROMOTION

THE TWELFTH STEP

February 7, 1979

About a year after my divorce, Julian Marsh called me into his office. He rarely spoke to me alone. In fact, I hadn't been invited back since my employment interview, and so, I had no idea what he wanted. My nerves were frayed. I was terrified I had done something wrong and was about to be fired, leaving me with yet another loss and absolutely nothing in my life.

"Good morning, Mr. Marsh. You wanted to see me?"

"Yes, Sean, sit down. We have a lot to discuss, so you'll be here for a while."

"Oh my G-G-God, it s-s-sounds serious. Am I in some kind of trouble? Look, I've given you everything I have, even at the expense of my marriage. I don't understand what's wrong."

"Sean, Sean, please relax. You've done nothing wrong. You are not in trouble. In fact, it's quite the opposite. Blackguard values you more than I can say, I'm almost jealous. But it would help if you calmed down. Perhaps some lunch is what you need, I'll send for Rachel to get us something."

"Yes, sir, I'm sorry."

"You've been with Blackguard for almost five years now, and you have certainly proved your loyalty. You're a brilliant technician, and we trust you to keep our confidentiality agreement. You must hold what I'm about to tell you in the strictest of confidence, and it's only between the two of us."

Even though I felt somewhat relieved, I still felt a sense of dread. Was Marsh about to set me up for something I would later regret? I remembered Marlene's words: *'Money isn't everything.'* Instead of feeling elated, I was guarded and weighed carefully what he was about to tell me. He escorted me to the conference table. Rachel brought our lunch and I settled in, nervously anticipating what my boss was about to say.

"Sean, you've been our team leader ever since Travis left."

"Yes, sir, that's been a while. Is he okay?"

"I'm sure he's fine. I know the two of you are close friends, so I want to relieve your mind. My boss informed me he contracted a serious ailment that requires professional medical treatment. Because they want only the best for him, they sent him to one of their specialists in Toronto. I contacted his family and told them what I'm telling you, but they are not satisfied with my explanation.

They're very upset and informed me that if they don't hear from him soon, they'll conduct their own investigation. So, Sean listen to me. If they contact you, you now know as much as I do. My last contact with him was last August 10th—the morning Blackguard flew him to some island in New York to install the new security system we designed for them here at Area C. That's all I know."

"Now I'm sorry I didn't ask you sooner about him. I feel that he may have needed me. Mr. Marsh, I hate all this secrecy. It has affected my relationships and was a big reason for my divorce."

"Look, Sean, I understand how you feel. I feel the same way, but we need to move on with our discussion. As of this moment, I'm relieving you of your duties here as interim team leader. The Carcassonne office has instructed me to move you up the ladder to serve as their technical liaison. You will travel to some pretty glamorous locations all over the world—Europe, Iran, Turkey, India, Russia, and China."

"Why me? You must have plenty of other qualified people here in Area C."

"Yes, we do, but they specifically asked for you. Trust me, Sean. We will miss you around here."

"And what do you mean the Carcassonne office? I thought you ran Area C."

"I do run Area C, but I also have bosses. You may be interested to know that I have never met or seen or been in personal contact with any of them. My orders are passed down to me from their personal assistants."

"Mr. Marsh, be straight with me. What will they expect from me?"

"My job over the next couple of weeks is to prepare you. So, we need to get started now. I've been with Blackguard for about twenty-five years now, and I can tell you some things about this organization. It's made up of ten wealthy humanitarian families. They are concerned about the state of the world and, in particular, the Cold War between Russia and the United States. Several of these families live in Europe, and they remember only too well the destruction Hitler brought to their countries. They shudder to think what would happen if someone like him got their finger on the nuclear button.

"They also see the moral decline taking place here in America. The drugs, sexual promiscuity, lowered education standards, and social divisions are all very disturbing, especially on our campuses. They believe if this collapse continues, America's strength will decline until we will no longer be able to contain the communist threat. Even more important, they want to help eliminate hunger and disease all over the world. For the sake of people everywhere, their scientists are busy creating vaccines to help build immunity against the worst of these viruses."

"That's amazing, I really didn't understand how important our work is. Now I see the reason for all the secrecy. Count me in; I'll do whatever I can do to serve Blackguard."

"Sean, my boy, now that's what I wanted to hear. I will train you to install their intranet equipment, as well as other projects we have on the drawing board. You don't know this yet, but Area C is working on some amazing new technologies, things right out of science fiction. You will also travel by private jet to their other three divisions: Area A in Austria, Area B in Cyprus, and Area D in Belgium. Each of these locations was chosen to avoid attention, much the way Area C is hidden here in this old Packard plant."

"Mr. Marsh, I've never traveled like this before. I'm speechless. I have no idea what to wear or how I'll get around. Now I know how James Bond must have felt when he was first assigned to Her Majesty's Secret Service."

"Sean, do not delude yourself. You are not a spy, you will not chase bad guys, you will not drive an Aston Martin, and you definitely will not carry a weapon of any kind. Make no mistake about it. You are a team member and are in service to Blackguard. Let me remind you once again—you must hold everything you do, hear, see, or experience in the strictest of confidence."

"When will I start this *dream assignment*? Will I be able to come back to Michigan? What should I tell my friends and family? They're going to have a lot of questions."

"Over the next three weeks, I will personally prepare you. Don't worry, you'll be fully equipped to take on all your new responsibilities. After you complete the installations, you'll return to Detroit and we'll update you on all the new technologies we're working on."

My training went smoothly and I felt fully prepared for what lay ahead. On the day I left for New York, Marsh gave me a medallion that the security team had developed years before. I had never seen anything like it. It was about six and a half centimeters in diameter and one centimeter thick attached to a metallic chain. It was made of a strange alloy that changed in color from bronze to silver to gold depending on the lighting conditions. The face was embossed with a stylized hand holding a globe of the world. Under the hand are ten stars, and engraved above the hand are the words *Invisibilia Manus*. The reverse side has a round, hermetically sealed glass lens that displays an electronic cipher. Marsh instructed me to wear it always while I was working. He told me that doors, elevators, and gates would only open with it. To gain access to their facilities, I must present it to the security guards for scans.

The next morning, I boarded a private jet to a small airport near New York City. A limo awaited my arrival, driven by a smartly dressed and talkative chauffeur, ready and waiting to escort me to some of the city's most exclusive men's shops and tailors. Several weeks later, I left the U.S. fully prepared to begin my new career abroad as a technical liaison for Blackguard. But nothing relieved the nagging paranoia. What was I getting myself into? My first stop was in Austria, in a deserted castle they called the Area A Banking Division. Then, I was scheduled to go to the Area B Media Division in Cyprus and, from there, to the Area D Information Division in Belgium. Each of these places was hidden away, just like Area C.

The next couple of years were the most exciting time of my life. It was exactly what Marsh described: interesting job assignments, exotic locations, glamorous nightlife, and plenty of female companionship. It was like a dream come true. But as with all dreams, it came to an abrupt end.

It was May 1981 when I received my next assignment to go to Carcassonne, France. It was the first of the ten family offices on my itinerary. Thankfully, I wasn't scheduled to go there until the end of the following June, so I decided to spend some time in Marseilles. The glamour of my job was great for a while, but now I needed some relaxation time and pure luxury. I booked in at a recently completed five-star luxury beachfront hotel, where I decided to work on my Genesis project. That's when I met Camille, and my somewhat predictable world completely changed forever!

CHAPTER 11

SUDDEN PANIC

July 20, 1981
Marseilles, France

Camille was constantly on my mind while I was away on assignment in Carcassonne. During my stay I was forbidden to have contact with anyone. At night they had me sequestered in a makeshift bedroom with no windows, keeping me from any outside communications. The work was stressful, as their security team constantly kept their eyes on me, and cameras everywhere. Since I was not allowed to talk to anyone, other than the technicians who were assisting me, time seemed to crawl. Finally, three lonely weeks later, after I completed my work, I flew back to Marseilles. My heart was pounding with anticipation. The first thing I did was to go to a market near the hotel, bought a dozen roses, picked up some wine and gourmet delicacies, ready to lavish her with my affection.

As I stepped into her apartment, a chilling silence enveloped me, thickening the air and constricting my chest. The faint scent of her perfume lingered, teasing memories of her laughter and warmth. But now, there was only emptiness, an eerie void where her presence should have been. I set down the roses and wine on the nearest surface with trembling hands, the vibrant colors of affection stark against the backdrop of desolation. My mind raced with questions, each one more terrifying than the last. Where was she? Why had she vanished without a trace? Panic clawed at my throat, threatening to suffocate me.

I searched every corner of her apartment, desperately hoping to find some clue, some sign that would ease the growing dread gnawing at my soul. But there was nothing—no note, no hint of her intentions, just the unsettling stillness of abandonment. I rushed to the front desk frantically, my heart pounding a frantic rhythm in my ears. The security guard's eyes held a mixture of pity and concern as he confirmed my worst fears—Camille had been missing for weeks.

Fear gripped me like icy tendrils, squeezing the breath from my lungs. What had happened to her? Was she in danger? Had she left willingly, or was she taken against her will? The possibilities loomed before me like specters in the darkness, each one more terrifying than the last.

I stumbled out of the building, the world spinning around me in a dizzying blur. Every shadow seemed to hold a lurking threat, every sound a whisper of danger. My mind raced with images of Camille, alone and afraid, lost in a world she didn't understand. I vowed then and there to find her, to unravel the mystery of her disappearance no matter the cost. As I ventured out into the cold, unforgiving night, I couldn't shake the feeling that something sinister lurked just beyond my sight, waiting to consume me whole. And in that moment, I knew that the nightmare was far from over.

Even though we were only together for a few weeks, I felt this enormous sense of loss and a life without a future. I returned to my hotel room, packed my suitcase, and opened the hotel safe to get my belongings. As the door swung open, my heart plummeted into the depths of despair. My journals were gone! How had she gotten into the safe? What sinister motive drove her to steal my most precious possessions? A cold sweat broke out on my brow as I envisioned the consequences of their contents falling into the wrong hands. Every detail of Area C, the Blackguard's clandestine operations, my interactions with their personnel—everything was laid bare in those pages, a roadmap to my downfall. Fear clawed at my mind, twisting my thoughts into a tangled web of paranoia and desperation. The threat of their henchmen loomed over me like a shadowy specter, ready to pounce at the slightest misstep. I cursed under my breath, my hands trembling with impotent rage. How could I have been so careless, so blind to the danger lurking just beneath the surface? With a sinking feeling, I realized that I was utterly and completely exposed, vulnerable to the whims of forces beyond my control.

I considered my options. I could disappear, but that would make me a fugitive, always looking over my shoulder. I could confess to my boss, Julian Marsh, what I did, but that would no doubt put me in a concrete coffin at the bottom of the Detroit River. Or, I could pretend nothing happened, and pray she packed them away somewhere and forgot about them. In other words, I had no options.

Being deeply in love with someone you can't live without is devastating when they're gone. You don't think straight, you can't eat, you don't even want to talk to anybody. Camille came into my life as quickly as she left. I didn't understand. Did she find someone else? Did I offend her in some way? Did she lie to me about her feelings? Was I not the one she really wanted? Or worse yet, was she not who I thought she was? I needed to somehow find her, but how? Private detectives were out of the question. I didn't even have a picture of her. I had no idea where to begin looking, except maybe at the coffeehouse.

I first met Camille at a coffeehouse in Marseilles on a beautiful June morning. She dropped her purse on the floor next to my table. I stooped down to pick it up and handed it back to her. When I looked up, looking down at me was the most strikingly beautiful woman I had ever seen. I couldn't help but introduce myself. Thanking me for my chivalry, she asked me to join her. Our conversations were effortless; it was like we could read each other's minds. And with her charming French accent, I was immediately smitten.

After weeks of licking my wounds, it was once again time to go back to work and complete the installations at the other Blackguard locations. On top of it, Area C bombarded me with a barrage of new technologies that I needed to brush up on. Even though I found this routine monotonous, I put up with it because I had already made up my mind: I would retire when I turned forty-five, assuming I lasted that long.

The first time I ever experienced loneliness was when I was away from Marlene during basic training. Those same feelings had returned. I needed to do something to distract myself, so I delved back into my Genesis project. Its thirty-one verses always fascinated me. To me, they were more like a scientific summary of the origin of the Earth, plants, animals, and humans, than the six-day Divine Creation Story that I was taught in religious school. I soon came to realize that the original Hebrew Creation Story had been lost by the many translations and religious interpretations that followed. But, if my theory had any chance at all of seeing the light of day in academia, I needed to somehow prove its scientific accuracy. The last phrase of the Creation Story especially intrigued me. After God created everything, the verse reads, *'And God saw every thing that He had made, and, behold, it was very good.'*

Originally, the earth and its ecosystems were pristine and untouched by human activity. Being the nature lover that I am, I was struck by the contrast of how contaminated our environment was today compared to when the author wrote those words. Humans have polluted and destroyed many of the natural habitats to the point where countless species of both plants and animals were going extinct at an alarming rate. Anyway, in my spare time, armed with countless binders full of notes and reference books, I continued my quest. With the voluminous amount of information I collected, dealing with it all was far too complicated. So, I decided to put together a coherent timeline and a synopsis that I thought would make my work intelligible to others. Then, I needed to have my findings confirmed by the experts if they were to have any relevance at all. However, I wasn't even close to that point, and I worried I would never be able to finish it.

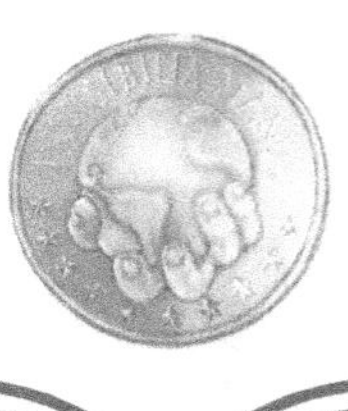

CHAPTER 12

THE CODEX SINAITICUS

November 13, 1982

Even a year and a half after Camille left me, thoughts of her still haunted me. In an attempt to try and forget about her, and while I was in Detroit, I thought it would be a good idea to kill two birds with one stone. I wanted to touch base with Bob Townsend, a college professor of mine in Ann Arbor. Even though he was highly skeptical, he had always shown an interest in my Genesis theory. I made quite a bit of progress since my college years and I wanted to see if I could make him a believer. I knew he would be a harsh critic, but if I could get his approval, my enthusiasm to continue with the project would be reignited.

It had also been quite a while since our divorce, so I decided it was time to reconnect with Marlene and sort out my feelings for her. I looked her up and found out she was still living in our Orchard Lake home. So, I went.

With open arms and a heartfelt hug, I greeted her, "Wow, Marlene, it's great to see you. It's been a while. Thanks for seeing me, especially without giving you much notice. How are you doing?"

"Sean, I have to say, it's really good to see you, too. I'm doing great—never been happier. A lot has happened since we last talked, and I'm sure you have a lot to tell me too. I really wish we could spend more time together today, but I have to pick up the kids from daycare in about twenty minutes."

"Kids? Wow, I had no idea. Who's the lucky man?"

"Sean, please don't get upset with me. I am so sorry things didn't work out for us, but I'm happy now, and he's a wonderful man."

"No, no, I'm not upset. I am happy for you, other than being disappointed that I don't have another chance with you. So, who's your prince charming?"

Hesitatingly, she replied, "It's Danny."

"D-D-DANNY? Danny Kirchner—my friend D-D-Danny?

"Sean, you promised me you wouldn't get upset. We're perfectly suited for each other, and we love each other very deeply. He's a good, fun-loving man, and he's great with the kids."

"Upset? Believe me, I'm way beyond upset. Oh my God! You mean to tell me you married my best friend? And now you and him live together in our house? I can't fucking believe it."

After she shocked me with that announcement, my depression and loneliness only deepened. What the hell was I thinking? Did I actually think that she would wait for me until I got my shit together?

THE FOURTEENTH STEP

November 15, 1982
Professor Robert Townsend
LSA Physics
University of Michigan
Ann Arbor, Michigan

After the shock of Marlene and Danny, I drove to Ann Arbor to see Bob Townsend, hoping he would be a distraction, even if it were for just a short time.

"Professor Townsend, it's great to see you again. I really appreciate you taking time out of your schedule to see me."

"Sean Phillips, the Curiosity Kid! It's great to see you, too. What in the world have you been up to?"

"Believe me, Professor, when I say there's not enough hours in the day to answer that question."

"How 'bout you call me Bob? We don't need to be so damned formal anymore."

"Wow, that feels kind of weird, but yeah, that would be great."

"You mentioned on the phone you wanted to talk to me about your Genesis theory, and since you're still at it after all these years, I'd like to give it a go. But you do realize, like always, I'll be a tough critic."

"Yeah, I understand, but that's exactly what I need right now."

"Before we start, I have to ask you, why are you still so obsessed with Genesis?"

"Well, for one thing, don't you think it would be quite amazing if I can prove that the creation story is actually scientifically accurate, even though it was written over 2,500 years ago? The other reason is the last phrase:

"'And God saw every thing that He had made, and, behold, it was very good.'

"When those words were written, the earth was pristine and the ecosystems were unspoiled by the pollution nightmare we'd created by our overconsumption. Compare that phrase to what humans have done to the planet today. We're polluting ourselves into extinction. It's a long shot, but if I can prove that the thirty-one verses of Genesis 1 are scientifically accurate in a world obsessed with materialism, maybe people will wake up and realize this pollution disaster we've created in the process and do something about it before it's too late."

"Wow, Sean, I must say, you have some pretty lofty goals. Ha, you want to save the world."

"Yeah, I guess so. Anyway, I've come a long way since we last talked. No pun intended, but I'd like to begin in the beginning. So, if the Big Bang was the beginning of everything, then interestingly, it correlates with the first three words of Genesis 1—*In the beginning.*"

"Yes, Sean, I already know what you're going to say. Before the Big Bang discovery, we believed the universe was eternal—it always existed. You held it over my head for many years. So, in this instance I'll give it to you, Genesis is correct and science was wrong."

"Thank you. Anyway, I'm only prepared to discuss the first creation day. I haven't even gotten to the Second Day yet, and I'm not going to waste any more of my time if you win this debate today. Let me show you what the author wrote in the first verse.

"*'In the beginning God created the heaven and the earth.'*

"Interestingly, he included—"

"Wait a minute, Sean, stop right there. You're a science major, you can't possibly believe there's a God who *created* everything in six days."

"Of course, I don't. At least not in six *twenty-four-hour* days."

"Well, what other kinds are there? That's the only kind I know of."

"You may not know this, but the Hebrew language only consisted of 7,800 words to express their thoughts, many of which have multiple meanings. So, no, I don't believe the verses refer to six literal days. Actually, '*day*' in Hebrew has eight definitions. Hebrew scribes used each one depending on the context of their writing. I've been studying this stuff for so long, I've memorized them:

"'Period of light, as contrasted with the period of darkness'

"'A general term for time'

"'Point of time'

"'Sunrise to sunset'

"'Sunset to next sunset'

"'A year in the plural'

"'A time period of unspecified length'

"'A long, but finite span of time such as age, epoch, season'

"In this case, I believe the Hebrew author used the last definition."

"Okay, Sean, but the verse implies God created both heaven and Earth at the same time, and of course we both know that's not true. The Earth accreted nine billion years after the Big Bang."

"But the author did not say they were created at the same time. For example, the verse does not read, *'At the beginning God created heaven and earth,'* which would imply an exact point in time. Instead, it specifically reads, *'in the beginning,'* meaning a general period of time. And another thing, *'the'* precedes both *'heaven'* and *'Earth,'* with *'the heaven'* first, and *'the Earth'* second. Keep in mind the Hebrews had no concept of billions of years. And to be clear, *'the heaven'* in Hebrew means visible heavens, the sky, or realm of the stars."

"Go on, you make a compelling argument. So far, I'm impressed."

"Well, guess what? The next verse also correlates with the science: *'Now the Earth* was *unformed and void.'*"

"Again, Bob, I'm not telling you anything you don't already know. The Earth was indeed an unformed molten inferno, void of any of the features that we are all familiar with: no oceans, lakes, rivers, mountains, forests, or plains.

"Then the next verse goes on to read*: 'And darkness was upon the face of the deep.'*

"As the Earth's crust cooled and then hardened, the gasses condensed and rained down as water. Those torrents of rain lasted for hundreds of years. We also now know that massive, icy asteroid and comet bombardments brought more water and covered its surface, '*the face,*' with a sea, '*the deep.*' What amazes me is the author somehow knew the Earth was initially covered with water. There was no land. He also knew that this early atmosphere consisted of a dark cloud layer that covered '*the deep in darkness.*' How he knew these things, I have no idea."

"I agree that is remarkable, especially in light of the fact that we didn't know until this century that Earth was initially a water-world, without any of the continental land masses."

"I'll tell you what, Bob, this next verse really threw me, though, and took me years to understand.

"'*And the spirit of God hovered over the face of the waters.*'

"Hard as I tried, I couldn't figure it out. That is until I found out many scientists believe the same comets that brought water to our Earth now theorize they also brought the building blocks of life that evolved into microscopic organisms."

"Okay, okay, slow down. You're losing me here. Until now your theory has made sense, but I don't see how the '*spirit of God*' has anything to do with science. Unless you make the case that it does, we're done here today. What do you say we go to my favorite new watering hole, and you can tell me all about what you've been up to since you graduated? I'm particularly interested in the careers my students have landed."

"That sounds great, but first you need to know that phrase has everything to do with science. You see, it turns out '*the spirit of God*' in Hebrew, translates into the breath or the wind. These are ancient terms for the 'life energy' that animates every living thing. The other verses describe the physical world: earth, water, light, dry land, plants, and animals. However, like you said, this phrase is different because it seems to describe a supernatural event, but such is not the case. In fact, there are other verses in the Bible that make my point.

"For example, Job wrote: *'The Spirit of God hath made me, and the breath of the Almighty hath given me life.'*

"The Genesis 2 author wrote, *'And the Lord God formed man of the dust of the ground, and breathed into his nostrils the breath of life; and man became a living soul.'*

"And then, there are the Old English translations of the Bible where *'spirit* was replaced by wind, and written as a reference for the life force. The Greeks, a contemporary culture of the Hebrews, described *'spirit'* as pneuma, a pressure like the wind. They did not think of *'spirit'* in the traditional sense, but rather as an invisible, animating life energy. These early translations described the *'spirit of God'* as the animating life energy that *'moved over the face of waters.'*

"The Judeo-Christian religions refer to *spirit* as the soul, the life essence, or the energy that sets in motion an individual life and then continues after death. Other cultures have various names for the life energy. The Chinese refer to it as Chi or Qi. The Japanese call it Ki. Hindus call it Prana, and the ancient Egyptians refer to it as Ka. So, *'spirit of God'* is the energy that animates all living things, enables plants and animals to reproduce, to grow and to heal themselves from the physical stresses they must endure."

"I must say you've certainly done your homework. When you said asteroid and meteor impacts brought the building blocks of life, I assume you were correlating that event with *'And the spirit of God hovered over the face of the waters.'*"

"Exactly, and there's another thing. All life requires liquid water to survive. This verse makes this biological correlation clear by combining the *face of the waters* with *the spirit of God* in the same verse. Earth is the only known planet where liquid water occurs on the surface. As you know, everywhere else it's either ice or water vapor."

"I've got to say, Sean, you're making it very difficult for me to argue with you."

"Thank you, but I'm not finished. As you know, scientists have no idea what the life force is; they describe what it does. Living things evolve, move, reproduce, take in nourishment, then excrete waste, and they heal themselves. But what is the energy that allows non-living, organic compounds to come alive and do these things? It's the same for human consciousness that allows us to even discuss these matters. We can describe consciousness with words like wisdom, knowledge, creativity, genius, and so forth, but what is it? We don't really know."

"Hmm, I guess I never really thought about it that way. Sean, it sounds to me like you believe in God."

"God? I don't know about that. But I do believe there's the other side of the coin that science has not considered, perhaps a spiritual dimension we can't see or quantify. Anyway, I'm almost done making my point. The next verse reads:

"*'And God said: 'Let there be light.' And there was light. And God saw the light, that it was good; and God divided the light from the darkness. And God called the light Day, and the darkness He called Night.'*

"From the scientific point of view, when the atmosphere began to clear, some light made it through the perpetual dense cloud cover, and it probably looked much like a dark, overcast sky we would see today—'*and there was light.*"

"You know what, Sean? As I'm listening to these events and the way you describe them, they seem to coincide with the first geologic period of time—the Hadean Eon."

"Yeah, I know, and thanks for following me on this. But lastly, there's an important point I haven't figured out yet. Each of the six days ends with, '*And there was evening and there was morning: one day, a second day, a third day,*' and so forth.

"The problem with this phrase is that it doesn't match any of the eight Hebrew definitions for day. A day does not begin the evening and end in the morning. So, there you have it, Bob. Here's a summary page from my synopsis for of the First Day. Now, I'm ready for that drink."

Synopsis
Genesis Correlation of the First Day

Genesis 1:1
The Big Bang
13.80 billion years ago
***In the beginning
God created***

Genesis 1:1
Galaxies
13.60 billion years ago
the heaven

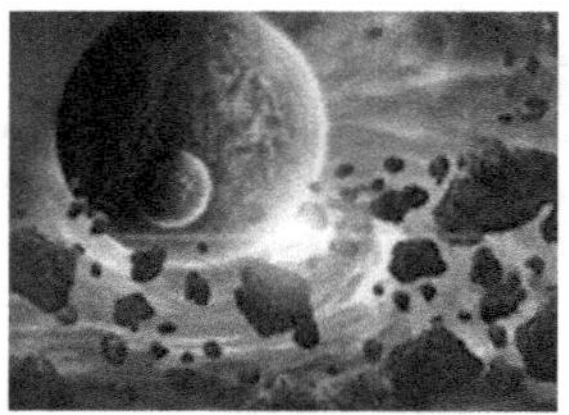

Genesis 1:1
Earth's Formation
4.54 billion years ago
and the earth

Genesis 1:2
Earth covered with
molten lava
4.54 billion years ago
***Now the earth was
unformed and void,***

Genesis 1:2
Dense atmosphere over
the sea of water
4.40 billion years ago
*and darkness was upon
the face of the deep*

Genesis 1:2
Building blocks of life
brought by asteroids and
comets
4.00 billion years ago
*and the spirit of God
hovered over the face of
the waters*

Genesis 1:3
Atmospheric Clearing
3.80 billion years ago
*And God said: 'Let there
be light.' And there
was light.'*

Genesis 1: 4
One Day
The Hadean Eon
*And God saw the light,
that it was good; and
God divided the light
from the darkness.*

Genesis 1:5
*And God called the light Day, and the darkness
He called Night. And there was evening
and there was morning, <u>one day</u>.*

"I have to say that's great work, Sean, but you've only correlated the first day, and you have five more days to go. I've read the Creation Story several times, and quite frankly, I don't know how you'll do it. You're a smart guy and all, but I think it will take more than just your brain to correlate all six days."

"Yeah, I know you're right, Bob, but thanks anyway for your input. I really do appreciate it. Anyway, I miss Ann Arbor and would like to take a look around."

"Sean, wait a minute. Before we go, I just thought of something. I have some interesting photos I'd like to show you. There's a rare bookstore here in Ann Arbor, near the campus, where I go when I have the time. I can't afford any of the books, but the owner lets me browse. One afternoon, I was looking at a collection of rare Bibles he had on display, which got me to thinking about you and your Genesis theory. I mentioned it to him, he sounded interested, and remembered something that he had locked away years ago."

"That does sound interesting, but what does it have to do with my correlation?"

"Have you ever heard of the Codex Sinaiticus?"

"No, I have not."

"Well, I hadn't either, until he described it to me. It's a 400-page, parchment leaf manuscript that comprises most of the original written text of the Old Testament. Because of its age, the pages are extremely delicate. Even so, they were carbon-dated to the second half of the fourth century. Scholars consider it the original Hebrew to Greek translation of the Old Testament, and it's been locked away in the Vatican library since the 1400s. It's not known exactly when they acquired it, but it's included in their 1475 catalog listing."

"You're not going to tell me the bookstore owner has an original page from it?"

"No, no, but he does have something just as interesting and which may apply to your correlation."

"Okay, I'm listening."

"It's an ancient Latin manuscript that's been dated to the 1600s. Many of the pages have deteriorated, but some of the writing can still be made out. He knew a little Latin, but not enough to accurately translate it on his own. So, he took it to St. Francis Church near here, and a priest offered to translate it for him. Now, here's the interesting part. There's enough script left to see that it references Genesis."

"Bob, let me get this straight. You've seen a Latin manuscript written in the 1600s that mentions Genesis. I have got to see this."

"Calm down for a minute, I'm trying to make a point. If you remember from your history lessons, the Greeks believed in the geocentric model of the universe."

"Yes, but what does that have to do with my correlation?"

"I'll get to that. I'm sure you remember that at the heart of the geocentric model is the sphere. They considered it to be the ideal shape that reflected God's perfection. They believed the universe was a sphere, and the earth was at the center of it. To them, all the heavenly bodies were implanted on other transparent, rotating spheres that revolved around the earth. They imagined them to be like jewels placed on transparent glass globes.

"They thought these spheres were composed of an ethereal, transparent material, with the stars embedded on the outermost sphere, while the sun, moon, and planets were embedded on the inner spheres. This is the same belief the Catholic Church adhered to. They believed the Earth and humans, along with God, were at the center of everything. Now, here's where it gets interesting."

"Oh yeah, I remember now. The 1600s were at the time of the Inquisition."

"That's right. Copernicus, Galileo and other scientific thinkers proved the geocentric model was wrong. Copernicus proved it with his meticulous calculations, and when Galileo pointed his telescope at Jupiter, he saw moons orbiting it. He realized the Earth was not at the center of everything and figured out the sun was at the center of our Solar System, and the planets orbited around it."

"Yes, I know all that, but what about the Latin manuscript?"

"Well, it refers to an addendum that was added to the original Codex Sinaiticus in the 1600s, which refers to Genesis 1 and links it to the Copernicus and Galileo observations. Like you said, it was written at the time of the Inquisition, and the scientific discoveries made by these men were considered heresy. If they were made public, it would have completely overturned the geocentric model and the teachings of the Catholic Church. So, the Vatican has kept the Codex Sinaiticus and the addendum locked away ever since."

"Good Lord, Bob, can we go to the bookstore? I need to see this."

"I don't think he has it anymore. He told me he was going to sell it, but I did take pictures. Let me get to the point. From what I remember, the manuscript claimed the Codex Addendum revealed that the creation story is, in fact, much older than Genesis. Here, I'll give you the pics, I don't need them. But, unless you know Latin, you won't understand any of it."

"Bob, this last sentence seems to stand alone from the others: *'Caelum et terram naturaliter sunt facta.'* Do you know what it means?"

"I probably did at one time, but like I said, it's been a while and I honestly don't remember any more."

That meeting with Bob Townsend gave me back the enthusiasm I needed to continue with my theory. I left Ann Arbor with renewed energy, but unfortunately that feeling did not last long. My job had become increasingly more demanding, and because Marsh never took the time to train an assistant, he became more and more dependent on me. As the years passed, the combination of jet lag, working with technicians and engineers who could barely speak English, plus the pressure he passed on to me, all took a toll. I felt if I didn't find a distraction, I would crack. But it was the combination of Bob Townsend's encouragement to continue with my correlation theory, the pressure to get some relief from Blackguard, and forget about Camille that gave me the desire to find a getaway retreat.

CHAPTER 13

THE ISLAND LIFE

"Much as we may wish to make a new beginning, some part of us resists doing so as though we were making the first step toward disaster."— William Throsby Bridges

THE FIFTEENTH STEP

August 18, 1988
The Caribbean
St. Martin Island

I needed a place of my own where I could relax, so I decided to buy a vacation home. The only trip that Marlene and I ever went on together was to the Caribbean. At the time, her friend Laura's husband set us up at a beautiful resort on the island of St. Lucia, a tropical paradise that time forgot. Charming villages, banana plantations, the Pitons, volcanic calderas, tropical jungles, and waterfalls made it the perfect Caribbean experience. I never forgot it.

Over the years, I traveled to other beautiful and exciting places, but the islands of the Caribbean always held a special place in my heart. They captured a place in my imagination with exotic names like: Martinique, St. Croix, St. Martin, Curacao, Trinidad and Tobago, Montserrat, Turks and Caicos, to name a few. During the off times while on assignment, my head was filled with images of a romantic past. Pirate ships, treasure chests of gold, bottles of rum, and swashbuckling buccaneers stirred my imagination. I wanted to soak up as much of that feeling as I could.

After visiting many of these colorful, picturesque islands, I settled in St. Martin—a beautiful half French, half Dutch tropical isle located in the Lesser Antilles about 190 miles northeast of Puerto Rico. I took the time to explore all the nooks and crannies of this beautiful island paradise and talk to many of the islanders whom I found to be friendly and very charming. They suggested the best places for me to explore. I wanted to find the perfect location for my sanctuary, one surrounded by palm trees on a pristine beach, near any one of the charming villages.

That's when I met Lila Knowles, an easy-going, twenty-five-year-old real estate agent. Born and bred in St. Martin, she knew the island inside and out, and seemed to have an instinct for her customer's needs. She led me to the perfect property, located on a secluded beach near the town of Anse Marcel, away from the crowds of tourists who routinely arrived by cruise ship on the Dutch side of the island. The perfect weather, beautiful beaches, swaying palm trees, and the friendly locals made it the ideal location. But most of all, I would be isolated at a place where I could forget the stresses of my job.

After the closing, I wanted to show my appreciation, so I invited her to have dinner with me at one of her favorite island bistros. Because I really didn't know anyone, she was the perfect companion to educate me about the ins and outs of island life. Lila was an unpretentious island beauty, with long black hair and a healthy complexion that needed no makeup. With her charming island accent, she possessed an inner warmth that gave people the feeling she really cared about them. Her outgoing personality was the perfect antidote for my quiet shyness. She introduced me to her friends and took me to the places where everyone knew her. I especially enjoyed her favorite beach bars where they created some of the best drinks I ever had. My favorites were the local concoctions made from the legendary Sint Maarten Guavaberry liqueur. I was also addicted to the toasted coconut rum that reminded me of what the Caribbean days of yore must have been like. We relaxed on St. Martin's beaches and snorkeled in the pristine, hidden turquoise lagoons. Even though I had an extreme water phobia, she taught me how to scuba dive in some of the deeper coral reefs that surrounded the island. I felt very safe with her. Then, there was the dancing. Ah yes, the dancing. Lila was a fantastic dancer with her sensuous, uninhibited moves. To my surprise, I did pretty damn good as we danced to the rhythms of the island music. The times we shared together were a 180-degree contrast from my job. It was precisely what the doctor ordered, and I could see myself retired in St. Martin for the rest of my life.

It wasn't long before I met her family. She introduced me to her older brother Dominic, whom I soon became close friends with. Dominic was physically trim and, with his military-style haircut, looked like a tough Marine drill sergeant—not somebody you wanted to mess with. But underneath his bulldog exterior was a warm laidback islander with an intimidating sense of humor. He loved to laugh when he would catch me off guard. I never knew if he was serious or not, and when he got me, he would say, "Ha, ha mon, gotcha again." He ran a small fishing boat charter that provided him with enough money to give him a carefree lifestyle without a wife and children to tie him down. Dominic used to tell me he envied my freedom to travel around the world and wanted to experience things he could only dream of. He told me Lila was serious about me, and could not understand why I would want to tie myself down with her. Being the overprotective older brother, he cautioned me that Lila was not like him and someday she would want a family of her own.

Each time I returned to St. Martin, the first thing I did was to meet up with her. Always anxiously awaiting my arrival, it was evident that her feelings for me had become more serious. Lila was someone I could have shared the rest of my life with, except I was afraid the same issues that caused my split with Marlene would do us in. And sadly, even after seven years, the memory of Camille was still with me. During the day, I yearned for her, and at night, she haunted my dreams. There was little I could offer Lila, and so I put my feelings for her on hold. We continued to see each other, but I intentionally kept our relationship casual and fun-loving, and nothing more.

In her heart, however, she believed her love would prevail, and we would ultimately tie the knot. I did everything I could to convince her I was not the marrying type, but she refused to believe me. So, our relationship continued, and we were together whenever possible. Even though I was gone much of the time, she never pestered me about my job, questioned me about what I did, or nagged me in any way. She was always as sweet as she could be. There was one thing, however, that really worried her. In her soft, sweet way, she was reluctant to tell me what had been bothering her for some time.

"Sean, when you are gone for so long, I miss you and wait patiently for you to come back. But when you're here, it's difficult to keep your attention. Your mind always seems to be elsewhere. Please tell me what's wrong?"

"Oh my God, Lila, I am so sorry. I know I can be a little obsessive, but I assure you it has nothing to do with us. Before I met you, I needed some distraction from my job, so, I began working on a project I started in college. I call it the Genesis Correlation."

In an attempt to understand, she asked, "That sounds interesting. What is it?"

"Well, I have this theory that the Creation Story in the Bible is scientifically accurate. So far, my research proves that the first book of Genesis perfectly correlates with our current knowledge of geology and evolution."

"But, Sean, that's not possible. The Bible is ancient. Those people at that time could not have possibly known what you're talking about."

"Yes, I know it may seem that way. I still have a long way to go to prove the entire correlation, but so far, all the pieces of the puzzle seem to be falling right into place. I don't want to bother you with a long, tedious explanation. So, I've condensed my research into a short synopsis that you may want to read someday. Regardless, I promise I'll put all that aside when I'm with you."

"Thank you, Sean. Now I feel better. I thought I was losing you. And yes, I would love to read it when you're ready to show it to me."

Seven years later

On December 31, 1995, I turned 45—my long dreamed of retirement age. Memories of Camille finally faded, and my feelings for Lila changed. I loved her, and she was the one I wanted to spend the rest of my life and raise a family with. So, for the second time in my life, I proposed marriage. Her enduring patience paid off, and with tears of joy and happiness, she accepted my proposal. We sealed our commitment with a loving embrace and a kiss that sent chills down my spine. Once again, my life finally seemed perfect.

After the passion of the moment subsided, we set a wedding date, but made the decision to wait until I was officially retired from Blackguard. As it turned out, our island was the perfect wedding destination for my family and friends. I hadn't seen my mother and father for almost a year, and it was at least five years since I last saw my sister, Susan. Lila wanted a June wedding, which was fine by me. We set a date for the following June 8th. Finally, I could see a future with a wonderful woman who was still young enough to have children. Best of all, I would be retired and could be there for them. Since Blackguard had paid all my expenses, I managed to acquire a sizable bank account. And along with the retirement plan spelled out in my employment contract, my resources were more than adequate so I would never have to work again. So, I called Julian Marsh to let him know I would be flying back to Detroit in February with my exciting news.

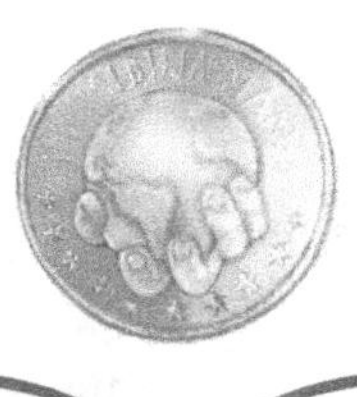

CHAPTER 14

AN ABRUPT TURN ON THE TRAIL

THE SIXTEENTH STEP

February 12, 1996
Area C
Detroit, Michigan

Sitting erect at the conference table, Julian Marsh began, "Hey Sean, it's been a while, welcome back. Before you meet with your team, I have some exciting news for you."

"Yes, sir. I have some exciting news for you, too."

"Yeah, that's right, you mentioned something on the phone. Why don't you tell me yours first?"

"Okay, Mr. Marsh, hold onto your seat. I'm getting married!"

"Good Lord, my man, congratulations—it's about time. Ha, ha, I was beginning to wonder about your tendencies. So, what's her name? Have you set a date yet for the big event?"

"Yes, sir, we have. Her name is Lila, and we're tying the knot this coming June. She'll be sending you and Mrs. Marsh an invitation. Make sure to set aside at least a week. I'm sure the two of you might want to spend some time on our island after the wedding."

"Oh, we will! I'm burned out and my wife, bless her heart, needs a well-deserved vacation."

"We're having the reception on our favorite St. Martin beach. The next day we'll leave on our two-week honeymoon. I have always loved the Caribbean, so we plan to hire an island hopper and explore the islands down there. And then, when we come back to St. Martin, we'll settle into our new life together. I can't wait. I'm ready. Also, I want to show you our new home, I think you'll love it."

"Settle in? No, no, no, Sean. You'll come back to Detroit after the honeymoon, and I'll tell you why. Now hold onto your seat for my announcement. I'm almost sixty-five. I've devoted forty years of my life to Blackguard, and I have to tell you, I'm ready to retire. So, the Carcassonne office is appointing you to take over my position here as director of Area C. You'll no longer have to travel. You can live right here in your hometown and raise your kids near your family. You have impressed my superiors with your performance over the last twenty years. They have complete confidence that you are the perfect fit to run Area C. Of course, you'll have to select someone from your team to replace your position as technical liaison."

"W-W-W-What?"

"That's right, I'm not getting any younger. Mrs. Marsh and I have looked forward to retirement for some time now."

"That's a flattering offer, Mr. Marsh, but to be clear with you and the Carcassonne office, I will retire this year, marry Lila, and raise our kids in St. Martin. So, I must turn down their offer."

"Well, okay Sean. Then I must be clear with you—there is no turning down their offer. Blackguard has a huge investment in you, not only money, but also the years we trained you. With your experience, you are extremely important to them, and I can assure you they will not allow you to leave. Sean, they own you."

"What in the hell do you mean, they own me? As far as the money is concerned, I gave them their money's worth. I never used any of my sick time. I never heard any complaints about my work performance, and I kept their trust all the years I worked for them. As far as wanting me as your replacement, you never mentioned anything to me about that before. And besides, when you hired me, you told me I could leave at any time, without consequences."

"Yes, Sean, that's all true. But, if you had actually read your contract, you would have noticed that clause only applied during your initial trial period. It did not apply after twenty years of employment. It does not say anywhere that you can leave without consequences. So, here's how it will be: After your honeymoon, you and your bride will move back to Detroit. I will train you to take over my duties of Area C. We'll take as much time as you need so you can settle in and make sure you are fully prepared. Of course, you can keep your St. Martin house and vacation there as often as time permits."

"Wait a minute, what the hell kind of consequences do you mean?"

"I have no idea, Sean. I don't make the rules—they do."

Julian Marsh's demands more than upset me. I could see my life with Lila in St. Martin suddenly vanish. Would she be willing to move to Detroit and leave her friends and family behind on her beloved island? Could I handle replacing Marsh as director of Area C without having a nervous breakdown? He never traveled to the other locations and never saw or heard what I did. Questions spun in my head. Did I know too much? What did he mean by consequences? For two hours, I had to listen to Marsh try and smooth things over. He knew I was upset and tried to convince me losing my retirement benefits is what he meant. I knew that was a crock of bullshit, and that would not be the only consequence I would suffer. After I left his office seething, I drove to my Bloomfield Hills apartment to call Lila and let her know I was on my way back to St. Martin. Only this time I would be arriving on a commercial airline, instead of the private jet. She immediately knew something was wrong.

The next day when I arrived home, she ran to the door. "Sean, what's wrong? I've never heard you so upset."

"What's wrong? What isn't wrong? Marsh is retiring and has ordered me to move back to Detroit, and the bastard didn't give me any choice. He said if I refuse, I'll lose my retirement benefits. Frankly, I'm sure that's not all I will lose."

Confused, she asked, "What do you mean?"

"Well, from the very beginning, I have always felt a veiled threat if I ever left Blackguard. The places I've been, the people I've met, and the things I've seen are all highly restricted. Not even Marsh has seen them. So, to protect myself, I kept a journal, in case I needed it. But now that's gone, and that's another story."

Lila responded in her usual supportive way. "It sounds to me if you accept the position he offered you, everything will be okay. If that's what you think is best, you'll get no argument from me. We'll move to Detroit, build our life together, and make the best of it. Sean, please don't worry, I'm sure we'll be fine."

"Lila, you're amazing, and you're more than understanding, but I'm finished with Blackguard, Area C, and Marsh. I have to nip this problem in the bud right now. If giving up my retirement benefits is the price I pay, I'll do it in a heartbeat. They paid me well over the years, and I stashed away a small fortune in a Swiss bank account. I assure you, money will not be a problem. My mind is made up. I'm not going back to Area C or Blackguard ever again. I'm mailing my letter of resignation to Marsh first thing tomorrow."

THE SEVENTEENTH STEP

June 8, 1996

Excited by my decision to leave all the grief and aggravation behind and start a new life with Lila, we spent the next several months planning our wedding. She wanted a full-blown ceremony and reception on the shores of the turquoise blue Caribbean. So, we sent out the invitations that she designed and penned with the most beautiful calligraphy I ever saw. She arranged to have the food and drink catered by our two favorite restaurants, Ile de Jardine and Brise Tropicale. The dance music would be played by our much-loved steel band, The Island Rovers, pictures taken by her favorite photographer, and the flowers flown in from San Juan. Our wedding attendants included several of her friends, and some friends of mine from Michigan. You can bet your life, Danny Kirchner was not one of them. I asked Dominic to be my best man. He, of course, accepted and welcomed me into the family with open arms and a gigantic bear hug. Then, he got that big broad smile of his. With his intimidating tone and dry, off-guard sense of humor, he looked me straight in the eye and declared, "Sean my good friend, if you ever make my little sister unhappy, I will *keell* you."

Lila and I were both as happy and excited as we could be. With beautiful weather and balmy breezes, we were married in front of our families and friends on June the 8th, exactly like we planned. All was perfect, except for the nagging threat Blackguard posed.

The next morning, eager to explore the Caribbean islands together as man and wife, we boarded the small, two-engine Beechcraft that I chartered at Grand Case-Espérance Airport, a small island airstrip near our village. The weather was perfect for our honeymoon flight: clear skies as far as you could see, calm seas, and ideal conditions to begin our long-anticipated honeymoon. Delirious with joy, Lila sang her favorite island tunes at the top of her lungs and giggled as she coaxed me to sing along with her. We brought a bottle of champagne to toast ourselves on the ceremonial journey that would personify our lives together as husband and wife.

While we sat in the back of the plane, the pilot with a baseball cap, earphones, and mouthpiece seemed oblivious to our antics. Lila continued to celebrate as she poured copious amounts of Dom Pérignon into the pricey crystal wineglasses she packed in the handmade French picnic basket her mother gave her as a child. I, on the other hand, did not hold my booze as well, and suffered from a major celebration hangover. The engines revved up, and the plane taxied down the runway for a takeoff that would put us on course for the British Virgin Islands, the first stop on our itinerary.

As the plane took off and gained altitude, we saw our cherished St. Martin and the nearby islands nestled in the turquoise blue waters below us. We could see the lush island of St. Bart's off in the distance, dozens of sailboats as they traversed the ocean below, and several cruise ships departing the port of Sint Maarten on the Dutch side of our island.

But then it happened! About fifteen minutes after takeoff, without warning, and for no apparent reason, both engines simply stopped. With little altitude, the plane started to nose down about a quarter-mile offshore from the southern end of nearby Anguilla Island. Lila dropped her glass, grabbed my arm, and screamed as the blue-green waters of the Caribbean enveloped the small aircraft.

In the eerie silence that followed, I struggled against the darkness, disoriented and engulfed by the cold ocean depths. As I fought to regain my senses, a primal fear gripped me. Seconds stretched into eternity as I battled against the weight of the water pressing in on all sides. With each passing moment, the realization of our dire situation sunk deeper into my consciousness. The plane, once a place of safety and security, now lay at the mercy of the sea. In the darkness, I reached out, desperate for any sign of life, but all I found was emptiness, the void swallowing my cries for help as easily as it had swallowed the aircraft. Then, everything then turned to black.

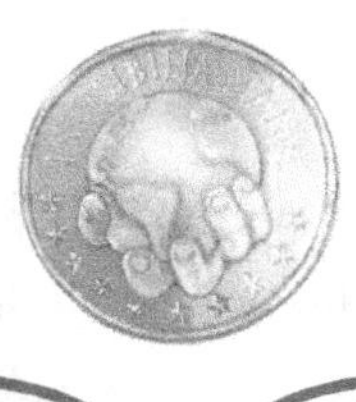

CHAPTER 15

THE ALTERNATE UNIVERSE

THE EIGHTEENTH STEP

June 9, 1996
Anguilla Island
The Caribbean

"Sean, my love, wake up—please wake up! You're okay, you're safe now."

Grasping my head with a splitting headache, I moaned, "M-M-My God, what happened? Where are we? I can't see anything."

"Don't worry, we're in a cabin on the south end of Anguilla Island. You were knocked unconscious when our plane hit the water. I pulled you to shore and you've been out since yesterday. Be careful though, you have quite a gash on your forehead. I wrapped it with some gauze and it covers your eyes."

In a state of shock, I mumbled, "Is the pilot okay?"

"Sean, my love, don't worry. I'm fine, and so is Lila."

"W-W-W-What do you mean L-L-L-Lila is fine? You're not Lila?"

In her soft French accent, she replied, *"Allez, est-ce que je ressemble à Lila?* You really are delirious. No, I am not Lila. But I did see her swim to shore and walk toward Long Bay Village. I'm quite sure she can find her way home from there."

Still dazed and confused, I demanded, "If you're not Lila, then who in the hell are you?"

Teasing me, she answered back, *"Tu sais qui je suis Sean."*

"No, it can't be! Take this damn gauze off me now! CA-CA-CAMILLE?" Shaken by the apparition looking down at me, I cried out, "What the hell, did I die? Am I dreaming? Is that really you?"

"You did not die, you are not dreaming, and *oui,* it is me. I will explain everything. We'll have plenty of time for that later. But for now, we must get out of here. I have a helicopter waiting outside. We need to leave immediately."

"What do you mean, a helicopter? Where are you taking me?"

"I flew a helicopter here earlier this week from San Juan, and now, we're going back there to my hotel room where you can take some time to recover."

"San Juan, Puerto Rico? For heaven's sake, why?"

"Please, Sean, no more questions. I will explain everything tomorrow after you've rested."

Still dazed, I slept during the entire flight. After she returned the rented helicopter, we took a cab to the hotel.

We spent the next several days in her room as she tried to explain the unexplainable.

San Juan, Puerto Rico

"You have no idea the misery and sleepless nights you've put me through for the last fifteen years. And another thing, where did you take my journals? I've been worried sick all these years. You've literally had my life in your hands."

"*Mon aime,* don't worry so much, I have your journals. They are safe, and no one has seen them. Believe me, with what you wrote in them, if anyone in my family had seen them, you would not be here now."

"Your family? What in the hell are you talking about?"

"I'll tell you, but first let me explain. Sean, I want you to know that I staged the plane crash. I brought an air tank with me so we could remain submerged until Lila was safely ashore. However, I did not anticipate the impact would knock you out. It was quite a struggle keeping you submerged long enough until she was out of sight. She will report to the officials and the local paper that after the plane went down, she never saw either of us again. Everyone will believe we both drowned. Even so, we can't take any chances in case someone happens to recognize us. We're both in extreme danger. We have no choice but to change our identities: new passports, IDs, clothes, even a different hair color. I will dye mine blond and get it cut. And may I suggest that you grow a beard?"

"I'm really confused. Who are you? I really don't know you."

"Okay, Sean, I'll start at the beginning. Remember the first time you and Julian Marsh met for your employment interview, and he told you Blackguard completed your background check?"

"Julian Marsh? You know Julian Marsh?"

"Yes, I do. If you remember, he also said you passed with flying colors and were exactly what they were looking for. Do you also remember, back in Marseilles, when I told you I worked for my family in the employment office?"

"Of course, I remember."

"Well, about a year before they hired you, I began working for my family. My job was to perform background checks on all new employees. Sean, I'm the one who hired you, and my family is part of the Blackguard organization that you worked for."

"Holy shit, you work for Blackguard?"

"Please, you must believe me. I did work for them, but I can assure you, not anymore."

"Ha, I can't wait to hear this. There were a lot of other candidates for Area C. So, why exactly did you pick me?"

"Before I go on, there is something else you need to know. Blackguard is an alias. Their real name is Invisibilia Manus, Latin for invisible hand. Blackguard is not what Marsh told you they are. Of course, you sensed that, and it's why you wrote in your journals."

"Just like in Marseilles, more lies and more deceit. You really do think you're in a James Bond movie. I'm done with you, whoever you are. Just leave me alone."

"Sean, stop, and please listen. My father wanted me to hire you because with your credentials and background, you were exactly what he was looking for. But the reason I wanted you, is because we both share the exact same birthdays. I simply had a feeling about you, something I couldn't explain. It was like a sign. I'm also the one who instructed Marsh to promote you to technical liaison. Over the years, I personally monitored your progress until we met in Marseilles. That's when my father sent me there to check you out. He was already thinking ahead and considering you as Marsh's replacement after Blackguard *retired* him."

"What in the hell do you mean—your father?"

"Okay, here goes. My alias is Camille Deneuve, but my birth name is Camille-Gabriella Martel. The Martel family is one of ten families that are Invisibilia Manus. And my father, Valentin Martel, is Chief Council for our family."

"Oh my God, whoever you are, you're crazy. You actually think you can make me believe all this crap."

"Sean, will you listen to me before you have a meltdown? I purposely dropped my purse in the Marseilles café, knowing you would pick it up. So, even though I came to you on business, everything changed after we actually met in person. The feelings I expressed to you back then are real. I was devastated when we were forced to part, especially after I left you with no explanation. Since then, you were all I thought about, but I had to figure out a way for us to be reunited. You gave me that opportunity when you sent your resignation letter to Marsh. He immediately briefed me when you left Blackguard and told me where you lived, your wedding date, honeymoon plans—everything. When I told my father what you had done, he, of course, was furious. I never saw him so angry. Since I'm the one who hired you, he sent me to St. Martin to personally eliminate you. That's when I devised my plan. I rented a helicopter, hired in at the airport as a pilot, and then faked the crash."

"You know what? I feel like you have totally played me, going to Marseilles and seducing me with that innocent French accent of yours. As far as I'm concerned, more of your lies that in some way or another will implicate me with Blackguard, your family, the Invisible Hand, whoever."

"I understand how you feel, Sean, but at least for now, please trust me."

"I don't know who I can trust anymore, except Lila. Good God, she must be going crazy. I need to get back to her—NOW! Ouch, ouch! Damn, my head is killing me."

"Sean, sit back down and listen to me. You're not ready to go anywhere yet, and you can never go back to Lila, or have any contact with her ever again. If they find out we're alive, they will send their *assets* after all three of us. I have never lied to you, not even a little, except about my family, and that was to protect you. I vow I will never lie to you again. Listen to me, I have put my life on the line for you here. The feelings we expressed to each other are real. It's like we are twin souls. I cannot be away from you any longer. I believe we were brought together for a reason."

"Brought together for a reason? What in the hell do you mean by that?"

"Over the years, I've given my feelings for you a lot of thought. I believe the answer lies in our passions."

"Our passions? Yeah, your passion is to fuck with my head."

"My God, Sean, I'm trying to be serious here. Will you please just listen before you decide to leave me? You told me in Marseilles that your passion was to prove your Genesis theory. Well, my passion is to defeat the evil that has taken over my family. These passions are not random. They have given us the inner fire, and the motivation to suffer for what we love and believe in, so that we can fulfill our destinies together. I don't know how or why, but maybe the two are somehow connected. For now, though, let's just trust our instincts and see where they lead us."

"That's all very poetic and all, but believe me, I'm far more worried about what your assassins will do to me if they find me. Then, I won't have any passions. I need to change my identity right now."

"*Oui,* and I'm one step ahead of you. I've already arranged for passports and IDs. Please forgive me, but I didn't have much time to select a new name for you. Your alias is now Sean Thompson."

"You've got to be kidding me. Look, I need to get to Zurich as soon as possible."

"Zurich, really. Why Zurich?"

"My bank accounts, I need some money."

"*C'est parfait,* that's also where I keep my accounts. I didn't know you traveled to Zurich. Since that's the case, I have a big surprise for you when we arrive. We should catch a flight as soon as possible. Do you think you'll feel well enough to travel by tomorrow?"

"Look, Camille, I don't know how I'll feel tomorrow. I've been with Lila for the last seven years, and we were just married. Then, in an instant, Lila is gone and you're back. My God, my poor Lila. The grief she is feeling must be pure agony. I need to somehow let her know I'm okay."

"Sean, listen to me. For the last time, you can never talk to Lila again!"

"Alright, alright, I'll give you the benefit of the doubt for now, and assume you did what you had to. I'm sure my head will feel fine by tomorrow, but trusting you again is another thing."

The next day, we caught a flight out of Puerto Rico and landed in Zurich ten hours later. We found a hotel room, had lunch, and took a cab to the bank, where coincidently we both had our accounts. I wanted to trust Camille, but her sudden return and shocking revelations left me shaken to the core. My journals were another thing. Where did she take them? Then, there was the matter of her big surprise. After all the surprises she already laid on me, I cringed at the thought of what might come next. After arriving at the bank, we made our withdrawals and I grabbed the Genesis files from my lockbox. She took some jewelry from hers, along with a small handgun that she slipped into her purse. But then, I froze in my tracks. I spotted a red leather-bound book with a familiar symbol embossed on the front cover. It was an exact replica of the medallion I wore while on assignment. I had no idea what were in those pages. Was it an incriminating dossier about me, taken from the pages of my journals? And I was terrified what her big surprise might be.

After we left the bank, we went back to our hotel room. I had a lot of questions and she had a lot of explaining. "Before we get down to business, is there something you want to tell me? I saw you put that handgun in your purse."

"I know you saw me. I didn't try to hide it from you. For heaven's sake, Sean, you need to calm down. I didn't want to draw attention to it in the bank. I understand your anxiety. Marsh didn't allow you to carry a weapon, but you no longer have to accept his demands. We are vulnerable, so you need a gun too, and as soon as possible. I know several black-market dealers here in Zurich."

"I also saw your surprise, Camille. Enough with the surprises. I want to know what's in that red book."

"Sean, please, why are you being so abrupt with me? Don't worry, I will give you the book, and after you read it, you will understand the magnitude of the atrocities my family and Invisibilia Manus are engaged in. You will realize that with what we both know, we may be the only ones on earth who stand between them and the global takeover they have planned. These two documents are our aces in the hole."

"A global takeover! Are you kidding me? And, what about my journals, or did you forget about them?"

"Sean, what will it take for you to trust me again? Did you not hear me? I said two documents—your journal and my red book. You have to realize that Invisibilia Manus is the most powerful criminal, terrorist organization on Earth. They can and will do anything they must do to survive. I have your journals, and I will give them back to you after we settle in. One other thing, *mon amour,* the red book is not your big surprise, so enjoy the anticipation. But for now, we have other priorities."

CHAPTER 16

THINGS DON'T ADD UP

June 15, 1996
The Offices of Chief Council Valentin
Martel Carcassonne, France

"André, get in here now, we have a big problem! I just received a message from a reliable source that Camille died yesterday in the plane she was flying on the island of St. Martin, down in the Caribbean."

"Oh my God, Father, Camille is dead! No, it's not possible. Who told you this?"

"She was responsible for hiring that traitor Phillips and felt it was up to her to eliminate him. So, I sent her there. She told me exactly how she would do it and I have to tell you André, her plan was foolproof. I wanted a clean, verifiable hit, and I agreed she should do it. However, I never told her I was also sending one of our assets there as a backup. He called and told me, but I don't believe it either. André, I want answers and I want you to fly there to get them. Listen to me son: don't come back until you find out exactly what happened to her. Now, get the hell out of here and don't waste any time. And there's one other thing—this whole matter is strictly between you, me, and Antoine. No one else is to know, especially your mother."

St. Martin Island
Grand Case-Espérance Airport

In as stern a voice as he could muster, mild-mannered André yelled out, "Where's the airport manager?"

"I'm the manager. May I ask who you are?"

"No, you may not. Look, I want answers and I don't want any of your bullshit. I flew all the way here from France to get them. I'm warning you, do not waste my time. I want to know exactly who flew the plane that went down the other day."

"Yeah, she was a mystery woman all right. If I remember correctly, her name was Pauline. She said she was thinking of moving here and wanted to line up a job. Since this is the French side of the island, her request sounded reasonable. She was absolutely gorgeous, and along with her sexy French accent, I couldn't resist her. Oh yes, I absolutely wanted her, if you catch my drift."

"Listen to me, what in the hell do you mean, you think her name was Pauline? You don't know for sure? She must have filled out a job application or gave you some kind of aviation documentation. Where's your logbook? I want to see it now."

"She didn't want to fill out paperwork until she knew for sure she would be moving here."

"Are you telling me she didn't show you her pilots license? Then why did you let her fly that plane?"

"No, she had her license alright. I made a copy of it. Do you want to see it?"

"You're damn right I do."

"You really are an idiot. This license is a fake. So, how in the hell did you know she could fly an airplane?"

"She wanted to give me a demo ride to prove her skills. Her takeoffs and landings were flawless and she performed her maneuvers perfectly. She knew exactly what she was doing. I put her through some pretty tricky exercises, especially ones that are required to fly here in the islands. I asked her what she would do under extreme weather and wind conditions. Her answers were always right on."

"Did you take the time to log the flight?"

"Yes, sir."

"Why did you let her fly one of your customers if you didn't actually hire her?"

"She told me two of her best friends were getting married and wanted to surprise them with their honeymoon flight. At the time, it seemed like a reasonable request."

André opened his jacket to reveal a Glock 19. "Where do these friends of hers live and what are their names? I hope you're not as stupid as you look, and you have a record of the booking."

"Okay, okay, mister, calm down. The flight was booked under the name of Lila Knowles. Actually, I know Lila personally. Knowles was her maiden name before she married Sean Phillips. She's a local and lives in Anse

Marcel, not far from here. She's easy to find; everyone knows her."

Shocked by the airport manager's revelation, André yelled out, "SEAN PHILLIPS! *Merde sacrée!* Is the booking, by any chance, in the name of Sean Patrick Phillips?

"Here, let me see. Well, not exactly, the signature is Sean P. Phillips."

"Okay, since you know where she lives, you can drive me to her house—NOW."

Ten minutes later

"*S'il vous plaît excusez-moi,* Mrs. Phillips. May I ask you a few questions about the terrible ordeal you recently suffered?"

"Why, who are you?" she asked.

"I'm a friend of the family of your late husband, Sean Phillips."

With tears of grief welling up, André consoled her. "Oh my, please don't cry. I didn't mean to upset you. I simply want to find out what happened to him. I heard that you and Sean went down in a plane crash and he and the pilot drowned. Do you have any idea what happened? Do you know what caused the plane to go down?"

"I already told the authorities everything I know. You should talk to them. I'm too upset to talk to anybody. I was only married to Sean for a matter of hours and now I'm a widow. I still have a hard time believing it. We were together for over seven years. Then in an instant, he's gone out of my life."

"Mrs. Phillips, I can't even imagine your pain. I'm grief-stricken, too. I flew all the way from France to offer my condolences and to help you in any way I can."

"That is very kind of you."

"May I ask you a question? When you were on the plane, did you, by any chance, meet the pilot?"

"The pilot? No, I don't think so. Sean and I were both hungover and still celebrating on the morning of the flight. My God, I can't believe it."

"Do you remember anything at all about the pilot?"

"No, not much, other than the pilot was a woman. Her back was to us the entire time, and I don't think she ever said anything. She was all business. Although, the more I think about it, she wore a baseball cap with her hair tucked up under it. She had on sunglasses and headphones with a mouthpiece. Oh yes, one other thing. I guess I didn't realize she was a woman until I heard her talk on the radio to get clearance. I remember her French accent. Actually, it was quite similar to yours. That's all I know."

"I read in the paper the plane went down about twenty minutes after takeoff, near Anguilla Island. Can you tell me what happened next?"

"Sean and I were singing, laughing, and toasting each other with champagne. Everything seemed fine. Then, both engines just stopped, and the plane plummeted into the water. He was not a strong swimmer. I opened the door and tried to get him and the pilot out, but the plane was sinking too fast. I saw blood streaming from his forehead. They were both unconscious and realized I couldn't help either of them. The currents in that area were very strong. I left them in the ocean to drown while I swam to shore. You have to understand—I couldn't do anything to save him. I lived and he didn't, and now I will have to live with the guilt for the rest of my life."

"Mrs. Phillips, don't be so hard on yourself. You did nothing wrong. Personal survival is an instinct. Besides, from the sound of it, I don't see how you could have done anything. I do thank you and appreciate your bravery for reliving this nightmare for me."

Realizing she had a sympathetic ear, she asked, "I'm sorry, I didn't get your name."

"*Excusez-moi,* Mrs. Phillips." He offered his hand with sincere compassion. "I am so sorry for my rudeness; my name is André. I do have one more question, and then I'll leave you alone. Did the authorities ever send divers to search for the plane?"

"Oh, yes. They tried, but the water there was far too deep."

"I must leave soon, Mrs. Phillips. I haven't seen Sean for quite a while. I'm curious, what did he do for a living? Did he ever talk to you about his job or who he worked for?"

"All I know is he was some kind of electronics expert. He never talked about his job, so I figured there was a good reason. I didn't feel I should pressure him about it."

"Okay, Mrs. Phillips, I must go now. I have a flight to catch. Thank you so much for your time, and please take care of yourself. You're a very special person. I can see now why Sean married you."

Voicemail to Valentin Martel

"Hello, Father. I don't have much time to talk. I wanted to let you know that things here don't add up. I spoke with the airport manager about the plane crash, but he was not much help. I also met with the woman who was on that flight. Her name was Lila Knowles, and she was on her honeymoon flight. She told me both engines simply stopped, and the plane went down near Anguilla Island, like the papers said. She managed to swim to shore, but her husband and the pilot, whom I am now sure was Camille, both drowned.

"After I left her house, I went to the beach on Anguilla, near where the plane went down. I combed the area and found an abandoned cabin back among the trees. It was obvious that somebody had recently been there. I don't know if it means anything or not, but I found a bloody bandage. I assume Mrs. Phillips went there after she swam to shore and tended to her wounds. Also, there's no need for us to eliminate her. She knows nothing about Phillips' work or Blackguard. Phillips never disclosed anything to her about us or what he did."

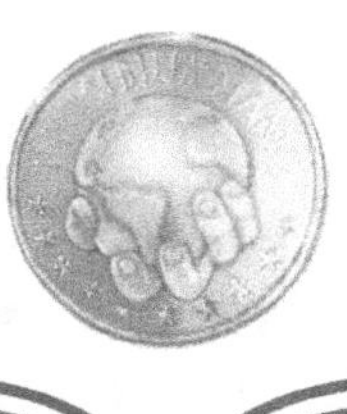

CHAPTER 17

TWIN SOULS

THE NINETEENTH STEP

September 26, 1996

As the months rolled by, Camille proved beyond a doubt that her feelings for me were real, and I began to trust her again. We needed a home base, so we purchased a house on the beautiful Lake Zurich, a home intended to make our lives in Switzerland very comfortable. It was a spacious four-bedroom multi-level with all the modern amenities, including an indoor pool. The landscaping blended beautifully on the wooded property, and the majestic backdrop of the Alps provided a panoramic view that could have been on the cover of any architectural magazine.

Being a car enthusiast, I splurged and bought a sports car, a luxury I had fantasized about ever since my teen years in Detroit. I decided on an Aston Martin DB7 Volante convertible, and Camille bought a Mercedes-Benz SL-Class convertible. Riding in style, we spent the next several months together in complete freedom, away from the dictates of her family and Blackguard.

Finally able to relax, the Genesis correlation was once again on my mind. I had completed the correlation for day two and day three, but I was still not certain of my conclusions. I needed the same kind of reassurance I got from Bob Townsend back in Ann Arbor. With nobody in Europe to turn to, I decided to pick Camille's brain for her thoughts.

"Sweetheart, I have a favor to ask you. I need your help."

"Sean, you never ask for my help. Can I take this as a sign that you finally trust me again?"

"Yes, you know I do. Anyway, I would like to discuss the Genesis correlation with you. My ex-wife thought it was ridiculous and didn't agree with any of it, so I'm not sure what you'll think."

"Look, the sooner we can figure out how my family and your Genesis theory are connected, the better."

"Okay then. It turns out I have, in fact, correlated the Day One of the Creation Story. I went out on a limb and shared my findings with one of my science professors in Ann Arbor. I thought he would tear it apart, but quite the contrary, he couldn't find any real faults with it. But he does think correlating all six days will be next to impossible. Regardless, I decided to continue, and now I think I may have also correlated the Second and Third Day, but I need some honest feedback from you."

"Okay Sean, but keep in mind I'm not a science professor."

"*Oui*, of course. Why don't you bring me up to date?"

"Sure! I have hundreds of pages of notes where I used the original Hebrew words. You can read them if you like."

"You're right, I need to understand. When we're done here today, I'll study your notes."

"That would be great. Anyway, on the Second Day, the verse reads, *'Let there be a firmament in the midst of the waters, and let it divide the waters from the waters.'*

"Because this verse falls in the correct sequence of the Earth's developing atmosphere, I concluded that is when the second atmosphere, the intermediary one between the first and the third atmosphere, began to form. Let me explain. Scientists have concluded our atmosphere was formed in three stages—the first, the second, and the third."

"But, how do you know that's what *'firmament'* means? I've never heard it explained that way before."

"Well, I found out it originated from the Latin term 'firmamentum,' translated from the Greek 'stereomaoin.' This translation came from the Hebrew word 'raqiya' or 'raqa'. Raqa can mean either beat, stamp, beat out, stretch, or spread out. In other words, something spread out. The closest English equivalent is expanse—the expanse over the Earth."

"Okay, but I still don't understand. What does *'in the midst of the waters'* mean?"

"When the lighter gasses of hydrogen and helium escaped into space, water vapor and the heavier gasses were left behind and organized in layers, from the lightest to the heaviest. The gasses, *'in the midst of the waters,'* divided the dense clouds of water vapor in the upper atmosphere from the *'face of the waters,'* the sea on Earth's surface. The firmament was the second atmosphere. It was the atmosphere that eventually transitioned into the third atmosphere, and the air where we and all life on Earth exist."

"Wow, you must have spent years working on this theory. What about the Third Day?"

"On the Third Day, in verses 9 and 10, God said:

"*Let the waters under the heaven be gathered together unto one place, and let the dry land appear. And it was so.' And God called the dry land Earth, and the gathering together of the waters called He Seas; and God saw that it was good.'*

"This verse reveals a naturally occurring event caused when the Earth's buoyant granite crust literally floated above the rigid basaltic mantle to form the first continental landmass. It seems that comets and asteroids delivered the precise amount of water to the planet. If they had brought just ten percent more, the Earth would have been a permanent water-world. If they had brought ten percent less, Earth would have been a lifeless, arid desert. The volume of water on Earth's surface was the perfect depth for the dry land to appear. This was the land mass that geologists call Pangea."

"Sean, it's hard to believe that random, unrelated events could be precise enough to bring the exact amount of water."

"Yes, I agree, that is a mystery. But then, next came the plants in verses 11 and 12.

"*And God said: 'Let the earth put forth grass, herb yielding seed, and fruit-tree bearing fruit after its kind, wherein is the seed thereof, upon the earth.' And it was so. And the earth brought forth grass, herb yielding seed after its kind, and tree bearing fruit, wherein is the seed thereof, after its kind; and God saw that it was good.'*

"You may notice that *'Let the earth put forth'* as well as *'And the earth brought forth,'* are descriptive terms for the natural evolution of plants, and not a supernatural, instantaneous creation event. I found other evidence which comes from the Hebrew definition of *'brought forth,'* which in Hebrew means to sprout, to shoot, to grow. So, I have come to the conclusion that, *'In the beginning God created the heaven and the earth,'* along with the natural laws, but everything that followed is the result of those laws, including the evolution of plants and animals. In fact, *'create'* doesn't appear again in the entire story until the creation of man."

"Sean, I'm beginning to feel something about you that I never realized before. I think you lean more toward science than God. You seem to trust evidence more than instinct or faith."

"I don't know about that, but the words God and religion turn me off. I think it reminds me too much of my childhood when religion was pushed down my throat every day. If it's okay with you, I would prefer to call them something else. So, I think the Genesis Correlation is about uniting science with the spiritual dimension."

"*Oui*, I agree."

"You have to understand, when I'm working on the correlation, I try to think like a detective and go where the evidence leads me. And right now, I want to simply define the original Hebrew words that the Genesis author wrote."

"And that's another thing, Sean. Many of the words in these verses that you're showing me are not what I remember when I read the Creation Story years ago."

"That's true, because you undoubtedly read one of the more modern translations of the Bible. I can't read

Biblical Hebrew, so I used the earliest Hebrew to English version I could find."

"Okay, that makes sense. But why, then, did the Genesis author only list grass, herb, and fruit-trees in this verse? Why didn't he include other plant species, like flowers, evergreens, ferns, hardwoods, and palms? All the millions of other plant species certainly existed when he wrote Genesis."

"Yeah, that's a great question too. The Creation Story is an account of our origins and he personalized it as a story for the Hebrews. The origin of their food was very important to them. So, he only listed the food plants; for example, grass would have referred to wheat and barley. Herb would have meant such things as mustard and mint. And fruit-trees would have been fruit-trees like pomegranates and figs. These plants are mentioned elsewhere in the Bible; they were foods the Hebrews were quite familiar with."

"That's an amazing analysis. I've never heard anything like that before."

"Well, there is something else I struggled with, but I think I may have figured it out. Tell me what you think. The next phrase appears at the end of each of the six days: *'And there was evening and there was morning: one day, a second day, a third day,'* and so forth. The problem is, it doesn't fit any of the eight definitions for day."

"*Oui*, I see what you mean. A day doesn't begin in the evening and then end in the morning."

"Exactly. So, here's my conclusion. Geological eras of time don't have definite boundaries. Instead, they transition one into the other. Just as night does not immediately become day, it is preceded by the morning. Likewise, day does not suddenly become night, it's preceded by the evening. I contend the Genesis author literally described a geologic transition."

"So, what you're saying is that a *day*, in this case, could represent an eon of time.

"*'As the evening of the third eon was coming to an end, the morning of the fourth eon was about to begin.'*"

"Thank you, sweetheart, you get it. I'm going to go ahead and describe these events in my synopsis."

Until Camille came into my life, I had never experienced having a partner or any friends that understood me and my interests. She was truly my equal and my twin soul in every way, even in the way we thought. My logical mind along with her intuitive spirit were the perfect compliments, the Yin and the Yang, one might say. Even so, she was like a multifaceted diamond. With each new facet she presented to me, I never knew what to expect, and what came next was no exception.

Synopsis
Genesis Correlation of the Second
Day and the Third Day

The Second Atmosphere
3.80 billion years ago

Genesis 1:6

*And God said: Let there be a firmament in the midst of
the waters, and let it divide the waters from the waters.*

Genesis 1:7

*And God made the firmament, and divided the waters
which were under the firmament from the waters
which were above the firmament; and it was so.*

Genesis 1:8

And God called the firmament Heaven. And there was evening and there was morning, a second day.

Continent Formation
3.00 billion years ago

Genesis 1:9

And God said: 'Let the waters under the heaven be gathered together unto one place, and let the dry land appear. And it was so.

Genesis 1:10

And God called the dry land Earth, and the gathering together of the waters called He Seas; and God saw that it was good.

Synopsis
Genesis Correlation of the Third Day

First Terrestrial Flora
450 million years ago

Genesis 1:11

*And God said: 'Let the earth put forth grass, herb yielding
seed, and fruit-tree bearing fruit after its kind, wherein
is the seed thereof, upon the earth.' And it was so.*

Genesis 1:12

*And the earth brought forth grass, herb yielding seed
after its kind, and tree bearing fruit, wherein is the seed
thereof, after its kind; and God saw that it was good.*

Genesis 1:13

*And there was evening and there
was morning, a third day.*

CHAPTER 18

SHOCK AND AWE

THE TWENTIETH STEP

May 17, 1997
Zurich, Switzerland

Camille asked me not to ask any questions as she drove down a meandering driveway through an alpine forest to an austere building set on the campus of what appeared to be an educational institute of some kind. The sign at the entrance was placed on a beautifully landscaped facade that read, *Institut La Swiss*. After we walked into the lobby of the main building, she went straight to the front desk and, in a soft voice, whispered something to the matronly receptionist. The woman escorted us down the hallway to a small, empty room where she left us to wait.

"Sean, do you remember last year when I mentioned my big surprise?"

"Oh yeah, I forgot about that."

"Well, it's time."

After a few minutes, a middle-aged, academic type brought a teenage boy into the room. Camille immediately turned her attention to him as she held out her arms.

"Michael, *bonjour mon fils.* Come here, let me hug you. I don't believe it—you seem to have grown another two or three centimeters since I last saw you."

He replied, "Come on, Mother, don't embarrass me in front of this man. Is he the boyfriend you wrote me about?"

"*Oui.* Sean Thompson, meet Michael Deneuve, my son."

Shocked and not knowing what to say, I stuttered, "W-W-Wow, this is a s-s-surprise." Tongue-tied and red-faced, I turned to the boy, barely able to get the words out. "M-M-Michael, it's really great to meet you. Please forgive my clumsiness."

"My mother never brings men here. Who are you?"

Camille interrupted, "Michael, I have a wonderful surprise for you. Sean and I just bought a home not far from here. You're going to love it. It's the kind of house you and I have always talked about. It has an indoor pool, and you'll have your own room where you can hang out with your friends."

Suddenly feeling betrayed, Michael cried out, "You bought a house without telling me? We always talk about everything first."

As her eyes welled up, she proceeded to reveal her second surprise. "Yes, I know, and soon you'll understand why. But first, I have another big surprise for both of you. Michael, you're old enough, and this has to be said. I don't know any other way to do it. There will never be a perfect time."

"Wow, Mom, you're full of all kinds of surprises today."

Overwhelmed with emotion, she cried out, *"Oh mon Dieu*, this is more awkward than I thought it would be. Okay, here goes. Michael, I want you to know that Sean is much more than just a friend. We love each other very deeply. Sadly, circumstances tore us apart many years ago, but fate has brought us back together again." She held her son in a tight embrace and announced, "Michael, my dear boy, Sean is your father!"

Stunned, Michael tore himself away and said only one word, "MOTHER!"

She turned to me. "Sean, meet your son, Michael."

In that moment, my body suddenly lurched forward and my mouth hung open in utter disbelief. "W-W-W-WHAT?"

"I know this is unexpected, but it's time the two of you finally met. Meeting like this must be confusing for both of you, but when I explain the circumstances, I pray you will understand."

"Mother, what in the heck are you talking about?"

"Oh, my G-G-G-God, C-C-C-Camille, I agree. What in the hell are you talking about? This is not like you. I hope you're not trying to be funny. This is not funny."

"S'il vous plaît, will the two of you just listen to me? This is not easy for me either, but the truth must come out. Michael, please understand, the past fourteen years have been very difficult being both a mother and a father to you, but I did the best I could. And I promise you, your father was dealing with a very difficult situation that prevented him from coming into our lives until now. Let me assure you, with God as my witness, it's not his fault. He did not walk out on us. Please believe me when I say he is a wonderful, kind,

and gentle man. You should not blame him for his absence all these years. I hope you can forgive both of us, so we can be united as a family once and for all. Please, let's go outside and sit on the veranda and I will explain everything."

Ever since my first marriage to Marlene, I have longed to have a family. Then I thought my marriage to Lila would give me that family, but she was gone. Then, I met a son I knew nothing about. That meeting changed everything for me. In a single moment, I realized it was possible to have a family of my own with the woman I truly loved. I wanted to be the father Michael never had, but I have to admit that I worried that he might not accept me. To make things easier for him, we felt an abrupt change in his routine would not be the best thing for him. So, Michael remained at the boarding school and stayed with us on the weekends.

In the years that followed, my life with Michael and Camille was as perfect as it could be. As we got to know each other, we spent more and more time together. Although slight, I felt a bond begin to form with my son.

We went on family road trips all over Europe and visited the places on his wish list. The three of us played soccer, American touch football, and spent countless hours on the golf course. I taught him some science he was not learning in school, especially about the origin of the universe and the evolution of life. I also showed him some of the new technologies that were evolving and tried to prepare him for college the best as I could. Everything in our personal lives seemed great, or at least I thought so.

Michael was a smart, good-looking kid, but he was overly sensitive and small for his age. He didn't have many friends, but when they would come to the house, they hung out in his room a lot. They never played any of the sports I taught him—not even golf. I never heard them talk about girls or clown around like I did when I was a kid. Instead, they were unusually quiet, watched TV a lot, listened to music, played cards or board games, and studied a lot. Occasionally, they would go to the kitchen and get something to eat. Sometimes they would swim in the pool, but far less than we imagined. He was always polite around us and well-behaved—almost too well-behaved. I guess you could say Michael was a bit of a geek, like somebody else I know.

Camille begged me not to mention anything about the Martels to him. She was adamant that he should never be associated with them in any way. However, as he spent more time at the house, I knew he overheard things, not only about the Genesis Correlation but also about Camille's family and the Invisible Hand. Whenever we thought he was eavesdropping, we would change the subject, which must have sounded very suspicious to him.

Having time with my family was great, but Camille and I were still on a mission. It was during this period that we decided to collect newspaper articles, both old and new. We went to the library and searched through the newspaper stacks to look for news events we felt might be somehow connected to the Invisible Hand. The more articles we collected, the more we began to see a pattern. In virtually every case, the investigators didn't seem to have any clues or answers as to how or why these devastating events occurred, or who was behind them. Furthermore, the more articles we read, the more we became aware that government intelligence and surveillance agencies were far less sophisticated than we thought they were. Evidently, they were no match for an invisible enemy.

CAR BOMB DETONATES BELOW NORTH TOWER OF THE WORLD TRADE CENTER

New York, February 27, 1993 (National News)

A car driven by unknown perpetrators drove into an underground garage of the World Trade Center and detonated a bomb that shook the twin buildings in lower Manhattan with the force of a small earthquake shortly after noon yesterday. The blast was so intense it collapsed walls and floors, ignited fires, and plunged the city's largest building complex into turmoil with smoke, darkness, and terrified bedlam for thousands.

Police estimated that the blast killed at least five and left possibly more than 700 others injured with smoke inhalation, burns, and broken bones.

The explosion also trapped hundreds in debris and smoke-filled stairwells and elevators, and forced the evacuation of more than 50,000 personnel.

The explosion was felt throughout the Wall Street area and as far as mile away on Ellis and Liberty Islands in New York Harbor. Moreover, it knocked out the police command and operations centers for the twin towers.

By last evening, officials began a series of investigations into the cause of the explosion and possible culprits. They said that a terrorist attack has not been ruled out. Officials were baffled as to how easy it was for the attack to have occurred without being detected. There are no suspects as of this date.

MORE THAN 80 FEARED DEAD IN COMPOUND BLAZE

Waco, Texas, April 20, 1993 (National News)

A compound ten miles east of Waco built by cult leader Vernon Howell turned into a raging funeral pyre on Monday. More than 80 Branch Davidians are believed dead from a fire they apparently set. Howell, who claimed to be Christ, also died in the fire.

Federal Bureau of Investigation (FBI) agents said several of the nine surviving cult members reported that three separate fires were set with lantern fuel on Monday afternoon.

A former cult member from the Peoples Temple compared this suicide to the Jonestown Massacre on November 18, 1978, when more than 900 members of an American cult died in a mass murder-suicide under the direction of their leader Jim Jones.

On February 28, the FBI went to the compound on charges of illegal firearm possession and ordered the heavily armed Howell and his members to surrender. Howell refused, and after a shootout, four agents with the Bureau of Alcohol, Tobacco, and Firearms and as many as six Branch Davidians died.

A standoff ensued, and after 51 days, right before daybreak, the FBI notified the compound's neighbors, "It would end today." They made an abrupt change Monday morning from a waiting game to an aggressive attempt to drive the Branch members out.

Investigators believe this incident is one in a series that is linked to unknown sources who are responsible for inciting social division. Sources predict similar incidences will follow.

BOMB KILLS AT LEAST 31; 200 MISSING IN OKLAHOMA CITY INCLUDING 12 CHILDREN

Oklahoma City, August 20, 1995 (National News)

At 9:02 a.m. this morning, a thundering half-ton car bomb exploded, tearing through a federal office building, collapsing ceilings and walls, and killing at least 31, with that count expected to rise dramatically. There were others buried in the wreckage, with up to 200 missing, including as many as 12 children. The explosion could be felt for miles as the bomb destroyed nearly half of the nine-story building. Authorities described the bombing as the deadliest attack on U.S. soil in the last 75 years, in the capitol city of 440,000.

The governor requested the National Guard called in, and late tonight, limited martial law was imposed to keep the area clear.

So far, no one has claimed responsibility for the bombing. Federal agents have noted that this is the second anniversary of the federal raid on the Branch Davidian compound near Waco, Texas, where David Koresh and most of his followers perished. Authorities have found no evidence that today's bombing was linked to the Davidians. However, it was similar in strength to the World Trade Center bombing two years ago.

CHAPTER 19

IT'S CAMILLE'S TURN

"The world as we know it, is coming to an end. What was once unthinkable, will be inevitable."— J.K. Rowling

THE TWENTY-FIRST STEP

July 16, 1997
Zurich, Switzerland

With Michael now in my life, I finally had the family I always wanted. Even so, no matter how much I tried, Michael and I didn't seem to click the same way my father and I did. On top of it, Camille was a mysterious, enchanting woman, but so much of her past eluded me. Whenever we talked about anything while in Marseilles, she always shocked me with another surprise that left me feeling even more out of touch with her. After we finally settled into our new Zurich lifestyle, I needed a heart-to-heart with her. She knew far more about me than I did about her, so it was her turn.

"Okay, sweetie, it's a beautiful Sunday afternoon and we have nothing planned. I think today would be a great day for you to tell me more about your past. I really need a better idea of what we're up against."

"*Oh, mon Dieu,* there you did it again. I woke up this morning and the same thing occurred to me."

"Yeah, we do that a lot. Let's start with when I left you in Marseilles and went to your offices in Carcassonne on assignment. I'm curious, did I ever run into any of your family when I was there?"

"Oh no, you did not. If you recall, one of their security teams was always with you. It's a damn good thing you never met or saw any of them, or you wouldn't be here to talk about it. Keep in mind, Invisibilia Manus means the invisible hand. Absolutely no one outside the hive will ever know who they are."

"The hive? That's an interesting term for them. So, let me get this straight—the hive is the Martel family, Blackguard, and Invisibilia Manus. Is that right?"

"Not entirely, but my family is one part of Invisibilia Manus. But Sean, you must listen to me before we go on. Let me remind you, they don't know anything about Michael. His identity must remain hidden from them. His birth certificate shows his name as Deneuve. I do not want him or anybody else to ever know he is a Martel, or that he is in any way connected to them."

Half-jokingly, I made it clear. "Well, Camille, maybe his last name should be Phillips. So yes, you better believe I don't want Michael to have anything to do with your family either. But I need to know more about the both of you. Where did you live when you were pregnant and how did you hide it from them?"

"Michael was born and raised in Uzès, a little village between Marseilles and Carcassonne. When I worked for my family, I drove to their offices about an hour away, the same one you went to. Fortunately, my pregnancy didn't show much and I wore clothes that would hide my tummy, so they never knew."

"Well, I certainly understand why you despise your family. But I have to tell you, my connection to Blackguard is also troubling for me. I worked for them for over twenty years and then come to find out I really didn't know anything about them, except that I always felt something was very wrong. So, please enlighten me."

"Okay, but I'm not proud of what I'm about to tell you. The Martel bloodline has been traced back over 700 years. We are the descendants of the Capetian family from France. The Capetian's ruled out of the walled city of Carcassonne and amassed more wealth than any other family in Europe. I do have to say, my ancestors were a colorful bunch, with a sordid history to say the least."

"Colorful history? What do you mean?"

"Well, as an example, one of my cousins recently found an ancient Martel coat of arms hidden away in a castle garret room in Carcassonne. That symbol of our past has become a fascinating relic among family members. When I saw it, I couldn't believe my eyes. It's the perfect symbol to represent the Martels' bloody past."

"Yeah, I bet it's a dragon breathing fire on the world."

"No, actually it's worse. It depicts three hands that hold three severed heads by the hair, with blood dripping from their necks. The heads hang over crossed swords that also drip blood. Historians who have examined it suspect it dates to 732 from the Battle of Tours. That's when Christian leader Charles Martel overpowered the army of Spanish Moors and halted the Muslim advance into Western Europe."

"Yeah, I remember studying about that battle in school. And now fate has hooked me, a tech geek from Michigan, with one of their descendants. How ironic is that?"

"Sean, it's not fate that brought us together—it's your trail."

"My trail? What do you mean, my trail?"

"I'll tell you more when you're ready, but for now, let's get back to my family. Their history gets better or worse, depending on how you want to look at it. The Martel family has over three hundred direct descendants, and many of them currently reside in the Aude Province of France, where Carcassonne is located. And of course, you already know that my family has great wealth and wields tremendous power. Unfortunately, they use it for their evil agendas."

"My Lord, Camille, why in the world did you work for them in the first place?"

"Because of my father, Valentin Martel. He is the chief council for the Martel family. As his daughter, he demanded that I be actively involved in the *family business*."

"I'm sorry, but I still don't see the big picture. How does the Martel family tie into Blackguard?"

"First, let me explain the red book you saw. It's the 1978 Red Book. That book was given to me when I went to the 200th annual assembly of Invisibilia Manus in 1978. It contains a transcript of all the meetings that took place over those seven days. They have held these assemblies every year since it was founded in 1778, and each year, they publish ten red books, one for each family. My father has the complete library dating back to 1778."

"Wow, Invisibilia Manus is the name inscribed on my medallion. Maybe I should have read your Red Book first before we had this talk today. I'm not making excuses, but with getting settled in and building my relationship with Michael, it never occurred to me."

"No need for excuses, Sean, I understand. Blackguard is the alias for Invisibilia Manus, Martel family members also have an alias when out in public. It's Lemieux."

"Wait a minute, I'm still confused."

"I know it's complicated. Invisibilia Manus is a collective of twenty family members from each of the ten families; two hundred in all make up the hive. They work together on shared agendas without relying on internal hierarchies or chains of command. The perfect analogy is a beehive where each bee has a job to perform with one common objective, and that is to protect and provide for the queen and her eggs. The collective assures the survival of the entire hive. If an intruder invades the hive, they eliminate it. Invisibilia Manus also has one common goal: the survival of the collective. Each of the ten families has appointed a patriarch or matriarch to act as their chief council. He or she then appoints twenty family members to sit on their respective councils. Each individual family council works collectively with the other families. Together, they determine the strategies that the collective will employ to achieve their agendas. In this case, it's Agenda One, the complete and unconditional control for a total global takeover."

"My God, it's no wonder they're so powerful—there is no division."

"Exactly. The secret to their unrivaled power lies in their unity; they are of one mind. That is their secret to taking control of a divided world."

"That means two hundred people make up the collective. So, when they meet in person at one of their assemblies, how can they be sure an outsider has not infiltrated?"

Extending her left palm, she showed me. "Here, Sean, do you remember this?"

"Oh yeah, the brand I saw back in Marseilles."

"*Oui,* I was branded on December 13, 1963, when I turned thirteen, just like all family members of Invisibilia Manus dating back to its founding in 1778."

"How do you keep people from seeing that?"

"I have learned tricks to keep it camouflaged. I keep my left hand closed or my arm down next to me most of the time. Sometimes I put my hand in my pocket. When I'm out, I might wear gloves. These habits have become second nature to me. But whenever council members meet in person, the first thing they do is present their left hand, palm facing forward."

"That brand is an exact replica on the face of my medallion."

"*Oui,* it's proof you worked for Blackguard, and it allowed you entry into their facilities."

"So, my French woman of mystery, that means as a council member in 1978, you were a member of the Invisibilia Manus and you knew all about their Agenda One."

"*Oui,* my father insisted I attend that assembly. Like you, I was young and naïve. But once I realized the full extent of what they were up to, I knew I could not be part of it."

"You mentioned each of the ten families has a distinct role to play, so what exactly does the Martel family do?"

"They operate and manage covert operations. In essence, my family is an extremely efficient and dangerous spy organization. They gather information on all employees that work for them, dig up dirt on government officials, corporate CEOs, military leaders, university deans, you name it. Once they have completed their dossiers, my family uses it against the individual in order to intimidate and control them and get what they want. They also deploy their twenty-five assets whenever and wherever they are needed."

"Yeah, I've seen enough James Bond movies to know what assets are."

"*Oui, c'est vrai.* These assassins are highly trained and efficient killing machines. They have been put in key locations around the world, and within hours they can take out any designated target."

"My God, Camille, you were involved in all of that?

"You must understand that if I wanted to live, I had no choice. If my father ever suspected I was not loyal to the family, let's just say I wouldn't be here today. Anyway, my team was responsible for background checks on all employees, including you. We also recruited and trained proxies to infiltrate any organization my father instructed us to. But there's a dirty little secret that anyone who has ever worked outside of the collective or is in any way associated with Invisibilia Manus doesn't know. Once they have served their purpose, they will be eliminated. Invisibilia Manus is a master at covering their tracks. They've been at it for 220 years. Only identified family members, along with the individuals and the alliances they choose, will survive in the end."

"Geez, now I really see why my instinct to keep a journal was crucial."

"Sean, there's something else you need to know. You've been to fourteen locations, but there's a fifteenth one Marsh never mentioned. That's because it's so secret, we never told him about it."

"Really, and where would that be?"

"It's located in the Thousand Islands area between New York and Canada on Heart Island, one hundred feet below Boldt Castle. That's where Invisibilia Manus holds its annual assemblies. It's where I went for the 1978 Assembly and is the only place in the world where council members from all ten families can meet in private. I want to bring this up now because something happened there that you should know about. It has to do with Travis McShane."

"Travis, yes, of course. He was a good friend of mine. Marsh told me he had taken ill and Blackguard sent him to Toronto for treatment, but I never saw him again after that."

"That's because Travis was assassinated on orders from my father. Two assets disguised as pilots were sent to do the job."

"W-W-W-What? Why in hell would he want Travis killed? He never hurt anyone."

"They sent him there to install their new security system. Not only did Travis know about Heart Island, but he also came in direct contact with council members. Marsh directed him to fly to Toronto where the assets picked him up and then flew him there. They told Travis that after he completed his job, they would fly him back to Toronto. However, that's not what happened. Once they were airborne, they knocked him out, tied his hands behind his back with his shirt, acid-scrubbed his fingerprints, and threw him out of the plane. Several days later, two fishermen found his body. Now, Sean, it's closer to home for you. Now, you understand why we are in mortal danger and why I took the steps I did to conceal our identities."

"Holy shit, those damn bastards killed Travis for no good reason. He was one of the nicest guys I ever knew."

"Sean, I told you this so you would realize what we're up against. However, that pales in comparison to their ultimate goal—Agenda One. The Qing family from Shanghai is in the process of developing a virus that they will unleash on the world. Invisibilia Manus needs to decrease the world's population in order to take full control. They believe the planet is overpopulated and will continue to grow exponentially. In the end, they want one billion of the fittest individuals to survive. That was the world population in 1778 when their families still reigned over the world."

"How in the hell will they infect over six billion people?"

"They plan on sending diseased individuals, what they call carriers, to spread their weaponized virus to every country on Earth."

"That's crazy. We have to stop this now. We need to give your red book and my journals to the FBI, the United Nations, Interpol, or whoever as soon as possible."

"Sean, please slow down. We can't do that just yet. First of all, nobody will believe us. They'll consider us to be radicals and we'll lose any credibility we have. Also, don't forget that if we tip our hands now, we'll expose ourselves to my family. For now, we still have some time since the development of the virus is still years away. However, I see a more immediate problem. They will fly trial balloons with novel strains into the population. I suspect the HIV virus may be one of them. Trust me when I say that AIDS is just a sample of what they are capable of. They will continue to release many more of these pathogens until they figure out which one will work on a global scale."

"Damn it, Camille, this is way too much for me to handle right now. I need time to process all of this. I need to change the subject or I'll end up having nightmares. I have a question. When we were in Marseilles, I told you about my assignment at their banking division in Austria. Remember when I told you one of the vault doors was left open?"

"*Bien sûr,* you were not supposed to see that. Somebody really messed up."

"Where in the hell did all that gold in those vaults come from?"

"Invisibilia Manus possesses unimaginable wealth, not only gold and silver, but jewels and other precious objects they plundered from centuries of conquests and burdensome taxation on their subjects. During the 1778 Assembly, the leaders entered into a pact and formed Invisibilia Manus. Each family then looted the wealth stored in their treasuries well before they lost their power. Then, they chose the Burgruine Dürnstein, where you went in Austria, as the storehouse for their plunder."

"Well, I'll be damned."

"You told me you met Bruno Wagner."

"Oh yeah, you mean Mr. Personality."

"Well, Wagner isn't his real name, it's an alias. His actual name is Bruno Habsburg. He's chief council for his family in Austria and is the only council member that works outside the family collective. That's how important he considers guarding those vaults to be."

"I saw eleven vault doors. I assume each family has one vault. But what about that eleventh vault— the one that was left open, the one I saw?"

"*Oui,* you are right. Ten of those vaults belong to the families and that includes the Martel vault. However, what you saw in the eleventh vault was gold the Nazis stole from European families during World War II. Hitler's soldiers stored it, along with valuable art objects and jewelry, in an abandoned salt mine near Merkers, Germany. After the war ended, the U.S. military came into the region. The locals told them where to locate the mines, and allied soldiers then proceeded to restore the Nazi plunder to its rightful owners. The Nazis were fanatical recordkeepers, so it was fairly easy to return it. However, after completing their audit, they realized only half of the gold was in those mines. The other half was never found. That's because under cover of night, Invisibilia Manus removed much of it before the military arrived. Ever since then, perplexed treasure hunters and government agencies have searched in vain for this treasure."

"My God, Camille, that is one hell of a story."

"Sean, let me tell you, nothing has changed. Invisibilia Manus still plunders and hoards wealth right under everybody's eyes, only now it's under the guise of multinational corporations. Because money is now easier to trace, their media companies deflect this attention onto an elite group of multi-billionaire proxies. They are names everybody knows but who have been assimilated into the hive. But make no mistake about it; Invisibilia Manus is the puppet master who pulls the strings. Unbeknownst to this elite group, the ten families control and manipulate them to do their bidding. It's no accident. They do it by clearing the path for them to gain more wealth. What they don't know is, they are the unwitting puppets of the Invisibilia Manus' financial institutions and investment firms. Their greed blinds them."

"How in the world do you know all of this?"

"Their disinformation division wrote the propaganda script. Do you remember what Marsh told you to win you over? Blackguard is made up of ten wealthy humanitarians from around the world, blah, blah, blah. Sean, you're going to have to excuse me. I've also have had enough of this for now. You're the only one I've been able to talk about it, but now I'm beginning to feel sick to my stomach. I'm exhausted."

"Yeah, I know, me too. One more question. You mean to say that you gave up all that wealth and power and risked your life so you can be with Michael and me?"

"Absolutely. I don't care about the money if I'm not happy. You should know that about me by now."

"Believe me, I do know, I just wanted to hear it from your lips."

"Sean, you've put off reading the 1978 Red Book for far too long. You have to be fully aware of what we're up against. It's an edited transcript and covers the week I was there. To begin, you only need to read the opening remarks. It's basically a summary of Agenda One. But for now, we need to take a break. No more for today."

"Good, how about some wine? I purchased a couple of bottles of your favorite Merlot from the new wine store in town. What do you say we retire to our room and uncork them?"

"*Merci mon amour*, and yes, Merlot sounds wonderful. I need to get out of this bad mood, get comfortable, and be close to you."

Camille could have been a fashion model who walked on the runways of Paris. No one would have ever suspected she belonged to the most notorious terrorist group that has ever existed. And yet, destiny brought her to me as we sat at the table and she described the life she once led. To this day, I have no idea how she ever came out of that family. She also confirmed a feeling that I and many others have felt for years. Something that can't quite be put into words. Like an invisible puppet master that uses their media outlets to subliminally control us and our thoughts from behind the scenes. It was after that conversation that

I knew it was not my imagination. *Invisibilia Manus* is real and is out to destroy us to guarantee their ultimate goal—to control the entire world and assure their own personal survival.

Invisibilia Manus
200th Annual Assembly
August 13, 1978

Sunday Morning Agenda

Greta Stadtholder (Maastricht, Netherlands)
James W. Stuart (Providence, Rhode Island)
Camille-Gabriella Martel (Carcassonne, France)
Johanne Wilhelm (Frankfurt, Germany)
Mikhail Romanov (St. Petersburg, Russia
Kadir Seljuk (Istanbul, Turkey)
Tobias Habsburg (Vienna, Austria)
Ramanan Mughal (Maharashtra, India)
Mahmud Sufavi (Gachsaran, Iran)
Zhang Wei Qing (Shanghai, China)

Introduction
9 a.m. to 9:15 a.m

A Reflection	**Our Mission**
9:15 a.m.– 11 a.m.	11 a.m.– 11:45 a.m.

The Future	**Comments**
12 p.m.– 12:45 p.m.	12:45 p.m.– 1 p.m.

Zhang Wei Qing
(Conference Leader)

Welcome to the 200th annual meeting of this gathering here at Boldt Castle. Allow me to introduce myself. I'm Zhang Wei Qing. Last year, your families appointed my family to organize this year's assembly. I am honored that my father, the Chief Council for the Qing family from Shanghai, China, chose me to represent them. It's my job to convene each of the meetings, answer your questions, and keep us on schedule for the next seven days.

Before we begin, there are a few preliminaries. Each of you received an envelope with the schedule for this week. You will also see a new security medallion. Should you go up for some fresh air, you must wear it, and as a reminder, you may only go outside under the cover of darkness. Upon arriving last night, you entered through our new security gate. That gate, the elevator you descended on, and the doors in this facility will not open without your medallion. An Area C technician from Detroit has been here to install it for us since yesterday. You may have seen him last night going about his business. My chef, housekeeping staff, personal assistant, and physician are also here. We're very happy to have these loyal servants, who have been with our family for over twenty-five years. So, feel free to request anything you may need from them.

Now, as we do every year, we will reflect on our history. For our first presenter, allow me to introduce James W. Stuart of the distinguished Stuart family from Providence, Rhode Island. He has prepared this year's reflection, and even though it will be brief, I can assure you his words will be an inspiration. Mr. Stuart, please.

The Reflection
James W. Stuart
Providence, Rhode Island

Ladies and gentlemen, I can't even begin to tell you how honored I am to be here. I have come to learn how fortunate we are to meet in this facility. World War I forced our families to move from their previous stronghold in Belgium, where these assemblies had been held since our founding in 1778. This location was selected in 1918, and Invisibilia Manus has met here ever since. Now, in keeping with our tradition and out of respect for our heritage, it's my pleasure to reflect on the legacy our families have passed down to us.

I see several younger faces with us today, and some of you may be here for the first time. I'm sure you know your world history, but regardless, each year we reflect on the past to remind us how it relates to our future.

Invisibilia Manus is the collective that unites our ten families. Our ancestors were at one time the royal families that ruled China, Russia, Persia, India, and Europe. In fact, several of our families trace their bloodlines to well before 1000 AD. But over time, various political factions from all over the world began to sow the discord that brought about revolutions. In 1778, our forefathers convened a council in Salzburg, Austria. They were wise enough to realize the American Revolution and Napoleon signaled the beginning of the end for their world order. They correctly predicted that over time they would be replaced by various political experiments. As their power and influence waned, our forefathers united under the supreme instinct—SURVIVAL! They were resolute not to allow the power and wealth they once held to be thrown into the trash heap of history, and thus they founded

Invisibilia Manus.

Of course, they were correct, and as history has proven, these governments lacked the wisdom and foresight needed to maintain peace. As a result, they led us into the disastrous Napoleonic wars and into World War I. Then, twenty years later, in 1939, Hitler thrust into World War II. Several years after the Nazi invasions began in Europe, Japan attacked the United States at Pearl Harbor in 1941. However, as Japan later admitted, its decision to attack the American naval force awoke the sleeping giant with disastrous consequences to follow.

Commencing with the invasion at Normandy, the Allied forces defeated Germany in 1944. The United States then ended the Pacific War with Japan in 1945 with the detonation of the first atomic bombs they dropped on Hiroshima and Nagasaki. These game-changing weapons ushered in the nuclear age, followed by the Cold War between the Communist Soviet Union and the United States. It was this conflict that came dreadfully close to a nuclear holocaust during the Cuban Missile Crisis.

The resulting fear and paranoia have encouraged these two superpowers to ramp up production of thousands of ever more powerful atomic weapons and intercontinental ballistic missile systems in an arms race which critics call MAD—mutual assured destruction. This terrifying war game is a military strategy in which the full-scale use of nuclear weapons, if employed by either side, will cause the total annihilation of both. Whichever country initiates a first strike will trigger an equal or greater response from their opponent, and thus their own demise. At the same time, neither side can disengage from this standoff without the threat of a first strike from the other. This insanity continues to this day.

In 1965, the United States foolishly entered the Vietnam War with the intent to halt the advance of communism and Cold War threats. Only now, thirteen years later, is this war ending. However, Washington and the U.S. military have failed in their mission. The grave and futile incursions by inept politicians and misguided military advisors must end at the risk of destroying our families in a nuclear holocaust.

These reckless governing schemes replaced the authority our great ruling families once held and are now on the brink of destroying us. World peace is not possible, and it is foolish for anyone to think it is. Three primary power structures dominate world politics: the 'militarists' of the communist regimes, the 'religionists' of the Middle East, and the 'monetarists' of the West and Europe.

The insatiable Western governments, what Eisenhower called the military-industrial complex, are empowered by greedy politicians, their lawyers, and their political action committees. These PACs influence political agendas, usually for their own selfish and greedy benefit. They pool contributions from members and then donate the money to political campaigns for or against candidates and legislation that will personally benefit their reelection campaigns. Interestingly, there is no accounting system or watchdog organizations to track these multi-million-dollar funds. Once these politicians have acquired their personal golden parachutes, campaign promises are forgotten. Little, if anything ever gets done, and nothing more is promised until the next campaign cycle, when the same promises are made, over and over and over again.

These political schemes are entirely at odds with one another, and it's a mistake for anyone to think anything could lead to lasting world peace as long as these politicians stay in power.

They must be abolished forever!

In fact, there are no liberal democracies, strong-man dictatorships, philosophies of communism, socialism, or totalitarianism that have been able to end political, economic, ethnic, cultural, or religious conflicts. And this is exactly the reason why we are here this week. As the week progresses, you will see how history dictates what we must do as we move forward to the future.

Our next speaker today is Greta Stadtholder. She will outline the purpose of this year's assembly, namely Agenda One. Once we put it in place, instead of us, these failed political systems will be thrown into the trash heap of history. In their place, we will create a new world alliance without borders or walls, and with one central currency. Under our control, wars between nations as well as regional wars will be contained, and nuclear weapons of all kinds will be destroyed. No more international competition that creates artificial shortages and price manipulations. And, of course, we will once again reign over the world, but with three billion less people. My friends, we gather this week as a collective to outline Agenda One, which will guarantee the future of Invisibilia Manus. To do so, it will require us to build our one world society from the ground up, and we will do so with the power and wealth our forefathers bestowed on us. So, without further ado, I hand the next segment of this morning's presentation over to Greta Stadtholder, our representative of the Stadtholder family from Maastricht. This morning, Greta will discuss how, why, and when we will implement Agenda One. Thank you, everyone, for being so attentive.

Agenda One
Greta Stadtholder
Maastricht, Netherlands

James, thank you so much for this year's reflection. As always, when we look back at our history, it puts these annual assemblies in the proper perspective so we can bring about the world we have long dreamed of. So, let's get started. Our founding fathers established Invisibilia Manus two hundred years ago this year. As planned, they passed the torch to us, and by God, I joyfully take on the responsibility of continuing their legacy, as I'm sure you all do. But what is the reason we are here this week? We have gathered at this year's assembly for one primary purpose—to outline Agenda One and assure the survival of our families. But you may ask, survival from what? It's not only from inept and dangerous governments and militaries but also global overpopulation density. This chart will make my point clear.

—

World Population Statistics

Dawn of human history	(100,000 years) 1 billion
1800 to present (1978)	(178 years) 4 billion
1978 to 2020 (projected)	(42 years) 7 billion
2020 to 2050 (projected)	(30 years) 11 billion

—

Looking back to when Invisibilia Manus was founded, the world population has grown from one billion to four billion in just 178 years. As you can see, it is projected to grow to eleven billion by 2050. Simply put, the planet cannot sustain this kind of population density without severe consequences, with aftermaths we can't even imagine. If left to continue, we won't survive. World leaders are not dealing with these numbers. They are only interested in their own personal, short-sighted agendas. The communist regimes of China and Russia, with their massive populations, are the worst offenders. They have buried their heads in the sand and are far more interested in plotting world conquest. We see these ineffective bureaucracies come and go with each generation, along with their own political and economic programs. Paradoxically, we face two survival problems. The indiscriminate annihilation from a nuclear holocaust and the opposite problem: unrestrained overpopulation growth.

Before I detail our ambitious goal, I want to mention communications. Each of our ten families will have a separate and distinct role to play in bringing about Agenda One. Therefore, we will need a faster, more precise, and safer method to communicate with one another. Currently, several private companies are reconfiguring a new communication tool for commercial use. It was first developed by the U.S. Department of Defense in the late 1960s, something they call the 'internet.'

When this new technology is available, it will be used in the public domain. The challenge we face is that communications between each of our families could easily be breached by anyone with even minimal computer skills. Four years ago, we gave our Technology Division in Detroit the order to design and build a private 'intranet' exclusively for our own use and separate from the worldwide web. Julian Marsh just told me they have completed the design, and they will soon provide each of us with this new technology. Our distinguished member, Johanne Wilhelm from Frankfurt, will explain this amazing tool in far greater detail later in the week.

Once we are able to effectively communicate with each other, the question is, where do we start? The answer is that we will start by chopping off the head of the snake—America.

As a side note, many of you are not yet aware of our restructured information division or, as I like to call it, the disinformation division. They will place specially selected and trained educators in high schools, colleges, and universities throughout America. We have not yet ironed out the details, but when complete, it will be a crucial component to the dumbing down process of the gullible, apathetic American public.

To begin, we must first weaken their will and reeducate, or, as I like to call it, 'socially engineer' the rebellious American youth. It will be carried out by our alliance of political and social activists, psychology organizations, educational institutions, legal entities, and, most importantly, our media companies. We will create chaos where order now exists. We will divide America where unity now exists. Historians will have no idea how the decline of America happened so unexpectedly, so dramatically, and so quickly.

So, how will we achieve this seemingly impossible agenda? It's actually quite simple. We will give the self-indulgent, narcissistic Americans exactly what they want. And what is that? Instant gratification! *'If it feels good, you are entitled to do exactly as you please.'* Allow me to introduce our four-stage program. The first stage is to transform the hearts and minds of the impressionable American youth. To lay the foundation for this discussion, we need to look back to the 1960s when the counterculture movement first began. After living through the Depression and World War II, parents around the country had the desire to give their children everything they never had.

Ironically, it was these over-indulged offspring who made up this movement. These spoiled, rebellious youth are the ideal pawns to serve as the model for our first stage. Their rallying cry of sex, drugs, and rock 'n' roll perfectly represents America's self-inflicted moral decline.

The second stage is to abolish God from government, a process that our politicians and lawyers have already begun. Our educators in the public schools and universities are teaching these impressionable students that organized religion is a scheme used to control them. Modern religion grew out of the tribal rituals of ancient cultures that created gods to protect them from the ravages of nature: droughts, famines, earthquakes, floods, and so forth. Powerful priests and shamans created this illusion, especially when the power they had to control was at stake. They would then make a public spectacle of human and animal sacrifice to appease the gods. But in reality, these rituals were designed to literally terrify their subjects into submission. Today, many of the modern religions apply a more subtle approach to guilt and the fear of hell to terrify their followers and then relieve them of their money.

Many students were raised in religious homes. To help shift their beliefs, they will learn that organized religion is a profit-driven business that uses fear and guilt to coax contributions from their families. Money is the ticket to gain redemption for their sins, and tithing is a way to earn their entrance into heaven.

This generation of students will come to view both religion and patriotism as manipulations used to control and keep them from getting what they want, when they want it. Moral behavior, discipline, and common sense will give way to narcissistic feelings and emotions. *'If it feels good, do as you please.'* Science will be their new god and show them the path to enlightenment. God will have no place in a modern, progressive society.

For the third stage, America's naïve youth will be taught to believe such things as family, patriotism, traditions, and marriage are old-fashioned, outdated customs. They may have served a purpose in the past, but in their brave new world, these archaic practices will do nothing but impede their progress. They will be taught to value their feelings and emotions over facts and reasoned argument, friends and community over family, personal independence over marriage and children, international equality over national patriotism.

The fourth stage of Agenda One is the most important of all. It will be the first order of business for our Disinformation Division. The self-indulgent, narcissistic behavior of this generation is the key to our endeavor, what ancient societies called the 'Seven Deadly Sins.' And deadly they are because they are the behaviors that ultimately destroy the body, the mind, and the spirit of the individual. They lead to addictions, physical and mental illness, hatred, depression, loneliness, and even suicide. Each one of these deadly indulgences has its root in the human desire for more and more. Idleness and apathy will then naturally follow and was the cause for the demise of many civilizations of the past. Once in place, moral judgments between right and wrong will no longer exist. We will promote sins or indulgences as emotionally positive states of mind. In effect, what was once considered vices will be now be considered strengths.

Pride will be 'Self-Admiration'
Greed will be 'Show Me the Money'

Envy will be 'I'm Entitled'
Lust will be 'Free Sex'
Gluttony will be 'Indulge Yourself'
Sloth will be 'Live for Today'
Wrath will be 'Hate Your Victimizer'

I am amused that everyone will believe, in one way or another, that they are victims or are being victimized. Whites are racist. Men oppress women. Straights detest gays. The 'haves' exploit the 'have nots.' The educated exploit the ignorant. The youth mock the elderly.

We will eliminate the middle class so that there are only the rich and the poor. We will then tax the rich out of existence to pay for the poor. When we reach this point, it will be easy to take control of the food supply, the health system, and take away their guns. Ultimately, we will bring about one class where everyone is under our total control.

I can assure you, this list is just the beginning of what to expect over the next seven days as the plan to fully implement Agenda One becomes clearer. We'll outline the individual role each family will have to realize the full impact of our four-stage program until we're ready to unleash the full power of Invisibilia Manus. Then, when Americans are weakened beyond the point of no return, it will then be time for 'The Purge,' which we will go into much further detail this afternoon.

Thank you for being so attentive this morning.

Zhang Wei Qing

I must give credit to our two speakers this morning. I never imagined how powerful the opening to this year's Assembly would be. Once again, Greta, thank you so much for such a well-defined summary of how we will implement

Agenda One and our New World Order. But before we adjourn this segment, let us take the time to introduce each other and open the discussion for questions and comments. For those of you who are not familiar with our protocol, I ask you to first stand, present your left palm facing forward toward me, and then introduce yourself.

I am Ramanan Mughal from Maharashtra, India. I would like to know what the next step after we leave here next week?

Each of you will be given a transcript of these meetings. As a representative for your family, it's incumbent upon you to take them to your councils so they can ask any questions, concerns, or thoughts they may have. When all ten families have completed this process, the transcript will be compiled and published in the 1978 Red Book Edition. For this reason, it's imperative that each family adheres to complete transparency so everyone is given a unified plan—one the collective can all agree on.

Okay, I'm getting a heads up. We will soon take a short break. We have time for one or two more questions.

Bonjour à tous. I am Camille-Gabriella Martel from Carcassonne, France. I am quite sure everyone here today is well acquainted with my family. As you are well aware, we are responsible for all employee background checks. We recruit, coach, and prepare proxies for our international associations. We also train and send our twenty-five assets on missions as they are needed. In addition, we direct all covert operations and acquire information on our targets. To maintain complete anonymity, we go to extraordinary measures in our selection process. My question is, how will this new 'intranet' technology benefit us?

Again, that is a great question, Ms. Martel,
but since I am not technically inclined, I am
unable to give you a precise answer. You will
learn more later in the week.

[adjourn]

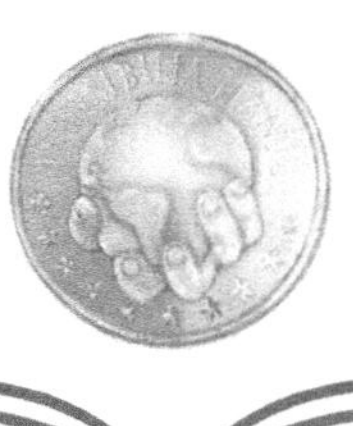

CHAPTER 20

CAMILLE'S INSIGHTS

THE TWENTY-SECOND STEP

February 15, 2001

I felt robbed for working all those years for Blackguard while I suffered unbearable loneliness. Needless to say, having Camille back in my life and spending quality time with Michael took precedence over everything else. However, five years had passed since we were reunited, yet her family was still a huge problem. The Invisible Hand also continued to spread its influence around the world. We were determined to stop them but had no idea where to start. We needed a plan and decided whatever we came up with would center on our life passions. We needed to prove the Genesis correlation, and she desperately needed to somehow expose her family to the authorities.

There had to be a common denominator and we were determined to find it.

"Sean, I've given a lot of thought to formulating our plan. I hope you realize we face an enormous risk. We really need to think this whole thing through very carefully."

"Yeah, I know, but we're running out of time."

"I'm at a dead end with my family, so I would like to focus on the correlation today. I know you're stuck on the Fourth Day. The thing is, I've read the remaining Genesis verses and to quote something you Americans say, you may be biting off more than you can chew."

"Believe me, sweetheart, I'm worried about it too, but I have come to a conclusion. I believe its power lies in numbers."

"What in the world do you mean by that?"

"Well, the way I see it, once people come to realize their lives and their loved ones' lives are at stake, instead of division, they will be motivated to unite around one common cause—survival. It's the same motivation that led the world to defeat the Nazis and Japan. You said it yourself: Survival is what unites your family with the other nine families."

"It's one thing to unite ten families, but how in the world do you plan on motivating six billion people to unite under something they have no idea about?"

"Right now, I have no freakin' idea."

"And there's another thing, Sean. Let me remind you, we need material evidence if we stand any chance at all."

"Material evidence?"

"The 1978 Red Book, your journals, and the Genesis Correlation are not enough. We have no choice—we have to go to Shanghai, get our hands on the Qing virus, and bring it to CIDEC."

"You've got to be kidding. I've been there, and I'm telling you, there's no damn way to get into the Qing tower."

"Sean, you have to stop being so negative. You've been there; you must know how that building is laid out and a way to get in."

"I'm telling you again, you're asking for the impossible. For one thing, the lab suites may not even be on the same floor where they used to be. I have no idea what the vials even look like or where they store them."

"You're probably right and it may not be possible, but I need to feel like we're making some headway. So, for now let's work on the correlation."

"Okay, here are the notes from my synopsis. You've already seen the first three creation days. But keep in mind, this correlation is extremely complex and it has taken years for me to get as far as I have. So, here's the Fourth Day."

After looking them over for a few minutes, she remarked, "My God, this is impressive work. You'll need to give me some time to think about it."

"Of course, take all the time you need. Here's the next verse, Genesis 1:14. Let me show you what I'm talking about.

"*And God said: 'Let there be lights in the firmament of the heaven to divide the day from the night; and let them be for signs, and for seasons, and for days and years.'*

"This verse seems odd to me, since it doesn't depict a creation event. Signs, seasons, days, and years are not creation events. I think you'll agree, they're human concepts of time."

"*Oui,* and my initial thought is perhaps the author did not mean to describe a creation event."

"Really? I don't understand. After all, this is the story of the creation."

"Exactly, Sean. Genesis 1 is a story and not just a list of events. It could be that at this point, the author diverged from the creation narrative to show the Hebrews the purpose of the *'lights'* in their daily lives. It would be similar to how he wrote about the food plants to illustrate to them how their food came about."

"Okay, I'm intrigued. I'm listening."

"Look carefully, and you'll notice the author does not say that God *'created'* the lights. Instead, the phrase reads, *'let them be for,'* which sounds to me like their purpose. I'm certainly not a linguistic expert, but it does seem logical that when ancient people observed the rising and setting of the Sun during the course of the year, they devised calendars to identify days and years. They made charts and studied the stars as *signs* to guide them on their travels. And when they tracked the summer and winter solstices, they recorded the seasons for the most favorable times to plant and then harvest their crops."

Amazed by her insight, I admitted, "I can't believe that I never considered that, but it makes perfect sense. Thank you, sweetheart, I think you nailed it. That's the rationale I'm using in my synopsis."

Anxious to be of more help, she asked, "*C'est marrant,* do you have more to show me?"

"Oh yeah. The next five verses seem to conflict with the first verse, *'In the beginning God created the heaven and the earth.'* Here, I'll show you what I mean.

"*'And let them be for lights in the firmament of the heaven to give light upon the earth.' And it was so. And God made the two great lights: the greater light to rule the day, and the lesser light to rule the night; and the stars. And God set them in the firmament of the heaven to give light upon the earth, and to rule over the day and over the night, and to divide the light from the darkness; and God saw that it was good. And there was evening and there was morning, a fourth day.'*

"So, here's how I see it. The first verse of Genesis reveals that on Day 1, God created the heaven. The Hebrews defined *heaven* as the visible heavens, the sky, and the realm of the stars. As you are probably aware, many religions teach that the Fourth Day is when God created the Sun, the Moon and the stars. However, this verse clearly does not say that."

"I'm sorry, Sean, but I still don't quite understand."

"Well, instead, it says God *made* them *to rule over,* again referring to their purpose. In this case, the author defined the purpose of the two great lights: *'to rule over,' 'to give light,' 'to divide the light from the darkness.'*"

"I see your point, but it seems odd he would use the term, *'to rule over.'* Again, that term seems to be the human concept of governing and not a creation event."

"Yeah, that's true. But the Bible is very clear that the Hebrews worshipped many gods. They believed, as a lot of the ancient cultures did, both the sun and moon were living gods who ruled over and protected them. They even gave them names. *Baal* was their sun god, and *Yarikh*, their moon god. But what I don't understand is why the author would write about them on the Fourth Day at this stage of the sequence. Up to this point all the verses are chronologically accurate."

"*Oui*, that's a good question, and again I see your point. Give me some time to think it. Hopefully, between the two of us, we'll figure it out."

Two months later

Camille was definitely a big help. She saw things from a completely different perspective than I did. Evidently, being a science nerd prevented me from seeing the obvious. Her intuition, combined with the way she could simplify complex ideas, definitely worked to our advantage.

"Sean, I think I may have figured out these Fourth Day verses. But first, go back one day and consider what event took place on the Third Day."

"Sure. that's when the dry land appeared, and when the earth brought forth the plants."

"So, besides water, what do plants and trees need in order to grow?"

"Well, they need sunlight."

"Exactly. You point out in your synopsis that the atmosphere developed through three stages, and then culminated with the life supporting third atmosphere. So, let's think about these verses from that perspective."

"Okay, but I don't see where you're going with this. For one thing, scientists are not certain as to the actual clarity of the Earth's evolving atmosphere, since gasses don't leave any evidence behind. They presume the first atmosphere was impenetrable and dark, the second atmosphere was opaque and overcast, and the third atmosphere was the beginning of our clear atmosphere."

"Sean, I'm pretty sure I see the correlation. Tell me what you think about this possibility.

"First, these verses list the lights in the order of their magnitude as seen from the surface of Earth: *'the greater light,' 'the lesser light,'* and *'the stars.'*

"Second, these celestial bodies, especially the stars, can only be seen with a clear sky.

"Third, these observations support the notion that the author was well aware of this fact, since he wrote these verses in the correct sequence for the evolution of the Earth's clear, life-sustaining third atmosphere."

Stunned by her perception, I said, "You're a freakin' genius."

"Well, I don't know about that, but I really do love your research. Even so, I hope you realize that if we actually correlate all six days, it will upset both the very theories and beliefs of science and religion. A lot of egos will be on the line. Their careers will all be at stake. They will do everything they can to undermine and discredit you."

"Yes, I know. But far more people, probably everyone, will be more than upset when they realize they will die from either an ecological catastrophe or Agenda One if those so-called experts don't start doing something about it now."

Synopsis
Genesis Correlation of the Fourth Day

Signs

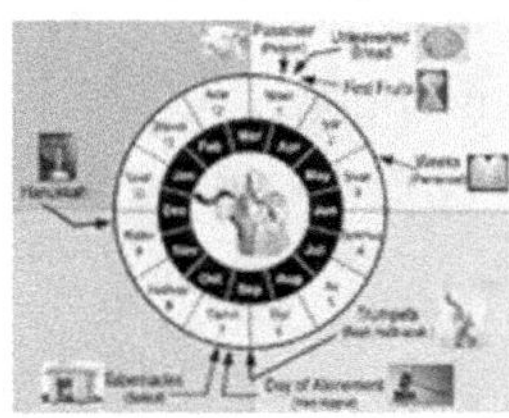

Seasons

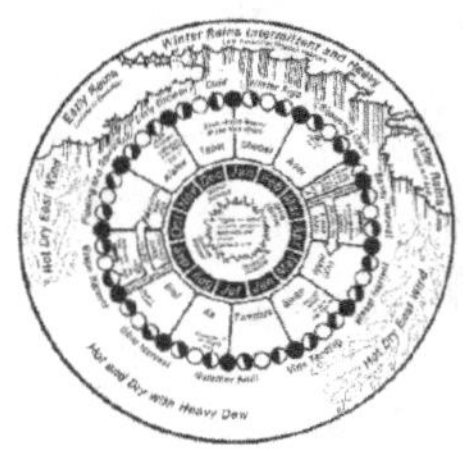

Days and Years (Calendar)

Genesis 1:14

*And God said: 'Let there be lights in the
firmament of the heaven to divide the day
from the night; and let them be for signs,
and for seasons, and for days and years;*

Genesis 1:15

and let them be for lights in the firmament of the heaven to give light upon the earth. And it was so.

The Third Atmosphere
Beginning 600 million years ago

Genesis 1:16

And God made the two great lights: the greater light to rule the day, and the lesser light to rule the night; and the stars.

Genesis 1:17

And God set them in the firmament of the heaven to give light upon the earth,

Genesis 1:18

and *to rule over the day and over the night, and to divide the light from the darkness; and God saw that it was good.*

Genesis 1:19

And there was evening and there was morning, a fourth day.

"Sean, I'm not sure I'll be of much help for the rest of the verses. I've studied them, and I can see why you gave up. And there's another thing. You realize people will want to know how the Hebrew author could have possibly known the science to write Genesis. So, I've been thinking, we need to find other historical evidence, if it even exists. We have to do some detective work, and at least give it a shot."

"Thanks for reminding me. I have some photos a college professor of mine gave me years ago. I think they might qualify as historical evidence. They're pictures of a Latin manuscript written in the 1600s that he saw at a rare book store in Ann Arbor. It describes an addendum that was added to a document called the Codex Sinaiticus written in the second half of the fourth century. The Vatican has kept the Codex and the addendum locked away for fear they would have undermined their teachings. It seems to say the Creation Story predates the Hebrews. There's also a passage in the Latin manuscript that reads, '*Caelum et terram naturaliter sunt facta.*'"

"That's unbelievable, Sean, that phrase literally translates to, '*heavens and earth naturally made.*'"

"My God, how in the world did you know that?"

"My naïve Sean, I know five languages, including Latin. I do realize all of this is important, but we have more pressing problems, like getting the virus out of China. And don't forget about our Michael. We still have a son who needs our attention. There's still a lot to do and time is running out." Suddenly getting in touch with her feelings, she cried out, "My God, all of this feels too overwhelming. These problems swirl around in my head all at the same time."

"Camille, trust me, I understand. But we made some great progress today, so if you can stay focused for a while longer, we might be able to get some of these verses behind us."

"I don't know. Don't expect a lot."

"You'll be interested to know; I've made some headway for the Fifth Day. Here, let me show you what I found."

"Okay, but like I said, these verses seem to be far more complex than the others."

"Yes, I know. At least let's give it a try. Here's the next verse in Genesis 1:20.

"*'And God said: 'Let the waters swarm with swarms of living creatures, and let fowl fly above the earth in the open firmament of heaven.'*

"The author wrote about fish and birds in the same verse. He then mentions '*winged fowl*' again in the next verse, Genesis 1:21.

"*'And God created the great sea-monsters, and every living creature that creepeth, wherewith the waters swarmed, after its kind, and every winged fowl after its kind; and God saw that it was good.'*

"At first, I couldn't figure out why he would mention *fowl* twice, that is until I realized he was conveying two different ideas. I believe verse 20 is simply a prelude to the next five verses, where he lists the five different classes of vertebrates. He simply pointed out that animals exist everywhere, from '*the waters*' up to '*the open firmament of the heaven.*'"

"What in the world do you mean by classes of vertebrates? The Hebrews didn't have biological classifications for animals back then."

"Maybe not with our words, but they did classify them with words they were familiar with. I'll get to that later, but first, I need to continue with my line of thought. I couldn't figure out what '*swarms*' meant. So, I looked it up in Strong's Concordance, and it can mean: insects, swarming things, teeming life, or teeming things. Since insects don't live underwater, it seems logical the author meant 'teeming life' in the waters. And then it hit me. Based on the fossil record, guess what happened next?"

"Okay, Mr. Scientist, I can't wait to hear what that was."

"Well, something happened about 540 million years ago that baffles evolutionary biologists. An evolution event took place quite suddenly, what they call the Cambrian explosion. They named it that because of the relatively short period of time—only 20 million years—over which the diversity of animal life first *exploded* all over the planet. The oceans suddenly swarmed with tens of thousands of exotic, complex animal species. It was a virtual menagerie of now extinct creatures and was the beginning point for the incredible diversity of animal life that would follow. And that includes the ancestors of the animal species that are alive today. Before the appearance of these strange Cambrian life forms, the fossil record is devoid of the Precambrian transitional fossils Darwin predicted should be there, but they are not."

"What do you mean by a relatively short period of time?"

"Okay, I'll put it in perspective for you. I made an analogy for the entire history of the universe, and the Earth, to a 24-hour clock."

- ▶ The Big Bang occurred 13.80 billion years ago. (12 a.m.)
- ▶ The Earth formed sixteen hours later, 4.54 billion years ago. (4:03 p.m.)
- ▶ The first microorganisms appeared in the ocean 4.00 billion years ago. (5 p.m.)
- ▶ From 5 p.m. to 11:03 p.m., not much happened, only simple Precambrian life forms.
- ▶ Then, in just 59 seconds, from 540 to 520 million years ago, at 11:03 p.m., the main pulse of the Cambrian explosion occurred, yielding the most concentrated explosion of complex life in earth's history

"That's amazing. So, you think, *'Let the waters swarm with swarms of living creatures,'* refers to the Cambrian explosion?"

"I sure do."

"You know what, Sean? The author may have also provided the answer for what caused the Cambrian explosion to occur."

Puzzled by her sudden insight, I questioned, "Really, what do you mean?"

"Well, you told me scientists don't know the actual clarity of the atmosphere during Earth's early history because the air didn't leave any physical evidence behind. However, these verses could explain what caused the Cambrian explosion to occur when it did."

"Okay, genius, I can't wait to hear this."

"The Cambrian explosion may have only been possible when the Earth's dark ages ended. That's when the third atmosphere was finally clear enough to allow direct sunlight to reach Earth's surface. It may just be possible that it happened because, after billions of years, the Earth was finally exposed to direct sunlight. A bright sun, instead of a dim, overcast sky, would have provided an abundance of plant life for this early Precambrian animal life to feed on and drive their evolution. It may be just that simple."

I was both thrilled and, at the same time, intimidated. "I can't believe it, but it's possible that you may be right. Camille, please tell me how in the world do you see these things? Biologists and geologists have wrestled with this mystery for decades, and they're still unable to come up with a theory that makes sense. Here, in virtually no time at all, you come up with a completely plausible explanation for the Cambrian explosion. I really don't know how you do it, Camille."

"Sean, I know you're tired, because I know I am. I really need to call it quits for today."

Camille's insights proved invaluable and I could not have gone on without her. The adage 'two heads are better than one,' in our case, was definitely true. She now fully recognized the legitimacy of my research. Even so, with everything we were dealing with, it left me feeling as if it was all a big waste of time.

Synopsis
Genesis Correlation of the Fifth Day

The Cambrian Explosion
540 million years ago

Genesis 1:20
And God said: 'Let the waters swarm
with swarms of living creatures,

and let fowl fly above the earth in the
open firmament of heaven.

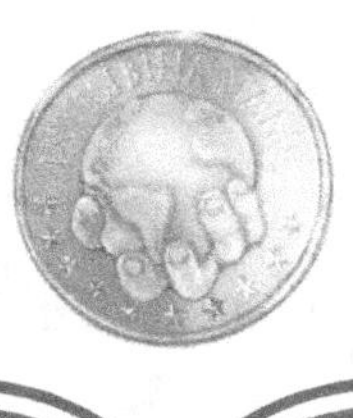

CHAPTER 21

THE SUMERIANS

THE TWENTY-THIRD STEP

May 13, 2001
Zurich, Switzerland

"Sean, what's this? I was cleaning out the den when I came across this box. I found it under a pile of papers in the lower desk drawer."

"Oh wow, I forgot all about that. When I was married to Marlene, the pastor at our church gave it to me. Go ahead, open it up. I have no idea what those things are inside. He purchased them in Jerusalem and thought they would make an interesting addition to his collection of ancient artifacts."

"*Très intéressant,* I've seen something like them when I went on a class trip to a museum in Berlin. Here, let me take another look. Have you ever taken a close look at what's etched on them? They appear to be figures of two men standing, and a seated figure at a table or an altar. It's hard to say."

"You know what, sweetheart? I made a promise to Pastor Jesse. So, if you're interested, I could use a vacation. How about you?"

"*Mon amour*, that's a great idea. I'll book the flight."

"Camille, I have to tell you, I'm really ready for a romantic getaway with you, but I'm not sure if Berlin is the place to go. Paris sounds much better to me. But yeah, I know what you're going to say—the museum is in Berlin."

So, we booked our flight, departed from Zurich about a week later, and landed at the Berlin Schönefeld Regional Airport. After arriving at our hotel, we took a taxi to Bodestraße 1–3. The Vorderasiatische is an archaeological gallery located in the lower level of the Pergamon Museum. It houses the world's largest collection of ancient Southwest Asian artifacts.

May 28, 2001
Vorderasiatische Museum
Berlin, Germany

"We need to find the curator's office. Let me do the talking. Germans are friendlier to a French female."

"Hey, wait a minute. Maybe the curator is female and prefers American men."

"Ha, ha, yeah right."

"Camille, here, this way. The office is over there. I see someone inside.

In her soft, charming French accent, she interrupted, "*Bonjour Monsieur,* may we have a moment of your time?"

Looking up from his desk, the man eagerly replied, "Oh yes, Fräulein, what can I do for you?"

"*Oui,* I'm Camille and this is my friend, Sean. I'm sure you are very busy, but if you would be so kind, we need your help to identify what's in this box."

"Okay, I'd be happy to take a look at it for you. Please, have a seat." After a few moments, the curator commented, "Hmm, these are very interesting. Where did you get them?"

"They were a gift from a friend of mine. He purchased them in Jerusalem, but we have no idea what they are."

Stroking his chin, he studied them for a while. "These are Sumerian cylinder seals. Most of the seals people bring here are forgeries, but at first glance, these look authentic. They are old, and probably date from well before 2500 BCE."

"*Monsieur,* I came here when I was a teenager, and remember seeing something similar to them."

"I'm sure you did, Fräulein. If you have a few minutes, follow me down to our Sumerian exhibit. We are quite proud of it. There is something I want to show you. Oh my, please forgive me. Allow me to introduce myself. I'm Wilhelm, Wilhelm Schneider."

"Camille and I really thank you for your time, but I'm sorry to say I don't know much about ancient history. So please, who were the Sumerians?"

"Of course, allow me to give you a short history lesson. A thousand years before the great Egyptian dynasties ruled, a mysterious but sophisticated civilization existed east of the Mediterranean. It was located in the southern marshlands near the Persian Gulf, along the valleys of the Euphrates and Tigris Rivers. Today, you know this area as southern Iraq and Kuwait. Eventually, this land came to be known as Sumer and its inhabitants were called Sumerians. The roots of this culture date back to 5500 BCE when the early settlers lived in villages, but archaeologists really don't know where they originally came from."

"*Monsieur,* what do you mean by sophisticated?"

"Well, these people laid the foundation for an economy and social order that was, how should I say it, completely opposite from their simple village lives. Seemingly out of nowhere, the Sumerians built a highly advanced and thriving culture, the first complex society known to exist. They established flourishing cities when everyone else was still living in villages and tribal settlements. We suspect the key to their development was the Sumerian language."

"I don't understand. How could a language account for their sudden development?"

"Camille, that's a great question. It's like the chicken or egg dilemma, so we don't really know for sure. Unfortunately, the lack of archaeological evidence ever since the first Sumerian artifact was discovered limits our knowledge of them. However, we do know their language was the first-ever put to the written word and dates to around 3400 BC. Strangely, no dialects that we know of preceded it. It also bears no similarity to any of the Mediterranean languages that followed: Assyrian, Canaanite, Egyptian, Minoan, Hebrew, Greek, Persian, or Phoenician. The Sumerian language seems to stand alone."

Enthusiastic about his knowledge of ancient history, Camille interrupted, "Okay, Mr. Schneider, now you have my attention."

"Oh, that's not all. The Sumerians were also the first to make objects from bronze, and in effect, launched the Bronze Age. They developed the first known system of law which they used to govern their most populated city of Ur. They originated the study of mathematics and astronomy along with many of the other sciences. They also established the first method to tell time and developed an accurate calendar system."

Out of curiosity, I asked, "Are there any theories as to how they could have accomplished all of this?"

"Not really, Sean. Although, you may find it interesting to learn about the Sumerian gods who they called the Anunnaki."

"Why would I find them interesting? Ancient gods are simply myths."

"Well, maybe so, but in this case Anunnaki translates to, *'those who from heaven to earth came.'*"

"That's incredible. I've been studying the ancient Hebrew culture for over twenty years, and didn't know anything about the Sumerians until now. I'm embarrassed to say it, but they do appear to be other-worldly."

"Yes, and I know there are a lot of others who would agree with you. I need to show you something truly remarkable. The Sumerians' most puzzling accomplishment was their knowledge of the heavens. They seemed to have had an extraordinary understanding of the solar system 4,600 years before Galileo in 17th century Europe. Here, let me show you what I mean."

Minutes later, we stood at a Sumerian display case. "Here we are. This is what I want to show you. Take a look at the three circles."

He continued, "We have many Sumerian seals in our collection, but this one, VA 243, is the most famous. You are looking at an ancient seal that depicts what appears to be the Sun with thirteen bodies orbiting it."

"That's crazy. How is it possible they would have known about the planets?"

"We have some theories, but we don't know for sure."

"But Mr. Schneider, I thought there were eight planets, not thirteen."

"You are correct Sean, there are eight planets: Mercury, Venus, Earth, Mars, Jupiter, Saturn, Uranus, and Neptune. However, there are also five dwarf planets: Pluto, Ceres, Haumea, Makemake, and Eris. Thirteen orbiting bodies in all are depicted on this seal."

Pointing to the two smaller circles, Camille asked, "Monsieur Schneider, why are those two planets so far away from the others?"

"That's a good question, Camille. Most likely because of their vast distance from the sun, compared to the other bodies."

"This is all very interesting. What do you think the seal represents?"

"After comparing it to other seals, we have concluded that the two standing figures are Sumerian farmers. They are presenting their agricultural gifts to the seated figure, perhaps an Anunnaki god. However, I should point out not everyone agrees with this assessment. Some of my colleagues think the thirteen spheres are a mere coincidence. They believe this seal may have been used for agricultural purposes. They suggest the spheres may have had something to do with the timing for planting their crops. But these are all guesses. No one really knows for sure."

"It sure looks like it could be our sun with the planets orbiting it. The numbers certainly add up. What about our seals? They are cylindrical, and your VA 243 is flat."

"Ah, Fräulein, you are not looking at the actual seal, this is a clay impression. The actual seal is locked up. In order to see what's on your two seals, we'll need to roll them on some clay. I have some here in this drawer. I'm anxious to see what you have here."

"Interesting, I would have never thought about doing that."

Wilhelm Schneider offered an explanation. "Okay, let's give it a go."

"Let's see. This first seal shows three figures and they appear similar to VA 243—two farmers and an Anunnaki god. All three figures are facing a tree. Based on other similar symbols I have seen; it could represent the tree of life. The farmers seem to be holding agricultural goods and the god points to the heavens. Behind the god is an incense burner with smoke rising from it. Also, there is what appears to be a table or altar, with an arrangement of symbols on it," he explained.

"What in the world does that all mean?"

"I don't know for sure, but the farmers could represent the physical earth and the Anunnaki god the spiritual heaven, or the afterlife. Okay, let's look at the other seal.

"This one appears to show the same three figures, except all three figures face away from the tree. The farmers hands are empty, the Anunnaki god's hands lay in his lap and the incense burner is extinguished. Interestingly, the symbols are missing from the altar. Another difference is that the tree is without leaves and appears wilted and dead. I think I might know what they mean, Sean, but I can't make a professional determination yet. Would it be alright with you if I showed these seals to one of my colleagues?"

"Absolutely. We could use any help you can give us."

"Okay, I'll see if Josef Brandt is available. He's a linguist in the ancient languages. I'll be back shortly."

After Schneider left the room, I asked, "So, sweetheart, what do you think?

"I'm not sure what to think. Let's wait and see what this guy has to say."

Several minutes later, Schneider returned with Josef Brandt. "Josef, this is Camille and Sean, the two I was telling you about."

Extending his hand, he welcomed us, "I'm pleased to meet you. Wilhelm tells me you have brought us some seals that he finds intriguing. Let me see what you have here." Squinting at the seals through his loupe, Brandt commented, "Very interesting. These seals certainly look genuine, and they are old, likely made between 2800 to 2500 BCE. They may well predate most of the seals we have here in our exhibit. My God, Schneider, you didn't tell me these were paired seals."

Camille interrupted, "Okay, but what do you think they mean, Dr. Brandt?"

He answered, "I'm interested that only the first seal has an inscription on the altar. My initial interpretation is that it's a cuneiform symbol that reads, 'AMITU TIIT DAMIQ.' But I have no idea what the English translation is. For some reason the symbols are omitted on the second seal. I would need to spend more time with them. Does our limited analysis mean anything at all to you?"

Feeling like the two men could offer little help, I responded, "I don't know yet. Camille and I have spent a great amount of time and energy attempting to understand an ancient mystery. Can you think of anything else, anything at all that might help us? Perhaps you have other seals that could offer some clues."

"It may help if we knew what you're working on, but not right now. We must get back to work." Obviously under pressure, the two men bid us farewell. "Sean and Camille, it was a pleasure meeting both of you. I truly wish we could have been of more help. I would like to spend more time to learn about this mystery you talk about. By the way, if you are ever interested in parting with your seals, as curator of this museum, I have the authority to purchase them. We would make you a very generous offer."

Thirteen Days Later
June 10, 2001
Zurich, Switzerland

"You know what, sweetheart? That trip to Berlin inspired me. I really want to get this correlation completed. When we were gone, I gave it a lot of thought. I have something I want to show you and I promise it won't take long."

"*Oui*, by all means." More than enthusiastic, she smiled and said, "I'm interested in anything that you think might move things along."

"Okay, great! The next verse, verse 21, reads, '*And God created the great sea monsters.*'

"When I was in grade school, our teachers taught from the King James Bible. In that version, the phrase was translated to read, '*And God created great whales.*' I realized that if *whales* were an accurate translation, it would have destroyed my theory. Interestingly, out of the many translations that exist, the KJV is the only one where *whales* are written."

"I'm sorry, Sean, I don't understand."

"Alright, I'll put this as simply as I can. The first vertebrate animals were the fish. Then, the amphibians evolved from the fish, and the reptiles evolved from the amphibians. But then, it gets tricky because the fossil record seems to indicate reptiles divided into several groups during the age of the dinosaurs. Mainstream biologists theorize the dinosaurs split into two branches. The avian branch that evolved into birds, and the therapsid branch that evolved into mammals. The problem is, whales are mammals. Mammals did not evolve from fish. That means the KJV translation is out of sequence with the fossil record."

"I think I can see where you are going with this."

"I'm sure you can. If Genesis 1 is indeed scientifically accurate, then, there had to be an explanation. So, I went to Strong's Concordance and it turns out *sea monster* is the expression for 'leviathan' in Hebrew, which can mean sea dragon or sea serpent. There were few words in the Hebrew lexicon to describe the countless species of fish that exist. So, 'leviathan' was apparently the closest word they had to describe these early Cambrian fish-like creatures. That was a fundamental discovery, which put me back on track again."

"*Oui*, that makes sense, but then, what does this next phrase mean? '*And every living creature that creepeth, wherewith the waters swarmed.*'"

"The reason I ask is because jumping forward, verse 25 reads, '*Let the earth bring forth the living creature after its kind, cattle, and creeping thing.*'

"Have you figured out why the author repeats '*creeping things*' in this verse? It seems redundant."

"I thought so too, but if you notice, he makes a distinction between them. In verse 21, he wrote, '*every living creature that creepeth wherewith the waters swarm.*' A creeping creature from *the waters* is an apt description of amphibians. But in verse 25, he equates *creeping thing* with the earth: '*Let the earth bring forth … creeping things,*' which is an appropriate description for reptiles."

"But, Sean, that could apply to other animals that crawl. What about crabs, snails, insects, spiders, worms, and so forth?"

"Not so, because when I looked up '*creeping things*' and then compared it to other verses throughout the Bible, none of the authors ever refer to any of these lower life forms."

"Professor Sean, your observations are quite impressive."

"I have to tell you, sweetheart, I feel a little geeky right now. If there's something else you want to do, go ahead. I certainly will not be offended."

"No, no, no, I am fascinated."

Together, Camille and I were able to correlate the fish, birds, amphibians, reptiles, and mammals to the Genesis verses. The modern term for these animal groups did not exist when the author wrote about them. Instead, he used descriptive phrases that the Hebrews were familiar with, which included *cattle* as an ancient term for mammals.

Synopsis
Genesis Correlation of the Fifth Day

The Amphibians
370 million years ago

Genesis 1:21

*and every living creature that creepeth, wherewith
the waters swarmed, after its kind,*

Winged Foul (The Birds)
300-200 Million Years Ago

Genesis 1:21

*and every winged fowl after its kind;
and God saw that it was good.*

Genesis 1:22

*And God blessed them, saying: 'Be fruitful,
and multiply, and fill the waters in the seas,
and let fowl multiply in the earth.*

Genesis 1:23

And there was evening and there was morning, a fifth day.

"I think we've almost completed the correlation, except for the most troubling verse. But I've had it for today. What do you say, we give it a rest?"

"That's fine by me, Sean. I need you to show me what you're talking about. Sometimes, answers to problems come to me in the middle of the night."

"So, we've correlated each of the vertebrates, except there's another animal mentioned in verses 24 and 25 that I have absolutely no explanation for.

"*'And God said: Let the earth bring forth the living creature after its kind, cattle, and creeping thing, and beast of the earth after its kind. And God made the beast of the earth after its kind.'*

"As hard as I try, I cannot fathom what *the beast of the earth* means. The thing is, we've come this far, and I won't give up now."

"Sean, we can't give up—our mission is far too important. I don't know, but perhaps, these verses refer to an animal that is now extinct, for instance, the dinosaurs."

"I sure wish I shared your optimism, but I'm tired. I've already combed through my notes at least five or six times. I tried to find other Biblical passages that might give me a clue. I've even searched through every reference book I could think of, but *'the beast of the earth'* doesn't show up anywhere else in the entire Bible."

It had been five years since Camille and I moved to Zurich. Other than the fact that I couldn't stop thinking about Lila and wished I could have given her some closure, that period of my life was the first time I did not feel under some kind of stress. I truly enjoyed my freedom with her, liberated from Blackguard. We were having the time of our lives as we traveled throughout Europe, experiencing things I only used to read about. Michael was away at college in New York and planned on going for his Master's at Columbia. In between our travels, we tried to find clues for '*the beast of the earth,*' but with no results. It seemed as if fate had brought us to another dead end.

HIJACKED JETLINERS CRASH INTO TWIN TOWERS AND HIT PENTAGON IN DAY OF TERROR

New York, September 12, 2001
(National News)

Hijackers slammed two jetliners into both of New York's World Trade Center towers yesterday morning, collapsing them to the ground in a fiery blaze as victims leaped out of windows. A third jetliner crashed into the Pentagon where 24,000 people worked. As of now, there is no official count of human tragedy from these attacks, but officials estimated it to be in the thousands. President Bush has ranked this as the most audacious terror attack in American history.

The attacks appear to have been expertly coordinated. All three planes were headed from Boston to California, loaded with fuel, with departure times within an hour and forty minutes of each other. A fourth plane leaving Newark bound for San Francisco crashed near Pittsburg. Officials believe it was possible that the hijackers failed to achieve whatever their mission was.

Continued on page 2a

"Oh my God, Camille, come here now! The World Trade Center has been attacked! Two commercial airliners hit them, both towers are on fire, and have collapsed. A third plane crashed into the Pentagon, and reports are coming in that a fourth plane crashed in a field in Pennsylvania killing everyone aboard. I'm really worried—Michael is in New York."

Panic stricken, she cried out, "*Oh mon Dieu,* Sean, I know, and I already tried to call him, but I can't get through. We won't be able to go there; I'm sure they've cancelled all flights."

"Camille, please, we have to stay level-headed. I really don't want to think the worst. I'm sure we'll get through to him by tomorrow."

Twenty-One Days Later
December 3, 2001

U.S. INVESTIGATION FAILS TO LINK IRAQ TO ANTHRAX ATTACK

Washington, Dec. 3, 2001 (National News)

Scientists confirmed that the anthrax bacteria used in the September attack was an American strain. Soon after the first anthrax casualty in October, the government conducted an all-out investigation to explore any possible link between Iraq and the attacks that continued even after the confirmation.

For the last several months, U.S. intelligence has searched for evidence of Iraqi involvement, and scientists have investigated whether Baghdad, in some way, acquired the American Ames strain of anthrax. However, a senior intelligence official stated that the connection simply was not there.

While looking for a perpetrator in the attacks that killed five people, investigators chased down tens of thousands of tips and conducted thousands of interviews. However, officials say that no likely suspects have come to light and they have run out of leads.

"Sean, we need to talk about this anthrax attack! It happened only one week after 9/11. I'm not surprised the authorities have no leads. I guarantee you, Invisibilia Manus is behind it, and I'm sure they also initiated it."

"I know you're right, but how could a band of Middle Eastern terrorists, who barely spoke English, hijack four commercial jetliners and fly them into the World Trade Center and the Pentagon without being detected? This attack was well-coordinated, with a lot of moving parts. How could they have possibly known all the details without raising suspicion, especially here in the United States? On the other hand, if one of their cells was behind the anthrax attack as well, they certainly weren't successful. Only five people died from it."

"You delude yourself if you think they weren't successful. This was another trial balloon, and I guarantee you many more will follow until Shanghai develops their ultimate virus. We have no choice; time has run out. We have to get a sample of the virus out of China as soon as possible."

The years flew by and we still couldn't figure a way to get in and out of the Shanghai labs undetected, but we decided to go ahead anyway. First, we had to find a place to stay for at least two nights near the Qing office tower. That was the easy part. We also had to be as inconspicuous as possible, since European visitors at that time in China were rare and stood out like a sore thumb. I knew where the research labs were, but security was tight and using my medallion to gain entry was not an option. Even if I somehow managed to get inside, I needed to maneuver my way up to the twelfth floor laboratory suite without being detected, assuming they were still there. Even more problematic was that I had no idea where they kept the vials. Whatever plan we came up with, it had to be flawless if we ever hoped to get out of China alive with the virus.

THE SARS EPIDEMIC—A DEADLY GERM FROM CHINA'S PROVINCES CREATES CHAOS

Atlanta, March 21, 2003, (World News)

On March 12, the World Health Organization (WHO) issued a worldwide health alert after cases of atypical pneumonia, known as severe acute respiratory syndrome (SARS), a form of coronavirus, did not appear to respond to standard treatments and has spread to medical personnel in Vietnam and Hong Kong. Before the spread of the disease in Hong Kong, a SARS outbreak was reported in the nearby Guangdong Province in mainland China. The outbreak was centered in the provincial capital of Guangzhou and the neighboring Pearl River Delta area. The outbreak purportedly started in November 2002 and has continued without relief, tallying up thousands of deaths.

The Dongyuan animal market was an hour south of Guangzhou, China, and was considered a possible source of the emerging virus. In hundreds of cramped stalls that reeked from the stench of animal entrails were wholesale food vendors readying a veritable zoo of chickens, snakes, turtles, cats, frogs, badgers, and rats for public consumption. According to WHO, this type of environment may present the perfect opportunity for the virus to cross from animals to humans. However, this theory has never been proven, and WHO has issued a global alert of a new infectious disease of unknown origin in both Vietnam and Hong Kong.

CHAPTER 22

THE QING TOWER

THE TWENTY-FOURTH STEP

March 28, 2003
Flight#1721
From: Los Angeles, California
Destination: Shanghai, China

"I bet you think this SARS epidemic we've been reading about is another trial balloon the Qing labs have deployed."

"*Oui*, I absolutely do, but it may also provide a valuable cover when we land in Shanghai. Look around the plane; many of the Asians wear face masks. We both have dark hair and the masks should conceal our identities from the security cameras."

"You do realize we have a bigger problem. I can't use my medallion anymore to get into the building."

"Okay, Sean, there you go being negative again. We've already talked this through. Somehow, we'll figure it out. You're really frustrating me, so for now, can we change the subject? We haven't eaten since we left LA, and I'm hungry for some authentic Chinese food. Do you have any suggestions?"

"Sure do. My favorite café is only four blocks from the office tower. I used to walk there every day for dinner. The owner, Liu Cheng, and I have become great friends. He would personally prepare his favorite classic meals just for me, and I paid him with American dollars. He wanted them so he could move to America and open a gourmet Chinese restaurant in California. But I don't know if he's made the move yet or not."

"*Magnifique,* that sounds perfect. I hope he's still there. I really don't feel like looking around for some place to eat."

With no actual plan, Camille and I landed in Shanghai, flagged down a taxi, and checked into a hotel near the Qing Tower. Needing some exercise after the long flight, we walked over to Liu Cheng's café.

The Precious Jewel Café
Shanghai, China

"Ah, Mister Sean, I barely recognized you. It has been many years. How good to see you again! Who is this beautiful lady? Is she your wife?"

"Liu Cheng, it's great to see you too. Allow me to introduce you to Camille."

He extended his hand and bowed. "I am pleased to meet you, Miss Camille."

"*Merci,* Liu Cheng. I'm pleased to meet you, too."

"We just arrived here on business, so we'll be here for the next couple of days. I told her about the Chinese delicacies you used to prepare for me. After we checked in at our hotel, this was the first place we came. We both hate airplane food and haven't eaten anything since we left the United States."

"Ah, I understand. I have a new chef and he is one of the best. I still love to cook for my customers, but I'm too busy making plans for my new cafe. I will have him prepare my special seven-course meal just for you. Nothing but the best for my favorite American customer."

"That sounds great, Liu Cheng. In the meantime, can you bring us some of your spring rolls? They're the best I've ever had, and I want Camille to sample what she's in store for."

"They're coming right up, Mister Sean. It is fortunate you came at this time. Remember my wish to own a cafe in California? Well, I'm almost ready to make the move and would like to request your help. Perhaps you may have some ideas for good locations in California and some contacts that can assist me."

"Liu Cheng, we would be happy to help in any way we can. I also have a request. You've known me for a long time, and you know I wouldn't ask you if it wasn't important. When I was in Shanghai, do you remember the office tower where I used to work? Can you tell me what you know about that place?"

"Ah yes, Mister Sean, nobody likes that awful place. I wish you could still come to my cafe, but I'm happy you don't work there anymore. Perhaps I will see more of you at my California café."

"Liu Cheng, what is it you don't like about it?"

"Hard to explain. The workers there are stern and not very nice. Everything there is different, very hush-hush.

Many comings and goings with trucks and official vehicles. It is certainly not a government building. No communist party or government emblems on the buildings or anywhere else on the grounds. The building seems out of place in our quiet neighborhood."

"Well, then, how do you know about the workers? The whole area is heavily secured."

"I know them because they purchase meals from me. Last year, I started a delivery service with my van."

"You mean the guards open the gate and allow you to enter?"

"Oh yes, Mister Sean, usually two or three times a week. In fact, I have a delivery tomorrow, precisely at noon. They are very strict about time."

"Where do you take the meals? There's no driveway to the front lobby."

"Oh, I don't go to the lobby. I drive my van to the service entrance. I beep my horn twice, the door opens, and I drive in. I get out of the van and unload the meals onto the table they set up for me. When the workers come down to pick them up, they take their selection and pay me. When I am finished, the guard opens the gate and I leave. It's the same every time."

"Liu Cheng, how long are you allowed to stay inside for those deliveries?"

"Usually about fifteen minutes. Mister Sean, I don't like the sound of these questions. Why do you ask them?"

"Believe me, my friend, for your safety, it's better you don't know. Do you think there's some way you can sneak me into the building and past the guards?"

"I don't like the sound of this at all, Mister Sean. If we get caught, it's lights out for both of us. You have a beautiful lady here with you, and I have a family. Allow me to think about this."

Several hours later, after we were done eating, Liu Cheng came back to our table. "Okay, Mister Sean, you are a good friend and I want to help you, but my participation must be very little. Perhaps you could hide in the back of my van, and I will distract the guards with small talk while you sneak out the back. But you will only have fifteen minutes before I must leave. I don't see how you will remain undetected once you are in the building. What you talk about is very dangerous. They mean business at that place."

"Liu Cheng, don't worry, that's my problem. Your help is of utmost importance. Someday I will explain everything, but not now. So, the plan is, I will meet you here tomorrow morning at 11:45 a.m., and you will drive your van to the office tower with me in the back."

"Yes, I understand, but I don't like it."

In her soft, warm voice, Camille remarked, *"Merci, Liu Cheng,* it's wonderful to meet you. Thank you for sticking your neck out for us. Regardless, we will be very happy to help you in any way we can when you are in California. I'm sure your new café will be a big success."

"Oh, thank you, Miss Camille, but you must excuse me. The new chef calls for my assistance in the kitchen."

"Wow, sweetheart, that was certainly unexpected. At least I have a way in and way out of the tower. But I still have to figure out how to get up to the twelfth floor, and hopefully the labs are still there."

"Sean, I have an idea. When you worked there, did you notice what the lab workers wore?"

"Yeah, they wore the typical white coats—oh, I see what you're getting at. Great idea. You know what? I know exactly where the laundry room is. I bet I can get in and grab one, and I'll wear my face mask. The only thing is, I won't have an ID tag, but I can always hold up a clipboard or a book. When I get up there, it will be lunch time, and if I'm lucky, everyone will be down in the cafeteria. The other problem is, I don't know how I'll find the vials, and unfortunately, I only have fifteen minutes for this crazy stunt."

"Sean, I'm terrified to think about what will happen if you're caught."

"To quote Liu Cheng, it will be 'lights out.'"

The next day, we went back to Liu Cheng's cafe at 11:45 a.m. and found him sitting in the driver's seat of his van. I got in like we planned, but he said nothing as he drove away with me in the back. Several minutes later, we arrived at the office tower, and just like Liu Cheng said they would, the guards opened the service entrance. He immediately drove in and distracted them with small talk. I slipped out, put on my mask, hurried over to the elevator, and stepped in. As it slowly clambered up to the twelfth floor, my attempt to do the impossible suddenly became real. What the hell was I doing? The clock was ticking with no time to spare. The first thing I needed to do was find a lab coat. Fortunately, as I stepped out, the laundry room was right there, only a few steps away.

Looking down the familiar hallway, I realized to my delight that they did not relocate the labs where I assumed they stored the virus. But as I worked my way to it, I encountered my first obstacle. There were several lab workers huddled together, discussing heaven only knows what. I needed to get in there. So, I waited out in the hallway, pretending to study the papers on my clipboard. Finally, after several nerve-wracking minutes, they left for lunch.

The fluorescent-lit room hadn't changed much since the last time I was there. Upon entering, I immediately spotted the row of freezers behind a large glass enclosure, with hazmat suits hanging neatly on the outside. I had no time to suit up, so I took a dangerous risk. I opened the glass door as a gust of pressurized air equalized with the outside air. I didn't know what I was looking for, but I opened one of the freezer doors anyway. That's when I knew I was on the right track. Inside were racks of hermetically sealed glass tubes, each containing what I could only imagine were some of the deadliest pathogens that have ever existed. Each tube was carefully labeled in Chinese and subtitled in English. As I looked through each of the freezer compartments, I finally came across an assortment of neatly arranged racks of tubes, labeled in red with 'Coronavirus 2003-03-26.' When I read about the SARS epidemic, I remembered articles that referred to it as a coronavirus. If SARS was a trial balloon as Camille had suspected, I assumed these tubes might contain the next generation of the deadly virus. I looked at my watch and realized I only had a few minutes left before Liu Cheng would leave. I grabbed one of the vials and wrapped it in the ice pack I put in my shoulder bag.

But then, just as I was leaving, the wail of alarms in the lab room and down the hallways suddenly broke the silence. The cameras had spotted me! The flash of the strobe lights blinded me and slowed my escape as I tried to run out into the hallway and find my way back to the elevator. When I finally got there, I realized the alarm system had disabled it. My only other option was to run down twelve flights of stairs and pray that Liu Cheng was still in the building. My watch showed that seventeen minutes had elapsed. The narrow stairwell had a double turn at each floor, which slowed my descent. The idea of tripping and falling into the hands of waiting guards terrified me. Finally, the service area on the main floor was within sight, but Liu Cheng was already backing his van out of the building. He was looking in my direction, but I wasn't sure if he saw me or not. Thank God, he slowed down. The guards, distracted by the alarms, were huddled together, yelling on their walkie-talkies, and didn't seem to notice Liu Cheng as he quietly drove out of the building—with me and the deadly cargo inside.

Back at the Precious Jewel Café

"*Oh, mon Dieu, mon amour*, thank God you made it out! Putting yourself in mortal danger like that, I pray you were successful."

"Yeah, I think so. Here, read what it says on the vial. I think it could be the next generation of the strain after SARS. But enough of that for now, we have to get out of China fast; I was spotted on their cameras. I can only hope their facial recognition didn't identify me."

"Sean, I have to tell you, I'm nervous. That building has airtight security. The Qing family is meticulous when it comes to guarding those labs. In my opinion you got in and out of that tower far too easily. I know only too well how Invisibilia Manus operates, and I am positive you were allowed to escape."

"Allowed to escape—are you kidding me? That makes no sense at all. Whatever, we need to get to the airport now. On the way back here, I asked Liu Cheng to call a taxi. It should be arriving soon. I thanked him for his help and told him the next time we would see him will be in California."

Moments later, Camille called me out. "Sean, the taxi is here. Our flight leaves in two hours. How long do you think it will take to get to the airport?"

"At this time of day, it shouldn't take more than forty-five minutes, but we still have to go back to the hotel and get our luggage. I put the vial in my shoulder bag and wrapped it in an ice pack. When we get back there, I need to repack it in my suitcase in order to get it through airport security."

"*Oh, mon Dieu,* I think there's a problem we have not taken into consideration."

"Really, and pray tell what is that?"

"The flight from Shanghai to Atlanta is nineteen hours, plus another hour to get the virus to CIDEC from the airport. I don't think an ice pack will last that long. Hopefully, when we get to the hotel, you can find something to keep the vials cold for as long as possible. But I'm not even sure that will work."

"I agree. However, luggage compartments are naturally cold, so it might be alright. You wait here in the cab while I take care of everything. It shouldn't take long."

Ten minutes later

"*Oh mon Dieu,* Sean, that took more than a few minutes. Is everything okay?"

"Yeah, the ice machine was out of order, so the manager gave me some from his office fridge. Anyway, we're good to go now. You know what, I'll give the cabby an extra ten bucks to get us to the airport in record time."

"Sean, when you were in the Qing Tower, I was thinking about Michael. If the guards had caught you, we would never have seen him again. We've been so wrapped up in getting our hands on this virus that I really don't remember the last time we even talked to him. Once we deliver the vial to CIDEC, we really should fly to New York and spend some time with him."

But then, unexpectedly, the cabby interrupted, "Mister, mister, I'm going fast as I can, but you should know that somebody is following right behind us, and it is not the authorities."

With all that we had just been through, now there was another obstacle in our way. The Qing guards may not have shot me, but even so, at this point, I literally thought I would die from a heart attack. After a thirty-minute grueling ordeal getting through security at the airport, we finally boarded. During the flight to Atlanta, we composed a letter for CIDEC that we included with the virus. We did not want to be identified, so I paid a courier to deliver the package. Even so, we constantly questioned ourselves. Did we miss something, like a stray fingerprint or a strand of hair? After the courier delivered the vial, we took another calculated chance. We had not seen Michael since well before the 9/11 attack and were anxious to get back on a plane to New York as soon as possible. But if Camille was right and we were being followed, we certainly did not want the asset to follow us there. So, we decided to wait several weeks in Atlanta to cover our tracks.

HANDLE CONTENTS WITH EXTREME CAUTION—DEADLY PATHOGEN ENCLOSED

April 4, 2003

Center for Infectious Disease and
Epidemic Control (CIDEC)
Atlanta, Georgia
Cathryn Ballantine, MD– Director

Dr. Ballantine:

We have gone to a great deal of trouble and put ourselves at enormous risk to get this vial to you. Our lives are in grave danger and, therefore, we are unable to reveal our identities at this time. We just arrived from China after smuggling it out of a covert laboratory in Shanghai. The lab is operated by the Chinese faction of an international terrorist cartel that calls itself Invisibilia Manus. They are made up of ten very powerful families from Europe, the U.S., India, Iran, Russia, and China. They have unlimited wealth and are using it to control societies and governments through their proxy organizations. Their goal, Agenda One, is world domination with a one world order under their total and complete control.

They have been planning this takeover since 1978, but it won't be completed until they have eliminated much of the world's swelling population. I suspect this vial contains the next evolution of the weaponized, genetically modified strain of the coronavirus they plan on using. You will have no defense against it. We know these must sound like outrageous claims made by crazed radicals, but you should assume our assertions are facts. We believe that when you analyze this sample, you will see the credibility of our claim and take us seriously.

This power grab is outlined in their 1978 Red Book, which we have in our possession. When the time is appropriate, we will give it to you. We are on record now, so when we make their identity known to the public, CIDEC will be a witness to our allegation. At this time, we can only provide this piece of evidence. We plan to go public with this information as soon as we can provide you with undeniable validation of their existence. We brought this sample to you as the first step. When available, we will come forward with more information. You may want to share this letter with the FBI and Interpol. For future correspondence, you will know us by our code name.

S-h-a-w-n.

CHAPTER 23

BLINDSIDED

"No memory is ever alone; it's at the end of a trail of memories, a dozen trails that each have their own associations."— Louis L' Amour

THE TWENTY-FIFTH STEP

May 2, 2003
Greenwich Village, New York

As he opened the door to his apartment with a smirk on his face, Michael sneered, "Mother and Father, I'm so *happy* to see you. It's certainly been a while, hasn't it?" After a deep breath, he continued, "Oh, wait a minute—you've never been here before. Well, I certainly feel honored. But that's okay, I'm sure you've been on one of your amazing adventures having a grand ole time. Oh, now I get it. I'm your next adventure. How wonderfully thoughtful of you! I'm honored by your presence."

"Michael, I don't understand—what's wrong? Your father and I have come here to visit with you. We certainly didn't expect a reception like this. We thought you would be happy to see us."

"What's wrong? You've got to be kidding me. Let's just say, like you, I don't understand."

Shocked by Michael's unexpected disrespect, I scolded, "Son, what in the hell is wrong with you? You look like a damn bum: long hair, ripped jeans, raggedy tee shirt, weird chains, tattoos. And what are those god-awful piercings? What have you done to yourself? Are you on drugs?"

"Father, Father—what makes you think I'm on drugs? This is the way my friends and I dress. *I'm sorry* you're so offended."

"Okay, cut the crap. You said you don't understand. What do you mean, you don't understand?"

"Oh, so now you want to talk. Well, sir, I'm quite sure you don't have enough time to hear everything I have to say. First of all, I never realized how little I know about myself until I came here to college. My friends talk about their families and where they come from. But when they ask me about my grandparents, aunts, uncles, and cousins, I know nothing. So, Mother, how come you never talk about our relatives? Who are my grandparents? Do I even have aunts, uncles, and cousins? I know we lived in France at one time, but exactly where? Before Dad came into the picture, I thought you and I were the only ones. And you have never told me anything about yourself before I was born. I want to know—am I adopted?"

"Michael, please, we did not adopt you. You are our child."

"And Father, where were you for the first fourteen years of my life? Actually, I'll give you some credit. At least, you did tell about my grandparents on your side and my aunt Susan. I know you grew up in Michigan with your fast cars, your college, and your Army years. So, Father, let me ask you: Where were you and what did you do before you came back to Mom? And you wonder if something is wrong with me. What a joke."

With tears streaming down her cheeks, Camille cried, "Michael, Michael, I am so sorry. We really do owe you an explanation, but it's not easy. For your own sake, I can't give you the answers you deserve right now. Please believe me, we love you from the bottom of our hearts, and I did everything possible to give you a normal childhood while your father was gone. Everything we've done has been for your well-being and your future. You must understand, our number one priority has always been to protect you from my family."

"You want to protect me from your family? Who the hell are they, the French mafia?"

"No, Michael, they are far more dangerous. Our family is one part of an international terrorist cartel. But, before you ask, I cannot tell you who they are. They have an agenda so diabolical that I can't discuss any of it with you. Believe me, the less you know, the better. I can tell you that I worked for them when I hired your father. We were both young and naïve, and at the time, I really didn't know how dangerous they really were. He unfortunately was also completely in the dark until just a few years ago. His boss told him he worked for a humanitarian group that wanted to save the world. I have so much more to tell you, but I really can't say more. I promise, in time, you will know everything. Michael, I beg you, for now, please trust us."

"You two are unbelievable, and you wonder if I'm on drugs! You live in some kind of delusional world that I want no part of. I suggest you both get some serious psychiatric help."

We were shocked when we saw Michael, how dramatically he changed, and how angry he had become. I was worried we may never have a close relationship with him ever again, especially once he found out what we were not telling him. Even more worrisome was what he might do when we revealed everything and he found out he is a Martel. On top of it, if he didn't believe us, how would we ever convince anybody else of the threat Invisibilia Manus posed? We came to the realization that our plan may never see the light of day, or worse yet, we may not even survive the ordeal. So, we flew back to Zurich to try and decide what our next step was and how to repair our relationship with him.

CHAPTER 24

THE TWINS

THE TWENTY-SIXTH STEP

May 6, 2003
Zurich, Switzerland

"Sean, I must say, it really feels good to finally pull into our driveway. I'm physically, mentally, and emotionally exhausted thinking about Michael. We should have never neglected him for so long. I know how sensitive he is, and now he feels that he has no family to rely on. We have lots of excuses, but we can't let them get in the way of our relationship with him anymore."

"You're right, sweetheart, and please don't think I don't care, but right now I can barely keep my eyes open. I don't remember the last time we got a good night's sleep. By the way, do you have the front door keys? I can't find mine."

"*Oui*, here, I'll open it. Hooray, back inside our home again! We've been gone for so long, it doesn't even feel real to me."

Puzzled, I asked, "Camille, the den lights are on. Do you remember turning them off before we left?"

"*Oui*, I always check to make sure all the lights are turned off and the doors are locked before we go anywhere." Then, after looking around, she yelled out, "*Oh mon Dieu*, Sean, someone has been in the house!"

After peeking into the other rooms, I went into the kitchen. It was then that I saw him sitting calmly in a chair with a glass of wine. "Ha, ha, Sean Phillips, *c'est tellement bon de vous voir.*"

"Who the hell are you, and what are you doing in our house?"

"You'll soon find out, Sean. I want you to calmly call Camille and tell her to come in here right now."

"Ca-Ca-Camille, come here! In the kitchen…"

"Okay, okay. I'm coming, I'm coming." When she walked in, she froze in her tracks and screamed, "*OH MON DIEU,* ANDRÉ!"

With a smirk on his face, he raised his glass and taunted her, "My dear twin sister, it's so good to see you. How have you been? Oh, wait a minute. I see you're just fine. Unlike what was reported in the papers, you are not dead. But, of course, I already knew that. In fact, I've known right from the beginning that you and Sean Phillips are alive."

Barely able to talk, Camille cried out, "How could you have possibly known?"

"Sister, sister, I thought you were smarter than that. Okay, if you must know, I'll tell you. Father sent me to St. Martin to investigate *your death*. I talked to that idiot airport manager, and I also talked to Lila. By the way, Sean, I see why you married her—she's a lovely woman. You should know she's absolutely devastated by *your tragic demise*. As tears streamed down her cheeks, she cried that she was a widow after only being married to you for a couple of hours. I actually felt sorry for her. Then, I'm sure you remember the cabin on Anguilla Island. Well, shame on you for leaving the evidence behind. That's how I knew."

"Evidence? What evidence? I was careful to clean up behind me, like I always do."

"Evidently, you've been away from your job for far too long. You've lost your touch. The bloody gauze gave you away, which, of course, I took back to France with me. It's truly amazing what DNA analysis can do, especially when I found out our lab had samples of both your and Sean's blood. Back then, it was protocol to test for drugs, so his was taken at the time of his employment exam. They compared them with the bloody gauze, and guess what? The DNA matched Sean's."

At a loss for words, I could barely speak. "This is unbelievable, Camille. You never told me you have a twin brother."

Embarrassed, she responded, "I really am sorry, Sean. This is my brother, André. I may as well tell you now, we also have an older brother, Antoine. And to let you know, I'm not proud that I'm related to either one of them."

Then, turning her attention back to André, she asked, "How in heaven's sake did you find us here in Zurich?"

"Camille, my dear sister, you underestimate the long arm of our family. I'm sure you have no idea how far our technology has advanced since you've been gone. You obviously thought wearing a face mask in Shanghai would hide Sean from facial recognition. You couldn't have been more wrong. Our new cameras didn't need to see his face; his eyes gave him away. Once they focused in on him, the director at the Qing Tower informed me. I thought to myself, 'wow, there's Sean Phillips, and he put his life in mortal danger just to get his hands on a sample of the virus. Why would he do that?' The rest is academic. I simply ordered our assets to follow you."

Confused, she asked again, "Okay, but how did you manage to find us here in Zurich? And how did you know when we would be here?"

"That was also easy. Our asset followed the two of you to Michael's apartment in New York. So, Michael told me."

Terrified, she screamed, "What do you mean Michael told you? You leave him alone. He knows nothing about our family, and I want to keep it that way."

"Oh, I already know that too. And by the way, I like your new name. Ha-ha, Deneuve is very clever. By the way, Michael and I had a wonderful conversation, although he does seem to be a bit screwed up. I'm sure you would like to keep him in the dark about our family. And you, Sean, you're Michael's father? I really can't wait to hear that story."

Feeling trapped, Camille could barely speak. "Okay, now that you have us where you want us, what are you going to do?"

"Well, let me put it this way: I did not tell Michael that I'm his uncle. As far as he's concerned, I'm a casual acquaintance he met at one of his hangouts. Although, I have to say, now that I know I have a nephew, it's more endearing than I ever thought it would be. Believe me, dear sister, if I were out to get you, you would have been dead a long time ago. Father and Antoine are completely in the dark about this whole matter. I have told them nothing."

"André, I really don't understand."

"*Oui chère soeur*, Camille, I am sure you don't. For now, let's just blame it on the fact that you are my twin sister and I'm Michael's uncle. And Sean, until recently, I didn't realize you share our same birthday. I can't wait to hear that story either, but not now. So, with that said, I never thought I would be saying this, but I do care about all three of you. Now listen to me. I don't know what the two of you are up to, but I'm here to tell you you're playing a very dangerous game. I've put my life on the line by even being here with you. If Antoine ever finds out about any of this, I'm a dead man, along with the three of you. So, I really don't want to know any more than I already do. Camille, I know you only too well, so I'm sure you have something big planned. But if you get caught, I can't help you. So, I don't need to tell you to be very careful."

Life is a funny thing. The roadblocks and the unknowns we came up against were beyond difficult; many seemed insurmountable. You never know what's next; dead ends and traps are around every corner. If

Michael did not believe us, how could we possibly convince the world that the Invisible Hand was real? And what in hell was André's angle? We needed to face the realization that any plan we came up with may never see the light of day.

But true to his word, we didn't hear from André or anybody from the Martel family. Michael eventually went on to get his Master's degree at Columbia, but decided to remain in New York. In a short email, he told us he had a job and wanted us to stop sending him money. We were heartbroken when he told us to leave him alone.

The Shanghai virus was another thing. We didn't see anything in the papers about the FBI or CIDEC, and so we didn't know if the crude ice pack we devised actually kept the virus viable or not. Time marched on, and the Invisible Hand was growing in power. And, of course, the Genesis Correlation had also come to a complete halt.

CHAPTER 25

AN ANCIENT MESSAGE

THE TWENTY-SEVENTH STEP

May 26, 2003
Zurich, Switzerland

"Sean, come here for a minute, I want to show you something. I've been looking at these Sumerian seals again and, in particular, the symbols on the first seal—AMITU TIIT DAMIQ. I thought we should find out what they mean, so I looked up an institute in Cambridge, England, that specializes in ancient languages. We've never been to England; what do you say we go there and give it a try?"

"I really don't see why. There's no evidence that links those seals to Genesis. To me, it will be just another dead end, and I'm sick and tired of dead ends."

"Well, I see the link. We're correlating physical science with Genesis in a spiritual book. And the Sumerian seals

227

link the physical with the spiritual. Remember Seal VA 243 and what Schneider told us about the Sumerian's knowledge of science as well as their belief in gods? There's your link. So, come on and humor me. We don't have any other leads. Besides, we have nothing better to do. I certainly don't view you as a quitter. I want you to put on your Sherlock Holmes hat, and let's get this Genesis Correlation figured out once and for all. And besides, we're certainly not getting anywhere with my family."

June 8, 2003
Mesopotamian Languages
Department of Archaeology
Cambridge Institute

When we arrived at the front desk, Camille approached the receptionist. *"Bonjour Madam.* We brought these artifacts with us that we believe your institute will find quite interesting. Is there someone here today we can speak with?"

"Yes, ma'am, that would be Professor Malcolm Little. I know he's in, but I'm not sure if he's available. Would you like to schedule an appointment for later in the week?"

"Oui, but perhaps we should show him what we have first. We flew here all the way from Zurich. If he's busy, we can wait."

"Okay, let me see what I can do." Several minutes later, the receptionist called our attention. "Excuse me, miss. I buzzed his assistant, and I'm sorry to say he's in meetings all day. However, he may have a few minutes to spare later. If you care to wait in the lobby, perhaps he can meet with you this afternoon."

Several hours later

"Professor, if you have a moment, these lovely people have patiently been waiting to have a word with you."

The professor, a tall, lanky man in a worn tweed jacket, approached us and extended his hand to each of us.

"Hello, I'm Malcolm Little. I apologize that you had to wait. What brings you here today?"

"*Bonjour*, Professor Little. I'm Camille Deneuve, and this is Sean Phillips. We're very excited to meet you— thank you for your time on such short notice. We came here to get some information on these Sumerian seals. We took them to the Vorderasiatische Museum in Berlin for authentication. The curator deciphered the symbols inscribed on them, but he wasn't able to translate their meaning. He told us they were quite rare and offered to pay us a generous sum to acquire them. We left them locked up at home; however, we did bring these clay impressions with us."

"Oh, so you met Wilhelm Schneider. I haven't seen him for years. I believe the last time was at a conference in Brussels. Anyway, allow me to take a look at them."

"We're working on something important to us. Any help that you can give will be welcomed."

After a few moments, he commented, "Okay, at first glance, I can tell you they are old. Oh, my goodness, I see why Schneider was so anxious to purchase them. These are paired seals. The message they contain can't be deciphered unless they are paired together. They're also quite rare. So yes, by all means, I am interested. I've heard about paired seals, but I've never actually seen anything like them before, other than in textbooks. I don't have the time to examine them today, so if you don't mind, I would like to show them to some of my colleagues. After we've collaborated, I'll draft a report that should answer some of your questions. However, since you didn't bring the actual seals themselves, the report will not be an official document of authentication. I can have it ready for you in about a week."

"*Oui*, Professor, that would be perfect."

"I really do hate to be so abrupt, but I'm in between meetings and I must get back. In the meantime, if you don't have other plans, you may want to explore our fair city."

"*Au revoir*, Professor, and thank you so much for your time. We'll see you a week from today."

Summary Report

An unofficial commentary strictly for private use only. It is not intended for commercial or educational purposes.

Date: August 17, 2003
Author: Malcolm G. Little, Ph.D.
Cambridge Institute, Department of Archaeology, Mesopotamian Languages
Prepared for: Camille Deneuve and Sean Thompson
Topic: Paired Sumerian Cylinder Seals

We have assessed the aforementioned "paired seals" and have made the following preliminary analysis:

Seal 1: There are three figures facing a tree. When comparing this seal with other seals from the same period, the tree could well represent the symbolic "tree of life." The seated figure sitting to the right of the tree appears to be a spiritual leader, most likely a Sumerian god. The incense burner placed behind him with smoke rising would represent favor from the divine entities. With his right hand, he points to the heavenly bodies, the sun, moon, and stars. His left hand holds a wand as he points it at the tree. These gestures represent the spiritual realm.

To the left of the tree are two standing figures who appear to be farmers. One is holding a ram and the other holds baskets of agricultural goods. We believe the farmers represent the physical earth. The tree sits atop what appears to be a small table or altar with Sumerian symbols inscribed on it. When transcribed, it reads AMITU TIIT DAMIQ.

Seal 2: It shows the same three figures;
however, on this seal, they face away from
the tree. Their backs are to each other and
to the tree. The Sumerian god no longer
points to the heavens, and instead, his arms
hang down. The farmers' arms also hang down,
and their hands are empty. Smoke is absent
from the incense burner and the symbols on
the altar are missing. The "tree of life" is
devoid of leaves and appears lifeless. We
have made an attempt to decipher the symbols
on Seal#1. In our opinion, it translates to
"BEHOLD LIFE GOOD."

Conclusion

Seal 1: When mankind is united with both the
physical and spiritual nature of existence,
life will thrive.

Seal 2: Denial and division of the physical
and the spiritual will lead to deprivation
and, ultimately, to death.

"Camille, take a look at this report. This is amazing. It seems to confirm what I have long suspected. Genesis 1 contains a 2,500-year-old message intended for our modern world."

"A message? I don't remember you ever mentioning a message before."

"I'm sorry, I thought I did. It's the last phrase of Genesis 1, in verse 31: *'And God saw every thing that He had made, and, behold, it was very good.'*"

"That verse is similar to the phrase on the first seal and was written when the Earth was pristine and unspoiled by pollution. Think about the contrast—and people are still reading that message today with the polluted world we live in."

"*Oui*, I agree that people can certainly be indifferent when it comes to the environment. I've been reading many articles about plant and animal species dying off in record numbers due to the death of ecosystems caused by manmade pollution."

"Wow, you really got that right. Actually, I think Genesis 1 is sending us two messages. Before I started working for Blackguard, Marlene and I went on a lot of nature hikes up in northern Michigan. That was in the 70s. Even back then, we could see how civilization was encroaching on the environment. I do believe this verse is meant to be a warning to wake people up before it's too late. So, Genesis, along with our seals, prove ancient civilizations that predate even the Hebrews lived in harmony with both the physical and the spiritual existence of nature. It was not possible for them to separate the two. Somewhere along the way, we forgot this ancient truth, and I suspect it started with Darwin."

"Why Darwin?"

"Actually, the split between science and religion is fairly recent. It really only began in the late 1800s, after Darwin published his book on evolution. The uproar then was over Darwin's idea that humans were descended from apes. As a result, many on both sides accused the other side of being the enemy. Unfortunately, this war became deeply engrained in many people's minds and has continued to influence thinking to this day. From what I've seen in both college and church and what I've read, this division seems more pronounced in America, where the battle tends to be much more bitter and divisive than in other countries."

"Yeah, Sean, and we both know why that is."

"But this is my point. Before the age of Darwinian thinking, civilizations going back to the dawn of recorded history, including the Sumerians, lived for thousands of years. Then along comes Darwin, and after only a couple of hundred years, we are on the eve of a man-made Armageddon."

"That may be true, but keep in mind, every one of those civilizations eventually died off."

"Yes, but they were replaced with others. Everything exists in cycles: birth, life, and then death, including civilizations. But this time, it's different. Previous extinction events, including the last one when the dinosaurs disappeared, were caused by natural events. But human ignorance and disrepect for nature has caused this one to happen."

"Sean, I know what you're saying is true, and I don't want to upset your enthusiasm, but we still have four more verses to figure out before the Genesis Correlation is complete. I also know we're working in uncharted territory here, but I really thought we would have made more progress by now. I think there's something holding us back."

"Holding us back? What in heck are you talking about? Nobody has ever even come close to what we're trying to achieve here."

"*Oui*, I know, but I've been wanting to say something to you for a long time now, but you have to be ready to listen. You seem to have accepted the unity of the physical and the spiritual. But, for you, I feel it's more about proving your Genesis Correlation than an actual and unconditional belief in a higher power. I know you're trying to prove the science in a religious book, but that is not what I'm talking about. Be honest and don't mince words with me, but do you believe in God?"

"Well, I can certainly tell you, I don't believe in religion. It's interesting though, you're the second person now to ask me that."

"Really, who else asked you?"

"My Army buddy, Eddie. He asked me when we were in basic training."

"Why did he question you about God? Were your lives in danger?"

"No, no, nothing like that. He was worried about going to Vietnam. But it was more than that. We used to talk about science stuff, like the Big Bang and evolution. He didn't understand how everything in the universe could have possibly come from absolutely nothing. And he couldn't comprehend how life and human consciousness could have evolved from lifeless matter. I remember he posed a couple of intriguing questions. He asked if scientists actually believed that Einstein's intellect came from stardust and his genius evolved from microbes."

"What did you tell him?"

"I guess I avoided the question and didn't really answer him."

"Sean, I have another question. Your pastor gave you these Sumerian seals. He could have given them to anybody. Why did he give them to you?"

"He bought them because he thought they might somehow expand his knowledge of God's word. I guess he probably gave them to me for the same reason."

"*Mon amour,* again, I ask this lovingly, so please don't take offense. Your parents raised you to believe in God, which, by the way, was far different from the way my family raised me. Then Eddie asked you a straightforward question, and you couldn't give him a straight answer. Then, your pastor sensed your disbelief and thought these seals might help you. You must see the pattern here."

"I never really looked at it that way before, but do we really have to talk about this now?"

"Yes, we do. You have to realize we will never complete the Genesis Correlation or expose my family until you and I are both on the same spiritual plane. Sean, you're my spiritual twin. We're here to fulfill our destinies together."

"Okay, okay, okay. I get it."

"No, you don't! Let me put it this way. We both believe the physical and the spiritual are two separate but equal entities. Two sides of the same coin, you might say. It's really no different for you and me. Let's say, for a minute, that you represent the physical and I represent the spiritual. We are also two but equal forces that must unite as one if we ever expect to fulfill our destinies together. If we don't, we'll never get past all the obstacles and dead ends that are surely yet to come."

"Yeah, I guess that makes sense."

"Sean, you have a dilemma that, unfortunately, I can't solve for you, and it's affecting us. You need solid evidence before you believe anything is true. Your motto should be, 'I'll believe it when I see it,' and that may be fine for science and physical things, but it's not true in the spiritual realm."

"Again, I have no idea what the heck you're talking about, Camille."

"Sure, you do. You're just being stubborn. The only way we're going to make headway is for you to believe. You must also live by another motto, 'I'll see it, when I believe it.' But that won't happen until you admit what it is you're afraid of, otherwise, your fear will continue to stop us."

"Afraid? Are you kidding me? I am not afraid. Well, I guess that's not entirely true. Maybe I'm afraid that after all the time and effort we've put into this stuff, we'll fail. So, I guess I'd say I'm afraid of the unknown, and I don't know where to go from here."

"Well, at least you're being honest. So, think about it this way. The past represents the *known*, and you can't change it. But the future holds the *unknown*, where unlimited possibilities exist. Focus your attention on all the opportunities that will best serve us and dismiss your negative thoughts. You can't always choose the way you feel, but you can choose what you think. It's like developing a new habit. If you focus your thinking long enough, your feelings will follow. But beware: thoughts can be either negative or positive. Negative thoughts will lead to negative outcomes. Once you grasp that simple idea, you'll soon realize you have nothing to be afraid of. Actually, that's the secret great people throughout history have mastered on their rise to the top."

I was intimidated and, at the same time, impressed. "Okay, my 'goddess of wisdom.' How did you ever come to know this stuff?"

"Sean, believe me, you can't even begin to imagine what it was like growing up with my family. My father ruled with an iron fist, and I always did exactly what he said, otherwise, I faced his wrath. As a sensitive child, to say the least, I was always afraid of one thing or another. I was literally taught to be afraid. Then, around eighteen, I began reading countless books about the spiritual side of life, and that opened a whole new world for me. I learned to pray and meditate twice a day to calm my mind, and for the first time, I experienced inner peace. I soon came to realize I actually possessed power over my own life—the same power anyone can have. All you have to do is ask for what you want. But the key is you have to expect to get it. Hoping, wishing, wanting, and so forth won't work—only expecting. Then, simply let go and trust that it will happen. So, ask for help when you need it and truly expect to get it—many times, in unexpected ways."

"Okay, let's say I'm open to what you're saying. I suspect you want to teach me how to meditate, but I feel like there's more to it than that."

"Sean, this is your journey. It's not a matter of what I want; it's what you want. All I can do is offer you some suggestions."

"Okay, what else?"

"You need to look back on your destiny trail."

"You mentioned this trail to me one other time. What in heaven's name is the destiny trail?"

"To answer that question, you'll have to start at the beginning and retrace the steps that led you to me and this point in time. To keep your mind focused, you should give this exercise a name. For example, you could simply call it 'The Trail.' The first question you should ask yourself is how and when it began."

"Okay, I think I get it."

"Alright then, I'll help you get started."

"Hmm, let's see. Well, I guess my trail began when you hired me; the time Marsh was looking for an assistant for Travis McShane. With my education and background,

I was the ideal candidate. But, of course, you already know that."

"Okay. What led to Blackguard hiring you?"

"It was my next-door neighbor, Don Campbell, who referred me to Julian Marsh."

"How did you happen to live next to Don Campbell?"

"That was when my first wife, Marlene, and I moved from our first rental into the one next to his."

"So, that was your second rental. Why did you move from your first rental into that particular one when you did?"

"That happened when I came back from boot camp. Our first landlady sold her rental house in Royal Oak. Marlene's mother knew the owner of the second one, and it happened to be available when we needed a place to live."

"Sean, I've always thought that after army training, soldiers were sent off to serve somewhere, like Vietnam."

"Yes, that's true for the Regular Army, but I enlisted in the Army Reserve."

"Okay, so how did you avoid getting drafted into the Regular Army?"

"Well, our minister, Pastor Jesse, was able to pull some strings, and he got me into the Reserve. That was really a close call. The day after I swore into the Reserve, I received a letter from my draft board announcing I was selected for the draft. I remember how damn lucky I was to have dodged it."

"So, why did you go to Pastor Jesse for help?"

"Marlene was raised in a different religion than mine. She converted so I could go to church with her. Pastor

Jesse's church was in our Royal Oak neighborhood, and that was where we went. He happened to be a volunteer on the local draft board."

"I see. How did you meet Marlene?"

"My ex-friend Danny Kirchner introduced me to her when we were in college."

"Well, now you have it, *mon amour,* the beginning of your destiny trail.

"First, Danny introduced you to Marlene; she converted from her religion to yours, and then you met Pastor Jesse.

"Then you married her. Pastor Jesse got you into the Army Reserve, and you dodged the draft and the Vietnam war.

"Before you returned home from basic training, your landlady sold her Royal Oak flat. Fortunately, at the time, Marlene's mother had a friend who owned a rental in Birmingham. That rental was next door to Don Campbell's.

"Don introduced you to Julian Marsh, and it was then that I hired you into Blackguard. We promoted you to technical liaison, which brought you to France.

"You first met me in Marseilles, where we fell in love, but I was forced to leave you. Feeling lost, you bought a home in St. Martin, you left Blackguard, and married Lila Knowles. That provided me with the perfect excuse to fake a plane crash and come back to you.

"And, you can figure out the rest from there."

"Wow, when you put it that way, I have to admit it is quite a remarkable series of coincidences."

"Sean, they are not coincidences—it's your destiny trail. You need to ponder that for a while until it truly sinks in. But you are not at the end of your trail yet. You still have more steps to go, only now you're not alone. We are spiritual twins and, now, united."

That talk with Camille was a turning point for me. For the first time, her words finally made sense. My stubbornness to completely acknowledge both sides of the coin had been my stumbling block for years. I was now ready to move forward with my eyes wide open—or so I thought. But as the years passed, the papers were still full of articles that reminded both of us just how crucial it was for us to complete our journey on the Trail together.

EDITORIAL: OKLAHOMA CITY BOMBING QUESTIONS STILL UNANSWERED TEN YEARS LATER

Oklahoma City, May 2, 2005 (National News)

Ten years ago, on April 19, 1995, Timothy McVeigh, a disgruntled military veteran, drove a truck crammed with fertilizer bomb explosives into downtown Oklahoma City and blew up a federal office building. That heinous act killed 168 adults, 19 children, and injured over 200 others. Approximately 90 minutes after the bombing, police pulled McVeigh over near the Kansas border, driving an unlikely getaway car—an old, sputtering rust bucket Mercury sedan without license plates, making him an obvious target for any highway sheriff patrol car.

The most troubling issue about the bombing, which was without a doubt the most devastating act ever carried out by a domestic terrorist against other Americans, is how little we still do not know and why so many questions remain unanswered. How could such a carefully planned attack come to such a bizarre and quick end?

The Federal Bureau of Investigation (FBI) immediately launched a massive investigation, and three separate trials were conducted against McVeigh and his co-conspirator, Terry Nichols, along with an enormous collection of court documents.

Continued on page 5a

Continued from page 1a

Even so, there is still no definitive answer to that question, and many other unanswered questions remain.

Investigators still don't know how McVeigh and Nichols learned how to build a fertilizer bomb with the mass and power needed to blow up a structure the size of the office building.

The identities of the other people seen with McVeigh on the morning of the bombing are still unknown, even though there were more than twenty eyewitnesses who told the FBI that he was not alone.

During the week leading up to the bombing, there was a second Ryder truck that was seen by witnesses at the motel in Junction City, Kansas, where McVeigh stayed, and at the state park, where the bomb was assembled. The investigation led to no answers as to why.

No explanation has been put forth for the other people that witnesses saw inside McVeigh's motel room.

Investigators could not provide a reasonable explanation for the fact that two people, neither of whom fit McVeigh's nor Nichols' descriptions, were spotted renting the bomb truck on April 17.

McVeigh provided no answers to these questions. In the end, he waived his right to further appeals and went to his execution in 2001.

Since the official account of the bombing is unfinished and unanswered, the questions remain. Who were these other people that witnesses saw, and what really happened?

CHAPTER 26

WHO AM I?

August 12, 2009
Greenwich Village, New York

"Michael, what can I do to help you out of this funky depression of yours? You've been moping around for far too long. Ever since you graduated, you've seemed lost. As your roommate, I have to live with you, so I deserve to know. Quite frankly, you're getting on my nerves and beginning to bring me down."

"Look, Jeff, I have problems you can't fix. I'm sure you won't understand—it even sounds weird to me when I say it—but I don't know who I am."

"Oh my God, what in hell do you mean by that?"

"Look, I'm twenty-seven years old, and I don't know the first thing about my roots or my family. I've never met any of my relatives—no grandparents, no aunts or uncles, and no cousins. All I know for sure is that my mother is French and my father is American. Other than that, I know nothing. My mother claims her family is part of a terrorist collective that has concocted some kind of diabolical plot to take over the world. She says she can't discuss anything about them with me or anybody else—and get this, it's for my own protection. I'm telling you, she's completely flipped out. I didn't even know I had a father until I was fourteen. Their story is that she used to work for her family and she hired him."

"Good Lord, Michael, now that I've heard everything, I guess I understand why you're depressed. But you can't go on like this. Let me ask you, do you think your parents care about you?"

"Yeah, I guess so. My mom did everything she could as a single mom to give me a good childhood. When my father came into the picture, he bent over backward to be a good parent. But they were gone much of the time on their so-called journeys. That's another thing—they did a lot of talking behind my back, which left me feeling like a total outsider. When they were away, I stayed at a boarding school near our home in Zurich. I just felt like I wasn't that important to them."

"Michael, you're not a kid anymore. If it bothers you so much, why don't you simply pin them down for answers?"

"No, way. The last time I saw them was six years ago. I told them back then that I wasn't interested in ever seeing them again."

"Have you ever thought about getting a copy of your birth certificate? I'm sure your mother has one somewhere. Maybe you should swallow your pride and ask her for it. Or, at the very least, ask her where you were born."

"I think I was born in a small town somewhere near Marseilles in France. I was young when we lived there, but

I do have some vague memories of it. Thanks anyway, Jeff, that's a great idea. I guess I could go online and find some genealogy websites."

Several days later

"Jeff, come here for a minute. I have something I want to show you. I downloaded a copy of my birth certificate today. It shows I was born on March 14, 1982, in Uzès, France. My mother's name is Camille-Gabriella Deneuve. But get this: it shows my father's name as Sean Patrick Phillips. That's weird because when I first met him, my mother introduced him as Sean Thompson."

"So, what are you going to do?"

"What do you think I'm going to do? I'm going to France."

"Michael, I have a bad feeling about this whole thing. If your mother is right about your relatives, I'm afraid you could get yourself into a lot of trouble. You did say your parents care about you, and it does sound to me that they are simply trying to protect you. As much as I would like to go with you, I hope you realize that I can't. My career and friends are here in New York. You should rethink this whole idea."

"Look, Jeff, you know who your family is. You can't possibly understand how I feel, and I don't expect you to help me—this is my battle. I've made up my mind, and I'm flying to France."

Seven Weeks Later
October 5, 2009
La Villa Rose Rouge

Uzès, France

"*Oui monsieur, puis-je vous aider?*"

"*Bonjour*, I'm Michael Deneuve. Do you speak English?"

"*Oui*, Mr. Deneuve, welcome to our hotel. We've been expecting you."

"*Merci*, I know I'm early, but by any chance, is my room ready?

"*Oui*, your room is ready, *monsieur*."

"One other thing—I haven't eaten in some time. Where would you recommend?"

"*Oui*, I would recommend the café right next door. When you arrive back here, your room key will be at the desk. In the meantime, I'll have room service turn down your bed for you. Enjoy your meal, Mr. Deneuve."

Le Café Du Jardin

"*Puis-je vous aider monsieur?*"

"I recently arrived in town, and I'm here alone. May I sit at the bar?"

"*Oui*, by all means, please seat yourself. I believe something is available next to one of our regulars."

Finding a seat next to a friendly face, Michael asked, "*Excusez-moi, monsieur*, is it alright with you if I sit here?"

"*Bonjour, mon nom est Jacques, et le vôtre?*"

"*Je suis désolé*, but my French is not up to par."

"*Oui*, you are a tourist visiting our village? Are you here for business or pleasure?"

"Both business and pleasure, I guess. I have come to Uzès to find someone. You asked my name, its Michael."

"Well, Michael, I've lived here all my life, and I know everyone. Perhaps I can be of some help. So, you are an American? But of course, you are an American, your accent gives you away, and you dress like an American. I'm not saying Americans are terrible dressers; actually, the British are worse. I'm sorry, I don't mean to insult you. My wife says I talk too much. Ah yes, my wife. I come here every night to get away from her for a while. She's a good woman, but she can drive me crazy. Michael, my friend, if you are married, you know what I mean."

"Jacques, you said you might be able to help me. I was born here twenty-seven years ago, and I came here to find my family. I was only six when we left, so I don't remember very much."

"Find your family? You mean, you don't know who your family is? My goodness, how tragic. Well, let me see. Twenty-seven years ago, I was thirty years old. Ugh, that makes me feel old. Anyway, I'm sure I must have known your mother and father. When did they leave here with you?"

"I only lived here with my mother, but I don't think she was born here."

"Michael, why don't you simply ask her about your family? That seems a lot easier than coming all the way here from America. Although, if you're going to be here for a while, I'm sure you'll fall in love with Uzès."

"I really don't want to get into that, Jacques. Let's just say my mother and I are not on speaking terms."

"Ah, I see. What's your mother's name? I'm sure I would have known her."

"Camille Deneuve."

"*Oh, mon Dieu,* of course, I should have known you're Michael! The last time I saw you, you were just a little guy. Wow, it's really good to see you. Everyone in town knew you and your mother. She was a real beauty and you were such a lovable little boy. I don't mean to be crass, but every guy in town had their eye on your mom, including me. I remember she didn't have many girlfriends. The young women in town were intimidated by her. But they really had no need to worry; your mother was not interested in any of us guys. Anyway, she didn't live here long. She arrived shortly before you were born and then left six years later."

"Okay, Jacques, but do you know where she came from?"

"Actually, nobody knew where she came from, but some of us had our suspicions. She was a mysterious woman, to say the least, and she definitely knew how to take care of herself. Money sure didn't seem to be a problem for her either. Interestingly, she didn't have a job, at least not here in Uzès. She rented a small house on the outskirts of town where the two of you lived. I remember she tended a beautiful garden that people would walk by and admire. Whenever she came into town, you were always by her side—she was very protective of you. But then, like I said, the two of you simply disappeared with no word. Michael, I'm interested, where did the two of you go?"

"Jacques, you said there were some who had their suspicions about where she came from?"

"Ah, yes, of course. The word was she left you at home with an au pair and would drive off toward Carcassonne, but she always returned home early the same evening. She usually went two or three times a week, always by herself. Some used to say that they thought she cared for a sickly relative, but that was just a guess. Like I said, she was a mysterious woman. She never talked about herself to anyone."

"You said she drove to Carcassonne?"

"You know what, Michael, I have an idea. I have to drive to Trebes next Thursday on business. It's on the outskirts of Carcassonne, and I could use the company. You are certainly welcome to join me."

"Thanks for the offer, Jacques, but I don't know how long I'll be staying there, it could be a while. Anyway, I want to hang around here in Uzès for the next couple of weeks and explore the area to see if I actually remember anything."

Several Weeks Later
Brasserie L'Escargot
Carcassonne, France

Raphael noticed a stranger sitting by himself. "Hey Patrice, look over there, a lonely American."

Patrice asked, "How is it you can tell which ones are the Americans?"

"It's easy. Look how he's dressed."

Patrice yelled out, "Hey Americano, you look lonely, please come and join us. We have room for one more here at our table, and the first drink is on us."

"Okay, guys, thank you. That would be great."

"I'm Patrice. Next to me is Raphael, across from me is André, and next to him is Lucas. What is your name, Americano, and where are you from?"

"I'm Michael, from New York."

"So, Michael from New York, what brings you to our historic city—business or pleasure?"

"I guess a little of each. I've been sightseeing for the last couple of weeks and just drove here from Uzès. I never realized how beautiful the south of France really is."

Patrice raised his glass as the others at the table toasted with him. "Let's drink to Michael, our new American friend. Even though you are younger than us, it doesn't matter. You are now officially one of us guys. We meet here often. The food is tolerable and you are our guest today, so please, help yourself."

"Oh my God, is that you, André? You must remember me—I'm Michael. We met in New York about five or six years ago at Sammy's Bar and Grille in Greenwich Village."

"Hmm, no, I'm sorry, Michael, you don't look familiar. You must have me confused with someone else."

Patrice interrupted, "Michael, our new American friend, we meet here every Wednesday and Friday afternoon. You are welcome to join us anytime you like." Laughing, he said, "But the next time you come here, you're buying the first round. For now, though, I have to get back to my office, so please excuse me. I must leave you gentlemen for now, and, oh yeah, you too, Lucas. I'll see you guys next week."

Lucas snapped back, "Ha-ha very funny, Patrice the comedian. The two of us must also go. What about you André, are you going or staying?"

"I haven't finished eating yet, and I want to give our new American friend some company until he's done eating." Then, teasing them, he quipped, "It's only polite, and unlike the three of you, I'm a polite guy. Besides, I'm interested in talking with Michael about American politics. So, I'll see you guys later."

Moments later after the three left, André leaned forward and quietly conceded, "Michael, now that we're alone, of course I remember you. Although, before you mentioned New York, I have to admit I didn't recognize you, especially with your short hair and new clothes. I can't believe you're here. How in the world did you ever find me? I never told you where I lived. I know I have a French accent, but France is a big country. So, please explain—how did you find me?"

Confused, Michael stammered, "I-I-I really don't know what to say. I'm as shocked as you are. I really have no explanation. You're right, you never told me you lived here. I came to France a couple of weeks ago based on the information on my birth certificate. And then I talked to a guy in Uzès who pointed me in this direction. Actually, the reason I came here has nothing to do with you. I'm here to find my family."

Alarmed, André tried to contain himself. "Your family! Why do you need to find your family? I don't understand."

"André, what's wrong? People track down their relatives all the time."

Hiding his shock with an excuse, he said, "No, no, you're right. I guess I was surprised because you can find things like that on the internet nowadays."

Michael continued, "I found out my mom and I lived in Uzès for about six years, before she moved us to Zurich. It seems the town people certainly remembered the two of us. The guy I talked to remembered her, but he didn't know what she did. It seems she never talked much about herself. He also told me she frequently drove to Carcassonne, but he didn't really know why. So that's what brought me here."

"Your family history must be very important to you."

"Yes, it is. Other than my birth certificate, I can't find any information about Deneuves in Uzès. So, here I am, and I'm not leaving here until I find out everything, even if it means getting a DNA test or hiring a private detective."

"*Merde alors,*" André shouted, "PRIVATE DETECTIVE!"

"My God, André, what's wrong with you?"

"I'm sorry Michael, I guess I've never heard anything like this before. It just seems extreme. Please go on."

"My mother has this fanatical idea that our family belongs to some kind terrorist cartel and wants to protect me from them."

"Wow Michael, that's a serious accusation to make of one's family. What do you think that's all about?"

"To be honest with you, André, I don't know and I don't care. I think my parents are both crazy. I don't want anything to do with either one of them."

Realizing time was critical, André excused himself, "Michael, I must be going, but I know somebody who may be able to help you. First, let me talk to him about your situation, and I'll get back to you next week. Do you have a number where I can reach you?"

The Following Week
The Office of Valentin Martel
Carcassonne, France

"*Bien, bien, bien,* who do we have here? Tell me my boy, what is your name?"

"*Bonjour, monsieur*, I'm Michael Deneuve."

"Hmm, very interesting, I know a lot people in France, but you are the first Deneuve. My name is Valentin Martel, but you may call me *Père*. I presume you do not speak much French, so to accommodate you, I will speak English. André tells me you want find out about your family."

"Yes sir, that is true. So, how do the two of you know each other?"

"Well, Michael, André is my son. But let's talk about why you're here today. I do believe I can help you. It's quite possible I may have even run across your mother when the two of you lived in Uzès. André tells me you were very young at the time. Tell me, son, what do you remember when you lived there?"

"Well, sir, I don't remember much, and yes, I was only six years old when we left. I do remember she would leave me alone with an au pair. The guy I met in Uzès knew her and said he thought she used to come to Carcassonne to take care of a sick relative."

With a sarcastic laugh, he scoffed, "A sick relative, ha-ha-ha how thoughtful of her. Tell me, Michael, where did the two of you move after you left Uzès?"

"We moved to Zurich."

"To Zurich? Hmm, it's interesting that she did not remain in France—such a lovely country. Do you know why she decided to move to Zurich?"

"Not really, other than the private boarding school she sent me to. She took good care of me when we were there, and she gave me much of her attention, that is, until my father moved in. He showed up in our lives when I was fourteen. That's when everything changed. After that, they were gone out of the country much of the time and left me there."

"Michael, tell me more about your father."

"Well, they told me his name is Sean Thompson, but that's another thing. My birth certificate shows his name as Sean Patrick Phillips."

Confused, Valentin leaned forward and challenged him. "Sean Phillips? No, son, you're mistaken. What you say is not possible."

"Oh my God, *Père*, why would you say that?

"Michael, my boy, please excuse me for questioning you. Did he ever tell you what he did for a living? What was his job? Who did he work for?"

"He said he was a technician, but other than that, I have no idea what he did or who he worked for. I do know he loved science and he spent hours teaching me some pretty amazing things."

"One other thing, Michael. What about your mother? When was the last time you saw her?"

"It was probably about six years ago, when they came to visit me in New York."

Shocked again by his revelation, Valentin couldn't contain himself. "What the hell are you talking about? Excuse me again, Michael, but I think you might be confused."

"No, sir. The last time I saw my mother and father was six years ago at my apartment in New York; I'm sure of it. That's when they came to visit me. By the way, what in the heck is wrong with the two of you? Everything I say seems to upset you."

"I'm sorry, my boy, for questioning you, I must have been thinking about someone else. I certainly understand the confusion you have about your family, because I certainly am. But for now, I need to have a chat with André, and we'll get back to you once we have some information."

"Thank you, *Père.* "

"André, I want to see you in my office—NOW!"

Later That Same Day
Brasserie L'Escargot
Carcassonne, France

"Michael, thank you for meeting me here on such short notice. We need to talk."

"Of course, André, no problem. By the way, other than being excitable and a little confused, I really like your father. He has shown more interest in me than anybody has in a long time. It's weird, and I don't know why, but he made me feel like I was part of your family. I actually believe he might be able to help me."

"Yes, he has a way of making people feel that way. Michael, I have to ask you to do me a big favor. My father and I have an awkward relationship. For reasons I can't go into right now, I ask you to never mention our meeting in New York—to him or anyone else. As far as you're concerned, that meeting never happened and our first encounter was right here, in this cafe."

"Sure, André, no problem, whatever you want. You have really been a big help, and I sure don't want to come between the two of you."

Feeling somewhat relieved, André continued, "My father was right when he said he has a lot of contacts here in France. I promise he will find out everything you want to know about your family history. Believe me, I'm sure you're going to hear more than you would like to know. And, be prepared, because my father can be blunt."

November 6, 2009
Martel Office Building
Carcassonne, France

"Michael, my boy," Valentin began, "we have a lot to talk about today. I want you to know my team has spent a great deal of time and resources to help you discover who your family is. It seems fate has brought you to the exact time and place to get the answers you came here to find. But be prepared; what I am about to reveal will not be easy for you. Nothing is what you think it is. This morning, I'll tell you all I know about your mother and father. Then, I'll present you with a life-altering question. This may well be the most important question of your life, and how you answer it may well determine your destiny."

"Okay, *Père*, now I'm really intrigued. You have my full attention."

"Michael, my boy, there's one thing I ask. Don't ask me any questions until I'm ready to answer them. I don't want to leave anything out. So, let's get started. First of all, allow me to tell you a little about myself. My family owns ten percent of a business we call Blackguard. The other ninety percent is owned by nine other very wealthy and powerful families who reside in other countries around the world. Our families can trace their lineage back over a thousand years, including my family, the Martel family. Collectively, we are a humanitarian group with one common goal: we want to make a better life for everyone, especially the disenfranchised. We feel there is far too much pain, hunger, disease, discrimination, and hatred in the world, and we want to do what we can to end it once and for all. However, the greedy, power-hungry governments, especially the United States', have much to lose if we are successful. So, we have developed a master plan to overcome these tyrants, but we still have a way to go. Thankfully, there are thousands of other people who are dedicated to our same causes."

Impressed, Michael commented, "I love that you want to make the world a better place for everyone, *Père*. I personally know a lot of people who feel the pain of discrimination and exclusion."

"Okay, Michael, no more about my family. We're here to talk about your family. Fate is an amazing thing. You left the United States and went to Uzès, your birthplace. Then, you met a random stranger at a café who told you your mother drove here to Carcassonne on occasion, so you came here. Then, quite by accident, you ran into André at a bistro, and he brought you to me."

"Yes, *Père*, that is all true."

"Well to begin, ironically, your mother was born right here in Carcassonne, and we hired her in 1972 to work in our employment office. She was one of the smartest, hardest-working young women who ever worked for us, and at the time, she certainly shared our core principles. You may find this hard to believe, but two years later, she actually hired your father. He was a brilliant young engineer with an amazing mind for science, exactly what we were looking for. She completed his background check and then signed his employment papers."

Realizing that Valentin had confirmed what his mother tried to tell him back at his apartment, Michael hesitated for a moment in amazement. "Oh my God, you've got to be kidding. You're telling me my mother worked for your company, and she hired my father?"

"I am not kidding about any of this, Michael. After only five years, she promoted him as our technical liaison and gave him the responsibility for the installation and maintenance of our new technologies. We provided both of them with the best of everything, including generous salaries, private jets, and plenty of time off. We gave them all they needed so their lives would be as easy and comfortable as possible. That's how much we valued them.

"Then in 1981, we scheduled your father to come here to Carcassonne to install our new computer system. Because your mother hired him and had never personally met him, I thought it would be a good opportunity for her to go to Marseilles, where he was staying, to personally meet with him before he came here. They were the perfect employees for Blackguard. That is, until 1996 when I heard of their plane crash in the Caribbean. Your mother was aboard that plane."

"*Père,* again, my mother did not die in a plane crash—she's fine."

"Please, Michael, I told you not to interrupt me. What I'm about to reveal is complicated and painful for me to relive. Yes, now I know she is alive. With the help of my assistants and discussions with André, we constructed a timeline to make sense of it all. But I must warn you, when you see this chart, it may confuse you."

Name	Age	Date	Event
Camille	22	1 Sept 1972	Hire date
Sean	24	20 May 1974	Hire date
Sean	29	27 Feb 1979	Promoted to Technical Liaison
Camille	31	20 Jun 1981	Met Sean in Marseilles

(9 months later)

<u>Birth certificate: Camille-Gabriella Deneuve & Sean Patrick Phillips</u>

Name	Age	Date	Event
Michael		14 Mar 1982	Birthdate
Sean	45	3 Jan 1995	Letter of resignation to Blackguard
Sean	45	10 Jun 1995	Married Lila Knowles
Camille	45	11 Jun 1995	Plane crash (pronounced dead)
Sean	45	11 Jun 1995	Plane crash (pronounced dead)
Michael	14	22 Jul 1996	Met father as Sean Thompson

After a few minutes of studying the chart, Michael remarked, "I have to say, *Père,* this whole thing makes no sense. So, I have a question. Why in the world would they want to fake their own deaths?"

"My dear boy, there is a whole lot more to the story, but I'm not convinced you can handle the truth. Now that you have the background on your mother and father, I believe it's time for your question. Your answer will be the biggest decision of your life. I caution you to think about your future very carefully, because once you give me your answer, you cannot turn back. You only get one shot at it."

"This is obviously a lot for me to take in, *Père*, but I came to France to discover the truth about my family, so I guess I'm ready for anything."

"Okay, son. André and I have given your situation a lot of thought, and we want to make you an offer. Your fate has played a large part in this, and you have gone to extraordinary lengths to find us. We believe you are here for a reason, and we would like to give you that reason. Michael, you're the child of our once most valued employees. We would like to hire you and offer you a position with us here at Blackguard. Our work is so critical that we must have a hundred percent commitment from you. You should know we take very good care of our people, no matter where they are in the world. But with that commitment from us comes a commitment from you. Employment with Blackguard is classified. If you were to break our code of silence, I can't help you. My boy, allow me to repeat, for your own sake, do not jump into this offer until you carefully consider it. And let me remind you again—once you commit to it, you cannot turn back."

"Wow, I'm overwhelmed. However, I really don't have much going on in my life right now. And your point about fate bringing me here certainly makes sense. For most of my life, I have felt different—like a part of me is missing. This feeling has gone on for far too long. I told André that I feel connected when I'm with the two of you. You have shown more interest in me than anybody else has in a very long time. I don't need to think about it, *Père*, I've already made up my mind. I want to be right here with you and André."

"Michael, my boy, you have chosen wisely. Welcome to the team."

"*Père*, is it alright if I call my roommate to let him know I won't be returning back to New York?"

"Of course. How about you make that call right now so we can move on with our discussion. Give me his number and I'll dial it for you on my phone. After you've had your talk and told him of your decision, I ask that you have no further contact with him or anybody else other than André and me for a while. And for God's sake, do not mention anything about us, Blackguard, or this Carcassonne office. You will be an important person in our organization and will learn a whole new way to communicate with people."

Twenty minutes later

After a last goodbye, Michael handed the phone back to Valentin. "Okay, Michael, now that you have accepted our offer—it's time."

Puzzled, Michael asked, "Time for what?"

"Michael, my boy, you have proven your allegiance to us, so I'm thrilled to tell you this. I have done a lot of things in my life, but I have never done or said anything like what I'm about to tell you. I am not a man to deliver news gently, so I'll get right to the point. Your mother, Camille-Gabriella Martel, is my daughter, which makes you my grandson. André is my son and your mother's twin brother. He is your uncle. You are a Martel, my boy, and we are proud and excited beyond words to welcome you into your family."

Reacting to the news and barely able to speak, Michael sobbed. "*Père,* I apologize—I can't believe it. I don't know what to say. I trusted my mother. Why did she hide me from you and my family all these years? And why did she move me away from you?"

"I knew this news would overwhelm you. Maybe we should take a break for now. I'll have some lunch brought in and the three of us can take some time to sort out this life-changing turn of events."

"Please, *Père,* answer my question. I need to know. It's important to me."

"Michael, I am sure your mother was a wonderful parent and did her best to raise you. I believe she felt she was somehow protecting you, but I really have no idea why. But in doing so, she brought disgrace on the Martel family when she turned away from us. What makes it so heartbreaking is that we have no idea why she left us. Perhaps it has something to do with your father. After the two of them met in Marseilles, her relationship with us changed. Isn't that right, André? André, let me ask you, you were close to your sister. Do you have any thoughts?"

Unexpectedly put on the spot, he answered, "Not really, Father. At one time, Camille and I were very close. We used to talk about everything. We didn't always agree, but that was usually over our competitive, sibling rivalry stuff. But you're right, her attitude shifted dramatically after she met Sean Phillips—or Thompson—whatever his name is."

Valentin continued, "Michael, did you notice anything much different about your mother after your father came to live with you?"

"Well, for one thing, they were very affectionate toward each other and she certainly seemed happier and more content when he was around. The only other thing I noticed that seemed weird, is they spent a lot of time reading the Bible, and talked incessantly about Genesis."

"Religion, really! Your mother and father have become religious," Valentin laughed. "It's interesting to me they turned to God. That is actually very funny."

"*Père*, you said I would have a lifelong position with Blackguard."

"Okay, son, let's get down to business. I told you the goals our family and business associates share. You are going to have a prominent role to play. We have a lot of enemies who are trying to stop us. They view our cause as a threat to their unbridled greed and lust for money and power. But we are powerful and well-organized, and in the end, we will prevail and bring prosperity and world peace to all. We will provide medicines and vaccines to eliminate pandemics, grow enough food for the hungry, and provide the basic necessities of life to third-world countries. But we need soldiers, and we want you to become the lead soldier for the Martel family."

"A soldier?"

"Yes, Michael, a soldier. You should know you have another uncle besides André, your uncle Antoine. From this point forward, think of him as your drill sergeant. He's going to whip you into shape and teach you skills you may have only read about in books or seen in the movies.

We want you to become proficient in the use of a large variety of weapons, tracking skills, fighting techniques, and other useful survival skills. Antoine will train you to become an extremely valuable *asset* to our cause. You will be sent all over the world to carry out our orders. That might mean eliminating some very dangerous people. Michael, do you think you're man enough to handle that?"

"*Père*, don't ask me to kill people. You must understand that when I was in college, my friends and I organized peace groups. We marched, held rallies, and handed out flyers to help bring peace and understanding to our generation. No, I cannot and will not kill people."

"Michael, okay, I see you're a very sensitive and caring young man."

Suddenly defensive, he immediately shot back, "Yes, but what does that have to do with anything?"

"Michael, Michael, please relax. I simply want to make a point. Intolerance is one of the most disturbing sins we are trying to eradicate. But holding rallies and handing out flyers is not going to get the job done. You have to go after the source of prejudice—those power-hungry, hate-filled elitists who think they are better than everyone else. Only then will we be able to bring about the lasting change you are fighting for."

"Okay, *Père*, of course I see your point, but I can't kill people."

"Michael, my boy, you must learn to fight the haters or we won't survive in this world. I haven't known you for long, but from what I can see, you seem to be a bright, passionate young man. At some point, you must take a stand. The time for that is right now. Do you understand what I'm saying?"

"Yes, sir, I do, but—"

"One other thing, I am going to restore your birthright. You are Martel family now, and I am personally going to have your birth certificate amended and make it official on our family tree. However, to the rest of the world, you will remain Michael Deneuve. Son, it's my honor to bestow this title on you at this stage of my life. Coincidentally, you came here to Carcassonne at a very important time for me. I'm an old man and will soon retire. To see my only grandson join our ranks is truly heartwarming. Since Antoine is my eldest, I will pass my duties over to him within the next couple of months. So, when you have completed your training, I expect you to carry out your orders without question and without hesitation. Michael, do not disappoint me. Is that clear, soldier?"

De: andré.lemieux1950@carca.fr
Á: camille120@swiss.ch
6 Novembre 2009

URGENT

Michael found his birth certificate and is in Carcassonne. Don't ask me how it happened because I honestly don't know. He found his way to Uzès and then, quite by accident, ran into me at a bistro here in Carcassonne. He told me he was not leaving France until he finds out everything, even if it means getting a DNA test or hiring private detectives. We cannot have detectives snooping around here. I had no choice and introduced him to Father yesterday. He now knows you are alive and where you live. He also knows Michael is his grandson, and has recruited him into the family as an asset. If he finds out I've known about the two of you since the plane crash, I'm a dead man. I made Michael promise me he would not mention my meeting with him in New York, so I certainly hope you taught him to keep his promises. One other thing, Father appointed Antoine to train Michael. Be careful, and do what you need to do.

CHAPTER 27

CRUSHED

THE TWENTY-EIGHTH STEP

November 6, 2009
Zurich, Switzerland

"Camille, you have to stop crying. I know André's email is upsetting, but Michael is a smart boy and has a promising future in New York. Plus, all of his friends and connections are there. I really don't believe he'll do anything foolish. Even though he hasn't shown it for some time, I know he loves us. Our prodigal son will return—I'm sure of it."

"I know you're trying to make me feel better, but we haven't seen or heard from him for over six years. I'm really sorry now we didn't try harder to patch things up with him when we had the chance. Now he's under my Father's influence, and you don't know Valentin Martel like I do. He's a master manipulator and will pull out all the stops to win him over. You have to understand, he doesn't care about

Michael. He only wants to use him to get even with me. He's a hateful, vengeful man and only cares about himself."

"I understand, but so far, your family has left us alone. You're right though, now it's personal between you and your father, and unfortunately Michael is caught in the middle. So more than ever, it's time to dig in our heels if we have any chance of getting him back."

"I know you're right, but I'm too upset. This is not a good time. Please be patient with me."

"I don't mean to add to your grief, but we have another problem. Now your father knows where we live."

"Believe me, I haven't forgotten. But I don't think he sees us as a threat. Like I said, he wants to punish me. At least for now, with Michael under his control, that's enough to satisfy him. But, if it would make you feel better, we can move somewhere else."

"I really don't want to, but I haven't forgotten what you said about ex-employees being eliminated."

"Sean, trust me, I'm sure he's not worried about us. Remember the Martel coat of arms? If and when he finds out what we're up to, he will personally lay Michael's head at our doorstep. So, no, my father is not ready to eliminate us just yet. For now, he has other plans. He wants to use Michael to torture me and make my life unbearable."

"Okay, let's think about this. He has Michael, his one and only grandson, so he's not going to harm him, especially if he can use him to get revenge. If you're right, I think we should stay here until we collect our thoughts, get our emotions under control, take a well-deserved vacation, and then reorganize our plans."

"I like that. I really need to get away from all of this. My nerves are shattered."

"I'll tell you what, sweetheart, let's leave tomorrow, and you choose where you would like to go. But this coming spring, I would like to go to Washington. Neither of us have ever been there before. There's a new exhibit at the Smithsonian I've read about, but it isn't scheduled to open until March. That should give us plenty of time to regain our composure over this whole thing."

"Sean, I don't know. I'll see how I feel by then, but don't count on it."

"Okay, but I've also been thinking that even though we don't have all our evidence ready, I really think we should go to the FBI as soon as possible. This latest development with Michael has also put me over the top."

"*Oui,* I agree, but without evidence, I'm not sure they will be willing to meet with us. And Sean, there's another thing—something I haven't told you. I don't want you to worry, but I've been having some weird symptoms for some time now, especially the peripheral neuropathy on my hands and feet and the vertigo. After running a series of tests, my doctors suspect it's something they call EMF syndrome."

Camille never complained about anything, so her symptoms suddenly became a red flag for me. Since I had never heard of this EMF thing, she explained that they are electromagnetic frequencies given off by cell towers, cell phones, and all the new cell technology that was popping up everywhere. But if we were going to the FBI, we needed to get on an airplane to the United

States. Big cities and airports are loaded with these EMFs, so my protective instinct was to go by myself. But after a very long discussion, she convinced me that she had to go too.

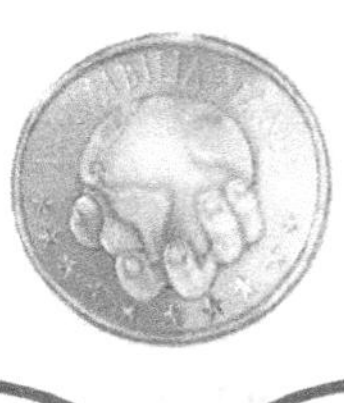

CHAPTER 28

BRING IN THE TROOPS

THE TWENTY-NINTH STEP

January 28, 2010
Meeting Room 312
Hotel Washington
Washington, DC

"Mr. Phillips, thank you for meeting with us today. I'm Special Agent Frank Sullivan, heading up this investigation. To my right is Special Agent Jim Gannon, and across from him is Special Agent Dianne McClellan. Agent Ed Clark can't be with us today. It's his job to compile the notes from your testimony and then correlate them with your journals. Anyway, his presence isn't essential, since we'll be recording this interview. One other thing, before we get started, I assume Ms. Deneuve will be arriving soon."

"I'm sorry, not today. Unfortunately, she suffers from a disorder, something called EMF syndrome. And for some reason, it seems to be far worse when she's here in the United States. So for now, she's up in our room until she feels better.

"Hmm, EMF syndrome—I've never heard of it. You do understand that her testimony is essential?"

"Yes, sir, I do, but I never know how she'll feel. When she gets anywhere near cell towers or is on her cell phone, she gets some pretty severe symptoms. The worst is vertigo, neuropathy, and headaches, and this hotel must be loaded with EMFs. So she'll meet with you as soon as she is able."

Sullivan continued, "Allow me to commend you, Mr. Phillips. Your journals have been an invaluable source of evidence for our preliminary inquiry. Like we discussed on the phone, you're here today to give us your verbal testimony regarding your involvement with Blackguard. What you disclose is critical before we can launch a full-scale investigation. This interview will no doubt take some time, but we have all day. Unless you have any questions, I would like to get started."

"Excuse me, Mr. Phillips," Agent Diane McClellan interrupted. "I have a question about the letter you sent to CIDEC. Your name is Sean, but you signed it as S-H-A-W-N. Why?"

"Because phonetically, both spellings are pronounced the same, so S-H-A-W-N is the code name I used."

Frank Sullivan then added, "That letter, along with the virus you gave them, is what alerted us, but I also have a couple of questions. You made that contact with CIDEC seven years ago; why did you wait until now to call us?"

"Well, for one thing, you would have likely thrown us in prison back then. It has taken us all this time to gather our evidence. What's your second question?"

"What if your testimony today is not enough for us to move forward? How will I convince the brass that the audacious claims you make are factual and not some outlandish conspiracy theory the two of you cooked up?"

"Yeah, you have a point. Okay, Agent Sullivan, I'll make this personal for you. Back when I was a kid and got sick, my parents called the family doctor, and he would come to the house to treat us. Usually, all it took was a shot of penicillin, some over-the-counter medicine, or sometimes a prescription from the corner drugstore. If the illness was more serious, he would send his patients to the hospital. That's the way it was all over America. We didn't have anywhere near the health crisis we have today. In fact, at that time we were considered the healthiest country in the world. Patients from everywhere came to the United States to get treated, and students came here to study medicine.

"You can check the statistics for yourself—the United States now rates 35th. We lead the world in all the major diseases, like cancer, heart failure, diabetes, obesity, and so forth. The record shows the pharmaceutical industry alone is expected to gross over half a trillion dollars this year, and total health care in the U.S. will exceed $3.65 trillion. In comparison, revenue for the entire technology industry is expected to reach only $407 billion. That makes healthcare costs in the U.S. nine times greater than all technology spending. So, there you have it, Agent Sullivan. America is the sickest country on Earth, and we spend far more money than anybody else on questionable cures. So, I ask you, what's happened to Americans since we were kids? Is that personal enough for you? Don't you want to find out why this has happened?"

"Okay, Phillips, let's say we believe you. What then? Keep in mind, we need tangible evidence of your claims. You gave us your journals, and you said Camille would give us the 1978 Red Book. But my bosses might look at them as complete fiction, a story the two of you fabricated. Even if they do believe you, they will still want key witnesses to corroborate your claims. One other thing, Mr. Phillips, you told me on the phone that you want to go public with this information. How in the world do you think you're going to do that?"

"How will I do that? I sure hope you don't expect me and Camille to do everything. Here's my wish list. And you will be responsible for arranging this audience, as well as the venue."

- ▶ All members of the UN General Assembly
- ▶ Representatives from every major religion
- ▶ Representatives from every branch of science
- ▶ Leaders of every industrialized country
- ▶ Fortune 500 CEOs
- ▶ Deans from every major university
- ▶ High-ranking generals from the military
- ▶ Leaders of WHO and CIDEC

"Phillips, you're crazy! This list is ridiculous. What you ask for here is not possible."

"Agent Sullivan, these are the same people who have stuck their heads in the sand for far too long and wittingly or unwittingly have participated with Blackguard. Believe me when I tell you that the only possible hope you have of defeating Blackguard is to unite this group under one common cause. The world united to win World War II, and we must unite again if we are to survive. So, no sir, I'm not crazy. I've never been more serious in my life. Please keep in mind, Camille and I are simply the messengers."

"Okay, Phillips, I'm still not on board with any of this."

"Oh, that's not all, Agent Sullivan. You see, there's a second enormous problem the world is going to have to deal with. Scientists call it the sixth mass extinction, a pollution disaster that is killing off thousands of species every year."

"My God, what in the hell is that? Anyway, right now it doesn't matter. Listen to me, Phillips. Even if we were able to somehow arrange this so-called meeting, where do you think we can accommodate that many people with the facilities required to secure them? Keep in mind they will also bring their personnel with them, not to mention the aircraft they will arrive on."

"You're a law enforcement officer. I'm sure you can figure it out."

"Okay, Phillips, go ahead with your testimony, but you better not be wasting our time here today."

"Sure, where do you want me to start?"

"Why don't you start at the beginning?"

Two Months Later
Washington Hotel
Washington D.C.

"Mr. Phillips, thank you for flying back to Washington to meet with us again. I would like to spend some time to chat with you, but we need to get right down to business. I have some good news for you. You gave us a lot of information, and Agent Clark correlated it with your testimony. His report indicates everything you claim checks out so far."

"Okay, that's great! So, did you go to all the locations I mentioned in the journals, especially Area C where I worked in Detroit?"

"Unfortunately, no judge will grant us a search warrant without the solid evidence needed for due cause, and Interpol will not cooperate with us for the same reason."

"Frank, I don't understand the system. You need to go to their offices and their four divisions to get the evidence."

"Yes, Sean, I know. Believe me it's very frustrating for us, too. However, you asked me earlier if the ice packs did their job, and I can assure you they did. CIDEC has spent a great deal of time evaluating those samples. They have concluded that it's a novel strain of the coronavirus, one they have never seen before. But, they also determined it lacked the characteristics to classify it as a deadly pathogen. Most likely it would produce symptoms no more severe than the common cold or flu. Their final conclusion is that the virus could be the precursor of a weaponized version. So, you see Mr. Phillips, that's the reason we were anxious for you to testify when you came to us. Like I said before, you hold all the cards. If we have any hope at all of exposing Blackguard, and now this mass extinction event you mentioned, it will be up to the two of you to bring us the additional evidence and the witnesses we need. Oh, and by the way, the brass contacted some leading scientists here in the United States to verify this sixth mass extinction you mentioned. Actually, it's quite terrifying what they had to say."

"So, what's the good news?"

"The good news is we believe you. But I do have one other question for you, Mr. Phillips. Why are you putting so much energy into all of this? What do you and Camille possibly have to gain, other than the impossible mission of saving the world?"

"It's simple. First and foremost, we want our son back. And also because we are running out of time before the Invisible Hand and the extinction event come crashing down on humanity."

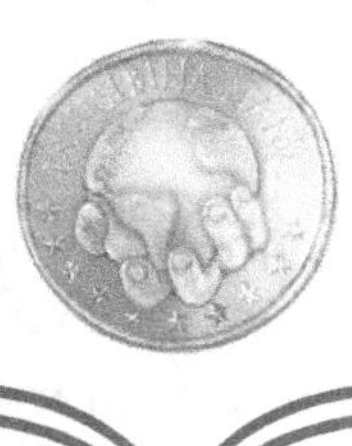

CHAPTER 29

SOMEBODY'S WATCHING US

THE THIRTIETH STEP

June 9, 2010
Hall of Human Origins
Smithsonian Institute
Washington, D.C.

"Sweetheart, I don't know if I thanked you, but I really do appreciate that you came here with me to Washington, even though I know your heart is not in it. I know these are challenging times and Michael is constantly on your mind, but we need to get back on track."

"You could have suggested a nice resort or someplace more relaxing. I do like Washington, and I know you explained it, but I really don't understand why you wanted to come here to the Smithsonian."

"Yeah, sometimes my need for efficiency sends mixed signals. There's a new exhibit about human evolution and I think it might help us. Since the next several verses of Genesis deal with human origins, I thought it would be helpful if we learned a little more about our prehistoric ancestors."

"Maybe so, Sean, but I really don't care about any of it right now. However, since we are here, I'll try and act more enthusiastic."

"That would be great. Is it okay with you if we stop by the gift shop for a moment while we're here? There are a couple of books I'd like to get. I'm hoping they might shed some light on verse 26, '*Let us make man in our image, after our likeness.*'"

"Sure, go ahead. I don't really care."

"Wow, Camille, look at those posters over there. Think about it; that's what our prehistoric ancestors may have looked like. Anyway, the creation of man was the final event in the Genesis timeline."

"Sean, please, I can't think about anything right now, especially Genesis."

"Unbelievable. You really are not interested."

Camille's indifference toward our research was on full display ever since she found out about Michael. I knew the only way I had of getting her back on track was to make some progress. I needed to find a way to get him off her mind. If I could distract her for even a short time, she might stop wallowing and come back around. So, I suggested we go back to our hotel, get some lunch, and relax by the pool with some drinks.

For the next several days, we toured Washington. We bought two-day tickets for the on-off trolley and explored all the sights our nation's capital had to offer. She really liked the Washington Zoo, especially the panda exhibit. And each evening we enjoyed the nightlife in Georgetown. My strategy paid off.

Later that week

"Sweetheart, before we plan our day, I need your help. I could barely sleep last night thinking about it. I promise it won't take more than a few minutes, and then no more Genesis talk. Whadaya say?"

"Sure, go ahead. I think I'm fine, at least for now."

"Okay then. Don't forget verse 26: *'Let us make man in our image, after our likeness.'* I have suspected for some time that it is a metaphor the author used to differentiate humans from the animals. So, I compared the words in Strong's Concordance. In Hebrew, *'image'* can mean either phantom or illusion, and *'likeness'* can mean resemblance, concretely, model or shape. In effect, this verse seems to imply that humans are physical beings with a nonphysical spirit. I believe it points out that man differs from the animals because we have a physical *'likeness'* to something we have not yet figured out, and a nonphysical *'image'* to Spirit. But unlike the animals, humans are a combination of both image and likeness. In other words, we are both spiritual and physical beings at the same time. The verse then goes on to read:

"*'And let them have dominion over the fish of the sea, and over the fowl of the air, and over the cattle, and over all the earth, and over every creeping thing that creepeth upon the earth.'*

"Again, according to Strong's Concordance, *'dominion'* has two meanings. One of them means we are a higher order than the animals. It doesn't mean, as many believe, that God said we could do with them whatever we wanted to with them, including killing them into extinction."

"*C'est voir*, but I still don't see how these verses correlate to science. Sean, we're wasting our time here. You wanted to come to Washington to have a vacation, so let's decide what we're going to do today."

"Alright, but stay with me for one more moment before I forget. The fossil evidence indicates primitive ape-like hominids, like the ones depicted on these posters, are the ancestors of modern humans."

"Okay, so what you're implying is the sequence of that split falls in line with the Genesis timeline. But we still don't know who the other half of '*us*' and '*our*' is."

Exasperated, I said, "Yes, Camille, I know."

"Good, can we stop this for now? You're driving me crazy. I want to do something else, Sean. I'm in no mood to figure out riddles today."

"Okay, thirty more seconds, I promise. Verse 27 reads, '*and God created man in His own image, in the image of God created He him; male and female created He them.*'"

"*Oui,* I agree that is a fascinating verse. Is that what you wanted to hear?"

"If you give me a minute, I'm simply trying to say that this verse contradicts Adam and Eve in the Garden of Eden story in Genesis 2, on a so-called seventh day."

"Yes, I know, Sean. Genesis 2 was no doubt written by a different author. The verse says that God took Adam's rib and created Eve—they were created separately, which of course makes no sense at all from a biological perspective. On the other hand, the Genesis 1 author made it a point to write '*male and female*' together in the same verse. It's all academic. I'm done."

"Alright, alright, but since we're, here I still want to go back to the hominid display. Other than enjoying a vacation with you, it's the main reason I wanted to come to Washington."

Later that day at the hominid display

THE ANSWER LIES NOT IN WHAT WE SEE, IT LIES IN WHAT WE DON'T SEE.

"Excuse me, Miss, that's an unusual title for a DNA exhibit. Can you tell me what that sign means?"

"Yes, sir, we get that question a lot. The exhibit points out how geneticists use DNA analysis to reveal human evolutionary timelines. We like to say fossils are what we see, but DNA tells us what we don't see. When they take DNA samples from present day genomes and then compare them to hominid fossil DNA, it provides a complementary method to date evolutionary events. Genetic changes happen at a steady rate, and those changes give us an idea of the elapsed time between the generations of hominid and human ancestors. Think of it like the ticks on a stopwatch—what we call a 'molecular clock.' When comparing these DNA sequences, we can reconstruct the relationships between different hominid groups and extrapolate their evolutionary history over extremely long timescales."

"Wow, that all sounds very interesting. Thank you. By the way, when does the next tour begin?"

"Sean, please excuse me, but we have to go back to our hotel. I'm tired and I don't feel well. We can always come back tomorrow. I don't like to complain, but my EMF neuropathy is really bad today, and I'm getting more symptoms that are starting to concern me."

"Oh my God, now what?

"Like I've told you before, the worst is the neuropathy on the soles of my feet and my palms, like hundreds of sharp needles stabbing me, and they turn beet red. Then, there's insomnia, which is definitely worse when we are here in the U.S. Usually, I can meditate, which thankfully helps me get to sleep. But when the symptoms are severe, my dreams can be quite disturbing. I've also been getting headaches, along with other symptoms I never used to get."

"Camille, you need to tell me when you're having these problems. I'm here for you, no matter what else is going on."

"I know you want to help, but if the doctors can't help me, I don't see what you can do. Please, let's just go back to our hotel room."

"Of course, I'll flag down a cab right away."

But then, suddenly startled, she whispered, "Sean, wait a second. Look over there, but don't make it obvious. See that man standing next to the vending machine, the one with the short hair and sunglasses? I could swear he's the same guy I saw at the airport yesterday, watching us. Maybe I've worked with my family for too long and am just paranoid, but I'm afraid it could be one of their assets. I thought if we waited long enough, we would throw him off. Regardless, we need to ditch him and move to another hotel right away."

SWINE-INFLUENZA A (H1N1) VIRUS INFECTION SWEEPS ACROSS THE WORLD

Atlanta, May 22, 2010 (National News)

On April 17, 2009, the Centers for Disease Control and Prevention (CDC) identified two cases of human infection with a swine-origin influenza A (H1N1) virus. The World Organization (WHO) reports the swine influenza strain has not been isolated in pigs and can be transmitted from human to human.

On April 25, the WHO declared a public health emergency of international concern, and on April 26, the United States declared a public health emergency.

On April 29, the WHO raised the pandemic influenza phase from 4 to 5, indicating human-to-human transmission of the virus was occurring in at least two countries.

By May 5, 2009, a total of 642 cases had been identified in the United States, and other additional cases had been identified in Mexico, Canada, and Southeast Asia.

According to the latest reports, death from swine flu has reached 1,235, with 123,397 people tested in India as of February 1, 2010. Of the people tested, 23.3% were suffering from swine flu. Symptoms include fever, cough, sore throat, body aches, headache, chills, and fatigue. Many of the severe cases have involved other chronic health conditions, with an increased percentage of patients reporting diarrhea and vomiting.

Between a third and half of the serious swine flu cases have occurred in otherwise healthy, young to middle-aged adults. Overall, the majority of infections have occurred in individuals aged younger than 25 years.

Researchers worldwide remain puzzled as to how the transmission from pigs to humans could have occurred naturally.

HEALTHCARE WORKERS VOICE DEEP CONCERN OVER DEVELOPING EBOLA OUTBREAK

Atlanta, August 15, 2015 (National News)

The latest news from West Africa reveals the rate of new Ebola cases continues to fall, and it appears that the newly developed vaccine is providing some protection against the deadly infection. But we are told by healthcare workers that reporting only on these optimistic developments ignores the bigger picture and the many overwhelming challenges that remain in bringing this disease under control.

This West African epidemic has caused at least 12,000 deaths since it was first reported in Guinea in March 2014. It is extremely tenacious, has proven hard to contain, and if left unchecked, may grow into a much larger pandemic. It could not have developed in a more underserved region of the world with the severe shortage of health professionals.

This silent epidemic of sickness and death can be traced back to late February 2014, from the illness of one woman from Sierra Leone. According to her neighbors and family, she became ill shortly after returning home after traveling in Guinea. She then crossed back into Guinea and died there while undergoing treatment.

Medical experts believe this strain of the virus is a mutation from earlier strains, but unfortunately, based on test results, they remain skeptical and cannot account for the origin of this novel strain and how that first woman contracted it.

EDITORIAL: THE EXACT ORIGIN OF THE FATAL AIDS EPIDEMIC FIRST IDENTIFIED IN 1981 REMAINS UNKNOWN

Atlanta, June 22, 2016 (National News)

In 1981, doctors from New York City and the San Francisco Bay area diagnosed a rare and often fatal disease in 41 homosexual men. Among the diagnoses, eight of the fatalities died within 24 months. The cause of this outbreak at that time was unknown.

Since then, researchers have identified a species of chimpanzee in West Africa as the source of HIV infection in humans. They theorize it is the source of the virus and was most likely transmitted to humans and mutated into HIV when humans hunted chimpanzees for meat and came into contact with their blood. This tradition has been practiced for centuries. So, the question remains: why did the virus transmit to humans at this time?

Continued on page 2

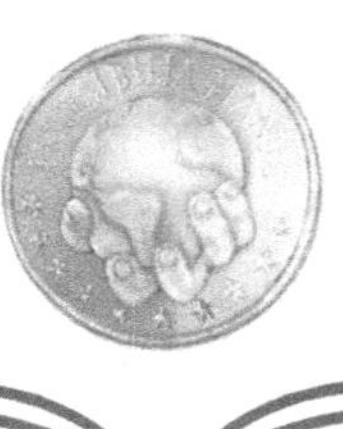

CHAPTER 30

THE BEAST

"This trail is never-changing, it won't lead you astray. It won't always be easy to follow and at times it will look too narrow. Follow it anyway, and you'll overcome every challenge you face."—Brittany L. Engels

After Camille's father died in 2018, Antoine took over as Chief Council of the notorious Martel family. He was young and ambitious, anxious to make his mark, and relentless in doing his part to advance Agenda One. The frustration we felt from all the dead ends and setbacks we encountered in stopping him and the Invisible Hand was akin to continually running into a brick wall. It was absolute torture knowing there was nothing we or anybody else could do to stop them or even slow them down. They were on the verge, perhaps less than a year away, of releasing their deadly virus on the world. In order to feel like we were making some headway, we continued to collect newspaper articles. With little left in our quiver of arrows, we spent many sleepless nights hashing and rehashing our frustration.

"Camille, we have to get the last piece of this Genesis puzzle solved. Time just keeps marching on, and we're getting nowhere. I've read in National Geographic, Discover, and a lot of environmental publications that more and more species are disappearing at an alarming rate. If this continues, we won't have to worry about Invisibilia Manus, an environmental apocalypse, or anything else for that matter."

"Sean, I know how discouraged you are, but I may have an idea. I've been thinking a lot about Father Larouche. He was the priest at Saint-Étienne, the church I went to when I lived in Uzès. He was a genius when it came to deciphering Biblical metaphors. He would weave them into his Sunday sermons, and he had amazing insights into the meaning of obscure scriptural passages."

"I'm sure they were great, sweetheart, but we don't know for sure if *'the beast of the earth'* is actually a metaphor. So, to be honest with you, I think going there will be a waste of our time."

"Sean, it sounds like you're poo-pooing my idea."

"That is definitely not true. Okay, I'll tell you what. Before we go all the way to Uzès, let me first show you what I discovered and then decide if we should go or not. I think it's important."

"Of course, Sean, whatever you say. I would never even think of poo-pooing your ideas."

"Ha-ha, okay, I get your drift. Anyway, I did some more digging and discovered the Hebrew word for beast has two grammatical forms, the plural and the singular. The singular form is 'behema,' as in *the beast of the earth.'* Interestingly, the author used that phrase in both verses 24 and 25.

"*'And God said: 'Let the earth bring forth the living creature after its kind, cattle, and creeping thing, and the beast of the earth after its kind.' And it was so. And God made the beast of the earth after its kind, and the cattle after their kind, and every thing that creepeth upon the ground after its kind; and God saw that it was good.'*"

"*Le bien* Sean, but I don't understand how that solves our problem."

"It's a subtle but important difference, because in verses 29 and 30, he wrote:

"*'And God said: 'Behold, I have given you every herb yielding seed, which is upon the face of all the earth, and every tree, in which is the fruit of a tree yielding seed—to you it shall be for food; and to every beast of the earth, and to every fowl of the air, and to every thing that creepeth upon the earth.'*

"In this verse, *'every beast of the earth'* is 'behemot' and is the plural form. It refers to livestock, or beasts of burden like oxen, sheep, horses, donkeys, goats, and cows. Now, here's the thing: the singular form, 'behema,' only appears in verses 24 and 25 and nowhere else in the entire Bible. Keep in mind, the Hebrew vocabulary was limited, so 'behema' must have been the closest word at their disposal to describe this mysterious creature."

"Okay, Sean, I get it. You have narrowed the Genesis correlation down to one word. But you still don't have any idea what it actually is, do you?"

"No, damn it, I don't. So, once again, you are right. We certainly have nothing to lose by going to see your priest. Besides, I would love to see where you used to live."

"*Merci*, Sean."

At this point along the Trail, my patience ran particularly thin, and I took it out on Camille far too many times. It seemed that the talks we had and her words, "*You'll see it when you believe it,*" still eluded me. It was frustrating, because only one word separated us from completing the Genesis Correlation. So, with few options left, we booked our flight to France.

CHAPTER 31

FATHER LAROUCHE

THE THIRTY-FIRST STEP

October 5, 2018
Uzès, France

Camille was very excited to return to the village where she spent six years of her life with Michael. After we got there, I realized why she loved Uzès so much. Situated on the picturesque Alzon River, Uzès was a fairytale village with manicured gardens, cobblestone streets, historic buildings, charming boutiques, and lively outdoor cafes. We arrived late Friday afternoon, the perfect time of day to get settled in, so we could go to market the following Saturday morning. That was Michael's favorite day of the week. She told me how he used to run through the streets, coaxing handouts from the merchants. We meandered down those same cobblestone alleys where fragrances of all kinds filled the air, along with the sights and sounds of the small French village. Vendors lined the narrow streets, peddling everything from olives, wine, cheese, and meats to embroidered clothing, lavender sachets, handmade baskets, and the myriad of confections Provence France is known for.

As we strolled through the town, I noticed people staring at us. They glanced at Camille as if they weren't sure if this beautiful woman next to me was someone they once knew. Not wanting to be noticed, she went out of her way to avoid eye contact or conversations that might announce her arrival. She was so excited to be back that she almost forgot the reason we were there. For the first time in a long time, Camille was relaxed and happy. Seeing her like that raised my spirits, and I actually felt like I did when we first met in Marseilles.

Sunday Morning
Saint-Étienne Church
Uzès, France

"Sean, I would love to go to Mass this morning, but I think it's best if we wait here outside until the service is over." After a few minutes, she added, "Oh look, there he is now, chatting with his parishioners. He loves to talk, so it could be a while."

"I have to say, it's great to see where you and Michael used to live. Now I understand why you loved it here so much."

"*Oui*, I knew you would love my little village. Okay, he's going back inside."

As she ran toward the aging priest, Camille yelled out, "Father Larouche, Father Larouche! One moment, please. Can we have a moment of your time?"

"*Oui, bien sûr*. You look familiar, my child, but my memory fails me."

"*Oui, Père*, it's been a long time since you last saw me. It's me, Camille—Camille Deneuve."

Excited to see her, a big smile lit up his face. "Oh, my goodness, Camille, it is you. Where have you been all these years, and who is this gentleman you are with? Are you finally married? Is he your husband? How is Michael? The last time I saw the two of you, he was very young. He's a man now. Where does he live? Where do you live? Your arrival has stirred up many memories. Please forgive me, my dear, for all the questions."

"Oh Father, I have missed you too, and yes, we have a lot to catch up on. I know it is Sunday, but I promise I'll be brief. I must say that I have missed your wonderful sermons, especially on Biblical metaphors. Do you still study them?"

"No, Camille, not like I used to. Unfortunately, that time has passed. I do believe the Bible contains many universal and timeless truths, but I have found the verses were written at a time and for a culture that is completely foreign to us now. As you said, I used to base my sermons around them. But nowadays, my people don't seem to show much interest, so I haven't been as enthusiastic about studying metaphors like when you were here."

"Father, I must apologize, I forgot to introduce you. This is my most special friend, Sean Phillips."

He grabbed both of my hands with a gentle shake. "Sean, my son, I think Camille is perhaps a bit shy about revealing her relationship with you. From what I see, you are much more than just a friend. I've been around long enough to see the difference. When she lived here, she had nothing to do with any of the other young men. You must be very special to her."

"Yes, Father, you are perceptive. I have to tell you, I am absolutely delighted to be here in Uzès and have the opportunity to meet you. On our way here, she told me how comforting you were to her when she was raising Michael. She has the utmost respect for you."

"*Oui* Sean, she was to herself much of the time, and I could see how lonely she was."

"Father, you have no idea how much I valued your friendship during those years, and I still do. And that's why we came here. We need your help. Sean and I are trying to figure out the meaning of a particular metaphor. Genesis 1:24 mentions '*the beast of the earth.*' Can you tell us what it is or what it means?"

"Camille, my dear, I'm curious. Of all the Bible verses, why are you so interested in that particular one?"

"It's a long story, Father, and I don't want to bore you with the details. But if you can reveal the meaning, we will be able to decipher an incredibly complex Biblical riddle. We'll be happy to share it with you once we figure it out. I'm sure you will find our discovery to be truly amazing, and perhaps help you deliver sermons that can give your parishioners much peace of mind and bring them closer to God."

"I'm truly sorry, Camille; I wish I could help. You may have come all this way looking for an answer I'm unable to provide. Unfortunately, I don't know what '*the beast of the earth*' means. Believe me, I have tried, but the Bible gives us no hints. There are others who are just as mystified about its meaning as I am."

"Father, you have questioned this phrase with others?"

"Oh yes, my dear, more than once. You are not the only ones who are puzzled by its meaning, as well as other verses in Genesis 1. Many of them are a mystery to us and seem to be out of context and in conflict with the Genesis 2 account of Adam and Eve in the Garden of Eden."

Disappointed, by his admission, Camille replied, "Father, it seems once again that we have come to another dead end. You know what? That's okay. Our visit with you has made our journey here more than worthwhile."

"Camille, my child, before you go, I would like to offer you some hope. If my memory serves me correctly, you might find the answer you're looking for from a priest in the town of Granada. I've never been there, but I think it's in the Andalusia region of Spain. I've heard from those who have visited there that it's quite spectacular. At one time, that area was occupied by the Moors and they built a fortress-palace, which they called Alhambra. Now it's a tourist attraction. I've heard that it's breath-taking. I'm not sure you will find the answer you're looking for, but I am sure you and Sean will both enjoy that area of Spain. Anyway, there's an elderly priest there who is much more of a scholar than I am and understands Biblical metaphors more than anyone I know. I haven't seen him for some time, so he may be retired now, or he may have left us."

"Granada, Spain? We'll have to think about that. Thank you, Father, it was wonderful to see you again after all these years. Now, I want to show Sean where I used to live before we leave Uzès."

"Bless you both, and have a safe journey."

As we walked away from Saint-Étienne, I could see in Camille's eyes how disappointed she was. "I want you to know, sweetheart, that I'm really glad I met your priest. I can see why you loved your life here in Uzès so much."

"Sean, you're avoiding the real issue here. I know you're as frustrated as I am. Will I have a problem convincing you to go to Granada?"

"Well, let me put it this way: I really don't think traveling all the way to Granada will be of much help. From what Father Larouche said, the main attraction there is Alhambra, not exactly the place to figure out *'the beast of the earth.'* He's a nice man and all, and I could see he was disappointed that he couldn't help us. So, am I excited about going all that way to Spain for hope? Personally, I need more than hope. However, if you want to turn over every possible rock, then for your sake, we should go."

Then, all of a sudden, her face turned sullen. "You're going to think I'm paranoid like I was in Washington. See that man over there in the park—the one with his back to us? It's hard to tell with his sunglasses, but I could swear I saw him photograph us when we walked over here this morning. I didn't want to upset you at the time; I thought it might distract you from our meeting with Father Larouche."

Camille's instincts were usually right on, but she had also been wound very tight ever since we heard about Michael. So, I discounted her concern. "Yes, Camille, I see him, but it looks to me like he's simply a tourist taking pictures. I don't think you're paranoid, but I do think you are on edge about Michael. To be honest, I did notice people staring at us yesterday, but I really do think they were some of the locals who thought they may have recognized you."

"*Oui,* you're probably right. Sean, come sit down with me over here for a moment—I want to show you this map. Granada is about 1,300 kilometers from here. It takes about the same amount of time, including connections, and layovers, whether we go by rail, fly, or drive. What do you think?"

"What do I think? Ha-ha, I think I want to go back to our room and sleep for the next three days. Just kidding. Sure, let's drive. Maybe we can rent the new Alfa Romeo 4C. I think there's a dealer in Avignon."

"You and your cars. But, sure, that sounds great. Since you want to drive, we can take the scenic route down through Barcelona and Valencia. I know your heart is not in this little adventure. But you always love our journeys, so I'm sure we will love Alhambra, and if we're lucky, maybe we'll find the priest Father Larouche mentioned. Let's go find some maps and brochures."

CHAPTER 32

CRAZY LIKE A FOX

THE THIRTY-SECOND STEP

October 10, 2018
On the road to Granada, Spain
45 Kilometers South of Barcelona

"I know you love going fast in these sports cars, but don't you think 150 is a bit much?"

"Sweetheart, I don't want to upset you, but I think somebody has been tailing us ever since we left the outskirts of Barcelona. I've been varying my speed for the last ten kilometers, and he's still keeping up with me. Like you, maybe I'm just a bit paranoid right now. Anyway, just in case, I put my handgun in the glove box after we picked up the car."

"Good, mine is in my purse. You know Sean, I've thought somebody has been trailing us for years now, ever since we were at the Washington airport, then at the Smithsonian, and then again in Uzès. My instincts are usually pretty good. I never told you this, but there were also many instances back in Zurich when I thought someone might have been following me."

"No, I did not know that. Now you've got my attention. I'll keep this cat and mouse game going until the next exit, and we'll see what he does."

Twenty minutes later

"Sean, get off at the Tarragona exit, and then drive to the police station. I'll get the location for it on my phone."

"Okay by me. Damn, he's following us off the ramp. Now, I am getting worried."

"The police station is right in town. There, over there, is the *Policía* sign. Take the next right."

With tires screeching, I tore into the parking lot. "Damn, here he comes." Then suddenly, "No, no, wait a minute. Thank God, he's driving on. But I think we should stay put for a few minutes and see if he backtracks."

Eight Hours Later
Alhambra Palace
Granada, Spain

After we arrived in Granada, we took a leisurely stroll through the massive Alhambra to savor the intricate architecture. Then, we spent several more hours wandering the beautiful grounds and the lush, manicured gardens that surrounded the palace. The park-like setting was overgrown with wildflowers and the air was filled with the sound of running water from the many fountains and cascades. Everywhere we looked, peacocks waited for handouts from tourists eager to have their pictures taken with the colorful birds. Alhambra was truly a paradise on Earth, just like the brochures described.

"Camille, come here for a minute. Do you have any euros for these binoculars? I think I see something. I want to take a closer look, but I don't have any change." Moments later, I added, "Here, take a look. You can see Granada's historic district up there. It's about a thousand meters to the north and overlooks the main part of the city."

"*Oh oui,* I see a little church or a convent next to those white buildings. I think we should get in the car and go. Maybe we'll find the priest there that Father Larouche mentioned. I love Alhambra, but I don't see anything here that can help us."

"I agree. Actually, he told us the priest was in Granada. Alhambra was merely his suggestion as an interesting side trip while we were here. Okay, let's go, but when we were driving around yesterday, I don't remember seeing any signs leading up there to the historic district."

"Sean, let's just go. It can't be that hard to find."

After a thirty-minute drive from Alhambra, we traversed the streets of Granada. We had been driving around in circles for at least an hour but couldn't find the way up to the historic district. Its ancient streets were narrow and all the signs were in Spanish. To make matters worse, they were crowded with pedestrians who, with no space where they could move aside, plastered themselves against the buildings so cars could pass.

I consider myself an excellent driver, but I worried I'd hit one of them. Our GPS was of no help either in the tangle of narrow streets. We thought about asking someone for directions and hoped they would understand English or French, but even if we did, there was no place to pull over and park. I began to freak out, but as usual, Camille remained calm and came up with a great idea. We paid a cabbie to drive up to the historic district, and we followed him there in our car.

* * *

"Wow, sweetheart, that was a great idea. We would have never found this place by ourselves. I drove past that same turnoff, but it looked to me like an alleyway where delivery trucks and dumpsters go."

"Sean, I love all these charming old buildings up here. Look over there, you can see across the valley where we just were at Alhambra. I wouldn't mind if we moved from our hotel and stayed here for a few days."

"Yes, my romantic Camille, it's really beautiful, but first things first. We came all the way up here to find that priest. First, let's find the church you saw. You said it's between some whitewashed buildings, but I don't see anything like them around here."

Then, after a few minutes of exploring the area, we realized the historic district is on several different levels. "Let's go up those steps over there. They go up to the next street level. My God, Camille, I didn't realize how out of shape I am. I'm already out of breath." But then, as we turned a corner, I pointed, "Good, I see them over here. Can you see the name street they are on?"

"*Oui,* I see a street sign—*Calle Santa Isabel la Real.* Let's start there." Moments later, she yelled out, "There, I see the church, the convent of Santa Isabel la Real."

As we approached the convent, a welcoming nun stopped us. "*Bienvenida a nuestra humilde convento, soy Hermana Dominique. ¿Puedo ayudarlo?*"

"*Ah, excusez-moi,* do you speak English, Sister?"

"*Si, Señorita.*"

"I'm Camille, and this is Sean. Sister, I really love your village up here. It's quite charming."

"*Si,* I've lived here all my life and have no desire to go anywhere else. What brings you here today? Are you on holiday, exploring our town? If you haven't been to Alhambra, I would suggest you see the gardens, they are quite spectacular."

"*Oui,* Sister, we just came from there. However, the reason we are here is because my priest in France told us we might be able to get the answer to a question we are looking for."

"May I ask, what the question is that brings you to our humble convent?"

"It's a Bible passage that contains a metaphor that has puzzled us for years. He told us there is a priest here in Granada who may be able to help us."

"*Si,* you must mean Father Rodriguez. He's retired now and somewhat eccentric in his old age. In his day, though, he was able to decipher many Bible verses others could not fathom. But, he's not here right now. I'm sure he's in town mingling with the tourists."

"Okay, we'll go back there and look for him, but how will we know who he is? We've seen dozens of priests walking the streets down there."

"Oh, you can't miss Father Rodriguez. He has a long, white beard and is dressed in a full-length white gown with a hood draped over his head. Over the gown, he wears three open robes: dark purple, dark green, and dark blue, all trimmed in gold. Around his neck, he wears three gold chains and a pendant with a five-sided pink crystal. We don't know why he wears the crystal, but it is beautiful. He thinks he's a prophet, you know, and dresses the part. The tourists all find him very charming, as he entertains them with his banter. However, we who know him think he is simply getting on in years, if you know what I mean." Moments later, "Oh wait, you're in luck. Here he comes now. He arrives here every day around this time to pray and to chat with us. We look forward to his visits. We never know what to expect."

"*Padre, Padre*, please come here for a moment. You have some visitors."

"Sister Dominique, how are you today, and who are these beautiful people that have come to visit us?"

"This is Camille and her friend, Sean. They have come all the way from France to ask you an important question."

Turning his attention to us, the elderly priest remarked, "From France? *Si,* what a lovely country. I have visited there many times. Come, let us go inside, out of the heat, and make ourselves more comfortable. You know, the sisters have a bakery here in the convent. They prepare the most delightful madeleines and other tasty confections—the best in all Granada. They sell them here at the convent for a reasonable price. You should buy some before you leave. I promise you will come back for more."

"*Oui* Father, they sound wonderful."

"So, my children, Sister Dominique says you have a question and seek an answer from me. How can I help you?"

"Sean, perhaps it's better if you ask Father Rodriguez our question.

"Well, Father, we're trying to solve a puzzle hidden in the Genesis Creation Story. We've almost completed it, except for one particular phrase. On the Sixth Day, in verse 24, the author wrote about '*the beast of the earth.*'"

"*Si,* my son, that is an interesting phrase, and I believe I can be of some help."

"Really? That's wonderful! You have no idea how we've struggled to find the answer."

"Ah, my son, I see what's wrong and why you cannot find the answer. Come, sit here next to me for a moment. You can't see the answer because the sunglasses you wear are clouding your vision. Here, give them to me and I will clean them for you." Several moments later, the aging priest handed them back. "There, my son. Now you will be able to see the answer you seek."

Frustrated and confused, I said, "Father, please, I don't understand."

"Oh my goodness, Sean, you will see it now—I'm sure of it. But I must leave you now and rest while I enjoy the Sister's delicious madeleines. Before you depart our village, you should purchase some cookies from them. That is how they earn their money. You won't be disappointed. The tastes they create are simply delightful."

After a few moments of bewilderment, I turned to Camille while we walked out of the convent. "That's unbelievable! Did you hear that guy? The nun said he's getting on in years. That's an understatement; he has completely lost it—he's crazy."

"*Oui,* I must admit, this trip here may have been a waste of our time. But I have to say, those cookies he talked about sound pretty good, and he did mention them more than once. I want to get some."

"Alright, alright, maybe their cookies will sweeten me up. Did you happen to see where we can get them? He never told us, and now they're both inside. I really don't want to go back in, and besides, I'm sure the doors are locked. The convent is not open to the public."

"Why don't we look around the courtyard before we leave? He said the bakery is how the nuns support themselves, so it must be here somewhere."

As we walked around the courtyard, we spotted a plaque over an old stone archway, but it was in Spanish, and we had no idea what it said. We went through it anyway and found a path to a cobblestone patio area adjacent to the side of the convent. Tucked away back in the corner of the patio, on the old stone building was a small, weathered wood door, about three feet off the ground, with an ancient brass bell hanging next to it. We had no idea what it was for, but I decided to pull the bell rope anyway. The door slowly creaked open, revealing an old wooden lazy Susan with samples of the nun's baked goods, along with an order sheet.

"Sean, the priest said he likes the madeleines. Let's get some; they're only two euros for six of them."

Moments after we placed our order, the lazy Susan turned to reveal the cookies. But then I saw something. Laying on the tray underneath them was an envelope that had obviously been used many times before. "What the heck is that? Do you think I should open it?"

"*Oui*, of course."

"There's a note written in broken English, and the scribble is hard to read."

"Okay, Sean, enough with the suspense. What does it say?"

"This is weird. It says, 'Now that you can see clearly, the answer you seek is hidden in plain sight.'"

"*Oh mon Dieu, Sean,* that priest really does have problems. Now I'm sorry that I encouraged this trip and another wild goose chase. Let's just go back to our hotel."

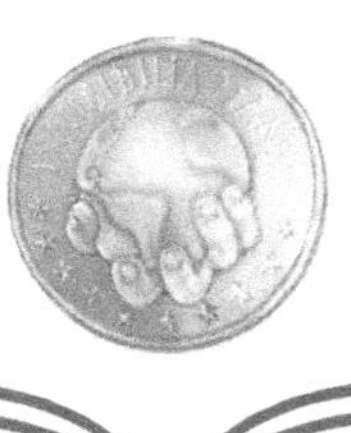

CHAPTER 33

THE ASSET

THE THIRTY-THIRD STEP

October 13, 2018

"Camille, let's face it—we have failed. The Genesis Correlation will never be completed. My vote is to get our luggage and get back on the road. We don't have to drive all the way back to Avignon today. We can stop for the night, drop the car off tomorrow, and then catch a flight back to Zurich. Whadaya say?"

"*Oui*, I agree. I won't argue with you, but I can't forget about that priest, he certainly was strange. His comment about your sunglasses was odd. Oh well, I'll try not to think about him anymore."

Camille was the most optimistic person I had ever met. Her frustration over everything we encountered in Granada was sad to watch. The Trail had led us in a direction where we thought we were making some great headway. But then, we met nothing but dead ends, more disappointments, and this was no exception. We were now both convinced the Genesis correlation would never be completely solved. I was at a point where I just wanted to forget everything: Genesis, the Invisible Hand, the Martel family, saving the world from extinction, and worrying about Michael. I was at my wit's end.

Before I bought my home in St. Martin, the charming little fishing village of Cadaqués on the coast of the Mediterranean had caught my eye. Since it was only 135 kilometers south of Barcelona, near the French border, I thought it would be an easy drive. I was exhausted, and it was practically on the way back to Avignon, where I rented the car. So we decided it would be a good place to relax for the night, a week, a month, maybe forever. Once we made up our minds, we got back in the car and set out on our way.

"Sean, I'm looking at accommodations in Cadaqués and we have a lot to choose from. Here's a nice, modern villa overlooking the bay. I think I should book it. It'll only be for one night."

"Fine by me. I'm exhausted, and it sounds perfect. After we get there, I just want to have a nice dinner and then settle in for the night. And, to let you know, I'm in no mood to talk about Genesis or that priest anymore."

"I know you can't look at this map while you're driving, but it is interesting. The road from the freeway to Cadaqués is only about twenty-five kilometers, and it will take us over the mountains. It's narrow, with a lot of switchbacks and one-way bridges. Spain is not good with their warning signs, especially on these back roads. I know how you are about the thrill of driving fast in these sports cars, so just be careful, especially as tired as you are."

"Sweetheart, you worry too much. I will be careful and protect you with my life. Just sit back, relax, and enjoy the scenery."

Twenty minutes from Cadaqués

Camille had been exceptionally quiet during the drive. I knew she was deep in thought, and I did enjoy the quiet.

"Sean, I have to say '*the beast of the earth*'is a real mystery. I'm sorry, but I can't help but wonder about it. And on top of it all, Michael is constantly on my mind. It's funny how my mind jumps around, so to distract myself, I scanned my Genesis notes again. Interestingly, it seems there are a lot of references to not seeing things—invisible things. Remember when we were at the Smithsonian and you were drawn to find out what that poster, '*The answer lies not in what we see, it lies in what we don't see,*' meant? Then in Granada, the priest cleaned your sunglasses and said you would be able to see more clearly. Then he gave you the handwritten note: '*Now that you can see clearly, the answer you seek is hidden in plain sight.*"

"Well, that may be interesting to you, but I can tell you what I don't see—the significance of any of it. Like I said before, I'm in no mood to talk about Genesis anymore. I've had enough. I'm done!"

"Alright, alright, but be careful. This road looks treacherous, especially for me sitting here in the passenger seat.

"Wow, sweetheart, these switchbacks are fun. This car really corners well on the tight curves. And look at this. I'm negotiating this hairpin, and I have perfect control. I really wouldn't mind having one of these Alfas for my own."

"Yeah, well, just watch where you're driving."

Then, out of nowhere, that chilling sound filled the air. "Holy shit, Camille, what was that?"

Terrified, she screamed at the top of her lungs, "SEAN, *OH MON DIEU!* The guy in that black SUV is shooting at us! I would know that sound anywhere. It's a Glock 19. He's serious. He wants us dead!"

"My God, can you see who it is?"

"No, I only see one shooter. Damn it, Sean, he got the windshield! Can you see?"

"Are you kidding me? I'm driving practically blind. That's the same damn car that followed us out of Barcelona. Camille, quick, get your gun. This couldn't have happened on a worse road. When I go around this next switchback, you'll be parallel to him. Get ready to take your shots."

"Sean, I can't, the window is locked. Quick, quick, unlock it!"

"Where the hell is the unlock button? You're going to have to shoot through the glass. Take your shots—NOW!"

"Damn it, I missed him."

"Camille, I can't see where I'm going. I'm losing control. Here comes another curve. We're headed down now, and no fucking guardrails. At this speed, I won't be able to keep control for much longer. Keep firing, keep firing! If you need more shots we're screwed. I didn't bring spare clips. Camille, quick—get my gun out of the glove box!"

"Damn it, Sean, I'm running out of rounds! Oh my God, I could feel that one fly past my head. Shit, it hit the rearview mirror. Sean, the glove box is locked!"

"Camille, you have to do something."

"I don't have time to get your gun. I have maybe two rounds left. I'm going for his tires. It's our only hope."

Thirty Minutes Later
Villa Grande Boutique
Cadaquéz, Spain

"Sean, we have a really big problem. This feels like my family sent an asset after us. Right now, I'm thinking the worst. You have no idea how vindictive my father was, and Antoine has followed in his footsteps. He wants the ultimate revenge."

"No, Camille, not that—he wouldn't do that. We need to go back to the crash site tomorrow morning. I want to know who was driving that car."

"Sean, there's another thing you should know: he won't give up and this won't end until we're both dead. You realize Antoine knows by now that we went to the FBI."

"Camille, please, this is way too much for me right now. Can we talk about something else? I need a glimmer of hope. Before all of this happened, you were trying to tell me something about not seeing things. No pun intended, but quite frankly, I was not seeing things through that shattered windshield. For Christ's sake, we almost died back there. I'm still in shock."

"I'm sure you are, but we did not die. So please, calm down."

That was the first time I had ever been shot at. And believe me, peeing my pants is an understatement. Camille definitely handled it better than me. And no wonder, after living the life she did before meeting me. But after a couple of hours, I finally settled down, and we were able to talk again.

"Sean, I was thinking… is it possible that the '*beast of the earth*' is right in front of our eyes and we don't see it?"

"You really are not going to give up on this beast thing, are you? Yeah, I guess it's possible. But can we backtrack for a moment?"

"What do you mean backtrack?"

"I think the sequence of these four verses is significant. Start with verses 24 and 25, where he lists the animals, including the '*beast of the earth.*'

"'*And God said: 'Let the earth bring forth the living creature after its kind, cattle, and creeping thing, and beast of the earth after its kind.' And it was so.*'

"'*And God made the beast of the earth after its kind, and the cattle after their kind, and every thing that creepeth upon the ground after its kind; and God saw that it was good.*'

"Then, in verse 26, the author lists animals again, but this time, he includes the creation of man.

"'*And God said: 'Let us make man in our image, after our likeness; and let them have dominion over the fish of the sea, and over the fowl of the air, and over the cattle, and over all the earth, and over every creeping thing that creepeth upon the earth.*'

"This phrase distinguishes man from the animals, but the question is, who was God talking to?"

"Okay, Sean, let me look at these verses from your logical perspective.

"First, we determined '*swarms of living creatures*' are the fish. Next, '*every living creature that creepeth, wherewith the waters swarmed*' are the amphibians. Then, '*Let the earth bring forth … creeping thing*' are the reptiles. '*The fowl of the air*' are the birds. '*Cattle*' are the mammals.

"And then, in verse 24 and 25, he lists the animals again, along with '*man.*' Then, in verse 27, the creation of man is complete.

"*'And God created man in His own image, in the image of God created He him; male and female created He them.'*

"But I still don't see who God is talking to when He says, '*let us make man in our own image.*' Can you see anything else?"

"You're asking me? Maybe the priest needs to clean my sunglasses again."

"Ha-ha, Sean, very funny."

But then, no sooner had that sarcasm come out of my mouth, it was like something opened up in my head. I saw it, or didn't see it, depending on how you look at it. For no apparent reason and beyond any logic, I saw the correlation. I saw who the '*beast of the earth*' is. Maybe it was because the shock of almost dying that opened a pathway into my subconscious—I don't know.

"Oh my God, Camille, I see it! I know who the '*beast of the earth*' is. The '*beast*' is the other half of '*us*' and '*our.*' So, Father Rodriguez was right."

"What do you mean? His note said, 'the answer you seek is hidden in plain sight.'"

"That is true, and he was exactly right. Think about it. Verses 24 and 25 both mention the '*beast of the earth.*' Now, compare those verses to verse 26. Do you see the difference? Verse 26 does not mention the '*beast,*' and that's because God was talking to the beast. I can't believe it, Camille, we're done with a project I've worked on for the last forty years. But, most important of all, you guided me through an intuitive world I had no idea existed. Together, we did it!"

"Unbelievable! Sean, that makes perfect sense! The '*beast of the earth*' is the hominid, like the display you took me to see in Washington. It's the link between animals and humans. Something that is written in Genesis 1, from 2,500 years ago, is something fossil hunters and biologists have only recently discovered. That's incredible!"

Sweetheart, I've been thinking; now that the correlation is complete, I would like to call it 'The Genesis Codex.' What do you think?"

"*Je pense que c'est parfait.*"

This insight into the world of Genesis gave us what we needed to prove what ancient societies instinctively knew. The science and the spiritual are united as one entity. The Genesis author proved it in a thirty-one-verse document that has survived to this day, when we need it the most. A scientific proof in a spiritual book—the Bible. But the thrill of this discovery didn't last long. We had other problems.

"Sean, I hate to spoil the mood, but time has gotten away from us and we have to go. We need to get back to the crash site as soon as the windshield is replaced. We need to confirm who shot at us, and I really don't want to believe it was Michael."

The following morning, we drove back to the crash site, but the SUV was gone. From the skid marks, it appeared as though it slid sideways and then ended up a couple of hundred feet further down the road and then slammed into a tree. How the driver was able to maintain control without tumbling down into the ravine must have required some very serious driving skills. When it comes to training his assets, Antoine is a master, and he didn't miss any tricks.

Synopsis
Genesis Correlation of the Sixth Day

Creeping Thing (The Reptiles)   Cattle (The Mammals)

315 million years ago   200 million years ago

Genesis 1:24
And God said: 'Let the earth bring forth the living creature after its kind, cattle, and creeping thing, and beast of the earth after its kind.' And it was so.

Genesis 1:25
And God made the beast of the earth after its kind, and the cattle after their kind, and every thing that creepeth upon the ground after its kind; and God saw that it was good.

The Hominids

200,000 years ago

Genesis 1:26
And God said: 'Let us make man in our image, after our likeness; and let them have dominion over the fish of the sea, and over the fowl of the air, and over the cattle, and over all the earth, and over every creeping thing that creepeth upon the earth.

Synopsis
Genesis Correlation of the Sixth Day

Genesis 1:27
*And God created man in His own image, in the image of
God created He him; male and female created He them.*

Genesis 1:28
*And God blessed them; and God said unto them: 'Be fruitful,
and multiply, and replenish the earth, and subdue it; and have
dominion over the fish of the sea, and over the fowl of the air,
and over every living thing that creepeth upon the earth.*

Genesis 1:29
*And God said: 'Behold, I have given you every herb yielding seed,
which is upon the face of all the earth, and every tree, in which
is the fruit of a tree yielding seed--to you it shall be for food;*

Genesis 1:30
*and to every beast of the earth, and to every fowl of the air, and to
every thing that creepeth upon the earth, wherein there is a living
soul, [I have given] every green herb for food. And it was so.
'And, behold, it was very good'*

Genesis 1:31
*And God saw every thing that He had made, and,
behold, it was very good. And there was evening
and there was morning, the sixth day.*

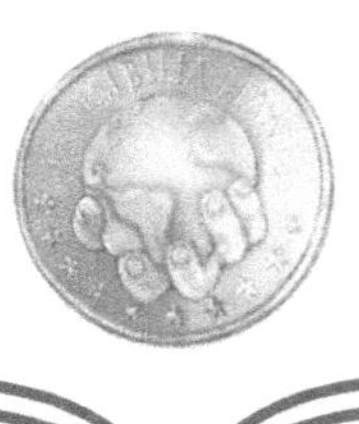

CHAPTER 34

FINALLY, SOME RESPECT

THE THIRTY-FOURTH STEP

October 20, 2018
Zurich, Switzerland

"Frank, it's great to hear from you. I can call you Frank now, right?"

"Sure, why not? We don't have to be so damned formal at this stage of the game; we're not being recorded. The reason I called is because I have some exciting news for you. The top brass here at the bureau read everything you and Camille gave us, and they wanted to move ahead and grant your request to hold the summit. It will be at Eglin Air Force Base in Florida, but there's a catch."

"I can't believe it—that's great news! Okay, so what hoops do I have to jump through now?"

"First of all, I personally read your Genesis Codex and want to apologize for underestimating you and Camille. I'm impressed, and so are my bosses. You realize, if we can get it authenticated, it will change everything. Nothing will ever be the same again, in so many ways."

"Yes, I know, but what do you mean by authenticated?"

"Well, Sean, it's not only me and my bosses who have read it. They gave your Codex to two of the top scientists here in the United States to authenticate your correlations. I really have no idea what they're so excited about, but after reading it, they believe you may have stumbled onto the discovery of the century. It's something they call the Cambrian explosion. They are also working on some other projects involving the Earth's early atmospheres, and told us you pointed them in a direction they have not considered. Anyway, we scheduled an appointment with them to meet with you next Tuesday."

"Wow, thank you, Frank. I don't know what to say, except I'll be there. I hope you don't mind if I bring Camille."

"Of course not, she should be there too. I hope she's feeling better. Okay, then, we'll make all the arrangements for the two of you. All you need to do is get on a plane, come to Washington, and we'll take care of the rest."

Ten Days Later
October 30, 2018
Room 115
FBI Washington Regional Office

As Camille and I entered the small, fluorescent-lit meeting room, two prominent intellectuals jumped to their feet. "Greetings, Mr. Phillips and Ms. Deneuve. I'm Dr. Steven Geyer, Head of Paleontology at the Discover Resources Foundation in Seattle."

"And I'm Sebastian Walters, Professor and Head of the Geology Department at Princeton."

Geyer continued, "Please have a seat and make yourself comfortable. We've read the Genesis Codex, and quite frankly, we've never seen anything like it. I understand neither of you are scientists or theologians. We are really quite impressed you were able to make these correlations, although we do have some questions. The one that especially intrigues us is your theory for the Cambrian explosion. Personally, I have been pondering its mysteries since before I went to college, as have many of my colleagues. There have been a lot of thoughts as to how it occurred, but in every case, nobody can provide a complete answer. So, here we have two amateurs who have proposed a plausible theory. We would really like to know how you managed to solve it."

Elated to have been recognized by two prominent scientists, I couldn't hold back. "Thank you, sir, but we can't take all the credit. The Genesis author provided the answers; all we did was correlate his verses with science."

Walters interrupted, "I completely agree with Dr. Geyer, and I must say your Genesis Codex is certainly impressive. I've read numerous Bible verses over the years, including the Creation Story. Now that I have read your Codex, I will never be able to look at those thirty-one verses ever the same again. But, there is something I would like to know. Do you have any theories as to who wrote Genesis 1 and where they would have attained this kind of knowledge 2,500 years ago?"

"That's a perplexing question, Professor, and I have pondered it ever since I first realized its scientific accuracy. Camille and I went to a museum in Berlin that specializes in ancient Southeast Asian artifacts. We found out archeologists don't know much about human culture prior to 5,500 BCE. Relics from the earliest known civilization, other than tribal settlements, can only be traced back to the Sumerians. However, the fossil record reveals modern humans date back far longer, at least 200,000 years, which makes those 7,500-year-old objects less than one percent of human existence. So, I guess it may be possible that there were far older, advanced civilizations that are buried under the ice ages. The Sumerians may have been one of their decedents, and this knowledge was passed down to them. It's my belief that Atlantis may not be just a mythical tale."

Walters remarked, "Mr. Phillips, I also have an interest in the Sumerian culture. So, what in particular drew you to them?"

"Well, sir, we were given a pair of rare Sumerian cylinder seals that we took to the Cambridge Institute and had them authenticated. Those seals, along with others we saw in Berlin, seem to indicate the Sumerians were not only a highly advanced culture, they also believed in gods they called the Anunnaki. Interestingly, Anunnaki literally translates to *'those who from heaven to earth came.'*"

"So, Mr. Phillips, are you saying the Sumerian's are the descendants of those civilizations? Or, are you saying they got their knowledge from extraterrestrials that visited them from another world?"

Feeling trapped by an unexpected question, I quickly responded, "Professor, I'm only guessing where the

Sumerian's attained their knowledge. What I'm saying is that I find them to be a very interesting culture. My passion lies in Genesis 1, the most read narrative in the history of the world. I'm interested in only one thing. The Genesis Codex proves ancient cultures that lasted for thousands of years not only believed, but they also lived the reality of existence. The physical and the spiritual are two sides of the same coin. And, if our world does not accept that reality, I believe we are doomed."

Geyer then asked, "Perhaps I'm being too bold, and please forgive my choice of words, but I have to ask. Are you and Camille people of God? I guess I'm asking, do you believe in God?"

Camille then spoke up. "Monsieur Geyer, I will only speak for myself. I believe in the Spiritual. I also believe that after many years of personal trials and tribulations, as well as numerous amazing discoveries, the Spiritual is what put us on the trail and into this room with you today. So, since we're being candid, Professor, I'll ask you—do you believe in God?"

Thrown by her candor, Geyer replied, "Well, Madam, I'm a scientist and I study the physical world. Personally, I am not familiar with the spiritual world." Put on the spot, he quickly redirected his question, "And, what about you, Mr. Phillips, do you believe in God, or the Spiritual, or whatever you would like to call it? The reason I ask is because you seem to be a man of science, and yet something drove you to the Bible for your correlation theory."

"Yeah, that goes back a long way—when I went to religious school and questioned everything. But there is something else. While correlating Genesis 1, I also uncovered a natural wonder that defies statistical logic. I call it, 'The Requirements for Life on Earth.'"

Puzzled, Geyer questioned, "Mr. Phillips, I have never heard of such a thing, and I don't see how this answers my question. But I am intrigued, so please continue."

"Interestingly, I identified at least eighteen requirements or conditions that must be met for human life to exist. My point is, if any one of them did not occur, life on Earth would not be possible, and you, sir, would not be here today to study it or to observe it."

"Okay, I'm listening."

"Dr. Geyer, I'm not a statistician, but it does not seem possible that these eighteen conditions could have possibly come about purely by chance. Statistically, the more of them that nature requires for human life to exist, the less likely they are just random events."

"Okay, Mr. Phillips, I'll concede that you may have a point. Do you have some examples?"

"Of course, I'll go through a few of them with you. Here, wait a minute, I think I may have my notes with me. You can read them if you like. First of all, I'm sure you're familiar with the Goldilocks principle. Earth is the only planet that falls within the habitable zone. It's neither too close nor too far away from the sun, and it's neither too hot nor too cold. If more distant, it would be a giant frozen snowball. If it were any closer, it would be a hot, arid desert. Its location is the perfect distance from our sun to sustain life."

"Yes, I'm quite aware."

"Well, Professor, there are many other examples. Earth is the only planet with liquid water, an Earth-Moon system, a magnetic field, an ozone layer, a clear atmosphere, breathable air, photosynthesis, nitrogen fixation, and I have identified at least a dozen more of these requirements. And I repeat, if just one of them were missing, we would not be here. To me, it seems statistically impossible for all of them to have occurred purely by chance on our tiny planet. Even our moon, which is critical for life on Earth, doesn't seem that it could have come about and positioned where it is, purely by chance."

Geyer responded, "Okay, Mr. Phillips, you make a compelling argument. However, I'm certainly not convinced God made them happen. You see, the universe is vast, with trillions of stars. So, it's statistically possible other solar systems could give rise to these same conditions."

Ready to take on Geyer, Walters took the opposing view. "Well, first of all, Geyer, absolutely no evidence exists to support that position. Mr. Phillips, you may not be aware of it, but many in my field also struggle with the same paradoxes that you do regarding the existence of a Creator. Our quandary has to do with the precise structure of the universe, what we call fine tuning."

Geyer argued, "Poppycock, Walters. I know exactly what you're going to say. The conditions that allow for life to exist can only occur when certain physical constants fall within an extremely narrow range. I've heard it more than once, and I've heard all the arguments."

Camille asked, "What do the constants of nature mean? And what does that have to do with a Creator?"

Walters answered, "Unlike Dr. Geyer, there are scientists who do not believe the universe is random and came about purely by chance. These constants are precise and they never change. Twenty of them have been identified, such as the mass of the electron, the speed of light, and Newton's constant of gravitation. In fact, Einstein erected his famous formula $E=mc^2$ around these constants. All the theories of physics are built around them, and they define the framework of everything that exists. But here's the thing. Nobody can explain how they came to be or why they have the unique numerical values they do. If they were even slightly different, complex atomic structures could not exist. The universe would not be able to accommodate the creation and expansion of matter and energy, the diversity of elements, or the formation of stars that ultimately gave rise to life. In reality, nature's laws and the value of the constants are absolute for life and for humans to exist. Like me, there are many others who believe there is an intelligence behind everything."

Feeling their arguments would not be resolved, I changed the subject. "Okay, gentlemen, that's great information, and you both have certainly given us a lot to think about. I'm pleased we had the opportunity to discuss our beliefs about God, but now we must get down to business and the reason we're here."

"*Excusez-moi messieurs*, before we go on, I have something I must say. Sean may have explained how the Cambrian explosion happened, but he couldn't have done it without me. In fact, he didn't figure out many of the other correlations by himself either."

Embarrassed, Geyer apologized and attempted to smooth things over. "Oh my, please pardon my rudeness. May I call you Camille?"

"*Oui, bien sûr.*"

"Camille, you are absolutely right, and I'm sure I speak for Professor Walters when I ask if you would accept our apology. So, yes please, how did you figure out these complex correlations?"

It was then, with this one question, that Camille voiced the perfect answer to a question that she and I had pondered for years. How was the passion to expose her family and my passion to solve the Genesis correlation connected?

"Gentlemen, like Sean said, all the great civilizations of the past, on all continents, knew science and lived the physical, but they also believed in gods and the afterlife, and they survived for thousands of years. The ancient Hebrews proved this connection in the Genesis Creation Story. However, the intended meaning in the original Hebrew text has been lost in translation by the many false translations and religious interpretations that followed. But beyond all odds, Sean and I proved that Genesis 1 correlates perfectly with the modern sciences of geology and evolution. This game-changing breakthrough provides the key to reuniting science with religion and gives a divided, skeptical world the power that is needed to fight the Invisible Hand. But here's the thing: we couldn't have done it without each other. We believe that the physical and the spiritual are two sides of the same coin, and both are equal. It's the same for Sean and I. He is a scientist and leans more toward science and the physical, while I'm an intuitive and lean more to the spiritual and faith—the perfect combination to solve this impossible riddle."

After a long pause, Walters didn't seem to know what to say. "I must admit, the two of you have certainly given both of us a lot to think about. Anyway, Frank Sullivan spent quite a bit of time explaining the importance of your speech. This is why we're here today—to authenticate the science behind the Genesis Codex. He mentioned you're going to expose this Invisible Hand we've been reading about in the papers. And to be honest, I have felt something amiss in the world for some time now. Things just don't feel right—as if some invisible master plan is controlling all of us. However, more importantly, and from our point of view, you're also going to deliver the dialogue regarding the crisis we're facing from the extinction of species. Geyer and I both believe if something isn't done about it—and soon—humanity will soon pay a price they are not willing to pay."

"Yes, and thanks for bringing it up, because we could really use your help. We believe this summit will have a far greater impact if two prominent scientists, such as yourselves, deliver this segment."

"I think I can speak for Dr. Geyer when I say we were hoping you would ask us. We may differ about the origins of the universe, but we do share a common concern for the world's ecosystems. Human activities are destroying the delicate balance that exists, and we won't survive if it is allowed to continue."

For the next twenty minutes, like highly emotional, fiery preachers, the two scientists lectured us about the pollution of the air, the water, and the land, from plastics, microplastics, heavy metals, industrial waste, toxic chemicals, pesticides, herbicides, petroleum spills, and carbon emissions. They carried on about the deforestation of our wooded lands, and especially the Amazon rain forest. The destruction of our most fragile ecosystems for building developments and roads, agriculture, livestock, mining, logging, oil drilling, and fracking. Walters seemed especially disturbed about the impact pollution is having on the coral reefs and sea life.

Not to be outdone, Geyer complained how many animal species are in decline due to overfishing, poaching, and hunting for their skins, plumage, horns, and meat. He pointed out how human activity is destroying their habitats by the atrocities Geyer mentioned. He was especially disturbed by the rapid decline of the pollinating insects from the misuse of pesticides and herbicides and warned that without them, our food supply is in jeopardy. They both agreed that the sixth mass extinction is real, and we're running out of time to stop it. I knew things were bad, but until then I really didn't understand just how critical the times we live in actually are. For the first time in recorded history, not one, but two catastrophic events have converged. These final and decisive battles have initiated devastating consequences no one could have possibly predicted.

"*Messieurs, merci beaucoup* for listening to us, but I must go now. Agent Sullivan has asked me to discuss the Invisibilia Manus 1978 Red Book with him."

In unison, all three men jumped to their feet, as Geyer repeated, "Camille, again, please accept our apologies for not acknowledging your contributions. Actually, you, more than anyone, have given me a lot to think about. My whole reputation has been built on a physical understanding of the world, and now I see there may be, as you say, the other side of the coin."

Walters spoke up, "Dr. Geyer echoes my sentiments exactly. You are delightful, and I am honored we'll be sharing the stage with you."

CHAPTER 35

240TH ANNUAL ASSEMBLY OF INVISIBILIA MANUS

NOVEMBER 1, 2018

Boldt Castle
Heart Island
The Thousand Islands
Alexandria Bay, New York

Invisibilia Manus
240th Annual Assembly

Thursday Morning Agenda

Herman Wilhelm (Frankfurt,
Germany) Conference Leader
Wang Yong Qing, (Shanghai, China)
Dorothea R Stuart (Providence, Rhode Island)
Mila Stadtholder (Maastricht, Netherlands)
Caspera Sufavi (Gachsaran, Iran)
Antoine Martel (Carcassonne, France)
Adele Seljuk (Istanbul, Turkey)
Dimitri Romanov (St. Petersburg, Russia)
Daamish Mughal (Maharashtra, India)
Sophia Habsburg (Vienna, Austria)

—

Review	9 to 9:15 a.m.
Message from Antoine Martel	9:30 to 10 a.m.
The Triad	10:30 to 11:15 a.m.
Our Progress	11:30 a.m. to 12:30 p.m.
Comments	12:30 to 1 p.m.

"Good morning, everyone. I hope you had a restful night after last evening's wonderful dinner and took the time to reflect on yesterday's meetings. It's already Thursday and I can't believe how fast these days fly by. We have a lot to cover today, so let's get started.

"I have never heard a more exciting report on the progress we've made since we began Agenda One in 1978. And now, after forty years of diligent efforts, The Purge is only one year away from becoming a reality. The dumbing down of the American public was far easier than any of us ever expected. The ignorant *sheeple*, as we like to call them, are completely oblivious, while they are obsessed with their cell phones, playing their internet games, fighting over their ridiculous politics, and complaining about each other on their social media. Every faction of their society is divided. They are so lazy and apathetic they will believe anything they hear or read on our media outlets.

"But for now, we have a far more urgent matter to discuss. I have an important announcement that will affect each of us here today, and our families. An unimaginable breach has taken place, and our security measures have been compromised! Our Chief of Security from Carcassonne, Antoine Martel, has come all the way here to reveal this unfortunate course of events. This violation has caused us to take direct and immediate action. When you arrived here at Boldt Castle on Saturday night, you entered through the security gate and elevator that has served us well for many years. But this entry point will be destroyed. It's only a matter of time before the persons responsible for this breach will bring the authorities here. We have spent a great deal of time and effort to find a new meeting place that meets our needs, like Boldt Castle, but to no avail. So, we will stay here. However, next year we'll enter through a new airlock system. An access point, located one hundred feet underwater, will be installed. A staging area on the mainland has been selected, where a state-of-the-art submersible watercraft will transport us on the one-kilometer underwater crossing to the airlock. I have seen the blueprints for this remarkable undertaking from Area C and am very impressed.

"During Sunday's introductions, you met Chief Council Martel. We are honored to have him with us this week. For the first time, and in the interest of full disclosure, a chief council has broken precedent and has come to Boldt Castle. So, without further introduction, allow me to present Chief Council Antoine Martel, from Carcassonne, France."

"*Bien, bien, bien,* let me begin by saying that personally, I am not honored to be here. Even so, I have to admit, this facility is quite impressive. As Herman mentioned, this is the first time a chief council has come to one of our assemblies, but I felt it was my duty to do so. Before I get started, what I'm about to disclose today is being recorded and will be available to each of your families. So, I will not answer any questions today. Let me start by saying, I am enraged beyond words to tell you that a family member of mine, along with a once-trusted employee, betrayed us and have gone to the authorities to expose Invisibilia Manus. When our informant told me the magnitude of this breach, I felt it was important enough for me to come here. But let me assure you, with help from my brother André and one of our trusted assets, this problem will soon be remedied.

So, who are these traitors? I am ashamed to have to admit it, but one of them is my very own sister Camille-Gabriella Martel. The other is her co-conspirator Sean Patrick Phillips, our once-trusted technical liaison from Area C. None of you were here at Boldt Castle for the historic August 13, 1978 Assembly, but she was here representing my family. And she was also responsible for hiring Phillips back then."

Shocked by Antoine's confession, nine horrified hands rose in unison, desperately awaiting an answer and a solution to a breach that could have devastating consequences for them and the future of Invisibilia Manus.

"Okay, okay, calm down. As I expected, you have questions, but there is no need to worry. Allow me to put your minds at rest. To begin, I assure you we have already taken the necessary countermeasures to clean up this mess. First of all, Area C has already been moved to another far more secure location—even more secure than the old Packard plant where they were located. Instead of relocating all the team members to another city, we felt it was important to leave them in Detroit. So, we purchased an abandoned factory in the south end that sits eleven hundred feet over a deserted salt mine. Area C will be relocated in those mines, and the entire ten-acre parcel is secured with razor fencing and a state-of-the-art security system. In addition, we have a special security team of highly trained armed guards with sentry dogs to patrol the perimeter 24/7.

"That brings me to our other three divisions and then our office buildings. Since the traitors have intimate knowledge of these facilities, we have already begun relocating them. Since the FBI has no jurisdiction in our countries, we feel we have some time to make the moves. However, Area A is a different matter. It will stay where it is. We simply cannot move the contents of those vaults without the possibility of prying eyes. We will destroy the existing entry point and create a new one, a kilometer away in the surrounding hills. When it is completed, no trace of the old entry point will exist, and Phillips will lead them to a pile of rocks. He will be laughed out of Austria as well as every other country, while he sends the authorities on a myriad of wild goose chases.

"Next, I would also like to put your minds to rest as to how we are going to deal with my sister and the traitor Phillips. I mentioned my brother André, and I also mentioned an asset. That asset happens to be my sister's son and my nephew, Michael Martel. We don't know how it happened, but as it turns out, Sean Phillips is Michael's father. My sister has kept Michael in the dark about our family for his entire life. So, here's the short version of what Michael initiated all on his own. He did some detective work, came to France, and, quite by accident, he ran into my brother André in Carcassonne. André immediately brought him to meet my father, Valentin Martel—rest his soul. My father let Michael know that his parents had denied him his family for his entire life. Michael, of course, was furious when he found out the truth. Not only did he vow he would never have anything to do with them again, but now he seeks revenge.

"Once my father felt Michael could be trusted, he brought him into the family as an asset, and I personally trained him. He has performed way beyond my expectations. I have seen Michael's skills, and as a man who does not frighten easily, let me just say, I would not want to be one of his targets. I'm telling you this because I've been told by our informant that Sean Phillips will expose us in a summit at Eglin AFB in Florida. But trust me, that meeting will never happen. Michael and André will make sure of that. So, there you have it. I'm going to turn the meeting back to Herman. Oh, and one other thing, let me remind you again—don't bother me with your questions today. Your chief councils can contact me directly."

"Chief Council Martel, thank you for coming here to Heart Island to disclose this tragedy. I can't imagine how difficult it must be for you to report this betrayal within the ranks of your own family. We all certainly stand behind you and are confident you will get the job done. Although I know and I speak for all of our families, your father would have never allowed this breach or let it get this far. The fact that Camille is your sister, I'm sure, played a part in your leniency toward them. The lesson to be learned here is that betrayal is to be dealt with swiftly, just like it always has been, since our founding in 1778.

"Next, I would like to introduce Ms. Dorothea R. Stuart, representing the Stuart family from Providence, Rhode Island. She is here to give us a clear understanding of the most significant component of Agenda One. Everything we have accomplished since our 1978 Assembly has led us to this moment in time when we can at last draw on the full power of the Triad to unleash the Purge. So without further ado, Dorothea, the stage is yours."

"Herman, thank you for that wonderful introduction, and also to you, Chief Council Martel, for your courage to come here this week. It must be incredibly painful for you to reveal this tragic event within your own family. I can't even imagine. But like Herman said, you have no choice now! You will assure us that the summit never takes place.

"But now we must move on, and it's my job today to explain the three components that make up the Triad algorithm. They are 5th Generation cell technology, also known as 5G, the virus that the Qing family has worked so diligently on to finally bring to fruition, and AI, or artificial intelligence. As you know, over the last thirty years, the Shanghai labs have sent multitudes of biological trial runs all over the world. Some were partially successful and made the headlines, but many others were complete failures. It seems the human immune system is far more resilient than we originally thought, even fighting off the novel strains Shanghai engineered. We also found out how fast these viruses mutate. With each successive generation, most of the mutations become less virulent. So, a virus with the potential to depopulate the entire planet is not plausible. As an example, even the Black Death in Europe only killed off half of the population. Therefore, we were forced to find another solution. Ladies and gentlemen, allow me to explain in detail how the algorithm Area C has developed makes the Triad possible."

CHAPTER 36

THEY'VE DONE IT

November 4, 2018
Zurich, Switzerland

De: andré.lemieux1950@carca.fr
Á: camille120@swiss.ch
4 Novembre 2018

URGENT

Antoine has completely brainwashed Michael against you and Sean. He has trained him and turned him into an asset. It's very difficult for me to tell you this, but Michael has completely embraced the dark side of his Martel heritage. I have personally witnessed his transformation and have never seen anything like it. It's at the point where I barely recognize him anymore. There was a time when I had a calming effect on him to help offset the hate that Father and Antoine instilled in him. But he won't listen to me anymore.

> Camille, you have no choice. You must come to
> Carcassonne as soon as possible. You have to
> face Antoine directly. It's the only chance
> you have of getting him to release his grip
> on Michael. Listen to me, I'm putting my own
> life on the line here for you if they're
> intercepting this contact.
>
> Take care, André

"Sean, come here. You have to read this email. I'm afraid André has confirmed our worst fears."

"For heaven's sake, now what are we going to do?"

"*Non, non, non,* not we Sean—only I. I must go to Carcassonne and face Antione alone. It's the only chance we have of getting Michael back."

"No, I won't let you go by yourself. Once you're there, he'll never allow you to leave. We have to go together. He wants me as much as he wants you."

"Sean, listen to me—you can't go. He will kill you on the spot. I'm his sister, his flesh and blood; at least I have a chance. And besides, you can't abandon all of our work now. It's far too important. Now that Sullivan has the Codex and everything else he asked for, he has lived up to his end of the deal. We made it happen. You're the only one who can write the speech and deliver it with the passion that will hopefully inspire and unify the world into action. Your speech is destined to be a world-changing event; you can't abandon it now. Besides, we knew this day would come and I would have to deal with unfinished family business."

"Camille, I'm terrified I may never see you again. If something were to happen to you, I really don't think I could go on."

"Sean, listen to me—you can, and you will continue; we are still a team. My half of the team will confront Antoine in Carcassonne and pray I can find his Achilles' heel. And your half of the team will prepare the most important speech ever delivered."

"What about your EMF exposure? You'll have no protection."

"*Oui,* I have already thought about that too. It may not be a problem, especially if I meet Antoine in his office. I suspect, for security reasons, there are no wireless connections, Wi-Fi, or even cell phones anywhere on the premises. So, my love, it's settled. I am going to Carcassonne and you're going to stay here and finish what we started."

"Alright, have it your way, but I don't like it. But since you've made up your mind, I ask one thing—please stay in constant contact with me."

Camille had been experiencing EMF symptoms for years. After considerable detective work, we discovered she suffers from electromagnetic hypersensitivity syndrome, also known as microwave syndrome. Evidently, the military has been aware of this problem ever since World War II, when microwave-generating equipment was first used during the development of radar. Military personnel with long-term exposure to those microwave frequencies often developed headaches, fatigue, loss of appetite, neuropathy, insomnia, difficulty concentrating, poor memory, and emotional instability. And of course, the government covered the whole thing up.

Since then, microwave frequencies have been used for numerous devices, including Wi-Fi, mobile phones, cell towers, and the 'smart meters' installed by the utility companies. Along with the widespread use of these microwaves have come increased exposure and an increase of these symptoms. Reports of these warning signs were ignored by the communication technology companies and the medical community. The excuse is always the same: We find no evidence that exposure to these EMF frequencies can cause any adverse health effects. But the data suggests otherwise, and reports of these symptoms are dramatically on the rise.

Why individuals like Camille are more sensitive than others is unclear. I like to call her my canary in the cage. She feels the EMFs others don't. However, just because she and people like her suffer doesn't mean the rest of us are immune. Newly published medical studies reveal these artificial frequencies are affecting everyone at the cellular level. Also worrisome are new studies and mounting evidence that they are killing animals, especially birds and insects. More importantly, they are killing the pollinating insects. Billions of years of evolution did not equip animal or human life to adapt to these powerful, artificial frequencies. Once we figured out what was causing her symptoms, we took extraordinary measures to protect ourselves from long-term EMF exposure at home. Thankfully, our efforts paid off, and her symptoms were significantly better. However, the Martel office building was another matter altogether. In my mind, Camille's theory that it was EMF-free was highly questionable. But I couldn't reason with her. Terrified I may never see her again, I reluctantly let her go.

November 15, 2018
Brasserie L'Escargot
Carcassonne, France

"*Excusez-moi,* I am here for a luncheon meeting. Has he arrived yet?"

"*Oui mademoiselle*, please follow me."

"*Oh mon Dieu, Camille*, I'm really happy to see you. It's been a long time. I can't believe it—we are the same age, but you don't look any older. What in the world is your secret?"

With a demure smile, she replied, "I don't know, André; perhaps it's clean living. How are you? You look good too, although perhaps not as much hair."

"Yeah, thanks for noticing."

"Okay, we need to get down to business. First of all, thank you so much for seeing me before I confront Antoine. I know you're taking a big risk even being seen with me, so I'll be brief. I have no idea what I'm going to say to him other than plead with him to let Michael go."

"I'm sorry to tell you this, Camille, but like I said in my email, Michael is too far gone. Antoine has followed in Father's footsteps and has completely brainwashed him against you and Sean. He has gone above and beyond with Michael's training. I hate to say this, but your son may be one of his deadliest assets. I've got to tell you, I'm really afraid for your life."

"Well, why then did you encourage me to come here?"

"Because I have important information."

"André, I want to let you know that we really appreciate your friendship and your loyalty. Thank God, we can trust you. And, don't let me forget, Sean and I have a big favor to ask you."

"No problem, Camille, whatever you need."

"So, what is it that I need to know?"

"Well, Antoine was at the annual Boldt Castle Assembly back in August."

"I'm stunned! A chief council went to Boldt Castle? That's a first."

"Right, but you also need to know that there's a mole inside the FBI that's keeping him informed on everything. He knows what the two of you are up to. He also knows that Sean has divulged the locations of the four divisions and all ten offices. So, they're in the process of relocating everything. As we speak, Antoine is moving the Carcassonne office. If or when the day comes, the authorities will find nothing."

"What about Boldt Castle?"

"Boldt Castle will remain, but the existing entry point has been demolished and replaced. The authorities will never find it. I don't even know where it is. Camille, there's another thing you should know. Antoine now knows about Sean's speech at Eglin. At first, he thought it was a big joke and laughed about it, but not anymore."

"So, tell me, André, what new information came out of that assembly? And what about the Shanghai virus? Sean and I went to great lengths and took tremendous risks getting it out of China."

"Camille, that was fifteen years ago, and everything has changed since then. It turns out Shanghai failed at developing a virus they could control and yet be deadly enough. But it doesn't matter anymore, because the Triad algorithm changes all of that."

"What in hell is the Triad?"

"I really can't tell you much. I wasn't there and haven't taken the time to listen to all the recordings yet. But from what I understand, it's a three-pronged weapon using 5G technology, the Shanghai vaccine, and artificial intelligence."

"*Oui*, I've read a lot about 5G since I suffer from EMF syndrome. But how is it used in this Triad?"

"EMF syndrome! Holy shit, Camille, what is that?"

"Yeah, I'll tell you about that some other time, but for now I need to know how they're going to use it."

"Well, 5G is short for 5th generation. Cell phones currently operate on 3G and 4G frequencies. But 5G technology is different. It's extremely powerful compared to its predecessors and has capabilities the others do not have. Invisibilia Manus is behind the global rollout and their technology companies have gone into hyper-speed to get it installed everywhere as quickly as possible. Camille, I have to tell you, it's a terrifying weapon."

"You also said they failed to develop the virus, so why would they create a vaccine for a virus that isn't lethal."

"Ah, the virus will still be deployed, but it's a deception. People will take the vaccine, thinking it's the cure for a deadly virus. Instead, the vaccine is laced with a unique material called graphene oxide, an electron transporter. These nanobot transporters, as they are called, are triggered using specific 5G electromagnetic frequencies that are activated using the AI algorithm. They're programmed to target and then destroy immune cells, leaving the body completely vulnerable to deadly diseases. They've also discovered that it's virtually impossible to isolate oneself from 5G frequencies, making the Triad the perfect bioweapon."

"*Oh, mon Dieu,* André, they've done it!"

"What do you mean they've done it?"

"When I was at the 1978 Assembly, they vowed that once people were sufficiently weakened, they would be ready for the Purge. So, when is this Triad supposed to be activated?"

"Very soon. Some smaller countries and municipalities are objecting to 5G installations, but in the end, their protests will fail. The Information Division has created an advertising campaign that is selling the public on the promise it will dramatically increase internet speeds and will give everyone the ability to tap into all the new technologies that are on the horizon, including driverless cars. Camille, I'm telling you, this 5G promotion is one giant Trojan horse of propaganda. And another thing, 5G can be modulated to any desired level they choose. They have the ability to ramp it up to 95 GHz. At that level, 5G inflicts severe pain on the skin. They will use it for crowd control or for whatever other intentions they choose."

"André, I don't know what to do. It sounds like they're winning. I came here to try and rescue Michael, but now that feels like a lost cause, too. What about mother? I haven't seen her in a very long time, and I really don't know how she feels about me."

"Father kept her in the dark about you. She thinks you still work for us and travel on business. You know how mother is. She keeps to herself much of the time and has buried her head in the sand about anything to do with the *family business*. She does see Michael occasionally, but he never mentions you to her. I do know she misses you, and I'm sure she would absolutely love to see you. Camille, you need to know, ever since father died, she has suffered from depression and intermittent dementia. So, we have her under twenty-four-hour care at the Cassis villa. I don't know how much longer she has. You may want to go and spend some time with her while you still have a chance."

"*Oui*, maybe you can arrange for the three of us to meet? I would feel better if you were there too."

"I'll tell you what, I know you're reluctant, but you have to confront Antoine first. Okay, I'll be blunt. Antoine is planning a hit on both of you before Sean ever gets a chance to deliver the Eglin speech. You know as well as I do who he'll appoint. So, before I arrange for you to meet with mother, you must first confront Antoine."

"André, there's something else I must tell you. He already sent Michael after us last month in Spain. I haven't been able to eat or sleep knowing my own flesh and blood tried to kill us."

Caught completely off guard, he pleaded, "Oh, my God, Camille, you have to believe me, I knew nothing about that! If I did, I would have contacted you immediately. I'm sure Antoine sent Michael after you, because he's desperate that Sean never delivers that speech. He won't be able to handle the aftermath from the other families if he's not successful."

"Okay, I'll go and talk to him. But like I mentioned earlier, I need a big favor from you. We need witnesses to back up the claims we make at the Eglin summit. André, you're the only one we can trust to do it."

CHAPTER 37

THE CONFRONTATION

THE THIRTY-FIFTH STEP

November 16, 2018
The Martel Office Building
Carcassonne, France

Terrified of what she was about to encounter, Camille courageously entered the office of her older brother, Antoine Martel. With a booming voice, he lashed out, "Camille, Camille, well, well, well, my one and only sister! What a wonderful surprise. Welcome home. How long has it been since you last paid a visit to see your family? It's been a while, hasn't it? What have you been up to? From what I heard, you and that traitor Phillips have been up to no damn good."

"Okay, Antoine, let's cut the bullshit—you know why I'm here."

"It's quite amazing, you haven't changed at all. You still look the same since the last time I saw you. Let's think about this for a moment. You know what? I think that was when Michael would have been about six years old. Hmm, let's see, that was in 1988. But, Camille, you never brought him to meet his family when you lived here. I certainly don't understand why. Are you ashamed of us? Come to think about it, that was thirty years ago. Michael is thirty-six now. You really should see him. I personally trained him, and he's no longer that frail, overly sensitive boy you once knew. He's turned out to be quite the man now. Maybe I can arrange for the two of you to meet here, so you can share some big hugs. That would be nice, don't you think?"

"Antoine, you haven't changed at all, you're still an asshole. I guess what they say is true: the acorn doesn't fall far from the tree. You and Father definitely share the same DNA."

"Don't bring Father into this, you traitor bitch."

"Okay, okay. I know I started it, but let's stay away from the name-calling. The only reason I'm here is because I want Michael back."

"Don't tell me what you want; you should tell him yourself. I'll call him to come here right now to give you that big hug."

"Why? So, he'll do your dirty work for you here. You trained him and sent him to Spain to kill me and Sean. But as you can see, brother, he has failed his mission."

"Camille, what a brilliant idea. I wish I would have thought of that. But what makes you think that was Michael?"

"Antoine, don't play games with me; I'm not stupid. I want my son back—he deserves to be with his family."

"You know what, Camille, it's really too bad you defected. We could really use you back in the family."

"Well, to be clear, that will be a cold day in hell."

"Okay, my dear sister, you win. *Oui*, I agree. Michael deserves to be with his family. And you know what?" Antoine screamed out, "He is with his family! Camille, let me remind you, whether you like it or not, Michael is a Martel and not the fake, bullshit name you gave him. What was that name again? Oh yeah, Deneuve. It's too bad you didn't level with him years ago; perhaps he would still be with you. Nobody forced him to come here. He found us years ago, all on his own. You know what he told Father after he had been with us for only a short while? He said he felt like he was already family."

"Antoine, you know as well as I do. Father manipulated him to get even with me. I'm sure he told Michael that Invisibilia Manus is a humanitarian group and that we're traitors. So, don't try and tell me Michael wanting to be a Martel is a clean deal."

"Okay, Camille, we're done here. If you want Michael back, I'm giving you one option. You see, we know all about the Eglin Summit you have planned for next August. You and Phillips have made my life miserable. I know everything. I even know about his journals. I must say, getting that virus out of Shanghai was a gutsy move. And there's a lot more I know too. But one thing I don't know is why in the world have the two of you become religious? You know what, never mind. I really don't care, because I can assure you not even God can save the two of you now."

"Okay, Antoine, so now you know everything. What is it that you want from us?"

"I'll try and convince Michael to go back to you if you and Philips call off the Eglin summit. That's the only deal you're going to get from me. Like I said, you have made my position as chief council very difficult."

"If we call it off, how do I know you'll keep your end of the deal? And how are you going to convince Michael to leave the family after all your brainwashing?"

"Well, I guess you're going to have to trust me, aren't you?"

"Okay, I see. But before I leave, I want to see Mother. She's old, and I don't know how much longer she has left. My guess is after Father died, you put her away someplace so she wouldn't be a bother to you."

"Who told you Father died?"

Hesitatingly, she replied, "Um, nobody told me. I figured it out all on my own when you said you were chief council."

"Okay, she's at the Cassis villa. And you're right, you should go see her. You and André, the twins, were always her favorites. Anyway, I enjoyed our little chat today. Make sure you think long and hard about our deal—and goodbye."

On the road to Cassis, France

After leaving the Martel office building, Camille drove the three and half hours to Cassis. After about twenty minutes on the road, she made a phone call.

"Sean, hi, it's me."

"Thank God, sweetheart, I've been worried sick. Are you okay?"

"*Oui*, I'm fine. I just left Antoine and I'm on my way to Cassis to see my mother. André told me she's in the early stages of dementia, and she may not have long."

"I'm really sorry to hear that. My grandmother suffered from dementia and she would fade in and out of reality every few minutes. It was sad. So, how did it go with Antoine? Tell me everything."

"Before I get into that, and just to let you know, after I leave Cassis, I'll be driving back to Marseilles to catch a plane home."

"Thank God, I can't wait until you're back home safe with me."

Back at the Martel Office Building
Carcassonne, France

"Hello, Michael, this is Antoine. Call me right back; we need to talk—NOW! Your traitor mother just left my office and is on the way to Cassis to see your grandmother. I don't know what you've been up to, but she informed me that you tried to eliminate her and that bastard father of yours when they were in Spain. Listen to me, Michael, I know how much you hate them, but don't you ever go off grid again without direct orders from me. Anyway, I'm really surprised and shocked that you failed. Even so, it doesn't matter, because now is the time. We can't afford to have them deliver the Eglin speech. So, Michael, your time has arrived. I want you to drive to the Cassis villa and do what you've been trained for. And for God's sake, this time, don't miss!"

The Martel Oceanside Villa
Cassis, France

"*Mère, Mère,* I'm so happy to see you! I finally have time away from my crazy schedule. How are you?"

Smiling, the old woman rejoiced, "*Oh mon Dieu,* Camille, I can't believe you're here. It's been such a long time since I've seen you. You must not stay away for so long next time."

"*Oui,* I know I have not been a very attentive daughter. Please forgive me. I have no excuses other than the family business keeps me away a lot. You know, traveling to all the different countries and all."

"Of course, I forgive you. I am so happy you are here now. I miss your father. You know he passed."

"*Oui,* I know, *Mère.*"

"My dear Camille, tell me again, why are you here? You know your father died. Where's André? You know, the two of you are my favorites. You know, somebody else comes here to visit me. I think his name is Michael."

"*Oui,* Michael is your grandson, *Mère.*"

"Oh no, Camille, you're mistaken, I don't have a grandson. My boys are not interested in having families. What a shame, don't you think?"

"*Oui Mère,* it is a shame."

Shaken by her mother's confusion, Camille stayed for a few hours, realizing the full extent of her mother's illness. She knew full well this was the last time she would ever see her again. Sobbing with a heavy heart, she said her last goodbye. "*Mère,* I must leave you now. This has been a wonderful visit and I'm so happy we finally had a chance to see each other." Holding her mother in a loving embrace, she cried, "I love you so much. *Au revoir, Mère.*"

Walking down the driveway to her car and crying from her heartbreaking visit, Camille suddenly heard a soft but firm voice, coming from behind her. "Get in the car right now. Do not say a word, and do not scream. I'm not going to hurt you."

"Who are you? Where are you taking me?"

Flashing his badge, "I'm Special Agent Edward Clark. Agent Sullivan personally sent me here to get you out of France. You are in extreme danger, Ms. Deneuve. Please get in the car. We don't have a lot of time. Michael will be here soon. I'll explain everything on our way to Marseilles."

Confused, she asked, "How in the world do you know I'm in danger? I need to call Sean."

"Sure, go ahead, but we have to get going now."

"Damn it, I don't have much battery life left. Do you by any chance have a phone charger?"

"No, ma'am, I'm sorry, I don't."

"Oh well, I'll call him and hope for the best."

"Hello, this is Sean. I'll be back in a minute. You know what to do."

"Hi Sean, it's me. I don't have a lot of time to talk; my battery is almost out. There's been a change of plan. I just left Cassis after seeing my mother. It's sad—she doesn't have much time left; at least I got a chance to say my last goodbye. Anyway, Antoine has gone back on his word and sent Michael out for me. Thankfully, Frank Sullivan sent one of his agents here to get me out of France. I'm in his car right now on the way to the Marseilles airport. Don't worry, I'll be home in a day or two, assuming we can catch a flight out today.

CHAPTER 38

GONE WITHOUT
A TRACE

THE THIRTY-SIXTH STEP

Four Days Later
November 20, 2018
Zurich, Switzerland

"Hello, Frank, this is Sean. I don't know if I should be concerned about Camille or not."

Puzzled, Frank Sullivan answered back, "Why would you be worried about Camille? Is she sick with that EMF thing?"

"No, no, I don't think so. Look, I don't want to overreact, but I haven't heard from her since this past Friday, when she called me from Cassis on her way to the Marseilles airport with your agent."

"With my agent? Sean, what in hell is she doing in France?"

Perplexed by the question, I said, "You know what I'm talking about. She went to have it out with Antoine to try and get Michael back. Then she drove south to Cassis to visit her mother."

"I'm sorry, Sean, I really have no idea what you're talking about."

"Frank, come on, you're scaring me. Antoine sent Michael after her, and you sent one of your agents to meet her in Cassis to get her out of France. She called me on Friday when she was in his car on the way to the Marseilles airport. She said there was a change of plan."

"Holy shit, Sean, I never sent any of our agents to Cassis. I had no idea she went there—you never told me anything about this. I really wish the two of you notified me first."

"W-w-w-what the fuck, Frank! What in the hell is going on?"

"Jesus Christ, Sean, you need to calm down. We'll help you figure this out, but first, you have to get on a flight to DC right away."

After several hours of mulling things over and feeling worried sick, I needed to talk to somebody I could trust. "Hello, André, it's me, Sean."

"Sean? What in the hell are you doing calling me? If Antoine finds out, we're both screwed."

"I know, I know, but Camille is missing. She took your advice and went to France to confront him. But it's been over three days now since she last contacted me. When we last spoke, she told me one of Frank Sullivan's agents drove her to the Marseilles airport to get her out of France and away from Michael. So, I called Sullivan, but he didn't seem to know anything about any of it. And then he told me to get on a flight to his office in Washington as soon as possible."

"Sean, are you sure you can trust Sullivan? I know you're worried, and now so am I. Listen to me. You need to proceed carefully—none of this is making any sense. I don't know who you can trust right now. I'm going to have a talk with Antoine to try and find out what happened, but I have to be careful how I approach him. I'm afraid his hatred of you two runs deep, and he's terrified of the Eglin speech. So, I don't know what to expect."

"André, thank you; at least I can trust you. I'm going to DC tomorrow to meet with Sullivan, and I'll let you know what I find out."

RESEARCHER PROVES THE CREATION STORY IN THE BIBLE IS A SCIENCE MIRACLE

Washington, January 15, 2018 (World News)

Amateur scientist Sean Phillips, along with Camille Deneuve, from Zurich, Switzerland, has proven his claim in a paper called The Genesis Codex. This paper proves that the Biblical account of the Creation Story in Genesis 1 correlates with modern scientific theories of the Earth's geologic origin and the evolution of plants, animals, and humans. Their research has been peer-reviewed by noted scientists and theologians around the world, which has led to a consensus.

Phillips claims this correlation has been hidden because of the many erroneous translations of the original Hebrew manuscripts over the past 2,500 years. Even though experts agree that their findings are accurate, there is a battle brewing in the worlds of both science and religion. This discovery has thrown years of scientific theory and religious dogma into chaos.

Of course, the question remains, how did the ancient Hebrews acquire this knowledge? Phillips does not claim to have the answer, but ancient alien theorists claim they do. Regardless, Phillips' discovery changes everything in the world of academia and organized religion.

January 17, 2018
The Home of Lila Phillips
Anse Marcel
St. Martin Island

Sobbing uncontrollably and barely able to talk, Lila cried out, "Dominic, come here quick—you need to read this! What they're saying in this article is not possible. Sean died twenty-two years ago this coming June in a plane crash. I was in the plane when it went down. I lived and he died. His forehead was bleeding. He was unconscious. I got out of the plane, but I couldn't get him out. It was going down too fast. He and the pilot both drowned—I saw them. I couldn't save either of them. My God in heaven, I relive that nightmare every day. I'm sorry, I know I keep repeating myself. You already know the whole story. You've heard it a hundred times."

"Lila, please stop crying. I know how painful that terrible day has been for you, but this article can't possibly be your Sean Phillips. You're right; he died in that crash."

"Dominic, you don't understand. The Genesis thing they mentioned in this article is what he was working on back then. He showed it to me—I saw it. But, it's not possible. Dominic, I saw him drown. I have to know what's going on. You have to help me."

"Well, the article says he lives in Zurich. I swear to God, if this is your Sean Phillips and I find out he's still alive and didn't come back to you, I will personally kill him myself, and he knows it. I told him on your wedding night, if he ever made you unhappy in any way, I would do exactly that, and I meant it."

"Dominic, no, no, no. Please control your anger. You're being a hothead. Dominic, listen to me—I don't want you to hurt him. He is still in my heart. I know there must be an explanation."

"Lila, my dear sister, leave everything up to me. I will get to the bottom of this, one way or another, and I will do what needs to be done."

"Dominic, don't overreact. You must wait before you go anywhere. We need more information, and I don't want you to go to Zurich. We'll decide what to do together, and if you go anywhere, I'm going with you."

"Okay, sister, I know some people in the military who might know people, who might have information on what's going on. Regardless, I can't stand seeing you like this. Like I said, we'll get to the bottom of it, and we'll go wherever we have to and do whatever needs to be done. If I find out he betrayed you, and is still alive without coming back to you, I won't rest until he's dead."

"No, Dominic, please you can't think like that!"

EXCLUSIVE REPORT

IT'S OFFICIAL: UNPRECEDENTED SUMMIT AT EGLIN AIR FORCE BASE

Washington, July 15, 2019 (DC Insider)

Three weeks ago, we reported to you that the Federal Bureau of Investigation (FBI) uncovered an international terrorist cartel. With a deeper understanding of just how widespread and dangerous this group is, authorities have changed their status to Level A- Terrorist Collective. This organization has one single agenda: a complete global takeover culminating in a one-world order under their total control.

Our insiders have confirmed that a summit is taking place at Eglin Air Force Base in Florida with high-ranking officials from around the world attending the event, including members of the United Nations General Assembly.

We have been told that this summit was organized by senior officials at the FBI based on compelling evidence from a single source. Authorities did not announce who they are, but an FBI insider named them as Sean Phillips and Camille Deneauve. Evidently, Phillips and Deneauve at one time worked for this collective of ten powerful families.

You may recall Phillips was in the headlines several months ago with the announcement of a paper he wrote, "The Genesis Codex." That paper is still sending shockwaves throughout academia and religious circles. How this paper has any bearing on this summit is still unknown.

CHAPTER 39

THE SPEECHWRITER

THE THIRTY-SEVENTH STEP

August 17, 2019
Seven Days Before the Eglin Summit
Building 427, Room 4A
Eglin Air Force Base, Florida

One week prior to the big event, I began working on the opening of my speech. If things went well, it could mean the beginning of a worldwide unification like nothing the world has seen in human history. But I was on my own. Camille, my inspiration, was gone, and I had no idea where she was or if she was even still alive. I shuddered to think that maybe Antoine had her locked up somewhere and would use her to stop me from delivering the speech. Or was she locked up in some dark underground bunker, being tortured and raped by some demented lunatic? I couldn't stop my mind from thinking the most God-awful thoughts anyone could ever imagine. It was a living hell. Without her, I didn't trust myself. I had a lot of misgivings about the summit and, on top of it, we didn't have the witnesses Frank Sullivan demanded. I worried that it could come off as some kind of fake conspiracy for the publicity. Or, since the FBI was involved, they might think that this whole thing was a play to somehow advance a government agenda. To overcome my doubts, I needed help to write a convincing speech.

"Mr. Phillips, please excuse me. Mr. Anthony Forsythe, your speechwriter, has arrived."

"That's great, he's right on time. Show him in."

Standing to greet him, I extended my hand. "Anthony, it's great to see you again. Please have a seat."

"Yes, yes. It's great to see you too, Sean. I hope it's okay with you if I call you Sean. We're going to be together for a while, and I abhor formality. I get enough of it when I'm writing these speeches."

"Yes, of course, as long as I can call you Tony."

"The last time we talked, you said you were going to prepare the opening of your speech, then I would take over from there and write the rest. Is that still the case?"

"That's right, so let's get right down to business. We don't have a lot of time. To speed things along, you may want to take a look at these two newspaper articles. One is from last year, and the other is from just a couple of weeks ago. They should give you a glimpse of what we are up against here and why it's so important for us to get this speech right."

INTERNATIONAL TERRORIST CARTEL NOW IDENTIFIED

Washington, August 30, 2019 (DC Insider)

The Federal Bureau of Investigation (FBI) and International Criminal Police Organization (Interpol) have come forward about a covert global terrorist organization, known as the Invisible Hand, a.k.a. Blackguard. They are linked to massive intrusions in geopolitical matters involving large-scale banking activities, extensive internet hacking and manipulation, drug trafficking, international terrorist activities, political collusion, and worldwide biological outbreaks, to name a few.

"There are no words to define what this organization is," said Frank Sullivan, a spokesman for the FBI. "Level A-Terrorist Cartel is the closest we have. They pose a threat to every nation on Earth and have infiltrated all levels of government, the media, our educational institutions, banks, corporations, and others."

"Our sources have collected undeniable evidence of their existence. Their invasions have created serious divisions within our societies ever since the 1970s, both nationally and internationally. This cartel has one focused agenda. They are on the verge of a total global takeover with consequences no one can predict," Sullivan added.

Details to follow

U.N. SECURITY COUNCIL CALLS FOR URGENT MEETING

Washington, June 5, 2018 (DC Insider)

A declaration signed by scientists from more than 100 countries warns the Earth is in the midst of a mass extinction event. The declaration cites evidence that 60% of animal and plant species from around the world have vanished since 1970, with many others on the brink of extinction. If this loss of life is left unchecked, scientists say the ecosystems human beings rely upon to survive will collapse.

"By some estimates, we must find a way to turn this trend around within the next 25 years, or it will be too late," said noted scientist Dr. Steven Geyer.

The last mass extinction occurred 65 million years ago during the age of the dinosaurs when 90% of all species on Earth died off. Scientists have traced that event to a massive asteroid that struck the Earth—a natural occurrence. This extinction event, however, is different. It is manmade and is the direct result of technologies that promised to make our lives healthier, easier, more comfortable, and convenient— our throwaway society.

Human activity is polluting the oceans, rivers, lakes, land, and air to a point when it will soon be irreversible, threatening all life forms and human survival. Especially toxic are the plastics and microplastics, heavy metals, industrial waste, toxic chemicals, pesticides, herbicides, petroleum spills, and discarded drugs finding their way into the ecosystems.

Dr. Geyer went on to say, "Global warming and species extinction brought about by pollution are major threats to human life and must be taken seriously."

He advised government agencies from around the world and the United Nations that they must concentrate on cleaning up and reversing this toxic mess that humans have created. He repeated that 25 years to rehabilitate the planet is simply an estimate; however, the time left could be far shorter.

"Debates and division of thought on this matter are not options," he emphasized.

"My God, now I see why I have my work cut out for me. Are you the source the article is referring to?"

"Yes, and also my Camille who is not here with me today because of them and that damn brother of hers."

"My God, Sean, I am so sorry. I promise I'll put my heart and soul into this speech. Let's get started. I recently completed work on a last-minute speech for the President to deliver at the G7 Summit in Biarritz on August 24. That's seven days from now, the same day when you're scheduled to deliver your address to some of these very same people."

"Yeah, we know all about the summit. We picked that particular date as a smokescreen to keep the press from snooping around here too soon. The G7 has been secretly canceled, and the delegates will meet here instead. So, let's get started. I'll show you what I've composed so far. Here are the first three pages."

Two Days Before the Speech
The Martel Office Building
Carcassonne, France

Infuriated by confirmation of the upcoming summit, Antoine Martel yelled out, "André, Michael, get in here now. We need to talk!" Nervously, the two men sat down across from the man who inherited the position of chief family council for the Martel family. "Listen to me. We have a huge problem, and I'm going to take care of it once and for all. Michael, I've been fucking around with that bastard father of yours for far too long. I really wish he had been here in France with your mother, so you could have blown their brains out at the same time. It certainly would have saved me a lot of grief. The situation he has put this family and Invisibilia Manus in is serious. I never thought it would ever get to this, but he's scheduled to give the Eglin speech in two days. He will expose everything he knows about us.

"If that isn't bad enough, as we speak, we have a much bigger problem. The other nine families are organizing a coup to oust our family if we don't end this disaster. They are already talking to the el Católico family from Spain and the de Medici family from Italy, and they will elect one of them to replace us. Maybe this will bring it home for you. I hope you realize if that happens, they will eliminate us and the entire Martel family. The Martel family line will cease to exist. So, I'm sending the two of you to Eglin to blast Sean Phillips from the face of the earth once and for all. Michael, you've been training for this day ever since *Père* brought you into the family. André, you're going with Michael as a backup, and you'll make all the necessary arrangements. I have complete confidence the two of you will get this job done once and for all. If you don't—make no mistake about it—their assets will perform their duties on us, quietly and efficiently."

One Day Before the Summit

On August 23, 2019, three men and a woman landed at Destin-Fort Walton Beach International Airport near Eglin AFB in Florida. At 10:05 a.m., two men arrived on flight 1014. At 2:36 p.m., the other man and a woman landed on flight 1315. They were all in possession of the required security passes that allowed them entry at the heavily guarded Eglin gate and into the secured area of the 640-square mile airbase. Security was especially tight in preparation for the influx of dignitaries who were scheduled to arrive for a speech that would undoubtedly have worldwide consequences one way or another. Since Eglin is the largest airbase in the United States, it was chosen because it could handle the aircraft that would be arriving from all around the world. Along with the temporary housing units that were being erected, the base had enough residences to accommodate this arrival of people, along with their aides.

Tony Forsythe and I had been at Eglin for the past week working on a presentation that would hopefully help unite this diverse group. Frank Sullivan made arrangements to have me housed in a secured guest residence within walking distance from Building 427, where we were busy preparing the outline and speeches for this seven-day event. As an added precaution, his agents shadowed me wherever I went. Of course, I was the star attraction and vulnerable to people who did not want that speech delivered.

Watching Frank along with his team secure the arena was like watching a symphony conductor. He personally supervised the carpenters who built the watch towers, the electricians who mounted the huge array of floodlights, and the technicians who installed the hundreds of security cameras. He told them exactly where the giant screens and speakers were to be placed, as well as the banks of monitors in the control room. He wanted my every nuance and emotion prominently displayed. At the same time, he supervised the activities of all the tradesmen, including the sound technicians, food concessionaires, and the tradesmen in charge of the multitude of other necessities that were needed to successfully pull off this event. Security was his top concern, and Frank Sullivan took his job seriously.

Everything seemed to be under control, except for the one person I cherished above all. Camille had been gone for over nine months. The loneliness and depression I suffered was unbearable. The only thing that kept me going was the thought that we were still a team. When I was especially down, her words would ring in my head: *'My half of the team will confront Antoine and pray that I can find his Achilles' heel. Your half of the team will deliver the speech of a lifetime to world leaders who have the power to destroy the Invisible Hand and save the planet from a pollution disaster.'* So, even though she was not with me in body, she was with me in spirit. My desire to honor our commitment kept me going through this trying time.

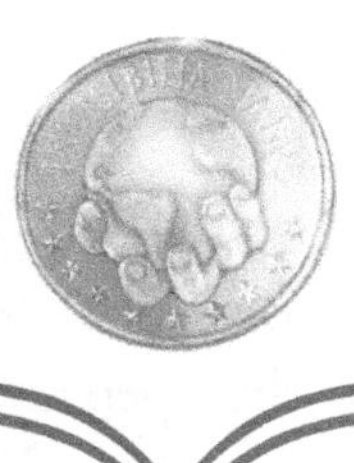

CHAPTER 40

THE WILD CARD

THE LAST STEP

August 24, 2019
The Morning of the Speech
Guest Residence House#15
Eglin Air Force Base

It was the morning of the first day for the seven-day event. The preamble of my speech was scheduled to begin at 10 a.m. Feeling the pressure, I, of course, couldn't sleep that entire night. I kept mauling over the key points and replaying them in my head. I couldn't get relief from the nagging doubt that my words would not be powerful or cohesive enough to make an impact. So, I decided to get out of bed, go outside for a walk, and attempt to clear my mind. As I stepped out the front door and walked down the stairs, the familiar face of Special Agent Sam Watts greeted me from the open window of his black SUV. I asked him if he would walk with me through the neighborhood so I could bounce some ideas off him. After about ten minutes, another SUV drove up to us, and the two agents discussed the upcoming events of the day. Sam let me know that it was time for his shift change and that it would be the last one before Frank Sullivan would personally come to get me for the preliminary sound checks. Watts walked with me back to my quarters as his replacement took position outside. I walked up the stoop, went back inside, locked the door behind me, went into the kitchen to make some coffee, and reviewed my notes. After a few minutes, I heard a knock. It was still dark so it was difficult to see him, but I could tell it was Sam's replacement standing there as he greeted me.

"Good morning, Mr. Phillips. May I come in? This is your big day, and we'll be together for a while. Agent Sullivan just called and told me to bring you up to date on what's going to happen this morning before he comes to get you. He made it very clear your safety is our number one priority."

"Sure, come in. I'm brewing some coffee. Would you like some?"

"That sounds great, but not right now. First, I need to take a look around and would like to start down in the storage area. Then I'll work my way up to this level. Sullivan instructed me not to overlook any detail. He wants no surprises."

"Of course, be my guest. Actually, I have never taken the time to go down there. Here, let me see if I can find the light switch for you."

As we proceeded down the narrow stairway, the agent drew his Glock 19, and in a firm, professional voice, insisted he would lead the way. Carefully surveying the dimly lit basement, he whispered, "Okay, this room is clear. I guess there are only two rooms down here. I'll get the other door. Moments later, he announced, "Okay, this room looks clear, too. I think we're good down here." Then, in a deep, concerned voice, he whispered, "Oh, oh, wait a minute. Mr. Phillips, come here for a moment—you need to see this. This is a surprise. You won't believe it."

I walked over and looked in the room. But then, for the second time in my life, I screamed out for the woman I thought was dead.

"CAMILLE!" And there she was, tied to a chair with duct tape covering her mouth, struggling to break free.

With a snide grin, the agent spoke. "So, Sean, my friend, we finally meet again."

Confused, I yelled out, "What the fuck do you mean my friend? Who in the hell are you?"

"Come on Sean, ole buddy, I know time has changed us, but are you sure you don't recognize me? Here, come closer, take a good look. Oh, wait a minute; maybe this will jog your memory.

"*'Hut, two, three, four—I don't know, but I've been told, Sean's got my back, but now he's gone. Ain't no use in feelin' blue, Sean left me here in Nam to stew.'*"

"EDDIE! Eddie Clark? Holy shit! No, it can't be."

"Aw, ain't that nice? You do recognize your old battle buddy! Your blood brother through thick and thin, you said. Surely you must remember the oath we made: 'We're battle buddies. We're blood brothers. We've got each other's back.' Well Sean, I must say that I'm very disappointed in you. Sean, my ole battle buddy, you did not live up to your end of the deal. While the Army shipped me off to Nam only to be captured by the Viet Cong, who inflicted three years of unspeakable tortures on me, you went home to live the life of Riley with your beautiful bride. And you know what, good buddy? You had the opportunity to get me discharged, and that would have changed everything for me. But unfortunately for me, and now for you, you didn't do it."

"Eddie, oh my God, I had no idea. I can't even imagine what you endured. But you knew full well that I was Reserve and you were Regular Army. You knew the risks. We talked about it many times. Regardless, there was no way I could have helped you."

"Damn it, stop talking. You could have helped me, but you didn't. So shut the fuck up—you're only trying to confuse me. And don't call me Eddie. My name is Edward—Special Agent Edward Clark. Sit down in that chair right now, and don't make a move. I don't want to hear any more of your bullshit. I'm going to get everything off my chest once and for all, so I can finally get some peace of mind, and maybe, just maybe, lead a normal life. On the other hand, you and your beautiful Camille have come to the end of your lives. But, before I kill the both of you, you're going to listen to my story. And Sean, my good buddy, you know exactly what I mean. I think it's only fair that I also have a chance to tell you my story too, don't you think?"

"Of course, now it makes sense. You're the FBI mole. You're the one who's been informing Antoine Martel. I remember now, you weren't at my testimony. At the time, Frank told me that you couldn't be there. You were the one who correlated the notes from my testimony with my journals. You had the details all along while playing double agent between Sullivan and the Martel family. So, of course you would have known everything. Hmm, you've been in a perfect position to keep tabs on us. You would have known all our comings and goings. Oh my God, you're the one who tried to kill us in Spain."

"Yeah, that was me all right. Too bad I missed. But that's okay, because even better, I will settle the score between us, here and now, on your big day. And as a bonus before you die, you're going to hear all about the tortures I suffered in Nam at the Hanoi Hilton. You should have been there with me, good buddy; you would have loved it."

"How in the world did the FBI ever hire you?"

"You forget, I have a law degree. After ten years of therapy, I applied everywhere for a job, but nobody would hire me. But then, a professor of criminology at a community college in Virginia showed some compassion and took me under his wing. I took his classes for two years, and along with my law degree and military background, he helped me put together a resume. He sent it out, and eventually the FBI hired me. I have to tell you, *Sean, my friend*, when Sullivan told me I would be working on your case, I suddenly became a believer. My awakening came as I combed through your journals and realized it was you. In that moment, I knew there was a God. Remember when I asked you if you believe in God? Interesting how fate works, isn't my old battle buddy? Anyway, it doesn't matter anymore because even God can't save you now. So, before I blow your brains out, I'm going to have the best therapy ever."

"Edward, Ed, Eddie, whatever your name is. Where did you keep her all this time? Damn it, did you hurt her?"

"I took good care of you, didn't I, Camille? Never mind, you don't have to answer me. But, don't you worry Sean, I didn't have my way with her—I couldn't. The Viet Cong took care of that. Anyway, if you're worried that I hurt her, I didn't need to. It seems that she suffers from some kind of malady I wasn't familiar with. She calls it EMF syndrome. I'm sorry Sean, I couldn't do anything to help her. Does that sound familiar, good buddy? Anyway, Camille and I did a lot of talking during her stay, and I believe she truly understands the misery I endured. In her own way, she tried to help me. She's been very compassionate. By the way, do you know what I think is really funny, good buddy? She's been in this house with you ever since yesterday afternoon, and you didn't even know it. If you were a better detective, you would have found her before now. Hah, you could have saved her. I must say, your batting average on saving those that are close to you is terrible. Now, you want to save the world, and you can't even do that. You really are a pathetic loser."

"How in the world did you ever get her here into Eglin without being detected?"

"None of your damn business. But if you must know before you die, I flashed my badge and told the guards that she was my assistant. They let us right in."

"Come on, Ed, you know how important this speech is. I'm supposed to be in the arena at ten o'clock. If you're going to kill us, can't you at least wait until after I deliver it?"

"You must think I'm stupid, so you can tip off Sullivan."

"No, no, I'm not going to say anything to him. You have Camille here as insurance. All I ask is that you kill us together—after I deliver my portion of the speech."

Grasping his head with both hands, he yelled, "There you go again, you're only trying to confuse me. SHUT THE FUCK UP—NO GODDAMN SPEECH!"

Then after taping my mouth shut, he proceeded to reveal the chilling tortures he suffered in Vietnam. The clock was ticking, and I could see on my watch it was almost 7 a.m. On top of it, in his demented mind, I didn't know what might set him off to pull the trigger. Our only hope was Frank Sullivan, but he knew I rarely got up that early. Ed Clark just kept rambling on. It was as if he felt dumping on me would somehow be a catharsis before he killed us. The only reason I could think why he saved Camille for this horror show was so he could torture me at the deepest possible level. But eventually, his tirade stopped, and he pointed his Glock two inches from Camille's forehead. It was weird though; as he continued to spew out the torment he was feeling, his tone changed. He seemed to calm down, to the point of being almost serene.

"So here we are, Sean and Camille. You may have stopped me from killing you in Spain, but unfortunately for you, your luck has run out."

Then, turning his head and looking directly into her eyes, the sick mind of a trained killer actually showed some remorse for what he was about to do. "Camille, I want you to know that I really do regret having to kill you. You have been good to me, so please don't take this personally. Although, I must say, I don't understand why you ever hooked up with this bastard." Then, turning his head to me, he uttered, "And as for you, my ole buddy, this is for your eyes. You can watch me spill her brains on the floor before I splatter yours all over this room."

Then, just as he got his final words out, the door burst open, and two armed guards entered the small room. Simultaneously, they opened fire, spending two shots each on the deranged killer standing before Camille, just when he was about to pull the trigger. Ed Clark dropped to the floor! As he did, his eyes never left mine. In some strange way, it felt like he was relieved that his years of mental torment were finally over. The guards quickly approached Camille, untied her, and carefully removed the tape from her mouth. Free from the sticky adhesive that silenced her, she shrieked, "MICHAEL! ANDRÉ!"

CHAPTER 41

THE REUNION

After freeing her from the chair that had confined her for the prior twenty-four hours, Camille reached out for Michael. With tears streaming down her face and with sobs of joy and happiness, she pulled him close to her, as they held each other in a warm embrace. After he untied me, I grabbed André in a heartfelt hug of unconditional gratitude. It was a surreal moment when I turned to Michael and hugged him for the first time in years. Then, the four of us just stood there, looking at each other and wondering if all of this was real or not. After a few moments, I walked over to Camille and grabbed her as we melted into an embrace of total relief and joy.

But then, without warning, footsteps thundered down the stairs and Frank Sullivan yelled out, "FBI, nobody move. Who are you two? Sean, don't tell me that's Ed Clark laying there." But before I could say anything, he instinctively drew his weapon from its holster and held it in a low, steady position. "Okay, everybody, drop your weapons and hands where I can see them. Sean, you tell me what in the hell is going on here—NOW!"

For the next twenty minutes, I explained who Ed Clark actually was. I gave Sullivan all the gory details: our army days back at Benning, the shots he fired at us in Spain, and how he had been tailing us for years. He listened intently about how his fanatical agent kidnapped Camille in Cassis and had her imprisoned somewhere for nine months. And then, I shocked him with the news that Ed Clark was a mole, a double agent for Antoine. Holstering his gun, he turned his attention directly to the two shooters and asked, "Okay, I understand why you shot Clark, but who are you two, and how in the devil did you manage to get in here? And, where in hell did you get those guard uniforms?"

"I'm André Martel, and this is Michael Deneuve."

Stunned, Frank Sullivan responded, "Holy crap, I thought you two were Invisible Hand. Well, that explains how you got in here. Evidently, your Media Division can counterfeit whatever you need." Then turning his head to Michael, he said, "I've certainly heard a lot about you. Let me ask you, how did the two of you happen to be in the right place at the right time to stop Clark?"

Michael responded, "Yes, sir. Well, first of all, we *were* Invisible Hand, but not anymore. Nine months ago, my mother met with Antoine and told him she was going to visit my grandmother in Cassis. Thinking it was me, she told him that I shot them in Spain. Since Antoine didn't order me to kill them, he thought I went off on my own. That's when he sent me to Cassis to finish the job. I really didn't know what he was talking about, but I learned to keep my mouth shut and do as I was told. When I arrived, an empty car was in the driveway, so I went into the villa. I asked my grandmother if anybody had come to see her. She, of course, was confused, but knew enough to know that a kind, beautiful woman had visited her."

Sullivan, in true detective style, asked, "Okay, that makes sense, but how did you know it was Ed Clark who kidnapped her?"

"Well, at first, I didn't know; that is, until I went back to report to Antoine and confessed to him that I was not the one who shot at them in Spain. That's when he told me Ed Clark was a double agent working for him. With no other possibilities, it was simply a matter of deduction. Clark was the only one who could have possibly known my mother's whereabouts. We figured out he was the one who had been tailing her and my father, but we couldn't figure out why he wanted them dead."

Sullivan continued probing. "How did you know Clark would come here to Eglin, and would end up in this house with your mother?"

"Agent Sullivan, don't forget that I'm a trained *asset*, and am very good at what I do, and I know how to track my targets. Ed Clark told Antoine that you assigned him to come here, along with Sam Watts, to guard my father. That was when Antoine called André and me into his office and ordered us to kill my father. So, we came here and posed as security guards. It was simply a matter of figuring out where Agent Watts was and asking him where Clark was."

"Okay, that makes sense, I think. I'll finish up with you two later, after I file my report. But for now, we're running out of time, and I need you and André on that stage today as my key witnesses. You're the only ones that can corroborate what your mother and father will disclose this week. And when we're done here at Eglin, the two of you are going to have to go into witness protection. I have to think about it, but it might be a good idea after the dust clears that maybe, I should talk to the two of you about careers with the FBI. And Sean, it's almost ten o'clock. I need to get you to the arena. André, you come with us. I think it would be a good idea if Camille and Michael stay behind for a while to get reacquainted. It's important not only for them but also for the integrity of the summit when they speak."

With that, the three of us left the guest house, ready to begin a presentation that would set the tone for the next seven days. Now alone, Michael and Camille finally began to say what should have said to each other sixteen years earlier. With tears of pent-up emotion and regret, Camille began. "Michael, I have to tell you, I don't know where to start. I am so sorry for not mending our fences when we had the chance."

"Mother, please, it's not your fault—it's mine. When you and Dad came to New York to visit me, I didn't listen to you about the Martel family back then. You were not crazy. In fact, they were far more dangerous than you were trying to tell me. I still find it hard to believe that I was suckered by the brainwashing *Père*, and Antoine subjected me, too, all those years. So, not only was I blinded by their propaganda, I knew they would never allow me to leave the family alive. And because of their utter hate—no I'll change that—actually, their utter fear of you and Dad, I guess I always knew they were preparing me to kill you. I was their ultimate weapon of revenge."

"Michael, you are not a Martel; you are Deneuve, the name you have on your birth certificate."

"Yes, Mother, in my heart I do know that. There is one other thing I am absolutely thrilled about. I had no idea Uncle André was keeping you informed about me all these years. When we were on the plane, I was terrified of Antoine and his orders to kill you and dad. I literally broke down in tears. It was then when Uncle André told me that we were not going after you; instead, we planned how we would get to Ed Clark."

In the warmest of embraces, Camille reached out. "Right now, Michael, I want you to know that I'm the happiest woman on Earth. But we must join your father on stage. He needs us now more than ever. I'll call Frank Sullivan to have someone come and get us."

10 a.m.

The Arena

Eglin Air Force Base

"Ladies and gentlemen, welcome to this world-altering event here at Eglin Air Force Base. I am Frank Sullivan, special agent with the FBI. For the last nine years, we've been investigating the notorious Invisible Hand. We would never have even known about their existence if it wasn't for the brave work of the two speakers you came to see, Sean Phillips and Camille Deneuve. Several months ago, we sent each of you copies of three documents: the 1978 Red Book that outlines Agenda One, and the journal that Sean so meticulously detailed. We also sent you copies of the virology report from CIDEC. Sean and Camille traveled to Shanghai and put their lives in extreme danger to retrieve a sample of the virus mentioned in the report.

"There is also a fourth document, The Genesis Codex, that you have undoubtedly read about in the papers. It has been authenticated by expert scientists and leading theologians from many of the countries you are here representing this week. We have read this document and can assure you it holds the key to uniting us against these dire threats we all face. A little later, Sean and Camille will go into some detail to explain the rationale behind this truly amazing document and how it will affect the decisions we make after we leave here this week. Ladies and gentlemen, these are troubling times we are living in, and you're going to hear some very disturbing testimony over the next seven days. So, without further ado, allow me to introduce our main speaker, Sean Patrick Phillips."

"Thank you, Frank, for that moving introduction. These seven days are going to go by quickly, so I want to get started right away. But before I do, I would like to say, even though my opening statement is from the American perspective, it applies to everyone here today, no matter what country you're from. We are all under siege, and we are all in this together. Later this morning, I'll go into much more detail about the terrifying Agenda One assault we face from the Invisible Hand. Then, this afternoon, you will hear from Dr. Steven Geyer, Head of Paleontology at the Discover Resources Foundation in Seattle, and Sebastian Walters, Professor and Head of the Geology Department at Princeton. They will be discussing the sixth mass extinction, the life-ending apocalypse caused by our thoughtless destruction to the environment. Your response to the evidence we will present during the next seven days is absolutely crucial, and you will be given the power, if you choose to use it, to determine the future of mankind. So, allow me to get started."

Introduction

To begin, I would like to look back in history and compare how dramatically attitudes have shifted. Beginning with World War II, people were compelled to unite under one common objective—SURVIVAL—and they willingly did so, regardless of their nationality, gender, education, race, religion, or wealth. This heroic struggle depended on one thing, the absolute and decisive defeat of the world's two deadliest enemies. The brave people of the world fought this war on not one but two battlefronts Nazi Germany in Europe and the Empire of Japan in the Pacific.

Men and women from all walks of life, young and old, volunteered to serve in the armed forces and go overseas to defend their country. Those patriots who were unable to fight stayed home and worked in the factories and workshops to help build the aircraft, tanks, battleships, and weapons needed in combat. Other able-bodied citizens assisted in hospitals and recovery centers to help heal and comfort the wounded. USO volunteers and celebrities traveled abroad and gave of their time and their talent to entertain and raise morale among the troops.

Uncle Sam asked everyone to forego creature comforts and contribute to the war effort. The government created a rationing system for automobiles, tires, gasoline, fuel oil, coal, firewood, nylon, silk, shoes, and other household items it diverted to the war effort. Americans used their ration cards and food stamps for household staples on such things as meat, dairy, coffee, cooking oils, and sugar. The Great Depression taught this generation of Americans to do without, and they understood how vital sacrifice was for the common good. They, in fact, gave of their time, their talents, and their treasure, and in actual, real-life terms, these brave Americans defined what patriotism is. Not just with words, but with actions and deeds. It was this commitment and their resolve that finally won the war. Historians refer to them as the 'Greatest Generation.'

Now, flash forward to the present day. Division has replaced unity. Greed has replaced sacrifice. Live-for-today attitudes have replaced morality. Cultural rivalry has infiltrated the very fabric of society. Far too many of our citizens have succumbed to greed, narcissism, self-indulgence, apathy, and hate. And to our detriment, these self-destructive sins have weakened all of our societies around the world.

Few believe we could ever unite under one common cause and survive what the Greatest Generation fought for. Of course, the two big questions are how and why. When asked this question, sociologists and historians alike admit they cannot pinpoint why this division has taken place so quickly and so dramatically. But this week, you will find out how and why. Looking at my country, the United States, as an example, just since the 1970s, many of our social and democratic norms that endured for centuries have been completely reversed. Let me give you a few examples.

> ► Americans were once considered to be the healthiest people in the world. Now, Americans are among the sickest. Based on the 2019 Bloomberg Healthiest Country Index, we rank 35th and lead the world in cancer, heart disease, stroke, diabetes, depression, mental disorders, as well as adult and childhood obesity. The CDC estimates there are approximately 20 million new sexually transmitted disease

infections, and half of them are among young people ages 15 to 24.

▶ Childhood suicide was rare. Now, the CDC has issued a report stating suicides have had a dramatic 40% rise in just the past fifteen years. Alarmingly, this trend is rising the fastest among the current generation of 13- to 20-year-olds. They also report that one-third of teenage girls are now suicidal. So, what makes this generation especially vulnerable? One possible answer is they are the first generation to grow up with cell phones and social media, beginning from childhood.

▶ The American educational system was once rated the best in the world. America was a place where students from all over the world came to study. Now, the PEW Research Center reports the U.S. ranks 24th in science, 39th in mathematics, and 24th in reading, among the industrialized nations.

▶ School shootings were unheard of, and public event mass killings were rare. Now, they make the headlines weekly. In addition to educating our children, schools are also mandated to take extreme measures to ensure the safety of their students from surprise attacks.

▶ Children were safe when they played in their neighborhoods. Parents allowed them to stay outside after dinner until the streetlights came on. They could walk or ride their bikes to school, run errands, and play in neighborhood parks in complete safety and without fear. Now, anxious 'helicopter parents' monitor their child's every move. And, for a good reason. Child abductions, child trafficking, and other crimes against children are pervasive.

▶ Our right to privacy is supposed to be protected under the U.S. Constitution. Identity theft, costly internet scams, social media bullying, camera snooping, and government intrusions were unknown. Now, these invasions of our privacy are commonplace and a threat to the freedoms we once took for granted.

▶ The threat of both foreign and homegrown terrorism was rare. Now, ever since the 9/11 attacks on the World Trade Center, the way we live, the way we travel, and how we view many of our fellow Americans with suspicion has created a culture of anxiety and paranoia.

▶ Pornography was low quality, hard to find, grainy films and photos viewed by adults. Now, graphic, hardcore videos and images are readily available to any child with a laptop or cell phone.

▶ The traditional family, with both a father and mother, was the norm. Now, the National Fatherhood Initiative states the absence of fathers is a severe crisis in America. According to the U.S. Census Bureau, 19.7 million children, more than one in four, live without a father in the home. Statistics from correctional institutions around the country reveal 85% of prison youth come from fatherless homes.

▶ Drug addiction was something you only read about, and even those drugs were far less potent than the designer drugs that are used today. There was no opioid crisis and little dependency on prescription drugs. Now, highly addictive and dangerous narcotics are not only used in the inner cities; they have also crept into the suburbs, every stratum of our society, and every age group.

This week, you will hear testimony from people who have personally been involved with the Invisible Hand and their Agenda One. Then, a little later on, you will hear some startling statistics from two renowned scientists, Dr. Steven Geyer and Professor Sebastian Walters. They're going to talk about the man-made pollutants we have put into the air, water, and soil, and what it's doing to the environment. Sixty percent of animal and plant species from around the world have gone extinct just since the 1970s, and many others are on the brink of extinction. If allowed to continue, this disaster will eventually cause a collapse of the natural ecosystems that humans rely upon to survive. Scientists and ecologists alike, refer to this doom as the sixth mass extinction.

In the final analysis, there are three essential questions we must ask ourselves:

One, how was this barrage of personal and socially damaging offenses allowed to happen?

Two, why did they all occur in such a historically short period of time?

Three, how can we reverse the course of these self-destructive behaviors before it's too late?

I have one final comment before we adjourn for a brief intermission.

LADIES AND GENTLEMEN, PLEASE WAKE UP!

After delivering my opening remarks, I did not expect what came next. As I stood before the expectant crowd, after pouring my heart and soul into every word, I could feel the weight of anticipation hanging thick in the air. The arena, a sea of faces belonging to VIPs and dignitaries from every corner of the globe, pulsated with palpable energy, charged with the promise of a seven-day event poised to reshape the very fabric of our world. But as the last echoes of my words faded into the silence, a deafening hush descended upon the room. Not a whisper, not a rustle of fabric, not even a breath dared disturb the stillness. It was as if time itself held its breath, waiting for the spark to ignite the dormant hearts of those assembled. For what felt like an eternity, I stood at the podium, grappling with the deafening silence that greeted me. Doubt gnawed at the edges of my consciousness, threatening to engulf me in its suffocating embrace. Had my carefully crafted words fallen upon deaf ears? Had my passion and conviction failed to penetrate the walls of indifference?

Then, like a solitary beacon cutting through the darkness, a woman rose from her seat. Her movements were deliberate, purposeful as she lifted her eyes to the heavens and raised her hands in a silent salute to the power of the human spirit. And then, with fervor that bordered on divine revelation, she began to clap. Her solitary act of defiance rippled through the crowd like a shockwave, stirring dormant souls from their slumber. One by one, they rose to their feet, a tide of humanity swelling with newfound fervor and conviction. The silence shattered, replaced by the thunderous roar of applause and cheers that echoed off the walls of the arena. I didn't know who she was—this woman who dared to defy the inertia of indifference with the force of her conviction. She was a stranger to me, a lone figure standing amidst a sea of unfamiliar faces. But in that moment, she embodied the essence of true leadership, her presence commanding the attention and respect of all who bore witness to her passion.

I cried at the microphone, "Thank you, thank you, thank you so much. We have so much more to reveal over the next seven days. But, before we continue, I must introduce the brave souls who are coming up on the stage. If it wasn't for them, I would not be standing here today. First, I must introduce the love of my life, the woman whose patience and commitment provided the backbone to bring us together today—Camille Deneauve. Next is my son, Michael Deneuve. If it weren't for Michael's bravery and the man standing next to him, André Martel, Camille's brother, Michael's uncle— and I'm proud to say, my brother-in-law—Camille and I would have both been shot dead not more than two hours ago, keeping us from this meeting with you. And finally, Special Agent Frank Sullivan, from the Washington Bureau of the FBI, who courageously went out on a huge limb to make this event possible."

After a thirty-minute intermission

"Okay everyone, I want to thank you again for that heartfelt acknowledgment of my opening remarks. But now it's time we get back down to business. When you arrived this morning, we gave you a packet and were asked not to open it until told to do so. The first item I would like you to take out is a paper called The Genesis Codex. Please open it to the first page. You may notice…"

CHAPTER 42

THE MYSTERY WOMAN

SIX MONTHS LATER

Emotionally and physically exhausted from all the hardships we had endured over the past several years, Camille and I left Eglin and went into the FBI's witness protection program. Sullivan wasn't about to take any chances from Martel revenge seekers. However, as it turned out, Michael had warned one of his friends, also one of Antoine's *assets*, what happens to all ex-employees of Invisibilia Manus. In turn, he let Michael know that on September 2, just two days after the Summit ended, the other nine families *replaced* the entire Martel family, including Antoine, and all of their employees. They would no longer be a threat to anybody.

After getting out of witness protection, Camille and I went back to Zurich and began planning our next adventure. We decided to fly to California and visit Liu Cheng in his new gourmet Chinese café. Michael and André moved to Washington and took Frank Sullivan up on his offer to join the FBI. And not wanting any association with the Martel name, André changed his surname to Deneuve. As far as Lila was concerned, I'm sure she found out about me from all the media attention the summit produced. Unfortunately, I never got over the guilt I felt for not personally letting her know what happened to me while I had the chance.

One of the most thrilling things Camille and I witnessed was the interest the Genesis Codex generated. Theories abounded as to how ancient civilizations could have possibly known the science contained in Genesis. In fact, there was a renewed interest in the science and engineering skills those civilizations left behind with their monuments, pyramids, and other archaeological discoveries that had been made.

The seven-day summit was grueling. Attempting to unify an arena full of bullheaded people did not go well. Animosities, diverse ideologies, and old scores to settle spread through the event like wildfire, and as a result, it ended without the alliance we had hoped and prayed for. But then, as the months rolled by, albeit slowly, these same people began to recognize the threat Agenda One posed and the atrocities we warned them of during the summit. They began to pay closer attention to the propaganda the media outlets were dishing out. They started to realize how the politics they play is weakening them. People's eyes were beginning to open, and they finally began to question why and how all the social norms and divisions I pointed out in my speech happened. But most importantly, people were finally beginning to realize that if we are to survive, we have to unite as one, just as the Greatest Generation did. Only then can the world defeat the two most devastating enemies in human history—Invisibilia Manus and the sixth mass extinction.

We owe it to the woman whose presence seemed to emanate an aura of mystery. None among us could decipher her origins or her purpose there. Yet, as events unfolded, it became abundantly clear that she was no ordinary participant. At first, she stood silent yet imposing, her gaze piercing through the veil of uncertainty. As she listened to my speech, she absorbed the essence of the message, distilling it into something palpable, something transformative. It was as though she possessed an innate ability to breathe life into the very soul of the gathering. While others listened passively, she absorbed the speech with an intensity that bordered on reverence. Each syllable seemed to resonate within her, igniting a fire of passion and purpose that blazed in her eyes. In her, we witnessed not just a listener but a conduit through which the collective aspirations of the group found expression. Though the speech was the same for all, it was she who truly heard it, who felt it reverberate within the chambers of her soul. For her, it was not just about the words spoken, but the profound meaning behind them—the vision, the mission, the unwavering commitment to integrity and truth. In her presence, barriers dissolved, and connections formed effortlessly among the diverse assembly. People who were once strangers found common ground, united by a shared sense of purpose inspired by her unwavering presence.

As the summit drew to a close, the mystery of the woman remained unsolved, her identity shrouded in the mists of uncertainty. Yet, her legacy endured—a testament to the transformative power of true leadership. For in every epoch of history, without fail, there emerges such a figure—an influential leader who, through their indomitable spirit and unwavering vision, leaves an indelible mark on the world. And in that fleeting moment, we bore witness to the timeless truth that such leaders are not born but forged by the crucible of their convictions.

JUST THE BEGINNING

www.ingramcontent.com/pod-product-compliance
Lightning Source LLC
Chambersburg PA
CBHW070523220726
48294CB00019B/141
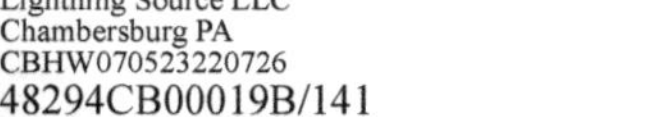